The Golden Vanity

The Golden Vanity

Isabel Paterson

With a new introduction by
Stephen Cox

LOST URBAN CLASSICS

Routledge
Taylor & Francis Group

LONDON AND NEW YORK

Originally published in 1934 by William Morrow and Company

Published 2017 by Transaction Publishers

Published 2017 by Routledge
2 Park Square, Milton Park, Abingdon, Oxon OX14 4RN
711 Third Avenue, New York, NY 10017, USA

Routledge is an imprint of the Taylor & Francis Group, an informa business

New material this edition copyright © 2017 by Taylor & Francis.
Copyright © 1934 by Isabel Paterson.

Library of Congress Catalog Number: 2016043148

Library of Congress Cataloging-in-Publication Data

Names: Paterson, Isabel, author. | Cox, Stephen D., 1948- writer of
   introduction.
Title: The golden vanity / Isabel Paterson; with a new introduction
   by Stephen Cox.
Description: New Brunswick : Transaction Publishers, [2016]
   Identifiers: LCCN 2016043148 (print) | LCCN 2016049628
      (ebook) | ISBN 9781412863421 (pbk.) | ISBN 9781412863650
      (ebook) | ISBN 9781412863650
Subjects: | GSAFD: Humorous fiction.|Satire.
Classifi cation: LCC PS3531.A774 G65 2016 (print) | LCCPS3531.
   A774 (ebook) | DDC 813/.54--dc23
LC record available at https://lccn.loc.gov/2016043148

ISBN 13: 978-1-4128-6342-1 (pbk)

Introduction

Important events do not always inspire important literature. *The Golden Vanity*, first published in 1934, is one of the few novels of the Great Depression that has enduring literary significance. It is a story in which women of different personalities, social positions, and social origins respond to the economic crisis. The novel's plot is fast but full; its characters are continuously interesting; its narration expresses the sophisticated wit of an author who knew the world. *The Golden Vanity* is a book that addresses the events of its day while revealing, just beyond them, the broad, rich vista of the American experience.

The author, Isabel Paterson (1886-1961), was well qualified to tell a big story about this continent's many ways of life. Born on Manitoulin Island, Ontario, into a large but unsuccessful family—last name Bowler—she spent her girlhood in the lumber country of Northern Michigan, the deserts of the American West, and the ranch country of southern Alberta.[1] She received only about two years of formal education (quite enough, in her opinion) and left home in her teens. While working in a hotel dining room, she taught herself shorthand and typing, skills that qualified her for subsequent jobs in the offices of bankers and lawyers. One of them was R. B. Bennett, who would later serve as premier of Canada. He offered to sponsor her education if she wanted to become a lawyer. She declined, but she accepted the informal education in politics that could be obtained by working with him.

In 1910, Isabel Bowler married Kenneth Birrell Paterson, a young salesman. Within a few weeks, the couple separated. Mrs. Paterson moved on to newspaper jobs in Spokane and Vancouver, writing editorials, dramatic reviews, and a few short stories. By 1924 she was in New York, working for *Books,* the weekly literary magazine of the *New York Herald Tribune*. It was a serious journal with a very large national circulation. Paterson's column, "Turns with a Bookworm" (signed "IMP"—"Isabel Mary Paterson") appeared in *Books* from 1924 to 1949. It gained her recognition as one of the wittiest writers in America, and one of America's most formidable literary personalities.

Besides scaring other authors with her mordant comments on their writing, and often on themselves, Paterson informed the nation about her views on society and politics. The views were unusual, to say the least. This was an era in which intellectuals quarreled about what kind of government intervention was necessary to achieve the good society, not about whether government should intervene at all. Paterson argued that government should function solely to protect individual rights, which ultimately consisted of the right to be left alone. The legitimate purpose of government was not to promote social well-being; the state was incompetent to do so, and the framers of the American constitutional system had, very wisely, never intended such a thing. "This country," she wrote,

> started on sound working principles. The main idea was that the Federal government was to be political, not economic. It was to protect human rights from the pressure of group interests and interferences, not to legislate people into either piety or prosperity or private morality.[2]

Paterson was an advocate of laissez-faire capitalism, a foe of socialism and the welfare state in any form, and an equally determined enemy of censorship and the prosecution of victimless crimes. She was a radical individualist, psychologically, politically, and philosophically, and she believed that she had the Constitution, as originally conceived and properly interpreted, very much on her side. To her contemporaries, she therefore presented the strange spectacle of a radical who was also a traditionalist. In fact, she was an early and powerful spokesman for the set of ideas and attitudes now known as "libertarianism."

In 1943, Paterson published *The God of the Machine*, a book that develops an original theory of history and society, along individualist lines. This work, and her writing in the *Herald Tribune*, gave her influence on both the nascent libertarian movement and the new conservatism that developed in the 1950s around William F. Buckley's *National Review*. She was a particularly strong influence on the most continuously popular author of the American Right, the novelist Ayn Rand, who called Paterson "the one encounter in my life that can never be repeated." In Rand's script for the film *Love Letters* (1945), she included an *homage* to Paterson. The hero (played by Joseph Cotten) picks up a ship model, smiles, and exclaims: "'The Golden Vanity!'"

Paterson's own career as a novelist began in 1916, when she published *The Shadow Riders*, a story about young people making their way in the new cities of western North America. A novel with a similar setting, *The Magpie's Nest*, followed in 1917. In the next decade, Paterson produced three historical novels: *The Singing Season* (1924), *The Fourth Queen* (1926), and *The Road of the Gods* (1930). Her last three published novels—*Never Ask the End* (1933), *The Golden Vanity* (1934), and *If It Prove Fair Weather* (1940)—are set in the contemporary world; they have different emphases and literary methods, but they are all stories about modern Americans trying to make sense of their experience.

Almost all of Paterson's novels enjoyed significant commercial success. *Never Ask the End*, a story of middle-aged Americans meditating on the unpredictable shapes their lives have assumed, was a big, unexpected hit. The novel is deeply reflective; there is little action, and the narration is handled with a stream-of-consciousness method that Paterson knew might be too challenging for ordinary readers. Yet *Never Ask the End* was a best seller.

By the time that book was published, she was already at work on another novel—*The Golden Vanity*. In letters of late 1932 she mentions "a new novel."[3] By summer of the next year she had "got to page 105," but it was slow going, and she lost writing time by building a house and visiting Europe. By December she was only about half done with the book, depressed by her slowness, and noting with some misgivings that "it doesn't look like other people's novels." At dawn on March 26, 1934, she reported to a friend that she was staying up all night trying to finish the book; she thought she was about fifty pages from the end.[4] Those fifty pages came hard. On August 15 she was trying to "finish it this week," despite an unusual amount of writing for the *Herald Tribune*. Her publishers were waiting for the completed manuscript, and she felt as if she were "carrying a grand piano upstairs, or something like that, and people telling me to hurry." Paterson was a very nimble writer of her newspaper columns, but in writing novels she ordinarily followed the time-consuming practice of revising as she went along, rewriting "each page, each sentence, till it's the best I can do—over and over and over. ... Amateurs are more apt to be satisfied; that's their mistake!" She completed the novel in mid-August 1934, and it was published by William Morrow and Company in October of that year.[5]

The cover featured tributes by critics from the *New York Post* and *The New York Times*, and by three prominent novelists: James Branch Cabell ("very beautiful and humorous, and not a little perturbing"), Nobel laureate Sinclair Lewis ("introduces Mrs. Paterson to the ranks of really important novelists"), and Ellen Glasgow, who came closest to capturing the novel's character: "As real as the hour in which we are living. A book of delicacy, charm, truth, interfused with the something different that is personality." Personality was something that Paterson and her works never lacked.

The Golden Vanity sold very well, with at least two printings in the first month. It was as much of a success in the marketplace as a serious novel could have been in the bad book market of the early Depression years.

Some of its success may have been owing to Paterson's individualist political ideas, which readers would have had a hard time finding in any other new book. It's certain, however, that *The Golden Vanity* is Paterson's most political novel. While writing it, she told fellow-critic Burton Rascoe that she was hoping to work some of her political and social ideas into the book, and she did.[6] She also abandoned the earnest stream-of-consciousness method of *Never Ask the End* and adopted a flexible omniscient narration that enabled her to shift easily from the thoughts of particular characters to her own assessments of their thoughts and actions. It allowed her to capture the sudden changes in her characters' lives without any laborious transitions from intimate, subjective views to larger, more objective ones. Her ability to move the story in this way gives a strong sense of action even to episodes that are more reflective than dramatic.

A lot happens in a novel that is not particularly long, and it happens to a lot of characters. Paterson was fascinated by the many worlds that Americans inhabit—either sequentially, in a society full of sudden change and motion, or simultaneously, in a nation dedicated to the proposition that individuals are free to live according to their own assumptions. She was entertained by the existence of these many worlds, becoming alarmed only when the occupants of one world tried to impose their vision on the others. A reflective passage of the novel, one of its most provocative, suggests that "in a complex society there are many moralities. They do not necessarily conflict, being complementary" (148).

The three principal characters of *The Golden Vanity* provide three different, though complementary, perspectives on the story. The three, all women in a novel dominated by women, have sprung from the same roots; they are members of the same extended family (cousins). But their relatedness merely emphasizes the greater importance of individual character and choice. In Paterson's phrase, "No two people are much alike" (240).

Gina Fuller is a genteel fortune hunter, worshiping riches and social position, but unsure about how to get and keep them. Mysie Brennan is a mildly successful actress who accepts the uncertain life of her profession. One of Paterson's letters describes her as a person who, "without exactly thinking of it, staked on individualism, adventure, just being herself and taking her chances and paying her shot with work."[7] Mysie's attitudes toward life are close to Paterson's. But the role of professional writer goes to a different character, Geraldine Wickes. Geraldine is a wife and mother whose stories enjoy an unexpected commercial success and make her the unacknowledged head of her family. Each woman inhabits her own world of friends, lovers, and social influences; each develops a separate history and a separate vantage point from which readers can view the intricate pattern of American life.

Paterson unifies her story by organizing it around her characters' reactions to the same set of events—the apparent prosperity of the 1920s, the Wall Street crash of 1929, and the first years of the Great Depression. For her, the boom and bust were more than distant rumors. Her friend Burton Rascoe describes the fever of investment that seized the New York literary world in the late 1920s:

> Everybody I knew, except stockbrokers, were in the stock market as daily traders—store clerks and traveling salesmen, bootblacks and truck drivers, but, above all, artists, cartoonists, novelists, playwrights, editors, musicians, critics, baseball players, actors, and press agents. At every literary "tea" (euphemism for cocktail party) the talk was of stocks, not of literary or intellectual matters; nearly everybody was boasting of killings he had made and exchanging tips on stocks.[8]

Paterson may not have caught the fever, but by the time it passed she was on her way to losing the equivalent of half a million dollars in today's money. Many pages of *The Golden Vanity* are devoted to the horror of discovering that one is falling deeper and deeper into a financial abyss.

Paterson did her best to preserve her sense of perspective. She reminded readers of the *Herald Tribune* that "in any economic system by which one can make a couple of million dollars, one can LOSE the same amount. The two possibilities, dear children, are equally inherent." Everyone makes mistakes, she noted, including such experts as Professor Irving Fisher, a prominent economist who had tried to predict what would happen in the marketplace, and failed. Fisher is also mentioned in *The Golden Vanity*, as evidence that some people get paid for making mistakes.[9] But the worst thing, in Paterson's view, was the role that politics played in inspiring, prolonging, and institutionalizing individual errors.

If government had been appropriately limited, she thought, individuals would have recognized their mistakes, liquidated their bad investments, and moved on. But government was not limited. It was ambitious and aggressive, and it produced an environment in which one could hardly tell the difference between politicians and the people now known as crony capitalists: "Government and business can be entwined only in the same way as Laocoon and the python, or whatever breed of snake it was. It doesn't do either of them any good."[10]

Between them, government and business spawned an official class whose function was to manipulate the economy, thereby ensuring that its own bad investments became everyone else's bad investments. In her column, she stated the recipe for a Great Depression in this way:

> First the statesmen of all nations must start a war with loud hurrahs, to make the world safe for democracy. Then the financiers must step in and give the impression that war doesn't really cost anything, because you can do it all on loans, and, in fact, everybody will make a nice profit out of commissions on the bonds. The industrialists don't need to worry about taxes, because they will also make a profit out of the war materials paid for by the bonds. And stocks will go up, so everybody can make a profit out of margins in the stock market.
>
> Then, mysteriously, the bonds begin to fall due. That was never expected. The immediate thing to do is to "refinance" them with new bonds, and new profits out of new commissions. This is called the New Economic Era. After this has gone on for some time it begins to look queer, but nobody can think why. The fact can be obscured for a little while longer by calling interest "debt service" and non-payment of debts "stabilization of the currency." Bad debts must be called "frozen assets," and "credit" means new loans that cannot possibly be paid. Finally the international financiers discover with dismay that they have destroyed the value of their own invested commissions. There is then nothing to do but add noughts [zeros] to infinity on the credit side of the ledger, call for a dictator and inaugurate a rain of paper like the ticker tape hurled out of the Wall Street windows on a parade day. Announce that democracy will not work in a crisis, and grab whatever any individual has left. And you have a lovely economics in which nothing need ever be paid, and if you think you have any rights you'll give everybody a big laugh.[11]

Paterson wrote these words shortly after Franklin Roosevelt's inauguration. But she hadn't begun to distrust the official class because of any disappointment with the incipient New Deal. She had opposed the policies of Woodrow Wilson and Herbert Hoover as well. The war to which she referred was "Mr. Wilson's war"; the New Economic Era was an optimistic term for ideas associated with Hoover.

The Golden Vanity emphasizes three aspects of American history, as Paterson interpreted it: the handling of the debts from World War I, the growth of statist sympathies among intellectuals and their wealthy patrons, and the manipulation of the economy by businessmen with access to state power.

Throughout the 1920s the United States government was involved in an effort to arrange repayment of Europe's colossal war debts and to stabilize the European nations that were supposed to repay them. The idea was for Germany, the loser in World War I, to pay reparations to the winners, who would then be able to pay their debts to the United States. Unfortunately, Germany could not pay, and America's former allies either could not or would not pay. Bankers and government officials therefore engineered a series of "plans"—the Dawes Plan (1924), the Young Plan (1929), and the Lausanne agreement (1932)—by which debts and reparations could be reduced or refinanced. None of these plans worked, and their failure was generally regarded as a major cause of the worldwide depression.

For Paterson, the drama of the war debts uncovered a world of ignorance and incompetence inhabited by seemingly well educated, allegedly responsible people. In a letter written in late 1931, she records a conversation with Stuart Sherman, her editor at the *Herald Tribune*, who was considered one of America's leading intellectuals:

> I remember ten years ago, no, eight, telling Stuart Sherman, with sudden exasperation, that Europe would never pay the war debts. He said, politely surprised, why won't they?
>
> I could only say, since it was impossible to deliver an explanation that would have had to be as long as Gibbon's *Decline and Fall*, *Because they won't.*[12]

Paterson was right. They wouldn't.

As an intellectual, Paterson was perpetually concerned about the failure of other intellectuals to think clearly about public issues. She was appalled by their complacent acceptance of nostrums, fads, and "movements"—the planned society, social engineering, technocracy, internationalism, primitivism, Soviet communism, Italian fascism. Wealthy beneficiaries of free enterprise were as bad, or worse. She didn't object to people having absurd ideas, so long as they didn't try to force them on others; and she had no objection to bankers or other rich people, so long as they didn't try to wield political power. She did resent the purportedly humanitarian attempts of wealthy people to dominate and reform everyone else: "Dumb people are dumb, no matter what environment you give them. We think they do less harm segregated in Newport, boring each other, than scattered about subsidizing kept thinkers and trying to run the country, with no regard for who will pay the bills."[13] The same sentiment appears in *The Golden Vanity*. If rich people would stay in their palaces in Newport, Mysie thinks, and manage to "keep quiet, nobody would mind" (239). But many of them—especially the "endowed" descendants of those who had actually made the money—felt free to inflict their social ideals on others, without experiencing any painful effects on themselves. What they lost in money (if they lost anything), they got back in power and self-praise.

In *The Golden Vanity*, the Dickerson family embodies two phenomena that Paterson often found in the same place: crony capitalism and the socialism of the endowed. Julius Dickerson is a banker who cashes in on the refinancing of the war debts; his son Roger agitates against the capitalist system. One of Roger's projects is *The Candle*, a magazine that promotes modern art, arrogant intellectualism, and Russian communism. Unwilling to deplete his own ample funds, he allows Arthur Siddall, another young man, to finance the journal and act as its figurehead-in-chief. Both father and son live comfortably on the wealth produced by others, and both use wealth to gain power.

The Dickersons (people who dicker away the livelihoods of others) owe much to the examples of Thomas W. Lamont (1870-

1948) and his son Corliss (1902-1995). The elder Lamont was a top executive of the Morgan Bank and in Paterson's view "a sanctimonious s.o.b."[14] He was a deviser of the Dawes Plan and the Young Plan, and his firm made money selling the bonds connected with the plans. In the words of *The Golden Vanity*, if your scheme is "big enough, even if it's a bust—look at the Dawes Plan and the Young Plan—you're a big man" (76). Corliss Lamont, who always expressed great respect for his father, was an eager advocate of communist causes. According to Paterson, he was "a none-too-bright Red," "a youthful millionaire Communist with a couple of half-baked books to his credit." His appeal, she said, was to "the upper classes, one of whom we are not which."[15]

The Dickersons are the villains of *The Golden Vanity*. The contrasting representatives of the wealthy classes are Arthur Siddall—Roger Dickerson's well-meaning dupe—and his grandmother Charlotte, a great heiress who lives up to her position. Paterson's liking for Arthur is plain. He is a nice young man—sweet, intelligent, well-meaning, bewildered. She seldom forgave political naiveté, but in *The Golden Vanity* she does. She feels the poignancy of the rich young ruler: "In his whole life, [Arthur] had never been really alone. Not without someone in the next room at furthest, aware of him, waiting for him. So he had never been really near anyone, on the intimate terms of equality" (17).

Charlotte Siddall is an even better example of Paterson's interest in individuals, as distinct from political and economic positions. Mrs. Siddall is a woman of vast wealth and narrow vision, a character who in another author's hands might have been nothing but a stereotyped target of satire. But Paterson's satire is gentle, and by the end of the story Mrs. Siddall has developed wholly unexpected capacities of heart and mind. In her final scenes, which are perhaps the most memorable in a book full of memorable episodes, she achieves heroic proportions.

No models for Mrs. Siddall have appeared among the people Paterson knew or knew about. She may have been conceived as a typical Manhattan dowager, until Paterson grew interested in who she might really be, beneath the type-casting, and her character grew in response. Arthur bears a surface resemblance to Vincent

Astor, heir to a Siddall-like fortune. Vincent's father died in the *Titanic* disaster; Arthur's parents are supposed to have perished in a similar catastrophe. Like the fictional Arthur, Vincent was a sponsor of magazines. But that's where the resemblance seems to end. Vincent played a role in running his own businesses; Arthur does not. Vincent was deeply engaged in political activity; Arthur is not. Vincent may have been bewildered, but he never realized he was; Arthur understands that he is. There appears to have been nothing of charm in Vincent Astor's life, but there is in Arthur Siddall's. Vincent is noticed in *The Golden Vanity* for the crudity of "offering to hand over to Uncle Sam his slum properties that are running in the red—he's willing to accept long-term bonds in payment. Ain't that nice of him?" (230).[16] This is not Arthur Siddall. Nor were the women of Vincent Astor's family similar to the women of the Siddall family. *The Golden Vanity* is a work of literary imagination, not of simple realism.

One character whom Paterson obviously enjoyed creating was Jake Van Buren, a friend of Mysie's who is closely modeled on Paterson's friend, the humorist Will Cuppy, author of such books as *How to Be a Hermit* and *How to Tell Your Friends from the Apes*. Paterson recognized Cuppy's talent and provided the eccentric author with much needed encouragement. In return, he dedicated his books to her. Cuppy's sense of humor closely resembled that of the fictional Jake Van Buren; Cuppy's nickname, in fact, was Jake. On several points, most notably Jake Van Buren's family history, his nonliterary profession, and the fact that Cuppy was homosexual and Jake is not, the two diverge; but it is clear that Paterson had fun putting Cuppy into her novel, just as Cuppy had fun putting Paterson into *The Decline and Fall of Practically Everybody*, where she appears as Queen Hatshepsut. *The Golden Vanity* is a harrowing story, but it is frequently a funny one, also.

An introduction shouldn't spoil a book by going into too much detail about what happens at the end. The best thing to say is that the stories Paterson wove together in *The Golden Vanity* have endings that few people would anticipate. It is a novel by an individualist, and it takes individuals seriously. The characters have lives of their own, and their choices are never predictably motivated by class, gender, occupation, or any other external marker of identity.

This may be the time, however, to discuss the title of the book. *The Golden Vanity* is named for an English folk song, existing in endless varieties, in which ships with such names as "The Golden Vanitie" meet an enemy vessel that is sunk by a sailor who is promised a reward he doesn't obtain. There is some relevance to the novel, but it is chiefly in the word "vanity." The book's last chapter conflates some of the usual phrases of "The Golden Vanitie" with usual phrases from another old song, "The Lowlands of Holland" ("My love he built a bonny ship ..." "The weary winds began to blow ..."). In that song, a ship sinks, killing a man beloved by the singer. Context makes it clear that Paterson's "Golden Vanitie" is America in the late 1920s—the vessel that suffered shipwreck in the Great Depression, destroying many an American's love.

Yet the novel is comic as well as tragic; and Paterson, who could have made it definitely one or the other, allows readers to weigh the effects for themselves. Mysie, the character whose ideas are most like Paterson's, finishes with skeptical and pessimistic thoughts. Yet the concluding action is comic. It recalls Paterson's habitual idea that Americans can easily save themselves if they recall the fundamental principles of their society. Again, I don't want to say too much about how the story ends, but one of the novel's prominent themes is the strange, unpredictable, extraordinary buoyancy of America and Americans, no matter what shipwrecks they endure.

Stephen Cox

Notes

1.   Unless otherwise noted, biographical information is derived from Stephen Cox, *The Woman and the Dynamo: Isabel Paterson and the Idea of America* (New Brunswick NJ: Transaction Publishers, 2004).

2.   Paterson, "Turns with a Bookworm," June 12, 1932; *Culture and Liberty: Writings of Isabel Paterson*, ed. Stephen Cox (New Brunswick NJ: Transaction Publishers, 2015) 34.

3.   For instance, Paterson to Garreta Busey, undated, late November 1932-early December 1932. Some form of *The Golden Vanity*'s opening pages may have been on paper before the Wall Street crash of October 1929. Paterson mentioned rereading some chapters of a novel she had started earlier than September 1929,

when she began *Never Ask the End.* The "laid-aside chapters looked thin," but she now knew "what to do with them" (Paterson to Lillian Fischer, September 8, 1932).

4.   Paterson to Busey, June or July 1933; Paterson to Busey, December 7, 1933; Paterson to Fischer, March 26, 1934.

5.   Paterson to Fischer, August 15, 1934; Paterson to Fischer, February 8, 1938; Paterson to Busey, c. September 8, 1934.

6.   Paterson to Burton Rascoe, undated, late 1933 (?), *Culture and Liberty* 164-65.

7.   Paterson to Busey, June or July 1933.

8.   Burton Rascoe, *We Were Interrupted* (Garden City NY: Doubleday, 1947) 262.

9.   Paterson, "Turns," December 31, 1933; *Golden Vanity* 128.

10.   Paterson, "Turns," February 12, 1933.

11.   Paterson, "Turns," April 23, 1933, *Culture and Liberty* 30-31.

12.   Paterson to Busey, November (?), 1931, *Culture and Liberty* 151.

13.   Paterson, "Turns," August 25, 1935.

14.   Paterson to Rascoe, undated, late 1933 (?), *Culture and Liberty* 164.

15.   Paterson, "What Do They Do All Day?", *Culture and Liberty* 83; "Turns," February 16, 1936; Corliss Lamont, *Yes to Life: Memoirs of Corliss Lamont* (New York: Continuum, 1991). Lamont's memoir demonstrates that sanctimony can be inherited.

16.   Paterson repeatedly criticized Astor for selling his "unprofitable slum properties" to the government, an act that she is unwilling to regard as a civic benefaction (Paterson, "Turns," June 30, 1935; see also October 25, 1936; March 17, 1940).

Grateful appreciation is expressed to the repository of the Isabel Paterson Papers, the Herbert Hoover Presidential Library and Museum, for permission to reproduce Paterson texts.

The Golden Vanity

One

When the telephone rang, Gina Fuller was looking in the files for a copy of the appeal for funds for the Chapel of St. Mary Magdalene. Dean Hervey was looking at Gina. He was not aware that he was looking at her, nor why. It was for religious consolation. As she stood with her back to the window, the morning light defined three points of gold on the nape of her neck, at the edge of her hair. He had never noticed it before, because her hair was dark, bronze-black, but shading to chestnut when the sun struck through it. Her head was bent and her lowered lashes made inverted crescent shadows. The ornament of a meek and quiet spirit, he thought. The Dean believed in God Almighty, maker of heaven and earth and of Mrs. Jelliffe Pearson. He gave God tactful advice every Sunday, but he was perplexed how to turn aside the wrath of Mrs. Pearson. The lady had been invited to subscribe to the Chapel Building Fund. By return mail, Mrs. Pearson reminded the Dean bluntly that as a divorcée she had been refused the benediction of the church upon her second marriage. Also it had been intimated to her that her voluntary resignation from active direction of the Flower Guild of Saint Stephen's would relieve the Bishop of serious embarrassment. Mrs. Pearson could not suppose that her money would be welcome where her presence was not. She had no doubt that enough stones would be contributed by eminent Pharisees to complete the Chapel.

Not a nice letter at all. The Dean was distressed. Ladies should be more—more—well, perhaps he meant less. They should not *say* such things.

They should be like Miss Fuller: modest, attentive, pious, diligent and serene.

Holding the letter as if he did not quite know where to put it down safely, he repeated: "Most unfortunate. The list—we must go over the list—" He started, and seized the telephone. It always made him jump. That was why Gina had muffled the bell down to a cicada's buzz. He wished she hadn't. It sounded more than ever like a rattlesnake.

He preferred not to explain the association, being ashamed of it as cowardice. Some impressionable years of his blameless infancy had been spent in the Southwest, where his father was a missionary. The image of Satan in ophidian form was a very lively one to the Dean, and the Unpardonable Sin was mixed up in his mind with the worship of the brazen serpent by the Israelites, though of course he knew better. He was small in stature, and seemed to have shrunk inside his clerical collar; his round face, puckered with shallow wrinkles, was that of a good child grown old without growing up. He could be pettish but not quite angry. He liked Gina because she was so respectful to him, just as if he were a man. His cloth was his sole protection against a brutal competitive world. Without it, he would have been one of those conscientious hirelings who spend fifty years drudging obscurely for one firm, and are overwhelmed by the gift of an inscribed watch as a reward for fidelity on retirement.

"Yes, yes, this is Dean Hervey. Oh, Mrs. Siddall, delighted, how do you ..." Under the mysterious compulsion which forces bystanders to listen to the cryptic half of a telephone conversation, or watch the paying of a dinner check, Gina remained immobile. Her devotional attitude, her veiled expression, had the patient nobility of one waiting upon some immediate revelation of destiny. Boredom is a part of every destiny. ... She thought, if the Dean's secretary was not recovered by next week, she must find him another substitute, and go back to her own work at the Settlement House; she had only been lent to the Dean. But then what? She had been at the Settlement House three years. Too long. She mustn't stay on with Geraldine either, a mistake altogether. ...

The Dean uttered sounds of ineffectual concern, slightly suggestive of a disturbed hen. "I cannot tell you how grieved. … If there
is anything. … I am sorry I did not catch the … You mean Miss
Fuller?" He put his hand over the receiver. "Miss Fuller, Mrs. Siddall
is asking if she may—ah—borrow you. Mrs. Benjamin Siddall."
The name carried its own emphasis.

Gina came out of her trance off-guard. "Mrs. Siddall—but she
has never seen me."

"Precisely. She will not be able to." The Dean beamed over his
own humor, before the inappropriateness of the occasion struck
him. He modulated into melancholy. "That is to say—I understand she has heard you. On the telephone. What she requires
chiefly is a *lectrice.* Since it is impossible to operate for some
months——"

"Operate?" Gina echoed. The Dean frequently took for granted on
Gina's part the extensive knowledge of his parishioners possessed
by his absent secretary.

"Her eyes—an impending cataract," the Dean elucidated. "She
liked your voice. 'An excellent thing in woman'—very true. But
the point is, will you? I need hardly say that Mrs. Siddall is——"

He need not. Gina said: "Of course."

The Dean lifted his hand from the receiver. "Miss Fuller
will be glad to—" He found himself addressing vacancy; the
invisible Mrs. Siddall had concluded the negotiations with
six words.

Gina enquired: "When would she want me?"

"At once, if possible. I think you will find," he ventured again
the note of deprecating humor, "that whatever Mrs. Siddall wants,
she wants immediately."

"Is she—difficult?"

"No, no. Decisive. With a broad grasp of affairs—but a heart of
gold." The Dean's avocation committed him to clichés. "I am sure
you will find the association most interesting. We shall miss you."
He sighed. His regular secretary, a devout spinster of fifty, had been
selected by his wife. He was inevitably henpecked. A sucking dove
would have pecked him. "Take the car—tell Dominic I shall not
need him until four o'clock."

Gina accepted gratefully. There is strong moral support in a limousine. She placed his appointment calendar before the Dean, left her desk neat; the car came around in five minutes.

As he leaned into the tonneau to unfold the rug, Dominic's liquid dark gaze slid down the chaste line of her throat. Swell dame, he thought, with a masculinity so direct that it became poetic: simple, sensuous and passionate. I like to get me one like that. Awri' for you, Nick; she don't even see you. Goddam uniform. S'pose I go in with Tony in the booze racket, big money, but my mamma she cry. Lookit Pete, she say; they take him for a ride, and Benny gets sent up two years. Wasmatter, you gotta good job, she say. Yeah, and maybe if I stick around some more first thing you know I marry Carmella, have nine-ten bambinos—watta hell. ...

He touched his cap. Gina said thank you, with the sickening sweetness of a lady being gracious to servants. She did not relax against the cushions; her appreciation of luxury was abstract, unrelated to comfort. She took out her vanity case and then forgot it for a few minutes, her face turned toward the window. Under the bland enchantment of October, the splendid materialism of Fifth Avenue became ethereal, rebuking the vulgarity of covetousness; this was the city of a dream. Gina ignored the spectacle. She looked beyond that even. ... She was trying to assemble the fragments of her information about Mrs. Siddall. An immense, almost legendary fortune, one of the famous fortunes. ...

Gina's reverence for wealth was mystical, partaking of the quality of veneration of the two extremes of pious minds, the childlike and the erudite. While aware of the physical substance, they conceive it to be transfused by a divine essence, which it imparts inexhaustibly by contact. So its possessors acquire merit, are superior beings, vessels of election. In her yearning toward them, Gina was not a simple mercenary snob, but a novice seeking admission to a difficult way of perfection. She intended to be rich. But she never thought of making money. Salvation was by grace; works would not avail.

She consulted her tiny mirror with austere impartiality. She was rather tall and slender, with pretty ankles and long fine fingers. Her face was a narrow oval, the profile delicately deflected; she wore her hair parted and brought down smoothly over her ears, giving a suggestion of a lady from a Book of Beauty. Her eyes were light brown, several tones lighter than her hair. The rose color of her lips was natural; they were shaped to an unchanging smile. She took some pleasure in the clear texture of her complexion, and rewarded it with a dusting of powder. Adjusting her smart little hat, she thought that the simplicity of her expensive blue frock was worth what she had paid for it. There was no complacency in the appraisal. Passably pretty, she knew, but somehow it was not enough. Men looked at her speculatively and kept a respectful distance; she didn't know why. And she told herself she didn't care, a kind of honest lie. In one way, she didn't, if they were the wrong men. (That, could she have understood it, was why; for they knew it.) In college, she cultivated the dowdy daughters of the rich, girls who quieted their feminine misgivings with vague aspirations toward good works or a career. The Settlement House had seemed the surest means of maintaining such connections. Now Gina wasn't so sure. It was suddenly become old-fashioned, and if it did not lead to meeting the right men. … For, after all, marriage was the only answer to her ambition. The endless stream of limousines gliding past were filled with women in Parisian frocks, in sable and silver fox and chinchilla, discreet strings of pearls and table-cut diamonds; but plain women, middle-aged, stout and dull. Wives.

Gina, though she did not look it, was twenty-six. She had not too much time.

She was aware that the Dean regarded her as a pattern of all the feminine virtues. The knowledge filled her with dismay. In due course, those virtues would render her indistinguishable from all the mouldy virgins and impoverished widows, handmaids of the Lord, who clustered about the higher clergy, exhaling the odor of sanctity and camphor. …

The sculptured beasts, who probably believed themselves to be lions, couchant beside the steps of the Siddall mansion, were absolutely right with the square greystone front. An advance post thirty years earlier, in the Nineties, when Mrs. Siddall had forced the rival leaders of New York society to concede her equal rank in a triumvirate, it was now a fortress of conservatism. It occupied a corner on the Avenue, and the porte-cochère on the side street marked its period. Carriages, the pre-motor age. ... Gina told Dominic to wait. The butler was English, and professionally decrepit, as became an old family retainer. Gina waited in the high gloomy hall, which exhibited baronial delusions of grandeur in the form of black walnut balustrades, a checkered marble floor, Italian dower chests and a Tudor court cupboard.

An uneasy sense of not being alone came over Gina. Of course, that was Sargent's portrait of the late Senator Siddall, above the mantel. An elderly gentleman with a neat grey beard; the features were impressive at first glance, but a second impression was shaded with doubt. All the dignity was in the whiskers; there was no force in the lofty forehead; the eyes looked away, but as Gina mounted the stairs she felt that they followed her—when she was not looking.

Of three people in the long drawing-room, there was no mistaking which was Mrs. Siddall. A pug-faced secretary hovered with a notebook. An oldish woman wore black and the indescribable gentility of a housekeeper.

Mrs. Siddall rose from a Louis XV sofa. She suggested a Chinese idol, short and solid, the same size all the way down. Nodding backward, she extended two fingers, a caste gesture, acquired with an opera box in the Nineties. "Yes," she said. "Very good of you to come. Sit down." The secretary diverted Gina from a chair which had attained its genuine antiquity by a complete inadaptability to the human form. Gina learned the chairs later: which were to be sat in, which were strictly objects of art. The secretary receded; the housekeeper presented some domestic requisition. Gina took her bearings cautiously.

The room expressed Mrs. Siddall's Victorian passion for superfluity, mainly in gilt, needle-point, and tightly stuffed satin. She was rich enough to defy interior decorators. Most of the paintings recalled that Corot stood for thirty thousand dollars a generation ago. And there was another Sargent, a plump young matron in a tight basque and a Langtry fringe. Mrs. Siddall herself.

The sun filtered through three layers of draperies at the windows: net glass curtains, filet lace, and rose plush. A mirror opposite betrayed a tall young man half hidden by the voluminous folds, at the far end of the room. His fair head made a spot of light. He couldn't get out of the room without passing the others.

"Very well, I think that is all," Mrs. Siddall concluded with the housekeeper. "Miss—" She deciphered Gina's card through a reading glass. "Miss Fuller—by the way, do your people live in New York?"

"No; in Washington." She forgot Geraldine and Mysie; cousins don't count.

"Indeed?" The word evoked gratifying memories to Mrs. Siddall, of herself as, in her own estimation, a great political hostess. "Any relation to the late Justice Fuller?"

"No, I meant Washington State." Gina added confusedly: "My father was in the law, though."

"Oh, the Far West." Mrs. Siddall's tone as much as the adjective indicated immeasurable distance. It put Gina outside of social classifications, a negative asset, like being an American in England. In Mrs. Siddall's girlhood, Chicago was the barbarous end of the world, and San Francisco belonged on another sphere. The tide of fashion flowed eastward across the Atlantic. She herself was neither east, west, nor midland. She was born in Lancaster, Pennsylvania, which is no mean city in the eyes of its honest burghers. The Siddall fortune had a double origin in the deep fertile earth thriftily cultivated by careful farmers, tenacious Pennsylvania Dutch blood; and the New England trading instinct. She was the great heiress, Charlotte Crane; her father, Heber Crane, from North of Boston, had married a Lancaster girl. Iron, coal and oil had turned to gold in the hands of Heber Crane. In her heart, Mrs. Siddall cherished a certain contempt for New York, as a congregation of the ungodly. She had cast her shoe over Edom; Moab was her washpot. The money drawn from the earth went back into it; the Siddall fortune was based on ground rents. Holdings of bank stock and trust companies were the natural outgrowth.

"I have never been to the Pacific Coast," said Mrs. Siddall, her manner allowing its existence nevertheless. "Senator Siddall used to say—Arthur!"

The image in the mirror had moved out of Gina's view. Caught escaping, the young man came forward. As a small boy he would have been called a towhead. An aspect of candor goes with that flaxen fairness, an effect of always facing the light. Blue eyes, inevitably. There was distinction in the shape of his head, the sincerity of his diffident bow. "My grandson, Miss Fuller ... Are you going out, Arthur?"

"Lunching at the Caxton Club. If you don't mind."

"Shall I see you at dinner?"

"Yes, grandmother." He showed no resentment at the catechism, and took his dismissal from her approving expression.

Mrs. Siddall resumed to Gina: "You might run over the news." She became slightly pathetic, staring about for the paper; a white film already clouded the iris of her eyes. "The president's message, and the leading editorial, or if there is anything new in the Stillman case." After fifteen minutes, she broke into the reading: "The Caxton Club! I must say, young men have changed—however, old books are a harmless hobby." She rang and the butler appeared. "Arkright, show Miss Fuller to her room."

Her room ... Gina said tentatively: "I came without—I'd have to go and pack."

By all means, Mrs. Siddall agreed benevolently; one could not depend upon maids.

Especially if there were no maids, Gina reflected, as Dominic drove her uptown again. Her cousin, Geraldine Wickes, lived in a featureless slab of an apartment house on Morningside Heights. Geraldine's husband, Leonard Wickes, was an instructor at the University. By abstruse juggling with a budget that never came out quite even, Geraldine contrived to pay for a cleaning woman once a week.

As Gina let herself in, Geraldine sat at an inconvenient little desk, writing steadily. There was something touching in the rapid obedient motion of her lovely feminine hands. Her hair, of an unusual pale red, was cut to a straight bob; she had a dimple in her chin, and a splash of coppery freckles across the bridge of her pointed nose. A little girl, about four years old, played with blocks on a cotton rug in a patch of sunshine. Geraldine paused, biting her pencil. It's getting away from me, she thought helplessly. There must be a happy ending. If I could only sell one story. Then Leonard needn't take that job with the drug company; he could go on with his chemistry research. … The little girl gravely said hello to Gina, and Geraldine turned her head. In spite of the difference in coloring and features, there was an indefinable family resemblance to Gina.

"Oh, Gina—is anything wrong?" Geraldine rose; she was heavy with child, a fact which her unbecoming blue linen overall had concealed until she stood up. How could she, Gina thought, on eighteen hundred a year and an instructor's prospects.

Gina explained hurriedly what had brought her home in the middle of the day.

Geraldine exclaimed: "Mrs. *Siddall!* You don't mean—" She paused, her mouth slightly open, as if overcome by awe. Gina knew Geraldine to be incapable of that emotion, and said shortly: "Yes." Geraldine recovered from the impact: "The last of the dowagers! I saw her, when I was at the Thompsons', but don't believe it. She actually did wear point lace and diamonds."

Gina flushed with a familiar annoyance. Incomprehensible that Geraldine should care to recall an interlude as a nursery governess, her employment with the Thompsons.

Geraldine pursued: "Isn't there a son and heir?"

"A grandson," Gina said. "I mean, I don't know if there are any more. …"

"That's right," said Geraldine, "there aren't any more—his father and mother, I've forgotten what but I mean they both died. He used to be in the Sunday papers, with dollar marks. Like The Interests. The Millionaire Kid. Is he married?"

"No." Gina corrected herself again. "I don't know. My trunk is in the basement, isn't it? Please don't bother; I'll find the janitor." She couldn't get away quickly enough. Poverty was contagious. … And the way Geraldine talked baffled her. Mysie was even worse. You couldn't get hold of anything they said. As if you reached for something, and it wasn't there, or it was something else …

When Gina was gone, Geraldine returned to her desk. But the thread of the story was broken. She said aloud: "Why did I ask if he was married?" And burst out laughing. The little girl laughed too; Geraldine stooped and kissed her. "Time for your nap, Judy darling." … She thought, a man needs to believe that he could make as much money as other men if he chose. …

Two

Mrs. Siddall emerged briskly from her bedroom, snapping on a pair of inch-wide diamond manacles, and followed by a yard of plum-colored velvet and her German maid, like a tugboat with a tow. A diamond collar indicated her neck; a tiara perched upon her sausage-roll coiffure. The state *parure* was in honor of Arthur's birthday. Her increasing infirmity of vision restricted her to a small dinner, only thirty people; about a hundred would come in after for dancing, not enough to make it a ball. "Where is the table plan, Janet?" Her secretary, Janet Kirkland, advanced with flatfooted alertness. Gina remained discreetly in the background. A tall sheaf of daisies, porcelain white, made a ruinous contrast to Miss Kirkland's swarthy cheek. She was younger than Gina, but with that complexion and two chins, what chance had she? Gina could afford to pity her. After six weeks, she no longer feared Miss Kirkland's veiled hostility. "Have the florist's men finished? My gloves, Trudi—thank you." Mrs. Siddall liked giving numerous orders at once; a tide of activity could be felt all through the house, setting toward her. This was what she enjoyed about a party; so did the servants. It gave them a sense of importance. They did not resent her brusquerie; it was personal like a box on the ear. Mrs. Siddall assumed that they were devoted to her; that was what she paid them for. And in fact her service was not difficult, since the commands she gave were practical and definite. "What did you say, Janet?"

Miss Kirkland said it again nervously: "A message from Mrs. Dabney—she's so sorry but she's got a black eye—I mean, she had an accident motoring, and can't come."

Mrs. Siddall made an unconscious gesture of annoyance. "Not serious? Remind me to enquire to-morrow." Too late to invite a substitute. "Go down and tell Arkright to remove—no, wait. Wasn't the Dean to take in Mrs. Dabney?" They studied the table plan with intense gravity. Mrs. Siddall said: "Gina, would you mind filling in?"

Would she mind? ... It was the first time Mrs. Siddall had called her Gina. Miss Kirkland's features took on a bluish tinge, the effect of strong suppressed emotion. Mrs. Siddall added: "I'm sure the Dean will be delighted."

He was. His gentle burblings helped Gina to composure, twenty minutes later. At first, the agitation of her nerves communicated itself to her surroundings; the lights and colors, the processional movement and hum of banalities between drawing-room and dining-room, blended into one indescribable general sensation. Like being waked suddenly, by a shaft of sunlight, in a strange room: a bright blankness. Then the scene resolved itself decorously: Gina stole a glance around the table.

The little man with the bulging shirt-front, on Mrs. Siddall's right, was an ex-ambassador. The man on her left, Julius Dickerson, was an international banker; he had a soft, bleached, greyish face, suggestive of a small-town preacher. Next him was Mrs. Avery, a survivor of the Four Hundred, exhibiting like Mrs. Siddall the rigid chin and glazed stare which were the hallmarks of their period. Her Roman nose and robust arms made her gold-sequined bodice into a coat of mail. The thin woman in black satin with dry henna hair, a rope of pearls, and her face obviously "lifted," was Mrs. Martin. Divorced, with enormous alimony, she represented the next generation from Mrs. Siddall. Except Arthur, Gina saw that she herself was the youngest person present. The thought daunted her; looking down, she found herself eating from a golden plate. The knife scratches on the dull yellow disk startled her again. She hadn't done that! No, how silly; they *used* such things! Yellow orchids in gold and crystal vases dotted the Venice lace cloth.

At the foot of the table, Arthur looked stranded. He had been talking to Polly Brant; when she turned to the man on her other side, he sat smiling shyly at nothing, and caught Gina's glance. All he saw was a young face, a contemporary; his sympathy went out to her unconsciously. Of course he had met all the others, knew who they were, in detail; but not much more. Except Polly.

Polly was his second cousin, a gypsy beauty, black-browed and red-lipped, immensely smart in the simplest of black frocks with a red flower on her shoulder. He had fallen in love with her when he was six and she sixteen; he could have recalled the exact occasion. She had swung him up to the saddle before her for a ride. When he was sixteen and she twenty-six he fell in love with her again. Unfortunately, it was her wedding day. He had never ventured to acknowledge to her, in the seven years since, that he was in love with her; he would have been shocked to learn that she was aware of it. She was still in love with her husband, but she felt possessively protective toward Arthur. She turned to him suddenly, intercepting his glance toward Gina. "Who is she?"

Arthur answered: "Miss F-fuller. She—she reads to grandmother."

"Reads what? Oh, I forgot. Though it's fairly obvious that Aunt Charlotte's sight is failing. Very pretty girl." Arthur's obvious lack of understanding of her meaning convicted her of vulgarity. Polly was no more of a snob than circumstances had made her. She amended: "I daresay Miss Fuller is quite charming."

Arthur muttered: "I suppose so; I've never talked to her."

"How long has she been here?"

Arthur reflected. "Must be a couple of months."

Polly laughed. Arthur really was a lamb. … Later, to placate her conscience, she went out of her way to "be nice to little Miss Fuller." The diminutive was an unconscious patronizing note; Gina was as tall as Polly.

The dinner had begun late and lasted long; Mrs. Siddall kept old-fashioned hours for large occasions. After dinner, Gina lingered unobtrusively, intending to slip away when the dance began. Nobody would notice her. She attached herself to Mrs. Perry, who was grateful for a listener.

The house was enormous, with a ballroom occupying one side of the ground floor. An old-fashioned conservatory projected from it, a blob of glass. Potted palms had sprung up in tropical luxuriance all over the place, and masses of flowers. Gina watched Mrs. Siddall receiving, before a lattice of red roses, with Arthur beside her. The dancing contingent arrived by eights and tens and dozens from other dinner parties; the young men mostly rather weedy but non-chalant or nothing; the girls in straight scanty frocks, their shingled heads neat and sweet. ... Arthur was slightly, unmistakably different. He had a rather engaging formality, the anxious hospitality of a child, as if he did not know the young people very well either. In fact, he didn't. ... He wasn't dancing yet. The others drifted onto the floor. A girl stopped near Gina and used her lipstick with the unconcern of a cat washing its face. Her partner said: "Come on, beautiful" ... Those girls had the glamor of an intimate group as seen by an outsider; the dance translated it into physical terms; they seemed to move lightly through another medium than common air. To be one of them would be happiness. Gina had never belonged to any group; her ambition had reached toward this always, even before she had seen it. She could not yet know that when an objective is attained, the illusion vanishes, to renew itself at a further distance. But only to the limit of one's vision.

Mrs. Perry was talking about Arthur. A faded widow of fifty, with crumpled eyelids and a band of black velvet around her neck, Mrs. Perry was a poor relation, a visitor in the house for indeterminate periods, not quite the same status as a guest. Aware that Mrs. Perry was negligible in her own right, nevertheless Gina cultivated her, acquiring bits of information which might help her to find her bearings. Mrs. Perry had a rule of never speaking ill of anyone, which produced in more realistic minds an extraordinary counteraction of blasphemy and uncharitableness. But not from Gina, who, in pursuit of her ends, was incapable of boredom. She had already learned from Mrs. Perry the story of Arthur's parents. They were drowned by the sinking of a great ocean liner. Twenty years ago. One of those senseless, sensational tragedies, which seem to have no other purpose than to furnish front page headlines.

"He looks like his mother," Mrs. Perry said mournfully of Arthur. "She was the belle of the season. In Washington—it was very gay that winter. An old Southern family, no money of course. John, that was Arthur's father, fell in love with her at first sight. They were married at a country parsonage; most romantic." The implication stirred Gina with some other emotion below her astonishment. An elopement! And with a poor girl … She'd never heard that … Mrs. Perry rambled on: "Dear Charlotte forgave them at once, insisted they should live with her. That was how it happened Arthur was left in her care when they sailed. Lucia, Arthur's mother, was to be presented at Court. Dear Charlotte has never been abroad since. Such a frightful shock. She sold her yacht. She has devoted herself to Arthur." Mrs. Perry's total lack of a sense of proportion sometimes made her narrative difficult to follow. "Of course, Arthur was too young to understand——"

"What is Arthur too young to understand?" Polly interrupted gaily. "Please introduce me, Aunt Annabel." She smiled graciously at Gina.

"Me too," Sam Reynolds put in. He actually resembled a hard-boiled egg, being bald and smooth-featured and curvilinear, with barely perceptible eyebrows and a slightly malicious grin. He was Mrs. Perry's brother-in-law. "Is Arthur up to anything, the young hellion? Then why isn't he? Ought to be ashamed of himself, mooching over a lot of old books, and the world full of women."

"I'm sure," Mrs. Perry exclaimed, "Arthur never thinks of women."

Sam found an unholy entertainment in the answers he provoked from Annabel. "He's not blind, deaf, dumb and paralyzed, is he? What ails Arthur, he's one of those bashful boys, waiting for some wild woman to drag him off screaming. I'm like that myself."

"You!" Polly said.

"Sure," Sam maintained. "I'm waiting right now for Mrs. Fuller to drag me off for this dance."

"Don't," Polly warned Gina. "It's enough to blast any woman's reputation to be seen speaking to him."

"I—I'm not dancing," Gina protested. But with his arm about her waist, she was obliged to accede. He danced well, and she cast about vainly for a pretext to stop. When the music ceased, they were by the conservatory. He said: "Let's see if the best rubber plants are taken. All this necking I hear about has got to be investigated."

She tried to disengage herself. "Are you one of those bigoted married women?" he asked reproachfully.

"I'm not married," she retorted, furious to the verge of absurdity.

"I'm sorry; thought Polly said Mrs. Fuller." He remembered; she must be Charlotte's new lady-in-waiting. "It's just my way of making myself agreeable. So many women get mad if you don't insult 'em. ... Where do you want to go?"

She walked blindly through the nearest door, refusing to speak or look at him again. The exit led to the hall and stairway. "The library?" Sam said. "Good idea. Mind what I told you; it's the truth; the first determined woman that goes after him will get him."

What a horrible man! She hated Mrs. Brant too. Since he had mentioned it, she certainly would not go to the library. It was at the head of the stairs. The house was so large, she didn't know it thoroughly yet ... She had not been in this room before. It was quiet, a cloistral atmosphere. Tall pointed windows, and a round green-shaded lamp on a long table. She sat down in a carved high-backed chair to get her breath. Not till then did she observe that the walls were lined with glazed bookshelves. It was Arthur's study, which held his collection of rare books. It opened off the library, at the back. The intervening door was slightly ajar. ... Men's voices were audible, muted, through the narrow aperture. ...

The ex-ambassador was saying that our prestige abroad suffered enormously from the lack of proper embassy quarters. The government should buy suitable buildings. Julius Dickerson's unctuous tones affirmed that Europe looked to America for leadership. Another voice regretted that the best people, young men of education and family, with independent means, did not enter politics. ... Coolidge was a safe executive. A business administration meant prosperity ...

This intellectual exchange soothed and impressed Gina. This was how people should talk. The voices had a padded, luxurious sound. Each remark was offered with the measured gravity of a butler presenting a letter on a silver tray. None called for any specific reply. They were like clearing house certificates, balancing accounts. They depended for their validity on the name attached. ...

She mustn't stay here. Nobody used this room except Arthur. But he couldn't come now; nobody would come. ...He had paid twenty thousand dollars for one book. Which was it? There were rows of small shabby volumes with dim titles behind the glass cases. More likely the manuscript lying open on the table: *The Legend of Good Women.* An initial was illumined with an aureoled angel, delicately drawn in its minute proportions, with grave rapt features and clear eyelids. Gina could hear the dance music, flowing through the talk in the next room. She did not hear Arthur enter; he moved quietly, because he did not wish to be heard.

He had stolen five minutes. Long enough to smoke a cigarette in peace. A birthday party, he thought, was ridiculous at twenty-three, but he couldn't object if it pleased his grandmother. His world revolved around her; he accepted this as the natural order. He was strongly attached to her, being of an affectionate nature, with no one else belonging to him. ... He did not know what to say to girls. He had no "line," and he danced badly. He respected girls. His mother was only a girl when she died; he thought he remembered her, and he owned a miniature of her. Very fair, with a gay proud flyaway expression. In college, he had been incautious enough to admit he'd never had a woman; it was turned into a joke against him. Some of the other fellows had got him tight. And took him somewhere, a drunken party; he didn't back out because he was ashamed of being ashamed. The liquor was bad and they mixed his drinks too. There had been several such occasions. Then he quit; he couldn't stand the next day. The girls had been drunk too; that was somehow the worst. ...

He crossed over cautiously and closed the door to the library. In his whole life, he had never been really alone. Not without someone in the next room at furthest, aware of him, waiting for him. So he had never been really near anyone, on the intimate terms of equality.

Gina heard the shutting of the door. She stood up; they were both startled. Arthur said: "Oh, please don't let me disturb you." She answered at random: "I only came in to hide for a minute."

"So did I." They both glanced about as if for pursuers; the absurd shared impulse mysteriously put them at ease. "Don't go," he said.

"I must," confusion had reduced her to naturalness. "I didn't touch anything," she looked down at the manuscript. "I suppose this is medieval?"

"Not exactly," his collector's enthusiasm gave him confidence. "Fifteenth century." Stupid, she told herself, of course Chaucer couldn't be earlier than the fourteenth. Arthur was opening a cabinet drawer eagerly. "Some of the finest manuscripts were produced just after printing was invented," he explained. "The scriveners tried to compete. But the earlier ones have more character. Here is the *Ancren Riwle,* thirteenth century; this copy is thought to be nuns' work, rather rare—it's a discipline for convents, you know."

"I don't, I wish I did. How bright the colors are, those tiny bluets and daisies." She pored over the thick black lettering, and murmured: "It says the anchoress mustn't wear rings or brooches or keep cows or any kind of beast, *except only a cat.* I'm glad she could have a cat. No, I must go now," she walked to the farther door, with a wistful and flattering air of regret. ... He thought, her face is shaped like the angel's, when she looks down. ...

"I'll show you some other time," he offered.

"Will you? I'd like to. Good night—I'm not going down again."

While he smoked his cigarette, he retained the image of her, in a white gown, bending over the manuscript, with those clear eyelids lowered. And when he had returned to his duty, he looked for her in the ballroom unconsciously, because she was not there.

Three

Gina had the afternoon off. Mrs. Siddall was closeted with her lawyers and business advisers. Her surgeon would have been greatly annoyed if he had known; the operation was set for next day, and he had ordered twenty-four hours of absolute quiet. He did not know.

In the atmosphere of secrecy proper to the discussion of large sums of money or other sacred subjects, Julius Dickerson explained that a holding corporation sometimes simplified the—ah—transfer tax. He avoided saying death duties. Mrs. Siddall was not discomposed. She had no intention of dying. The idea of trust funds gratified her by its implication of permanence, order and security. All obligations taken care of in advance, family, friends, good works. She gave a great deal to charity, in a fixed but handsome measure. She liked giving—as we should all like to give, out of an immense surplus.

Going out, Gina passed Janet Kirkland, hovering with a notebook in case Mrs. Siddall should call her. Janet's nose was glossy pink from weeping. She had the slightly imbecile expression of a loyal populace, on the route of royalty.

Arthur must be in his own library. Gina hurried; she was not prepared to encounter him. Since yesterday…

Standing on the steps, in the thin delusive February sunshine, lassitude invaded her, a spiritual fatigue. The massive weight of the great house at her back made itself felt, as if she had been trying to move it unaided.

So she had. The establishment, as such, was solidly against her as an individual. For her to become an integral part of it, the whole organization must undergo a relative displacement and adjustment. Had she moved it by the infinitesimal fraction of an inch in four months? Since the birthday dinner she had bent all her energies upon the almost impossible task. She sighed deeply, as if she had been holding her breath. Discouragement settled on her, localized as a physical chill between her shoulder blades, the coldness of a stone wall, shutting her out.

In a personal relation, there is an invisible boundary line you have to pass, at which it becomes personal, and you can't even tell till afterward. She couldn't now, about Arthur. She saw him every day. Mrs. Siddall found it humiliating to be led by her maid or secretary, and depended on Arthur. Every morning he came to her boudoir, to give her his arm when she went down to lunch. He sat about, his hands clasping his knee, pathetically masculine in a ruffled chintz chair, surrounded by knick-knacks and women: Mrs. Perry, Janet, Trudi. He was too polite to defend himself against tedium with a book. Gina was usually present, also waiting, in the background. She was glad it happened so; he grew used to her, his shyness wearing off with custom. He knew what she was there for, or he thought he did. She wasn't on *his* hands, not even when they were in his library. It seemed to happen by chance again, and he was pleased to show her his collection. The chance naturally recurred; he came to anticipate it, if he had something new to show. And they had a joke between them, looking over their shoulders for pursuers.

But yesterday evening …

No, she could not be sure … She hoped Mysie would be at home. She had an inward conviction that Mysie understood—about men.

A taxi drew up to the curb; Gina signaled it before recognizing the vacating passenger as Sam Reynolds. "Hello," he said cheerily, "any progress?" Gina regarded him with silent hatred and stepped into the cab. "There I go again," Sam said. "Ever hear of the goof that said to a girl: 'Oh, I know what you're thinking about'—and she slapped his face?"

The palm of Gina's hand tingled with the desire to do just that. The more because she was aware of an obscure counter-inclination to listen to Sam. As a man, he possessed that terrible profane knowledge which a woman could acquire only at an incalculable risk … She gave the taxi chauffeur his direction—Bank Street—in a low voice that nevertheless made him turn his head, startled by her tone.

Tears of anger brightened her eyes; Fifth Avenue shone through a crystalline veil. A light fall of snow, melting quickly, had washed the pavements clean; the shop windows were an open treasury of precious things, gold and silver and gems and rich fabrics, behind transparent walls that seemed as abstract as a mathematical line. People walking rapidly along the pavement stopped, stared dreamily into the windows, under a spell. … A couple in a taxi, blocked against Gina's when the traffic signal changed, leaned together for a kiss.

Gina's hand went to her breast. What had she to count upon? No more than that kiss, which could be taken and given so lightly. In his study, yesterday evening, Arthur had kissed her, with the awkwardness of a novice. He was enough taller, so that when she bent her head her face was hidden against his shoulder. And she didn't know what she should have done next. They heard someone in the library, it must have been the butler or footman mending the fire, who dropped the tongs against the fender. Gina's nerves were not equal to the external shock. She fled. Afterward, she could not sleep. She was not yet sleepy, but dry and tense.

Her will power broke suddenly; she tasted the luxury of abandoning hope, letting her mind flow with the current of the traffic and disperse with the crowd. For the moment she did not care; she was passive until the cab turned west from Washington Square. Heaps of dirty snow remained on the side streets; children splashed and shouted in the muddy runnels. Grimy curtains flapped from basement windows; and a slatternly fat woman leaned out of a half-basement window unexpectantly, her elbows on the sill. … Gina sat up straight again, recapturing resolution. This was the goal of drifters. … Never, never, never for her.

The taxi stopped before a large old-fashioned house with a high front stoop. The entry was dim; Gina peered at the row of cards. This was the right bell: Mysie Brennan. A fine staircase curved upward; but some of the spindles were missing, and the uncarpeted treads worn into hollows. Gina withheld her white gloves from the film of dust on the slender mahogany balustrade as she ascended.

On the third landing she flattened against the wall and shrieked, echoing the crack of a gunshot. "Gosh—excuse me," a young man materialized from the general obscurity, holding a .22 rifle. "Didn't see you coming up—I was potting at a rat—" Gina could only gasp, edging further away. The landing above was better lighted; Mysie's voice sang out.

"Shut up, Lanty, you're making it worse. Rats—for heaven's sake! Shoot your own guests, not mine. Come on up, Gina; welcome to Matteawan." Gina took the last flight breathlessly.

"Mysie, I'm so glad to see you." The plain truth. The cousins exchanged that quick, glancing salute of women who would never have chosen each other as friends, but are linked by some other circumstance.

They looked vaguely alike, a family resemblance which empha-sized the individual differences. Mysie too was neatly made, but not so tall and slender as Gina. Her square shoulders, beautiful flat back and straight thighs gave her the muscular balance of a cat. Her eyes were dark velvet brown, her nose slightly retroussé, and her smooth brown hair, bobbed, exhibited rusty streaks as the result of an injudicious experiment with henna, half outgrown. She had tried it for fun and discovered promptly that artifice did not suit her.

"Sit down, Gina; never mind Jake. Mr. Jakobus Van Buren. Make a nice bow to the lady, Jake."

Mr. Van Buren had already done so, rising politely from the sofa as Gina entered. Gina received a peculiar impression of a young man who was distinctly handsome and yet rather resembled a monkey in features. The bony structure of his face was well defined, especially about the eyesockets, so that his eyes, of a dark slate-color, seemed shadowed by an abiding sorrow, as with the more intelligent of the simian tribe. It is the face of comedy. Mr. Van Buren wore his clothes well, and had remarkably elegant ankles. His feet, unlike the average masculine extremities, did not seem to be in the way.

"Yes," he said to Gina, "it really is." Her startled gaze induced him to amplify. "My name—Jakobus. We hold a theory of patroon ancestry. Also President Van Buren. He can't argue about it now."

"Wasn't he the bachelor president?" Mysie interjected.

"He was a widower president," Mr. Van Buren explained. "That is immaterial; we claim only collateral descent. It's the Jukeses you mean; if you're going into that I'll be moving along. Lookit, I'll drop in on Lanty." He retrieved a hat and stick.

Gina could make nothing of the conversation. By the rules she understood, one must say certain things, indicated by the given occasion, to which the other person replied by certain other remarks according to suit; in short, the things that everyone said, current for the season. To Mr. Van Buren's suggested departure, she protested:

"Oh, not on my account."

"It is better so," he assured her earnestly. "But we shall meet again. I often meet people again. It is fate, don't you think? The mad Van Burens! They pop out at you. Why, I met Mysie once in the City Hall."

"Get out, you ijit," said Mysie. Mr. Van Buren obeyed; he even knew how to take leave gracefully.

Gina's curiosity followed him. Why did he put up with Mysie's rudeness? Gina was reasonably sure she was prettier than Mysie, better dressed, better mannered. But Mysie got on with men. Of course she cheapened herself, Gina thought; at home, Mysie had been "talked about." With Michael Busch, especially. And not so cheap, in one sense; Michael Busch had risked something; he had a good deal to risk. Still, it had done Mysie no good.

Was it—? They said you couldn't hold a man that way. … Gina observed now that Mysie was wearing a negligee of Swiss muslin, an irrational costume, since it was neither formal nor yet suggestive of the arts of a siren. White muslin, freshly laundered. Mysie was not made up, either. Gina could not account for Mr. Van Buren.

"Who is he?" Gina ventured.

"Jake? Nobody in particular; yes, he's a very rare bird, a native New Yorker. And an expert accountant, but he doesn't work at it all the time. Writes a little. He's threatening to do a play. His principal talent is fitting into any environment. That's why you nearly sat down on him. Protective coloration, like a zebra. You know, people often sit down on zebras, in mistake for tigers or something. Do you mind, darling, if I begin putting on my warpaint? I was asleep when Jake came; we had a rehearsal after the show last night." The darling was nothing but the habit of the theater.

"I see," Gina assented to the explanation about Mr. Van Buren's occupation. If he was writing a play, that would account for him. She surveyed the apartment. Without a single article of value except a grand piano, it was neat and comfortable. Being on the top floor, some conscientious Bohemian had torn out the ceiling to expose the beams and let in a skylight. Besides the large living-room, there were two small slant-roofed bedrooms, a kitchen and bath. The furniture looked as if it belonged to somebody, as if it had been chosen or inherited, not purchased hurriedly. Mysie shared the apartment with another woman, Theodora Ludlow, whom Gina had never met. Probably a chorus girl, Gina thought ... The guess was fantastically wide of the mark. Theodora was middle-aged and taught music in a girls' school ... Mysie's dress, which she fetched from her bedroom, needed a few stitches in the hem; she put on horn-rimmed glasses, and as she had taken off her muslin wrapper, she looked as unromantic in her petticoat, sewing, as a Degas ballet girl. ... She had none of Gina's virginal hardness of expression; in repose, her face was faintly melancholy in a contradictory way, for the corner of her mouth turned upward. It changed extraordinarily with a flicker of amusement. She was thinking, of course Gina would arrive at the right moment to be scared into fits by Lanty Webb and his probably mythical rat. Gina would forever retain the conviction that Mysie inhabited a rat-ridden shooting-gallery. Actually the apartment house was very quiet, and respectable enough. The ambiguous club on the ground floor rear might be a speakeasy; but where wasn't there a speakeasy? Mysie liked peace and to pass unnoticed. She liked Thea Ludlow's orderly habits and reserve. The room was very tidy. A back window overlooked the top of an ailanthus tree.

Gina uttered insincere regrets that she had not seen Mysie for so long.

Mysie said: " 'Sall right. I haven't been here much. The last show I had in New York ran for one consecutive week; then I had to go on the road. Got back about Christmas; and this show I'm in now, took over a part from Violet Warner, it's been running all winter and is likely to close soon." Gina reflected that Mysie obviously was not on the direct route to stardom. Mysie continued: "How's the whiteheaded boy?"

Gina failed to identify Arthur immediately by the description; and when she did, she was glad she had her back to the window. Mysie added: "It must be interesting, living with the wealthy rich for awhile. Of course they're petrifying bores, mostly; but seeing how the other half lives. What to do till the butler leaves. Geraldine told me about your job." She wondered what Gina wanted. Something— Gina never went out of her way without an ulterior motive. Funny how Jake knew that by instinct, at sight; he had an uncanny social perception. So he vanished—he would reappear with the same tact.

Gina replied noncommittally: "Yes," and scrutinized a photograph on the mantel. A substantial, prosperous man, in his forties. "Isn't that Michael Busch?" Gina's mother had retailed, by letter, further talk about him. His wife had begun suit for divorce, and then dropped it, nobody knew why; rumor was vague and contradictory.

"Uh-huh," Mysie bit off a thread.

"Does he ever come to New York?" Gina asked cautiously.

"Not that I know of," said Mysie. Her glasses masked her, but she grinned. Had Gina some remote design on Michael Busch? Gina had never met him, though she must have seen him. …

Gina thought, it's broken off, ended. To do that—for nothing. … Michael Busch was rich, not on the Siddall scale, but rich enough. He used to come up to their little town on Puget Sound, because the first source of his money was timber tracts, and he owned the sawmill which was, in effect, the town. Everyone knew him by sight. …

Mysie was then in the mill office, assistant bookkeeper. Five years ago. …

A picture formed in Gina's mind, against a black background. A starless night, with a smell of fresh-cut pine in the air, after rain; and flakes of light on the black water, where a motor launch rocked lazily against the float. Michael Busch was handing Mysie ashore. He was saying something in a low voice, and Mysie answered: No, better not. Mysie left him, running up the path in her white canvas shoes. Michael Busch stood gazing after her, bareheaded. He was visible only as mass and outline, yet his identity was unmistakable. He looked powerful, and helpless. He lit a cigarette and then threw it into the water, and still stood there, with his hands in his pockets.

Gina witnessed the scene by accident. She was going home from a church "social," by a short cut past the mill dock, with a youth she might have married, if it hadn't been for that. His father was the local banker. He was only an embarrassing memory now: a serious narrow-chested young man with a knobbly larynx, who read Bruce Barton for self-improvement. From that evening, Gina never wished to see him again. She was shocked at Mysie, and at the same time ashamed of her own suitor compared to Michael Busch. That was what decided her to go east and finish at one of the famous women's colleges, where she might make the right kind of friends. … But even assuming the worst, how did Mysie get Michael Busch, who could have had all the women he wanted? It was bad business for him, there where he was known, where everything became known sooner or later. … Gina had no mind to take Mysie's way; only if she knew what it was, she'd know why you couldn't hold a man that way. …

Mysie finished her sewing and slipped on the dress. "Were you going out?" Gina asked.

"No, I've been doing chores all day," Mysie assured her. "You don't have to hurry back, do you?"

But Gina said she had to, and went. Too much might happen in her absence, and the least chance might shut the doors against her. …

Left alone, Mysie gazed reflectively at the photograph of Michael Busch. I ought to write to him, she thought; but how can I tell him why I'm going back? I'm such a fool. …

Ten minutes later, a tap at the door announced the reappearance of Mr. Van Buren. "You must come and see *us* some time," was his cryptic greeting to Mysie. They disposed themselves at opposite ends of the sofa. Mr. Van Buren regarded his hat solemnly.

"Is that the cousin who came from the same town as you, with the unpronounceable name?" he asked.

"Sequitlam," said Mysie. "It's quite easy, if you work on it; not as if it were Puyallup or Snohomish. But you wouldn't understand." Merely a sleepy little town, thirty or forty frame houses climbing up the hill from the Sound. Like anybody's home town, the place you went away from. To see it, Jake would have had to see Gina as a little girl in a smocked frock and blue ribbon bows and Mysie in a middy blouse and her hair in a braid. "Sundays I used to practice walking over the logbooms down at the mill while the watchman was at dinner," she said, aware that it wouldn't convey anything to her auditor. The loggers in their spiked boots balanced by weight and muscular control; but if you were small and light and barefoot you had to do it with the tips of your fingers and the top of your head. Like a bird in the air. Sometimes a gull perched on the piling would watch intently as if it understood; and the water was deep green between the logs. Mysie had never been happier than when, at seventeen, she got a job in the mill office. She knew all the men by their first names, which Gina disapproved, as making herself common. But there wasn't anything else to call them; those were their names. They called her Mysie, with no familiarity, rather respectfully, because she was so young. She used to laugh a great deal … Gina's mother disapproved of Mysie; but Gina sometimes approached with cautious curiosity. It amused Mysie to evade the oblique inquisition. There wasn't anyone there Mysie could really talk to—except Michael Busch … She thought, perhaps she hadn't given Michael a square deal. A singular reflection, considering that she had been nineteen and Michael forty …

"But how did you get there?" Mr. Van Buren cogitated. To Sequitlam, he meant.

"By being born," said Mysie. "Grandpa Brennan went out to the West Coast by the Panama route in 1859, or 69, I forget which. I don't know why he didn't stop in California, but he went on up to Oregon and then Washington. Not many of the old-timers made money; they ended in the backwoods, same as grandpa. He married twice, so Gina is only my half-cousin."

"Who did he find to marry?"

"His first wife was a school teacher. And his second a hurdy-girl—a dance hall girl. One of his daughters married the super-cargo on a freighter, and came back around the Horn and settled in Hoboken. That's Geraldine's branch of the family tree. The prettiest

daughter was Gina's mother; she married a young lawyer in Seattle.
I don't think he amounted to much, but anyhow he died, and she had
to come home and live with Grandpa Brennan, and when Grandpa
died, he left her the house; it was all he had. My father was her
half-brother, Grandpa Brennan's youngest son; he died too, when
I was six. I've got a stepfather, you know. Gina's mother and mine
are only sisters-in-law, very distant relations. Don't try to keep track
of it; the complications are very complicated."

"It sounds just like the Van Burens," said Mr. Van Buren. "Except
that we seem to have petered out in aunts. Did I ever enumerate
all my aunts to you? No?—well you're in luck; stop me if I ever
begin." He lapsed into silence for a minute, and then said abruptly:
"You've decided to go through with it?"

"Wouldn't it be best to do it now?" Mysie asked with an impartial
air. Mr. Van Buren shrugged. "It would take only six months," Mysie
explained. "And I ought to visit my mother this year; she isn't well."

"How much will it cost?" Mr. Van Buren asked.

"Not a great deal. If you can manage to go fifty-fifty—that's fair
enough, isn't it? I expect I can find a job while I'm there; I don't
know if there's a local stock company now or not; there used to be.
But I'd just as soon take an office job."

"When would you be leaving?"

"As soon as possible. Then I'd have the summer away from
New York."

"My mother sent you her love," said Mr. Van Buren. "She'd be
glad to see you before you go."

"I don't know," said Mysie. "I like her."

"She likes you."

"But it isn't any use," said Mysie.

"I suppose not … Would you care to dine with me to-night?"

"Thea and I were getting dinner at home. Stick around if you
want to."

Mr. Van Buren strolled over to the piano. Mysie took up her
sewing basket again and darned a stocking. Mr. Van Buren hummed
to his own accompaniment, in a mild tenor. *It was not like that in
the olden days, that are gone beyond recall; In the rare old, fair
old golden days. It was not that way at all* … Mysie observed his

profile against the pale buff wall. He always had a very close hair-
cut, because his mouse-colored hair was turning prematurely grey
at the temples and he hated to see it. An intellectual head. If one
wished to draw the line that separates man from the brute kind,
it would be the curve of a human head from the eyebrows to the
back of the neck.

There was something uncanny about Jake, unclassifiable; he
simply did not obey any of the rules; he seemed to but he didn't;
so it was quite impossible either to judge or to predict him. He
was neither wrong nor right, by any set standard; he managed to
walk around the rules. So did Michael, but Michael would have
admitted that probably he was doing wrong, and gone ahead just
the same. …

It was going to be difficult, being in the same town with Michael
again for six months. He wouldn't make difficulties; he never did;
only the situation was impossible to resolve.

Though she hadn't mentioned it to Gina, she had seen Michael
six months ago, in Chicago, while she was on tour. He asked: Do
you like New York? She said: Nobody does. He said: You won't
ever come back? She said: What would I do back there? He said:
I guess that's right.

She thought, he's got trouble anyhow. But Mike took what trouble
was coming to him. … *When we all did just as we ought to do, or
if not, we ne-ever told …*

Theodora Ludlow opened the door; she was home early. She said,
without any formalities of greeting: "Where did you learn that tune,
Jake? It was before your time."

"Oh, I heard it somewhere," Jake said. He couldn't very well
tell Thea where. Thea took off her hat and sat beside him on the
piano bench.

"It goes like this," she played it over, imparting to the banal
musical phrases a brilliant and ghostly delicacy. Jake accepted the
lesson with docility. "Yes," he said, "but where did you used to tend
bar?" Thea didn't answer; she dropped her hands in her lap. She
was tall and bony and frankly her age, with strong aquiline features
surmounted by a crest of thick sorrel-grey hair, rather stately. …
She saw herself at twenty, in a yellow satin ball-gown, with an

eighteen inch waist, enormous puffed sleeves, and a yellow rose pinned to her corsage. Waltzing with Charles Ludlow. She used to waltz divinely. He proposed that night. She thought, it isn't possible. But which isn't possible, then or now?

Taking his departure later, Jake enquired of Mysie at the door: "By the way, did your cousin get what she came for?"

"She didn't say," Mysie said.

Four

In her own room, Gina seemed to hear the ticking of the nurse's wrist watch. An absurd fancy; it was her own traveling clock, of course; but her mind was elsewhere. She had ventured to pass by Mrs. Siddall's door at six o'clock, when the night nurses came on duty. The slight stir of the exchange roused Mrs. Siddall's curiosity; she was extremely bored after twenty-four hours of darkness and silence; and restless with discomfort. "Who is there?" she demanded. Mrs. Perry, already admitted, informed her, and Mrs. Siddall bade Gina come in. Since Mrs. Siddall ignored the surgeon's general instructions as soon as he was gone, the nurses did not know how to enforce them. She had refused to go to a hospital, and in her own house she was used to exercising unquestioned authority. It seemed inadvisable to give her any more sedatives.

"Don't sniffle, Annabel," Mrs. Siddall commanded. Propped against a mound of pillows in her immense canopied bed, against a headboard on which fat cupids were entwined with fat garlands of roses, she was still the dynamic center of her little world. The white stuff bound across her brow and secured under her chin lent her a Sibylline air. The visible portion of her face was slightly swollen and congested. The doctors said she had come through the operation wonderfully. Conscious of the exasperation of the nurses, Gina whispered: "Oh, Mrs. Siddall, I'm so glad ..."

Mrs. Siddall answered rather hoarsely: "You wouldn't expect that a bandage around your eyes would make it harder to breathe. It does, though." She turned her head impatiently. The nurse said: "Please, Mrs. Siddall, you mustn't tire yourself with talking."

"Very well," the old lady said. "Arthur!" She put out her hand. Arthur was on the opposite side of the bed, sitting in the shadow of a tall screen which cut off the light from the dressing room. He took the groping hand in his. "The doctor said he might stay half an hour, if he wouldn't disturb you," the nurse reminded Mrs. Siddall. The second nurse made a shooing motion; Gina backed out.

Miss Kirkland was sitting stonily in the library, resentful of exclusion. Gina went to her own room. She tried to read. Detached phrases irritated the surface of her mind. The book she had picked up at random was a romantic novel. Romantic novels told you nothing. Nor did the literal facts, which she had long ago gleaned academically from more technical treatises. Not only was there no help in them, they might be positively misleading, because they stopped short precisely where her experience stopped, giving no clue to the significance of facts. The same words, the same actions even, might mean everything, anything or nothing. What was the difference between Juliet bending to Romeo from her balcony, and the sullen, cheap, defiant girls whom the Settlement House workers strove to reform?

Gina didn't want to go to bed; the house was too still. Going out to the head of the stairs, she peered down. The upper hall was empty. She returned to her room, undressed slowly, and brushed her hair before the mirror. She observed the roundness of her arms, the smooth whiteness of her neck, against the old ivory silk of her kimono, which was embroidered with tiny yellow butterflies and blue flowers ... She stared into the mirror, facing it down. It had done Mysie no good, but what harm? You could lose either way. Her thoughts had a terrifying clarity and her senses were uncannily sharpened. A disturbance, felt rather than heard, brought her up standing. She went to the head of the stairs again.

Mrs. Siddall's rooms were on the floor below. There was a telephone at the end of the hall; a nurse was speaking through it, resting one knee on a chair and leaning forward. Obviously she was using this extension so that Mrs. Siddall should not hear. "Yes," she said, "the amyl capsules … we did … yes, yes … I understand, doctor … nothing else unless …" She went into some technical terms which Gina did not understand; then she replaced the telephone and hurried back to her duty. Her blue and white striped uniform and stiff winged cap struck a firm note against the dark-paneled wall … Gina stayed by the newel post above, waiting.

Very soon Arthur went along the hall below, in a dark blue brocade dressing gown, his hair rumpled. Then the doctor came up, grave and hurried, shedding his overcoat into the hands of the butler on the stairs. After five minutes of strained watchfulness, Gina returned to her room, leaving the door ajar an inch. She hoped intensely that nobody would call Mrs. Perry or Miss Kirkland.

Gina kept her vigil for an hour. It seemed interminable. If Mrs. Siddall were dying down there … Gina needed, desperately, a little more time. There would be no place for her in a house of mourning; she might never see Arthur again. As a child she was taught to pray; she had always prayed for some definite, tangible benefit. She prayed now for her chance.

It wasn't fair. …

She heard the doctor leaving, and stole out to the stairhead. A nurse, listening to final instructions, looked briskly cheerful. Arthur shook hands with the doctor, and accompanied him downstairs. Gina returned to her room. She sat for half an hour, telling herself she ought to go to bed. The door was still ajar. Before closing it, she listened again.

She could hear Arthur pacing up and down the hall below. She knew his step. He went by twice before he looked up and saw her.

"Gina," he said in a low voice, and came up.

"Is she better?" Gina whispered.

"Yes … Gina—can I talk to you?"

"Where?" She steadied herself by the banister.

"Anywhere. Couldn't you …" He looked about. "In the library?" She made a negative motion of regret, and he caught her sleeve. She looked over her shoulder.

"Listen," she said, "if you …" He followed her. Inside her room, she leaned against the closed door, with her hands behind her. "You won't think …?"

"No," he said simply. He was not thinking; he was comforted, enchanted by the atmosphere without perceiving the details which composed it: a silk slip lying across a chair, slippers decorously placed side by side, mirror and powderpuff and silver trifles on the dressing-table. The shaded lamp made a warm ring of light on the rose-colored rug. The room was shadowy and serene; he may have seen it before, but it seemed different, as if it did not belong to the rest of the house.

Gina slipped the catch of the lock. She said soothingly: "What was the matter? I was dreadfully worried, but didn't like to intrude."

Arthur answered vaguely; the doctor had been professionally incomprehensible. Nervous shock, syncope; the danger was averted; the patient was in a natural sleep. In short, the doctor preferred not to mention that Mrs. Siddall had over-eaten at supper; she believed in keeping up her strength, and as a result had come near putting all her other beliefs to proof.

"But she might have ..." Arthur rubbed his hand across his eyes and sat down on the chaise longue. He didn't want to put in words or remember the scene; he had been admitted to Mrs. Siddall's room while she was unconscious, fighting for breath. There was a ghastly indignity about it, violence to age and to the integrity of person-ality. His affection for his grandmother rested upon a foundation of respect; it was as if he had been forced to stand by helpless and witness the contempt of elementary forces for all human values. He had never seen death; the death of his mother and father was far-off, tragic and poetic. Youth turns to youth instinctively, in league against the knowledge of age and decay before them; he had been thinking of Gina, though hardly aware of it, when he looked up and saw her ... He shuddered slightly, drawing a deep breath.

"Don't, please please don't," she put her arm over his shoulders, moved for once to a natural and uncalculated gesture. "The doctor said there was no danger, didn't he?"

"Yes. But she's always been good to me." There was no dan-ger. ... He was quiet for awhile; the long silk sleeves sheltered him like wings. When he raised his head he saw the soft curve of Gina's arm and rested his cheek against it. He said: "I couldn't get to speak to you yesterday. You didn't come to the study. I thought you were offended." Gina thought dazedly, he expected me! She could only shake her head. He held her very gently, as if that were enough.

He had been reared by women, though less fortunate than Achilles among the maidens. Older women, a matriarchy. Had he been less masculine, he would have been less in subjection. He regarded Gina as if he had never seen a girl before, with his senses heightened to pure perceptiveness ... Delicate bones, fine fingers, a dent in her upper lip and at the base of her throat. He wanted to touch the corners of her mouth, and there, between her breasts. ... The folds of silk fell straight over her knees. ...

"I didn't know," she murmured.

"You went out in the afternoon."

"Only for a little while," she answered. His simplicity gave her no lead. She thought, but he hasn't *said* anything. She did not understand the oldest language, which can use any words and needs none. ... Her feet were bare, and she drew them under the hem of her kimono.

At her movement his expression changed. When he kissed her mouth she was afraid. She felt small and captive, ignorant that his strength was turned against himself; she turned away her face and he kissed her throat, and dropped his head on her breast; the warmth of his cheek came through the thin silk. "No, please," she whispered desperately, and struggled free, leaning back. When he lifted his head his eyes asked her. They were an intense dark blue, and he frowned against the light. She was to remember that look. He said: "I wouldn't hurt you." She knew it was true. His obedience gave her another kind of fear, not of him but of the unknown, the incalculable, the irrevocable. She could send him away. It rested with her. She knew it perfectly; and whichever course she chose, she might lose; there was no assurance.

She forced herself to remain passive. His unseeing look bewildered her and left her cold. When she kissed him she knew what she was doing. If this were her only chance. ... I can't, she thought. ... But I must——

Not in the light. She was never sure afterward if she said it aloud. In a panic of resolution, she stood up. The lamp was by the head of the bed; as she turned it off, the sudden dark dazzled her, and she seemed to have no weight in his arms. ... In deep water, if you let yourself go, you would be borne up safe; the tide would bring you in ... Or out ... But it wasn't like that for her. If only she need not be so terribly aware. This was what nobody could ever tell; it was shaming and absurd and trivial and final.

And after all. … She thought, he doesn't care, it didn't mean anything to him except. … She had lost. Was he asleep? How could he? …

The two windows were squares of twilight framed in darkness; she could distinguish the mirror over the dressing-table, by the dim silver columns of the candle-sticks reflected in it. The clock ticked away the minutes sharply.

She had supposed she would seem, to herself, a different person. It wasn't so. Except that she knew now how defenseless men and women are against each other, having once surrendered. Even if it meant nothing, there is nothing left to turn aside a word or a look. Her heart stopped and started again; Arthur said: "What is it, darling?"

"Nothing …" she thought, Mrs. Siddall might wake and ask for him; he would be missed.

"May I turn on the light?"

She remembered she herself had turned it off. … It blinded her, pressed on her eyelids. Oh, no!

"I want to see you," he said. "Gina, will you marry me?"

Her lips were cold, and she tasted the salt of tears; they flowed from beneath her closed eyelids. He dried them with his handkerchief, lifting her up against his breast. She couldn't stop the tears nor open her eyes.

"Gina, I'm so sorry. You won't hate me, will you—because I love you. Darling, you will marry me?"

She said in a drowned voice: "Mrs. Siddall won't let us."

"It doesn't matter—I mean, of course I'll tell her we're going to be married; but why should she object? When will you? To-morrow?"

The impulse to take him at his word was almost overwhelming. "We can't do that." Only as a last resort. Absolute secrecy would be impossible; his name was too well known. There mustn't be discoveries and accusations, a quarrel, appalling publicity. "Please don't tell her till she's quite well."

He thought her exquisitely unselfish, and was glad to keep something absolutely his own for awhile. … Her humbled head, the points of her wet lashes resting on her cheek, gave him a curious sensation, a twist under his midriff, a masculine pride he was unable to deny, however barbarous the tradition. … Those other women—he didn't want to think of them now, but the thought came in spite of him—the difference was, you couldn't exactly think of this.

"But grandmother will be pleased," he said ingenuously. "She wants me to get married." It didn't occur to him that most wishes are stultified by the terms of fulfillment.

Gina thought: It's real. He's sitting here on the edge of my bed; asking me to marry him. … She felt that she was within her rights, superior to other women. Her virtue consisted in fortitude and intelligence, justified by success.

"Is it very late?" she whispered. "If anyone should …"

Parting reluctantly, he kissed her hands. His flaxen hair dropped on his forehead in a fringe. "Good night—I'd rather say good morning," he turned at the door, came back and kissed her again. She stood listening, with a faint fear, after he was gone.

Sleep came on her as complete oblivion. She woke as suddenly to daylight. The housemaid was drawing the blind. For a moment Gina's mind was empty; she gazed at the maid's impassive back. Bessie. An angular middle-aged Scotchwoman. Bessie placed the matutinal tea-tray conveniently, and said: "Guid morning, ma'am" … An echo in Gina's brain said: Good morning—in Arthur's voice.

Fantastic. Like being invisible, with the cap of darkness, the shoes of swiftness, the sword of sharpness.

Five

"Really, Sam, at your age—" Mrs. Siddall smiled in spite of herself, and patted her hair with an unconscious reversion to long disused habit. Nobody in the world but Sam Reynolds would have the temerity to take her by the waist, or as much of it as his arm could compass, and imprint a mock-gallant kiss on her unyielding cheek.

"Hell, Charlotte, you didn't send for me to remind me of my age, did you? Have you no sentiment? Don't you remember the first time I bussed you?"

"The first—I should think you would prefer to forget it. In the kitchen garden, after I'd caught you pursuing the laundress!"

"Well, I had to square myself somehow. Fine figure of a gal, that laundress; I remember her distinctly, one of those outstanding Norwegians that look their best in the open air. And you handed me a haymaker that sent me through the ropes. Simply ruined the most promising young vegetable marrow on the lot; and I haven't been right in my head since."

"Nor before," Mrs. Siddall retorted. She tolerated Sam as a sort of court jester, a prerogative of her position. The exuberance of youth was his excuse in her eyes; he was twenty years her junior, and though not of her own blood, he belonged to the clan by marriage. Mrs. Siddall was the more indulgent because her father had been a jovial, blunt-spoken man; she rejected the legend that he had acquired his manner as a Yankee peddler. The Cranes were a fine old New England family. Perhaps she preferred even Sam's effrontery to her husband's suave deference, which always put him out of her reach. Since the money was hers, she had had her own way; yet after twenty years of conjugal courtesy, when he died she was left baffled, with the resentful feeling that he had not told her where he was going!

Besides her feudal attitude toward Sam Reynolds, she had a shrewder motive in condoning his disrespect. When necessary, she could get the truth from him. Her wealth created about her a maze of polite suppressions, diplomatic silences, and arrangements of disagreeable facts in a more favorable light. On the whole, she wished it so; it made for ease and consideration. But sometimes, she needed the truth.

"You have intelligence enough, Sam," she retracted, "but no ambition. I sent for you—" She paused, uncertain how to begin, or how not to be too explicit.

"To nick me for five dollars?" On principle, Sam would not allow her to play the patroness. "That's all the rich ever want of the poor—money." He had often told her it wasn't ambition but stamina he lacked. The main thing required of a great financier was the ability to exist for indefinite periods during important negotiations in a mental vacuum, listening to platitudes. Like Julius Dickerson, the sanctimonious s. o. b. … Sam knew he was labeled irresponsible. Charlotte gave him odd jobs; she never let him touch the big money. He had to extract some entertainment from the connection, or it was a dead loss. He was a lawyer, but had never got much corporation work. If Myrtle, his wife, had let him disport in his natural element— he often told her that he was born to be a Tammany politician, but Myrtle had set him polishing the doorknobs of respectability—if she had let him alone, he could have picked up enough honest graft to enable his family to relegate him to the background. His own social talent was best adapted to wearing a tall hat in a parade or at the funeral of a lamented district leader. Eminent Republicans, he affirmed, were not buried, but stuffed and placed in the windows of the Union League Club. When Sam was dragged to Charlotte's heavy dinners by his nervously aspiring wife, he avenged himself by breaking the china, the fragile proprieties. His wife and his sister-in-law, Mrs. Perry, were obliged to regard him in public as a humorist, though it was a severe strain upon their histrionic powers. In fact, there was a latent streak of vindictive envy in his clowning.

"Please listen, Sam, this is serious," Mrs. Siddall said, and stopped again. Even in her most private cogitations, she arrived at conclusions roundabout; and Sam had an embarrassing way of translating her phrases before he answered her. Being rich is a state of mind as well as a material condition. In order to derive the full benefit from wealth, the rich person whose natural talents are only mediocre or less must be convinced that he possesses some esoteric merit which has been rightly rewarded by divine justice. A blind spot in the mental retina must be maintained, to block out any object or idea that refuses to support such an assumption. Very few people are rude enough to the rich to drag inconvenient facts into the foreground and stress their significance. Sam would, and did. Mrs. Siddall considered that he had no sense of proportion. She didn't bother to adjust this view of his character with her recourse to him for direct, dependable information when she wanted it.

She had a strong aversion from morbid topics; that is, from the thought of death; hitherto she had not been afraid of dying because she simply did not believe it could happen to her. So she had suffered a profound mental shock, through her illness. She had very nearly died; she saw the truth in the expression of the doctor when consciousness returned to her. Though it was six weeks ago, she could not put it out of her mind. She was not disturbed solely on her own account. How could she leave Arthur with that vast fortune? It was the extension of her own ego, a double death to her if he could not hold it, or failed to carry on the line, leaving it to be scattered among distant relatives, sunk in the impersonal oblivion of corporate philanthropies, or dissipated in litigation.

"Sam, do you know anything about Arthur?"

"Know what? He's a good lad, that's all I know."

She fumbled with her lorgnette, watching Sam's expression.

"That is just why. ... You're a bad hat, Sam, so I'm asking you. Arthur is twenty-three and—and——"

"And a virgin?" Sam supplied.

"There is no need to be coarse. But he ought to marry."

"Well, what can I do about it?" Sam inquired. If she wanted it straight— "You'd better hire some able-bodied wench to rape him."

"Don't be so revolting." She was not discomposed; one had to set a limit with Sam, and call him to order when he exceeded. "Do you suppose there is anything—queer about him?"

"Not if he got a break. You've overlaid the boy."

"What do you mean?"

"Smothered him, with battalions of German nurses and French governesses and English tutors and Swiss cheeses. Might as well have put him in a convent—a damn' sight better. Don't you know a man can't marry his grandmother? You haven't even got a housemaid under forty, and plain at that. When you did let him go to college, didn't you send him with a bodyguard? That Oxford what-is-it. And I'll bet his valet reported to you once a week. If a live one had tried to pick him up, your flatties would have called the police. It's enough to make him queer, but he's all right. He wouldn't get so fussed when a skirt goes by, if he wasn't interested. Watch him piping that little Fuller gal."

"Gina Fuller!"

"Or Polly Brant," Sam amended hastily. Why should he crab the girl? She needed her job. And she was entitled to a shot at the prize. None of his business. "Fact is, Arthur's been mooning after Polly since he was knee high, but she's too square to encourage him. Big sister stuff. Anyhow, it's only because she's the nearest good-looker. All you've got to do is turn him loose."

"What an expression! As if he were not quite independent— ridiculous. He comes and goes as he chooses."

"Comes in every night and goes to bed at ten o'clock. You know where he is every hour out of the twenty-four, don't you?"

"Surely you don't imply that I should take no interest in him whatever?"

Sam said: "I don't imply anything. You asked me." He was annoyed at himself; wouldn't he ever learn to yes them? But there was no gain in taking back what he had already said. "All I can say is, you've got him in training for a bachelor. And if you want him to be queer, just put on a little more pressure." Compunction seized him; the old girl looked rather yellow about the gills. Perhaps he had hit too hard. "Oh, hell, Charlotte, I didn't mean that exactly; there's nothing the matter with Arthur except common decency. Get Polly to give you a hand. She'll marry him off before he knows what the shooting's about—and may God have mercy on his soul."

Mrs. Siddall's double chin quivered as if she were literally swallowing her pride. If she must, she would accept help—even from another woman. "Think it over," Sam repeated placably.

"Very well," Mrs. Siddall resumed her lofty tone; and Sam did not miss it.

"And of course," he said, "you'll never forgive me."

She could do the handsome thing. "No," she said, "I won't. I never forgave you for kissing the laundress first." They laughed together.

She thought it over, while Gina was reading to her next morning. Altogether the reading was wasted, for Mrs. Siddall paid no attention; and Gina read mechanically. Gina couldn't stand much more. She must chance it, let Arthur tell Mrs. Siddall, very soon. It would be so much worse if the knowledge came any other way. To meet one of the maids in the upper hall made Gina's heart turn over sickeningly—the way they were about at all hours. … And for a day she had experienced primitive terror. Afterward she recognized that what she feared might be the last resort necessary to hold Arthur, though it would be next to failure. She could almost have hated him for his unshared pleasure, bought with her unshared tears.

Mrs. Siddall's solid figure, in her winged chair, suggested the immovable body of the philosophical riddle. She too had had a bad night. She had dreamed that she lay swathed in some gauzy inescapable web, fold upon fold, all grey, over her face, wound about her limbs, till she could neither stir nor cry out, while she knew that something was happening, somewhere, which concerned her, though she was helpless to prevent or direct or even to discover its nature. A wretched dream; it must be the memory of going into the ether for the operation. Things came back like that occasionally; at long intervals she dreamed of her husband, dead these twenty years. In that dream, she was explaining some important matter to him, and he did not answer. She detested dreams.

"Eh?" Though she had been looking straight at Gina, she recognized her again suddenly when the end of an article was marked by silence. "Thank you," Mrs. Siddall said. "Yes, Janet?" Gina repressed a start; Miss Kirkland was standing in the door tentatively, and the least unexpected trifle now startled Gina. Miss Kirkland's sallow plainness was aggravated by a dress of the most unbecoming shade of brown, two inches longer than the current fashion. "Please telephone to Mrs. Brant," Mrs. Siddall requested, "and ask her when she can spare me an hour. If she could come to tea to-day... Go on, Gina; you might pick out the main points of the news from Washington."

Miss Kirkland reported almost immediately that Mrs. Brant was out for the day. "You left a message? Very well," Mrs. Siddall relapsed into her meditation. What light came into the room fell on Gina's demure figure. No make-up, Mrs. Siddall observed favorably. Modern girls were so hard, flippant and self-engrossed, painting their vacuous faces in public and bringing the manners of the demi-monde into the drawing-room. The things they talked about, under pretense of being honester than their grandmothers, who had borne ten children apiece and said nothing about it. Mrs. Siddall forgot that she herself had considered her duty done when she produced one healthy son. But they didn't talk about that either in her time; it was assumed to be the will of God. "Thank you," she indicated to Gina that the reading was over. "By the way, your parents are living, are they not?"

"My mother is," Gina had grown accustomed to Mrs. Siddall's mannerism of royalty, asking questions suddenly and dropping the subject with the same abruptness.

"And your brothers and sisters?"

"I have none." That seemed to be satisfactory; Mrs. Siddall nodded and indicated that Gina might go. Janet came in with the morning's mail and letters to sign. Poor Janet, Mrs. Siddall thought irrelevantly—a faithful creature, hardworking and capable. ... Usually, when Mrs. Siddall laid down the last letter and said with a rising inflection: "That is all, I think?" Miss Kirkland indicated zeal by hastening away. This morning, she lingered; and Mrs. Siddall asked ritually: "Yes, Janet?"

"There is something I must—" Miss Kirkland began nervously.

Some complaint of the servants, no doubt, Mrs. Siddall thought. Vexatious but unavoidable. If those empty-headed radicals who displayed their ignorance by talking about the idle rich had any idea of the task it was to manage a great household. ... Mrs. Siddall

was sincere in her conviction that "maintaining her social position" was her duty. Even the best of servants grew slack without
the immediate supervision of the mistress; she supposed hers had
become slightly disorganized during her illness. Mrs. Enderby,
the housekeeper, was growing old; it might be best to pension
her off, but then the other old servants would resent the orders
of a newcomer. Really, they were very trying, with their spites
and sulks. Most difficult with secretaries and governesses; Mrs.
Siddall couldn't stoop to personal cognizance of minor incidents,
but she could enforce her will when necessary, and listen when
it seemed advisable.

Miss Kirkland's approach to talebearing was correct but tedious.
If only she would stop fidgeting and rustling among the letters.
Temporary blindness had made Mrs. Siddall susceptible to noises.

"You may be angry with me, but I can't bear to see you deceived,"
Miss Kirkland said jerkily. Mrs. Siddall made a motion of impa-
tience. Miss Kirkland said: "Miss Fuller——"

Jealous, Mrs. Siddall thought. "Deceived? Really, Janet …" This
was going too far, impugning her intelligence.

A deep sense of injury flooded Miss Kirkland's maiden bosom.
It was shameful. The word slipped from her tongue.

"Miss Fuller—is taking a shameful advantage of your
confidence—to entrap Mr. Arthur." She stopped, gasping.

Mrs. Siddall's features settled into the semblance of a wood-
carving. One did not discuss the Family.

"Pray what do you imply by that statement, Janet?"

"I can't—don't ask me."

"I insist."

"I saw him—coming out of her bedroom. At two o'clock last
night. I thought you ought to know."

"What?" Mrs. Siddall gripped the arms of her chair. "I didn't
think he had it in him!"

Miss Kirkland stood stunned, amid the wreckage of her ideals.
She had brought the roof down upon her own head.

Mrs. Siddall said with firm persuasiveness: "Quite impossible.
Of course, you did right to come to me, if you had gained such an
impression, however the mistake arose. I am sure you will never

mention it again, to anyone. At two in the morning, one is apt to imagine things. I daresay you were not fully awake, and heard someone; Arkright goes round very late, locking up."

"I had a toothache ..." Miss Kirkland's carefully prepared story died away hopelessly. She wished she was dead.

"A toothache," Mrs. Siddall rose, sweeping aside the main charge, "you're not yourself. A toothache is very distressing; you must make an appointment with the dentist at once. As for this misunderstanding, I rely upon your discretion. It would be most unfortunate if it came to Arthur's knowledge. He is so sensitive and chivalrous. I am sure you realize. ..."

Miss Kirkland realized. So thoroughly, that she made an appointment with the dentist.

Six

Mrs. Siddall understood the immense power of inertia. If you let things alone, they usually worked out tolerably well. But that was only if one could say of the difficulty: It won't run away. Some problems will not wait.

Miss Kirkland, regarding only the moral issue, expected an exemplary manifestation. By no stretch of imagination could she have foreseen that her revelation lifted a weight from Mrs. Siddall's mind. She did grasp the meaning of Mrs. Siddall's emphatic incredulity. She had been put in her place. There were to be no scenes, no gossip. But Miss Kirkland still supposed that Gina would be sent away quietly and immediately. Ultimately, Mrs. Siddall would be grateful to her, would recognize her disinterested watchfulness.

Naturally, Mrs. Siddall did consider drastic action. No need to be brutal, or to betray her reason, her knowledge of the affair. Simple enough to decide to go down to Asheville, take Arthur along, and dismiss Gina; she did not need a reader. … And perhaps Janet really had been mistaken, had exaggerated some misunderstood incident. But then …

Mrs. Siddall rang and gave orders that she was not to be disturbed until Arthur came in, when she desired to see him.

But then … if Janet was mistaken?

Mrs. Siddall hoped flatly that she wasn't.

Young men recovered easily from puppy love or a casual affair. Sam phrased it vulgarly, but he ought to know; it was usually a matter of "the nearest good-looker." With Gina out of the way, nothing would be required but a little diplomacy and another, more eligible girl.

Mrs. Pearson had a débutante daughter, just out of a French convent. Rather foreign, but an attractive child. Still, those children of divorcées—a bad start. Mrs. Siddall had no abstract prejudice against divorce, except for the odious publicity. She wouldn't have endured Jelliffe Pearson's flagrant infidelity herself. But that was just the point; she didn't want him in the family, as Arthur's father-in-law. Besides, Mrs. Pearson was a *maitresse femme;* she would want to run the young couple.

There were the Townley twins. No, Arthur would jib. They belonged to the horsey set, smart laconic amazons, who lived in boots and breeches. Lily Adamson? As pretty as a china doll, and as silly. Eleanor Dabney? a man-eater and a jilt; she had broken three engagements within a year. Rosalie Sands? All that clan were spendthrifts, living beyond their trusteed incomes. They'd sponge on Arthur, divide him among them. Mathilde Avery, poor dear; her father had committed suicide to avoid some disgraceful exposure. It was hushed up, but everyone knew what his "appendicitis" was. Caroline Wiggins, a well-mannered girl, with money and sound connections, but so unnecessarily plain; it needn't come to that.

The ideal would be an orphan heiress of pleasing appearance, amiable disposition and distinguished name. Even so, heiresses were apt to be spoiled—too independent, Mrs. Siddall thought, serenely unconscious of irony. …If Gina had money and position. … Mrs. Siddall blinked, astonished at the direction of her own logic.

Arthur came in, bringing an outdoor air. He kissed her cheek as he had always done since he was a baby; he still possessed the naturalness of docile and affectionate children. She took him by the shoulders and searched his face.

He looked…innocent. Good and happy. She knew then that it was true.

She asked: "What have you been doing?"

At a book auction, he said; he had bought a first edition of Drayton; she tried to remember who was Drayton. A heavenly day, he added. I daresay, Mrs. Siddall reflected silently. He said he had walked through the park; she ought to go for a drive; wouldn't the doctor permit it yet?

"Perhaps," she said absently, "that is, next week. I remember when it was considered daring for a lady to drive her own turnout. A phäeton, with a parasol whip; that was when I was a little girl; then there were traps and we sat high up and very straight. My first riding habit had a long skirt and I wore a flowing veil."

"You must have looked magnificent," Arthur smiled.

"Chic," she said. "The Comte de Pourtales told me I reminded him of Princess Pauline Metternich." *Une jolie laide,* with black eyes. Mrs. Siddall deceived herself kindly, as most women do in remembering their girlhood; it is one reason why old women are often indulgent toward youthful escapades; they have a weakness for that other, partly imaginary self, the true self in their belief. And though Mrs. Siddall had been plump and fashionable rather than elegant, she had had the note of her period, as she now had the style of her age and her vast wealth. … Pourtales had kissed her wrist gallantly; that too was daring. She had been the leader of the dashing young matrons who broke the rigid ranks of New York society in the Nineties. In spite of the stuffy insolent old dowagers, she reflected reminiscently, still sublimely unaware of the humor of a completed cycle. … "But my dear," she exclaimed, "my mind is wandering; I'm getting old. That's what I wished to speak to you about; it would be a great comfort to me to see you married."

He was silent. Mrs. Siddall pressed the point. "Haven't you ever thought about it?"

He couldn't lie about Gina; she had only asked him to wait for a propitious occasion; surely this was it.

He said: "Yes."

"Someone in particular?" Mrs. Siddall proceeded carefully. "But you would tell me first?"

"She," he flushed at the pronoun, which had come to have a single meaning to him, "she said I must, as soon as you were quite well. She won't marry me unless you approve. But I'll never marry anyone else."

Mrs. Siddall had never heard that tone from him. He meant it. Of course, with time and tact—but time was the one thing she could not command. Those sensitive, unassertive people were the most difficult, in their own way. Arthur was like his grandfather, her husband. Without the Senator's adroitness, his political talent such as it was—Mrs. Siddall didn't draw any distinction between the opportunist behind the scenes and the man of genuine public abilities—but she felt in Arthur the same ultimate unreachableness. Even while apparently acquiescent, he would escape. Could she endure it again, to have him so near and yet so remote?

"Who is she?" Mrs. Siddall asked, since she didn't want Arthur to commit himself further on the point of honor.

"Gina."

Though she knew it perfectly, his utterance of the name was a blow to her. She forgot to play out the comedy. She didn't know why she said: "Your grandfather—" and stopped there. Her husband had belonged to one of the oldest New York families. She had never let herself know he married her for her money. And she kept a tight hold on the money. She said heavily: "This is a great surprise. It wants consideration. You can't expect—after all, it is hardly the match one would look for—" Now she was surprised by her own lack of resistance; she would never let herself know either that she was not unwilling to flout the old New York families, and their daughters. The Siddalls could do as they pleased. She had shown them once. Furthermore, Gina could never take Arthur away from her as long as she lived. Afterward, Gina would know how to manage him; the fortune would be safe. If Gina had been a flighty adventuress, she would have run off with Arthur. That was the underlying objection to any other marriage; by an alliance with an important family, Arthur would be detached to some extent from his grandmother, drawn into another circle. Not that Mrs. Siddall defined the situation in such plain terms. She merely felt that she dared not be too absolute; disinheritance would cut her more keenly than it would him; what else should she do with the money? She liked Gina well enough; there was nothing against the girl but her obscurity, and that was a kind of pledge.

"I think I had better see Gina, alone," she said. "Before you speak to her again—do you mind, my dear?" She had a vague hope of taking Gina unprepared.

"I'll wait in the library," Arthur said.

After Gina came Mrs. Siddall remained silent a moment, more from embarrassment than arrogance. "Sit down—never mind the papers now. There is something I am obliged to discuss with you. Perhaps you can guess. Arthur——''

Gina's lips parted and closed again; whatever happened, she must not allow herself to think of her actual relation to Arthur. It was like possessing a concealed weapon, too dangerous to display. ... Where was Arthur?

"Arthur has told me everything," Mrs. Siddall said.

Oh—he couldn't!

"He told you that he wants to marry me?"

Cleverly put, Mrs. Siddall conceded to herself. She nodded. "And that you refused, unless I gave my consent."

Gina wavered, uncertain if she were walking into a trap. She said in a low voice "I don't want to cause—an estrangement." But she had the power. "Because Arthur cares so much for you. And I should be sorry, on my own account. Because I value your—esteem."

"I suppose you are aware that Arthur has very little money of his own?"

"He said he had enough. I shouldn't care about that; you know he doesn't either." Clever of her again, Mrs. Siddall thought; Arthur would never have any conception of the value of money. He might become immensely extravagant without realizing it; he might, on the other hand, fail to realize what he was giving up until long afterward. "But he doesn't believe you'd be offended at him—for long," Gina continued, as if reluctantly. "So I have to consider—it's very difficult—I want him to be happy." She thought, why didn't Arthur warn me? What did he tell her? Has he promised not to see me again? ... She felt the empty pain of the deserted, and a sickness of fear.

"Would you release him if it seemed to be for his happiness to do so?"

She must chance it, since she could count upon nothing but his word. "If he came and asked me himself, I would," she said in a muffled voice.

"Not for any other consideration?"

"There couldn't be—any other consideration."

Mrs. Siddall inclined her head majestically. They had defined their terms. Gina offered allegiance; benevolence on one side, gratitude on the other. Mrs. Siddall offered cash down. But if Arthur was to be the arbiter—no, Mrs. Siddall knew the answer. She said: "You are right; money doesn't bring happiness." She was quite serious, and so was Gina. "You will find Arthur in the library. Kiss me, my dear; it will be very pleasant to have a daughter in the house." She could at least stipulate that they should live with her.

Arthur was walking up and down impatiently when Gina went to him; yet she perceived he had not been worried. "What did she——"

Gina said: "She was very kind. Let me sit down a minute." The sudden relaxation of strain was almost too much. And with his arm around her, she felt again that dark resentment of his good fortune, his ingenuousness, his delight.

The next morning, Polly Brant dropped the telephone receiver and upset her breakfast tray. "Bill!"

Her husband appeared from his dressing room, with a fluff of lather on his chin. He had an admirable physique, a drooping hay-colored mustache, and the mild brainless look of the true sportsman. By incessant effort he had risen to the position of substitute on the leading American polo team; and he took his vacations from this life work by shooting big game and exploring the more uncomfortable portions of the uninhabitable globe. He preserved devoutly complete files of the National Geographic Magazine, in which his photograph appeared occasionally in company with a defunct African koodoo, or Kodiak bear, or Ovis Poli, slain for the ostensible benefit of some museum of natural history.

"'Smatter? You nearly made me cut my throat."

"Aunt Charlotte! I cannot believe my ears!"

"Believe what?"

"Arthur is going to marry that Fuller person!"

"Who?"

"Gertrude the Governess. The girl who reads to Aunt Charlotte. You've seen her."

"I thought her name was Janet."

"I don't deserve this," Polly said in a suffering tone. "Even if I did marry you with my eyes open. I mean the other one. Gina Fuller."

"You said Gertrude," Bill objected.

"I know I did," Polly admitted. "Gertrude for short. Let's not go into that; I'd have to teach you the alphabet. It's partly my fault anyhow."

"What have you got to do with it?" Bill enquired placidly.

"Patting him on the head, when he was trying to escape from the nursery," Polly explained darkly. "The least I could have done was to break his heart. If it wasn't for you I'd elope with him this minute; it's my plain duty. But I suppose you wouldn't like it."

"I would *not,*" Bill grunted. "What's wrong with the girl, anyhow? I remember her now; she seemed a sweet little thing. No money, eh?"

"Sweet," Polly grimaced. "Oh, so sweet!"

"You women are always down on one another," Bill said, with unbearable masculine fatuity.

Polly moaned. "I don't see how it is possible to love such an absolute dimwit as you are, Bill. But I do. It's sheer atavism. If I were a Victorian, and you died, I'd feel an irresistible impulse to have you mounted with glass eyes and keep you in a case in the parlor."

"Quaint notion," Bill agreed. "I wouldn't put it past you. But cut out the elopements. When do they mean to walk up the aisle?"

"Oh, go away," said Polly. "In June, I suppose. People do."

She supposed correctly. Miss Kirkland sent the announcement to the newspapers, and fended off reporters. She knew she was typing her own sentence. The honeymoon would be spent abroad, and Mrs. Siddall planned to join the young couple later and winter in Egypt or on the Riviera. Mrs. Siddall had not been abroad for twenty years, dreading the sea; but this was a new start. She would engage a courier-secretary for traveling, she explained to Janet; but her old friend, Mrs. Trask, required a companion; Mrs. Siddall recommended Janet to her. Mrs. Trask lived in Lancaster, Pennsylvania, and was stone deaf, but very active and cheerful, Mrs. Siddall said encouragingly. The position would be restful for Janet, who looked tired.

Janet said nothing. … It was enough to make her abandon virtue altogether, if she had seen any feasible way. Much virtue in an if …

Seven

Mysie was an hour late, and she was in a hurry, and angry, and laughing. Teddy McKee stopped her as she was running down the steps of the theater entrance. She said: "Oh, hello," and waved to a taxi. He said: "I haven't seen you for a long time, Mysie: what are you doing this evening?" She said: "This *evening*—good heavens!" and sprang into the taxi.

Jake Van Buren would be waiting at her apartment to take her to dinner. When she arrived she was an hour and fifteen minutes late. She flew up the stairs and burst in; Jake was there. She exclaimed: "Don't bother to say it." She had a job as press-agent for Neale Corrigan, a grouchy little Irish producer with a face like a hickory knot. She rather liked him, in spite of his habit of counting the postage stamps and keeping her overtime. "Wouldn't you think," she said, "that at his age and him a good Catholic with the fear of death on him that he'd mend his manners—but it's unfortunate the Church doesn't tell you that you go to hell for that sort of thing. For you do. And then," she remembered what she had been laughing about, "Sid Walters came in while I was putting on my hat; there was a smudge of carbon across my nose; he clasped me to his manly bosom and said: 'My little wild rose.' Wild is no word for it, I just exploded laughing, and it hurt his feelings—that's his method, taking 'em by surprise, and he did all right—I had to bolt and leave him looking as if he had stepped on his foot. Blast, it's nearly eight o'clock, go out and get yourself something to eat while I dress."

"I had some," Jake replied. "I knew you'd be late. What about you?"

"I don't want any—" She vanished into her bedroom, and there were faint sounds of splashing.

Jake sat down again patiently, with his habitual air of a well-bred guest, at ease without presuming. Dress clothes became him; he only sighed at the discovery that he was wearing a hair shirt under the armor plate of white starch. He had been to the barber during the afternoon, and a few clippings had clung through a bath and change, with devilish persistence. Putting on horn-rimmed glasses, he took up a book.

Half an hour later Mysie called to him in muffled tones. He laid down the book exactly where it had been.

"Yes?" he replied. "Can I what?"

Mysie came out in a short black evening frock, with an erratic trail of silver lace at one side, and contorted her neck alarmingly, endeavoring to gaze down her spinal column. "Something is caught in the back, can you see what, and put it straight?"

"How can you tell when a dress like this is straight?" he enquired, making a careful, respectful survey. "Ah," he disentangled a fastener, without touching Mysie's bare shoulder.

Thea Ludlow appeared from the kitchen, and watched them. What an extraordinary relationship, she thought. She was the only person who knew or even suspected the nature of the relationship.

Mysie said: "Thanks—one minute," disappearing again. "I ought to have gloves," her voice floated out tragically.

"I will get you gloves to-morrow," Jake said.

"To-morrow! What good will that do to-night?"

"This book I was just reading," Jake said pacifically, "by Eddington Jeans Whitehead, explains that time and space are identical and interchangeable, and that if you work fast enough, you will overtake yesterday and get a million light years ahead of to-morrow, thus meeting yourself coming back for something you forgot, though it is possible that the whole universe is shooting sideways, which would make it harder."

"Well, then, I'll bet it *is* shooting sideways," said Mysie bitterly, "just to make it harder. The trouble with me is that I'm two million light years ahead already, so I've got behind again."

"There is that," Jake agreed. "Good night, Thea." Mysie snatched a green velvet evening cloak, and wrapped it about her as they went downstairs. They caught a taxi at once.

"If Geraldine is ready we can get to Gina's by ten o'clock," Mysie calculated, "so maybe I can be home at midnight and get some sleep. If only I had time to sit down and think——"

"What about?" Jake wished to know.

"Oh, shut up," said Mysie. The taxi stopped suddenly for the lights, jolting them together in a heap. They sorted themselves out politely. "This is known as the mad rush of New York's life, waiting for hours in taxis at crossings. It's five years since Gina was married—I don't know what that has to do with it, though. Only you don't see people for years, and then you gallop to meet them as if it were a fire." Someone had spoken to her on the steps …

Where had those five years gone out of her own life? Just as to-day had gone, running, breathless, accomplishing nothing. She was twenty-nine, would be thirty in six months. She had got nowhere in her profession, hardly was sure she had a profession any more. She was doing publicity as a stop-gap. Neale Corrigan had promised her a part; but his recent productions had nothing suitable for her type, his directors said. She was useful to Corrigan, knew how to get on with him, the feminine touch! …I'm one of those competent women, she thought with horror. I can always earn an honest living. So I'll never be kept in luxury. By a kind husband, or whatever. … My type! Blast, damn, hell! I can play anything. So they won't let me. There is no *acting*. Just walk-ons. No, I can't play anything, but if there is brains in it I can. If I'd learn to gurgle and swoop up and down on the lines—such lines, there really isn't anything else to do with them. Broadway comedy—synthetic gin. It makes me sick!

"There are no *plays*." She said that aloud.

Jake gave her his undivided attention and affirmed with passionate conviction that one of America's leading dramatists, whom he named, was a low-grade tomato worm. In Jake's opinion, the drama need not concern itself exclusively with subnormal creatures expressing themselves in a dialect compounded of East Lynne and Way Down East. "Not that I have anything against morons as such," he qualified, "but *does* the total absence of a sense of humor in itself constitute genius?"

"Among the Best People, it does," said Mysie. "I hope I may restrain myself at Gina's, and not dish your laudable ambition to chisel that job out of little Arthur. God knows I've tried hard enough to like the rich, for the sake of their money; but it can't be done. Once is enough to be told that Mussolini made the Italian railways run on time; and that Hoover has the international mind."

"Listen," said Jake. "I have told you and told you that it will get you *nowhere* to try verbal first aid on those cases. Why you go so far as to leap from the pedestal upon which I have enshrined you and scutter down to the abysms of such monsters and hold converse with them and put yourself in the way of receiving such surprising whacks over the pituitary I cannot imagine. Leave them alone! Leave them alone! They may serve some inscrutable purpose by saying those things—who are we to judge, after all, whom they were sent here to bore to death? If you start trying to enlighten one, you have to stand at the elbow of the patient forever, through long eternities, doing the same thing without any net results, for the remedy does not reach the real seat of the disease. I've seen you working on them. They finally get so they can't call their souls their own and say even worse things in their efforts to please. You believe in the possibility of ameliorating the condition of the mentally or spiritually submerged. You, a grown woman——"

"I don't," said Mysie. "All I ask is that they should go away and die somewhere out of my sight. They come up and speak to me. There are times, and plenty of them, when in self-defense you've got to use an ax."

Jake said: "It does seem the only way to get the sensation to the forebrain. But to-night——"

"Yes, yes," said Mysie. "I will, really. Besides, Arthur isn't like that himself. Of course he doesn't know the difference; he has never heard anything else in his born days. But he's rather sweet. You can tell. He has such lovely manners, and sees that everybody gets drinks, and looks bewildered because nothing makes sense. Usually only the nouveau riche are tolerable, because at least in early life they got it slapped into them. I've never talked to Arthur to any extent; Gina asked me to lunch a couple of times, but he was at the other end of the table. Then she dropped me because I didn't get my name up in electric lights. She's civil to Geraldine since Geraldine's novel went over. It's lucky I was there when she telephoned to invite Geraldine, so she had to ask me too. It tickled Geraldine to ring me in. Like most respectable married women, Geraldine sticks at nothing."

"Marriage blunts the finer feelings," said Jake.

"How do you figure that? I am sure you can, but your logical processes fascinate me, even after all these years."

"The very idea of going to bed night after night with someone you're living in the same house with—it's incestuous!"

"What would be your idea? Total strangers?" So we were, Mysie thought.

"Well, someone you meet on a moonlight night. For what is called romantic love, enormous obstacles are helpful."

"That's simple; if obstacles don't exist, you invent them. But there are so many strangers, how would you pick out one from another? I guess there's no real solution." She brooded.

Jake is cuckoo, she thought. He must be a genius, and a genius isn't human. I should have known at sight. However, there's no harm done, because if I don't make one mistake I make another … *Oh,* that was *Teddy McKee!* On the steps …

She felt a genuine horror and a great dismay. Reverse English, she thought; if your whole life should flash before your eyes, you'd go and drown yourself. … She had simply forgotten about Teddy McKee. Didn't even remember when she saw him. …

But she had forgotten deliberately, meant to wash it out. … The street lights slid by the taxi. They were dodging about under the Sixth Avenue Elevated, with intermittent maddening thunder overhead, trucks and street cars looming monstrous in the path; the taxi nosed through imminent destruction with fantastic insouciance. Had to go on, go through; there would be no point in stopping, either, in that spate of power pouring between artificial cliffs. There was nothing else to do, once started. And how even avoid starting? Mysie strained her eyes to catch a street number, and desisted. It didn't matter. She had looked automatically, on the instinct that you ought to know where you are and your direction and destination. But something happened to your sense of direction in New York. It had no relation to the sky and sun.

I am a lost soul, she thought. Not damned, just lost. But when did it really happen? When I was a child? ... You find yourself when you find what belongs to you, your own people. Where are mine? Jake isn't exactly; he's a fellow traveler. I don't know about Michael Busch, either—yes, somehow we belonged. But anyhow, Johnny Disston was a stranger, one of those strangers Jake means. Of course Jake is a stranger to everybody on this earth.

But it seems as if I got turned around, she thought, with Johnny. Until then I felt as if I were going somewhere definite, I didn't know exactly where, but there seemed to be a road and it seemed as if it would come out right, as if it must be my road.

While the street lights went spinning by, she thought back, with idle clarity. Beginning with Johnny Disston. She was barely eighteen, and working in the mill office, the summer Johnny came to Sequitlam. Could that be only a little over ten years ago? Johnny had come up on business, a projected farm land development, buying and clearing cut-over timber tracts, that kept him all summer but didn't keep him very busy. ... He was at least, she thought in self-justification, uncommonly good looking. Like Baldur the Beautiful; his face was broad across the cheekbones, slightly Scandinavian, and his hair was bright gold; he kept it clipped close to prevent it curling; he didn't exploit his good looks. And he had that exceptional vitality, an easy strength that is a kind of physical genius. When he moved, his coat moulded to the muscles of his shoulders. Both men and women liked him. Mysie had met him several times before the day he came into her office when she was reaching for something on top of the high old-fashioned safe. She was alone. The first thing she knew, she was swung into the air; he took her by the waist with his two hands and lifted her off her feet. Don't mention it, he said. ... After that, whenever she saw him she had a sensation of lightness and helplessness.

There was, actually, nothing to the affair. A brief flirtation. First love, or infatuation, is usually an accident of circumstance; the vague, enormous, dynamic potentialities of youth fix themselves upon any convenient object. Johnny had no idea of hurting her, no intentions of any kind. Men don't go around seducing girls. They don't want the responsibility. He meant nothing in particular even when he told her he was going away, kissed her good-by, and said: You'd better come along; how about it? She didn't say anything. She would have gone with him, though she couldn't say so, though she shook her head. She knew he didn't mean it. She could have made him mean it, if she had been older; but she didn't want to either, if he didn't want to himself. He went away, and for a long time afterward something of herself was gone too. She liked to talk to Michael Busch, didn't care what anyone thought, if they knew, because Michael was solid and centered, something to hold by. He was all there. She got from Michael some idea of people, of the world, and perhaps a valuation of herself. Michael valued her. Yes, she had treated him rather badly, through ignorance and inexperience. … The ache of loss persisted, even after she came to New York.

Everyone went rather mad in those years. She had thought, men don't let themselves go on caring when it is no use, or asking for what doesn't exist. They take whatever they can get, and seem well enough satisfied. I'll try it. … But Teddy McKee was just nothing. Teddy was puzzled; he never understood why she began or why she broke it off. A woman, she found, cannot live by the senses like a man—if a man can. Because her senses turn against her, are subject to her imagination. She should have realized that if it was no good with Michael Busch, it wouldn't be with a harmless amiable nonentity like Teddy McKee. She decided to wash it out. If there was nothing for her there was nothing, and no need to go through the motions.

Jake told her in a baffled moment: You'll die an old maid, no matter what…

Maybe he was right. For she did not believe it was Johnny Disston himself who counted; only he confused her, perhaps because she was too young. But how desperate a chance, if happiness is balanced upon so fine a point of sensibility that all one's life might go for one kiss, for a word or a glance occurring just so or so, at such a moment and no other … I've never met my man, she thought.

No, that must be wrong. One must make a life, out of the lump of raw commonplace, content with a kind of average return. Or fix upon some definite, tangible objective, and convince yourself that it's worth your whole effort. Men did that too, accumulated money and possessions and strove for importance. Mysie thought, at least Gina is successful; a great match is the legitimate traditional ambition for a woman, as much as place or power for a man. And Geraldine is successful, not because she has written a best seller, nor because she had got a husband; Leonard isn't much; but she has made something out of their relation, out of her marriage and her children; they belong to her.

For herself, Mysie had decided some years ago, she would have to work. Work was all right of itself. It wouldn't get you anywhere; she saw that. Presumably a career was as good for a woman as for a man, if no better; but she knew it would never be enough for her. After all, a man who has only a public life, even if he is a Napoleon, is somehow a poor creature, posturing and pathetic; and furthermore, Mysie had an inexplicable conviction that those apparently solid rewards were growing hollow, being eaten away by some spirit of the times, perhaps through being sought as an end in themselves. Everybody played the stock market for easy money; everything was flashy and tipsy and swift. And yet nobody really had any fun; there was always an aftertaste of bad gin in the pleasure. She did not like the way things were, the stupid drinking and promiscuous pawing and meaningless familiarity, in which all personal values went by the board and people seemed to derive an imbecile gratification from cheapening themselves. Work was better than that. Abstinence and virtue became attractive.

I suppose I'm a failure, Mysie thought. The simplest, most ordinary fool, crying for the moon. ... But isn't there something? I wonder what Gina has got out of her success?

The taxi turned, in the West Seventies, and stopped. Geraldine had moved to an apartment near the park, on account of the children.

Eight

Geraldine was almost ready; it is impossible to be quite ready in the bosom of one's family. She needn't hurry, said Mysie inconsistently, and laid off her wrap for a few minutes' grace. "I like this apartment; it suits you, Geraldine." The square old-fashioned heavy-corniced rooms were restful. "You know the Bible says Judas died and went to his own place—such a tactful way of putting it—I guess we all do here and now. Gina was bound to arrive on Fifth Avenue, and I have to live down town; and you can't escape from the West Side."

Geraldine reflected on the suggestion. She was sometimes surprised to find herself living on a scale which included a cook, a housemaid and a nurse. It happened gradually; after her novel established her reputation, her short stories began to sell, the money came in, and she spent it. "Grandmother lived in this part of town," she said. "Father's mother. We used to come over from Hoboken for Sunday dinner. Roast beef at two o'clock, and a coal-gas smell from those stingy black marble fireplaces. It was a brownstone house, of course. I always went into a coma on the stamped brown velvet sofa after dinner, with some deadly book. The Pansy Books. I liked Hoboken better."

"You didn't really," said Mysie, "live in Hoboken. Nobody could have. There is no such place."

"Maybe there isn't now," Geraldine conceded. "But there was. It must have disappeared, though; everything disappeared." There had been a small green-shuttered frame house in a slanting hillside garden; and father had a ship-chandler's shop near the docks; also a half interest in a cheap old hotel. Nothing was said about the hotel, especially before "company," because of the bar. Mother and the children never went near it. When father died there was trouble and delay realizing anything from the shop or the hotel; in effect, they disappeared. It was necessary for Geraldine to go to work when she finished high-school, any kind of work she could find, because she hadn't been brought up with the idea of working. She hadn't, so far as she could recall, been brought up with any idea at all. Mother and the children existed in relation to father. Perhaps they were a belated example of the traditional family, in which boys were expected to get jobs and girls to marry. There were no boys in the family, but Geraldine had two sisters; all three found husbands without effort. Geraldine was unable to account for her persistent impulse to write. She had gone about it unobtrusively, with no special hopes; and she used to wonder what a writer was like, never having seen one.

"I can't imagine your early life," Mysie said.

"I can't imagine yours," said Geraldine. "The West. It's a movie. But you talk about logbooms and sawmills and the sea. Besides, where did Gina come in?"

"Gina," said Mysie, "is from a small town. Her mother had white lace curtains and geraniums. Gina is one of those people that if anyone asks, do you know her? aren't you from the same place? you say, yes, I've met her. But Jake is a New Yorker; and you never even met him."

"If it was Murray Hill, that was another New York," Geraldine explained.

Jake said: "Well, my great-aunt Eugenia lived on Murray Hill. But the fact is, father owned a livery stable over on Third Avenue, and we lived on Eighteenth Street. The livery stable became extinct by degrees. Father had inherited it from the distaff side; you see my grandfather Van Buren married beneath him. Of course grandmother also married beneath her, because grandfather was the black sheep of his family as a young man, but he reformed later and became miserly after he inherited a bit of money and the house from his own father. Great-aunt Eugenia never married because it would have been beneath her, she being a Van Buren. I told you not to get me started."

"Goodness, Judy," Geraldine exclaimed, "haven't you gone to bed yet? Run along, darling." Nine-year-old Judy had been allowed to sit up to see her mother dressed for a party, and had lurked unobserved in a corner. She was a lovely child, with smooth dark hair, and eyebrows drawn in a delicate new moon curve, like Mysie's. Geraldine bundled her off and returned smiling. "She asked me: Why don't you have more people like Jake and Mysie come to see us?"

"The compliment of a lifetime," Mysie said. "Tell her there aren't any more; we're all the traffic will bear. Geraldine, for the sake of your innocent children you ought to reduce twenty pounds. Prosperity is ruining you. With your pink hair you could be very smart; you're really pretty."

"No, I couldn't," said Geraldine meekly. "I have no taste." She was getting fat, but her dimpled chin saved her; even the slight suggestion of bursting out of her clothes was endearing. "Do you think this frock will do?" she asked, brushing a sprinkle of powder from her black velvet bodice. "Your dress is stunning, Mysie."

"I bought it out of the wardrobe of a show that died unborn," Mysie said. "Thirty dollars for a two-hundred-dollar model." She reflected that she got a great many little luxuries and privileges through belonging to that esoteric fraternity of deadheads who frequently refuse as a gift what the rich stand in line to pay for. ...

Leonard Wickes, Geraldine's husband, appeared, slightly worn from the struggle with shirt-studs and collar buttons; he began mixing cocktails dutifully, though nobody wanted any. He was a mild, slender, dark, youngish man. "You should have got a new dress," he said to Geraldine. He was worried too because he couldn't drive them to the Siddalls' in his new car; he ought to have a chauffeur. He began to talk to Jake about the stock market. The enormous chemical corporation for which he worked, at seventy-five dollars a week, had made stock allotments to its employees. This paternal action had set them all speculating. Leonard had run up a shoestring to thirty thousand dollars, which was still spread out on margins. He expected to increase it to a hundred thousand and then invest it safely, for a life income. So he didn't mind Geraldine paying most of the household expenses out of her writing, temporarily. He thought of her writing as an interesting accomplishment, bringing her pin money. He honestly thought of it that way. He admired Geraldine, and never looked at any other woman.

Jake said: "All I know about the stock market is that if you buy a stock it goes down, and if you sell, it goes up."

"I thought you were an accountant," Leonard said.

"I am," said Jake. "That is how I discovered the fact I have just stated."

"Are you really?" Geraldine enquired. "I thought you were writing plays."

Mysie explained that Jake really was an accountant, rather mysteriously, since he refused even to keep a checking account for his own private finances, whatever they were, and existed on a cash or nothing basis. In a peculiar abstract way he had a good head for figures, and had been pitchforked into an accounting firm by a friend of the family when he left college. After a few years of routine employment, he decided, with immovable vagueness, not to hold a regular job; but he took on special work when his old firm was rushed. He had, of course, been writing a play for years; that was another matter. "How did we all commence telling the story of our lives?" Mysie broke off. "We're just typical New Yorkers, from Hoboken and points West. Listen, Geraldine, I was going to tell you our nefarious object in crashing Gina's party to-night. You know Arthur has bought a little magazine?" Mysie had heard so through professional sources.

"Why?" asked Geraldine.

Mysie waved her hands. "I ask you! If I had two hundred and fifty dollars what the hell would I want with a sawmill? It's an orphan magazine. The man who had been supporting it went crazy; I mean they finally took him to an asylum; and someone wished the magazine on Arthur. Jake desires to become its dramatic critic. They haven't had one, but they might as well have a dramatic critic as what they've got—cock-eyed drawings by Picasso and photographs of steampipes, and shredded modern verse without capital letters. Jake is qualified; he was dramatic critic for three months on the Wall Street Journal."

"The Wall Street Journal?" Geraldine repeated.

"Yes," said Mysie, for it was true.

"I have a theory," Jake propounded, "that if I could see enough plays, I might discover what a play is, and thus be enabled to write one. It is a distinct handicap not to know. My dialogue is said to be too good; but I am informed that a plot is indispensable, I don't know why. It seems to me there should be a place for the pure dialogue play."

"There is," said Mysie brutally. "Cain's storehouse." Jake gave her a wounded look, and she was sorry, not for him but because she would hear about that for weeks and months, maybe years.

"What is the name of Arthur's magazine?" Geraldine naturally was most interested in gossip of her own shop.

"The Candle," said Mysie.

"Why, I sold them a short story last year," said Geraldine thoughtfully. "And you say the editor was crazy?"

"He might have had a lucid interval," Mysie became tactfully evasive. "Let's go and get this over with." She hated wirepulling, but as this was not for her own benefit, she lumped it with her publicity work, which she didn't mind because it was a job. "You've got Gina's address—didn't you say she has a house of her own now?" Geraldine had the address.

Gina's house was on the side street, and joined by a party wall and a connecting door to the Siddall mansion, which occupied a Fifth Avenue corner. Mrs. Siddall had purchased the new house and presented it to Arthur and Gina as a birthday gift on the arrival of a grandson. The baby was now nearly two years old; Geraldine said he was a duck, and resembled Arthur.

There was a red carpet and awning out for the party, and the requisite number of men-servants, but Arthur, catching sight of Geraldine, came into the hall, with a quick instinctive wish to give a special welcome to Gina's kin. "I'm so glad you could come." With her hand in his, Mysie thought: He means it. He really is sweet. ... While they laid off their wraps, Mysie reflected that the house was like Gina, furnished with all the expected objects. Consoles and vases and the indicated panel of tapestry to go with the gilt-framed Louis XIV sofas. Gina herself was part of the scheme, the high note, in a gold lamé gown. The Siddall pearls had descended upon her, and the exquisite texture of her skin sustained the comparison. Her eyes wandered, while she kept her fixed smile turned upon the immediate arrivals. Arthur presented Mysie and Geraldine and Leonard and Jake to Mrs. Siddall, with his special air.

Mrs. Siddall stood on fixed post, with the train of her maroon velvet gown disposed just so, sweeping to one side. She recognized Geraldine, and passed Leonard and Mysie with, "Very good of you." To Jake she said unexpectedly: "Van Buren? Any connection of Eugenia Van Buren?"

"Great-aunt Eugenia?" Jake sustained the charge with his most deceptive ingenuousness, becoming wholly a nephew.

Mysie got away safely, none too soon. She was bursting with a giggle. She edged Geraldine into a corner, and said sotto voce: "The old lady is simply mythical. Did you see me—honestly, I didn't know I was doing it, couldn't help it—I ducked her a curtsey!" An abrupt nursery bob, sliding back one foot. The funniest thing was that Mysie couldn't imagine where she had learned the gesture; it does not belong to the ritual of childhood among the poor; it came out of some book and her dramatic sense. She reflected that great wealth really had a stylizing effect; at least, it had on Mrs. Siddall. "She's like—like a whale in its native element. An ocean of money. And then I noticed there was a biscuit crumb on her bosom. On the plush upholstery. But look at Jake prattling at her knee. He's marvelous." Jake's long training with his numerous aunts, or some other occult influence, had perfected a natural talent for respectful dissimulation toward age and authority. He encountered bores with the same elaborate mendacity, a defense mechanism which sometimes defeated its own purpose, so that he spent much time evading invitations he had brought upon himself, to quiet home dinners, spinsterish teas, and drunken parties, all of which bored him equally. Since the death of his mother, he occupied upper rooms in the old house on Eighteenth Street, held in life tenure by two of the aunts, whom Mysie had never seen and hoped never to see. Apparently he was seldom at home, and he kept his telephone plugged as a double precaution. He had a hide-out cottage in the country also. Mysie never tried to communicate with him; sooner or later he came around.

As the drawing-room filled, Geraldine appraised the other guests with the writer's eye. They were mostly elderly. "The old lady's friends," she commented, and owned herself a cat for the observation.

"I'm afraid there's going to be music," Mysie whispered sullenly. "The rich lead dreadful lives. They have to sit and sit and be shushed and entertained. ..." She guessed right; there was music, an opera singer and a pianist.

During an interval, a stout woman with blued white hair and much diamante trimming informed Geraldine portentously: "I have read your book." Mysie basely deserted. Perhaps there was some obscure spot where she might smoke a cigarette and yawn. She bumped into Arthur. "Can I get you something—a glass of punch?" he asked cordially.

Through a half-open door Mysie caught a glimpse of a buffet supper waiting for the appointed hour. She exclaimed: "Oh, I'm starving, I had no dinner." Arthur acted promptly, leading her to the table. "Thousands of those pâté sandwiches," Mysie said. "Will anyone catch us? if I am discovered eating all the provisions, Gina won't ask me again." Arthur carried her plate into a small breakfast room adjoining, and sat on the arm of a chair opposite her.

This is just dumb luck, Mysie thought; I mustn't keep him long, but while the music goes on, he won't be missed. And I can diplomatically prepare him for Jake. "There would be no social unrest," she said, "if the poor were supplied with champagne and pâté de foie gras. Instead of being investigated and surveyed at great expense by a lot of ghastly sociologists and uplifters, who then inform them that they are poor. They know it. I'm glad I was a barefoot child in the backwoods."

"Aren't you from the same town as Gina?" Arthur looked amused but puzzled.

"It's a town, but all inland is wilderness, slashings. But Gina wasn't a barefoot child; she was always a little lady," Mysie qualified. He can't imagine being poor, she thought. Absolutely nothing to go by. A nursery, and estate grounds to play in, and always walls around everything. So when he thinks he comes to a wall in his mind. That's worse than being poor—even the slattern poverty Mysie had known and hated. She had really hated it, from her first consciousness, because of her stepfather. Her mother had to carry the burden, a tired woman with the weight of a large family in a small house on her slender shoulders. Mysie didn't exactly hate her stepfather; she despised him too thoroughly for that. An able-bodied shiftless man who wouldn't hold a steady job even when it could be had; he sat on a tipped chair on the rickety porch in fine weather, and by the kitchen stove in bad weather, whittling little wooden boats and complaining of lumbago, the government, and his luck in having been born too late for opportunity. He was simply useless. There is that fact which sentimental sociologists do not take into account; some people are useless. It doesn't matter whether they sit in club windows and turn purple over the insolence of workingmen demanding higher wages, or sit in the kitchen grumbling about the injustices of capitalism; they are a dead loss. What are you going to do with them? They are more useless in a job than out of it. They have to be carried. I don't mind you riding your end of the cross-cut saw, but will you kindly not let your feet drag. ... Mysie used to wish disinterestedly that her stepfather would die. He wouldn't, of course. He would never die. His kind are notably long-lived, since they do not deplete their energies by excessive toil or mental exertion. Since for years Mysie had sent money to her mother, his lumbago had become chronic.

It was grimly humorous to be thinking of him here, opposite Arthur Siddall in this Louis XIV breakfast room, with a Wedgwood plate of pâté de foie gras and thin gold-etched wine-glasses on the table between them.

Nine

I suppose Arthur is useless too, Mysie thought, but at least he is ornamental. His white waistcoat alone is worth the upkeep. "There's something I want to ask you," she said. "A favor."

"What is it? I'd be delighted," Arthur said rashly.

When he turns his head, Mysie thought, you see pure light on it, like water flowing over a smooth surface. One hundred per cent blond. It's fascinating. She gazed at him with complete æsthetic detachment; and Arthur thought she had lovely eyes. And the dent in her upper lip, her ear and the line of her cheek. ... "Yes," she said mischievously, "we do. But we aren't."

"Do what?" he echoed, taken aback.

Mysie said: "Georgie—I mean Gina—and Geraldine and I do look a bit alike, a family resemblance. I can guess when anyone begins to notice it, sort of a haven't I seen you before expression. But we're completely different." Geraldine, she thought, has a surprising resistance under her quiet manner; Gina is as hard as nails, and I'm tough.

"Did you call her Georgie?"

"When she was a little girl. Don't tell her I told you; she never liked her name, Georgina." Not after she learned about her namesake, Mysie reflected. "It's better than mine. Girls hardly ever like their names."

"Mysie is a charming name," said Arthur. "I like it."

"Maybe you don't know the worst; my name is Artemisia! What parents will do to their helpless offspring—the name belonged to my grandmother, and they couldn't bear to throw it away."

"I don't like Arthur," he confessed.

"I do—now," said Mysie.

He said: "I always wanted to be called Bill or Jim or Joe."

"How would it be if I called you Spike or Butch?" Mysie offered.

"I'd be flattered," Arthur laughed with unexpected heartiness.

Mysie said: "How on earth do you manage to keep so clean? I mean, in New York—do you have to launder yourself every fifteen minutes, or doesn't a slight layer of coal smoke and miscellaneous show on your color scheme? I should think it would stand out prominently."

"It does," Arthur was still laughing. "Every fifteen minutes is the answer. Was that what you wanted to ask me?"

"No, but it was preying on my mind. I'm one of those pests who say whatever comes into their heads—if they think they can get away with it. What I was leading up to is, I hear you've bought a magazine."

"Why, I have, but how did you know? It isn't announced yet."

"Oh, I have to keep posted, in my business," said Mysie. "I expect you'll have a lot of fun, making it over. Why don't you get Jake Van Buren as dramatic critic? He has really new ideas about the theater." She grinned. But Jake could write. His occasional essays had a grave unearthly humor of logic pursued to its furthest limits that produced a sensation of a dislocated universe. "Of course you'd want to talk to him, judge for yourself." You poor dear, she thought, but I'm doing you a good turn.

"I'll be glad to discuss it with him," Arthur agreed. Mysie rose. Her diplomacy consisted in stopping at the right moment. She mustn't get into Gina's black books. They went back to the drawing-room.

The singer had ceased; and Jake was listening patiently to a very young man with a superior accent, who was discoursing on Russia. Mysie could imagine nothing Jake would rather hear less about. Mr. Dickerson, Gina introduced the very young man; he was tall and weedy, with a small head, the sapless collegiate type so frequently found among the sons of the well-to-do. They are sketchy, never filled out.

Gina's eyes still wandered abstractedly. She thought, Polly Brant isn't coming. It's a deliberate slight.

Young Mr. Dickerson was endorsing the class war and the dictatorship of the proletariat. Mysie said: "I wouldn't know about that; I belong to Local Number Ten of the Truckdriver's Union; we're aristocrats. Anyhow, why wait till dawn?" She managed to detach Jake, saying: "Arthur wants to talk to you about the big idea." Jake took the hint, with a glance of warning and reproach. Mysie remembered her promise to behave nicely, and thought sadly, I've crashed again. Arthur made an appointment with Jake for the next day; so that was as good as settled. It seemed safest for Mysie to find Geraldine and stick by her.

Geraldine was still in the clutches of the lady who had read her book, and who evidently meant to get her money's worth one way or another. Mysie intimated that she had some matter of urgency to impart, and the constant reader finally went away. Geraldine said expectantly: "Yes?" and Mysie explained: "Nothing; it was only to get rid of her. Those people have to be nipped in the bud. Who is that woman in green? I'm sure Gina hates her, she's being so cordial."

It was Polly Brant, making apologies for being late. A tiresome dinner had detained her, she said; and she had to go on immediately to a supper party. Polly's opulent beauty was undimmed; she was biscuit brown with the fashionable sun-tan, and her hair was brushed back severely, smooth as jet. She held herself as if she were walking through a public place. "So sorry," she repeated to Gina, and moved on to kiss Mrs. Siddall and speak to Arthur. "No, I can't stay. Prince Olaf insists upon seeing a speakeasy. And a Harlem cabaret." The supper was for an authentic scion of Scandinavian royalty. "Shall you be at the Helders' at Southampton this week-end? No?—you're sensible; it's simply deadly with the polo team in training; the men fall asleep in their chairs after dinner. Bill goes to bed at ten and gets up at five and is out all day; I might as well have married a stable boy. Oh, there are the Dickersons; I must do the civil to them, since our bread and butter depends on Julius. They're too weird, aren't they? Mrs. Dickerson is a dry, and she always has the most awful foreign guests, fourth-rate British authors and knighted British grocers, and they stay for months and talk about the League of Nations. Mr. Van Buren, do you know Katryn Wiggins; she was a Van Buren."

Jake said cautiously: "I think she is my second cousin; is she a friend of yours?"

"Are you hedging?" Polly enquired.

Jake replied ambiguously; "I haven't seen her since she was ten; I dare say she's changed considerably."

Polly had a rippling laugh, extremely effective. "Do come and see me, Mr. Van Buren; and I'll get Katryn. I'm at home every Friday after November first."

Jake bowed: "I shan't forget."

Polly progressed, with renewed aloofness, to the Dickersons, and then made her exit.

Gina missed nothing of the performance.

Sam Reynolds was an altogether unwelcome guest, but Gina had seen no way to avoid inviting him. Mrs. Siddall had an almost feudal regard for family ties, and her relatives were on all her party lists. Under the eye of his wife, Sam was behaving tolerably well; at least, so far as Gina was aware. He was talking about the Siddall Building to Julius Dickerson and Mrs. Siddall; and though it was bad form to drag in business on a social occasion, the Siddall Building outsoared its commercial aspects. It was to be the tallest building in the world. Every new skyscraper is. Mrs. Siddall had a growing pride in the project. It would be a landmark and a monument to the name. She acquired the merit of being public spirited at a profit. Half a block of long-term tenancies had recently expired, leaving the Siddall estate with obsolete buildings which wouldn't be easy to let again. Julius Dickerson had arranged to float thirty millions in bonds for a skyscraper, which would pay ground rent for the land on a fifty-year lease. Since Sam had heard of the project, he had been figuring how to get a cut on it. He said heartily to Julius Dickerson: "Why don't you sell me a few of those bonds? I've been giving 'em the once-over for a client. They look like a good thing—for somebody. The deferment and cancellation and pro-rating clauses especially. Copper riveted proposition. Safety first." He beamed at Julius. "I was thinking of dropping in on you next week, if you've got an hour to spare. Don't want to bother Charlotte about it."

"Certainly, certainly," Dickerson assented, his creased eyelids drooping. "By the way, who is your client?"

"Oh, nobody you'd remember; just one of the little fellows who take whatever securities their banks hand 'em," Sam assured him. "How about Tuesday at ten?"

"Tuesday at ten—drop me a note to remind me," Julius agreed.

Sam said: "O. K. You see, my client bought some Mexican bonds a few years ago, and it made him an investor for life. He's got 'em yet. Well, I'll be seein' you," for Dickerson was receding. … Sam thought, if the so-and-so doesn't declare me in on the syndicate commission, I'll tip off Jerry Delane, and we can get him on the building inspection laws, with the plans. Delane was the lad who'd been stuck with those Mexican bonds, put out by Helder & Dickerson; and he took it hard. Delane was influential in New York municipal politics, but Helder & Dickerson, one of the largest private banking houses in New York, were fairly well out of reach of local reprisals. Helder & Dickerson had weight in national and international finance; of late years they were openly called into consultation at Washington, and quoted as oracles of prosperity. Times had changed; Sam could remember, not so long ago, when an Administration was compromised beyond explanation if caught colloguing with Wall Street. The panic of 1907 marked the beginning of the change. When Teddy Roosevelt knuckled under … But Sam had a shrewd idea that Dickerson would shell out a little discreetly by way of legal fees or a small share in the flotation syndicate, carried on credit, rather than let Sam start Charlotte asking questions. Though the work was already begun on the foundations of the Siddall Building, Sam was reasonably certain that not more than half the bonds were sold. There were awkward possibilities in the situation. Dickerson, of course, had no concern with the actual construction work; he was a banker with a bond issue to dispose of; but he was also Charlotte's investment adviser, probably down as trustee in her will; his bank carried considerable sums of Charlotte's money, a discretionary account; and altogether he'd look silly, have difficulty in unloading the remainder of the bonds, if work stopped sensationally on the building. He might not even care to have

Charlotte know the bonds weren't all sold and that the remainder might come back on her private estate corporation. There was a joker in the ground-lease which sounded like a precautionary provision on behalf of the estate, but could as easily work the other way. ... Sam reckoned that watching Julius Dickerson pay out graft as if he were slipping a sealed envelope into the offertory at Saint Stephen's, was worth nearly as much as the money. Dickerson's unction was deeper than hypocrisy; whatever he made and by whatever means he made it, he felt it was sanctified to him, as a temple priest might feel about tithes.

As for Charlotte, Sam had no serious scruples. If she would give him a break, he could save her five times what he would charge her. But she would, like most of the rich, Sam knew, value a service or possession at the price she paid for it. The size of a transaction is what counts, Sam thought cynically; if it's big enough, even if it's a bust—look at the Dawes Plan and the Young Plan—you're a big man.

Sam was so well satisfied with having got something on Julius—a sort of inverse snobbery—that he didn't commit any noticeable *gaffes* during the rest of the evening, and his wife was profoundly relieved. Only when Mrs. Perry said of Julius Dickerson: "What a wonderful mind, wonderful, and so natural and democratic, really a great man," Sam almost gave way, and his wife had an uneasy moment, marking the lunatic gleam in his eye.

Mysie was a trifle surprised at Gina's cordial manner to Jake, when they said good night. Jake had a diabolical intuition of the reason. In the cab, going home, Mysie said: "Have you really got a Great-aunt Eugenia? I nearly expired when the old lady accused you. And what about this Katryn Higgins?"

"I suppose this means one of your tantrums," said Jake. "The name is Wiggins. But she is nothing to me; all that is over, long ago. The truth is, I met my second cousin Katryn precisely once, when we were both about ten; and a more poisonous brat I trust I may never set eyes on. It was at my Great-aunt Eugenia's; all the most remote off-shoots to the ninth and tenth generation used to be taken to call on Great-aunt Eugenia, in hope of being remembered with a slight legacy. Katryn and I were thrust into the back parlor together and told to make friends with your little cousin. She had curls and pink eyes. In a thoughtless moment I showed her my best chorus girl cigarette cards. She demanded them for keeps, and when I refused, she said she would tell her mother that I said something nasty to her. I am sure she was fully capable of inventing the suitable remark, too. Little girls are fiends in human form. That is why they grow up into what they do grow up into."

"Small boys," said Mysie judicially, "should be exterminated. You can't deny that everybody hates them; and there must be a reason. I was a very nice little girl."

"I," said Jake, "was a perfect little gentleman. All that saved me from growing up like that young Mr. Dickerson was the livery stable. I used to sneak over and spend all my spare time there. My father of course never appeared on the premises; he didn't run the livery stable, he owned the building and it was rented to a liveryman. The stable-men never gave me away. It was a liberal education."

"Isn't young Mr. Dickerson the son of Julius?" Mysie enquired. "I should say off hand that he is a snit."

"You overstate," said Jake. "He is ectoplasm. And you nearly ruined everything by treating him as such. He is the son, and he is going to be Arthur's associate editor on that magazine. Don't ask me why. The fact remains that I have got to keep in with him."

"Your method," said Mysie, "is wrong. The way to do with him is to step on him promptly. But I still don't believe in your Great-aunt Eugenia."

"How could I have met Katryn at her house if I hadn't a Great-aunt Eugenia?" Jake enquired Socratically. "I admit I never fully believed in her myself. You could have knocked me down with a poker when Mrs. Siddall evoked her venerable shade. She died a dozen years ago, at the age of nine hundred and eighty-seven or thereabouts—not Mrs. Siddall, Great-aunt Eugenia. She left no legacies whatever; everything was mortgaged to the roof. She wore crape-bordered veils, and had a pug dog; and the last inch of space in her house on Murray Hill was infested with photographs in plush frames and china shepherdesses and snowstorm paperweights and silver filigree baskets. The woodwork was all carved, with a grille and portières in an archway; and there was a corner what-not. And bracket shelves. I thought she had delusions of grandeur; she held as an article of faith that the Astors and Vanderbilts had paid her butler enormous sums for a copy of her calling list. Upstarts! As far as I know, her calling list consisted of half a dozen moth-eaten antiques of her own vintage, all widows; besides the expectant relatives. But Mrs. Siddall said she was on some reception committee to Prince Henry of Prussia. They were on it together. That must have been the last time Great-aunt Eugenia tottered out. She didn't even go to church in her later years; I gleaned that Grace Church wasn't what it used to be since the sexton, a person named Brown, passed away. I could never fathom how it was that a sexton named Brown was somehow an arbiter of New York society, but it seems he was. I guess he knew who to bury next to whom. Anyhow, Great-aunt Eugenia gave me a morbid horror of ever getting within a mile of society."

Remarkably, Jake had escaped the curse which usually falls upon the impoverished descendants of families once socially eminent. He had no vain regrets for vanished splendors. Except that he wished his proud progenitors had left him some money. He was grateful he had escaped. All he had ever heard from the aunts struck him as absolutely mildewed. ... It was rather an appalling suspicion to harbor, but Jake did suspect that father was what is known as a prominent clubman. All father ever did was to go to his club. He died when Jake was in his early teens. Jake recalled most clearly the way mother used to look at father, with a faint tolerant astonishment. ... Mother was different. Jake had never known anyone quite like her. Except in books. She reminded him a little of an eighteenth century French *dame bourgeoise,* the sort who would have had minor Encyclopædists to dinner. There were none available in New York, so mother made no social efforts; she read a great deal, kept house admirably, and wore a habitual air of placid amusement. She wasn't French, of course. Plain American. A little plump woman, with a bun of brown hair on the back of her head and a quizzical glance. Once when Jake was not more than six, he asked her: Mamma, where did I come from? She replied: My son, I have wondered about that myself.

Jake knew that Mrs. Siddall's recognition of him as a Van Buren had impressed Gina. Mysie said: "Gina invited you to call; I guess you'll have to. Don't you think she's pretty?"

"Yes," said Jake. "But she's a stopper."

"A what?"

"A stopper. Whatever remark you may offer to her drops dead on the spot. The matter ends there. You have to start all over again. Or keep going continuously."

"Mrs. Brant is more your style, isn't she? Shall you take her up?"

"No," said Jake, "she's a snatcher. Smart society. In her set, the women exist by grabbing one another's men. Not that they care for the men, but to score off." Imagining him certified by Mrs. Siddall and approved by Gina, Polly had acted automatically to annex him.

"How do you know?" Mysie demanded. "Have you mingled much with the smart set?"

"Enough," said Jake. "Listen, my child, you either know things or you don't. Those who don't never will. How about yourself? You went through that crowd to-night with the old spiked boots on. You learned all about the Four Hundred in a logging camp. And you're dead right."

"I didn't," Mysie protested. "I was a miracle of tact. Didn't I land the job for you, with Arthur?"

"Naturally," said Jake. "The unfortunate goof is in love with you. He is putty in your hands."

Mysie gurgled faintly and gave up. Jake could always win an argument, by an insanity of extravagance in his assertions, innocent of the remotest approximation of reality. In fact, he carefully avoided ever touching upon a home truth, as bad manners. He was the soul of discretion. Mysie knew less than nothing of his private life; and if he knew anything of hers—she reflected rather mournfully that there wasn't much to know for some time past—he never betrayed it by the most obscure allusion.

Ten

Mrs. Siddall felt that the evening had gone very well. She had the special point of view of a veteran hostess, not unlike a commander-in-chief holding a review. The right names, the household guards, filed by, saluted, deployed, and presently moved off in good order. There had been no hitch. Mrs. Siddall thought that Mrs. Martin was ridiculous showing her thin legs in a Patou model at her age, and her hair brittle with dye. And Mrs. Jelliffe Pearson had gone to pieces noticeably, but what could one expect—at forty-five she had married a man of thirty, and the five years since had been disastrous. She was strained and haggard, keeping her husband practically on leash. Mrs. Siddall made these mental observations impartially and impersonally, without prejudice to her guests as such. Mrs. Martin and Mrs. Pearson were people one always invited. There was, of course, a human aspect to the routine, threads of genuine friendship and intimate association woven into it. George Martin, Mrs. Martin's husband, who died ten years ago had been best man at Mrs. Siddall's own wedding fifty years ago. Mrs. Siddall had shared her first box at the opera with Mrs. Pearson's mother. The Dickersons were comparatively new people; it was only twenty-five years since Julius Dickerson had attained a junior partnership in the old firm of Helder & Company; but in so doing he had attained an equivalent social rating, carrying on an established line by adoption.

To Mrs. Siddall New York society was homogeneous and self-ex-istent, perpetuating itself by natural laws of succession. Having married a Siddall, Gina thereby belonged. She took her place beau-tifully, Mrs. Siddall thought, gratified by her own perspicacity in having chosen so wisely for Arthur.

The last guest was gone. Mounting the stairs, Mrs. Siddall looked down benevolently at Gina and Arthur, who had seen her home, through the inner corridor between the two houses. Mrs. Siddall felt a closer tie, a warmer affection, for Arthur than ever she had for her son, Arthur's father. She hadn't seen so much of her son during his childhood; those were the years of her large social activity as Senator Siddall's political helpmeet in Washington, which she took very seriously; the boy had been in the nursery, and afterward nat-urally he went to boarding school. Before he was out of college he had made his runaway marriage; that was so unexpected, and his death four years later so appallingly sudden—vanishment rather than death, for his body was never recovered—there was a strangeness and astonishment in her sorrow. She had hovered over Arthur with a shade of remorse at first, until he became almost completely identi-fied with the lost boy and doubly dear to her. She had kept him near her; his marriage with Gina made no break in the household. There they were under her wing, and the baby safe asleep, an assurance of the future, wisdom justified of her children.

Mrs. Siddall's velvet train spread two steps below her; she had the sensible egotism to dress her part. Against the black walnut paneling, under the crystal chandelier, she was exactly the right figure. Her dia-mond tiara, the solid bands of diamonds on her fat wrists, the diamond dog-collar supporting her double chin, took on their proper value. They did not glitter; the old-fashioned cut and massed setting subdued them just enough. She went on upstairs, the rich folds of maroon velvet trailing after, and all her period, her society, went with her.

Gina and Arthur returned through the corridor to the new house. The drawing-room was filled with a bright desolation. Arthur stopped to speak to the butler. Gina went up her own stairs, in her golden dress. Her stockings were of gold thread, her slippers were gold; her hair was waved and cut close to her pretty head, bringing out the bronze-gold lights in the bronze-black depths; her light brown eyes took on a golden reflection. The square diamond on her finger caught a ray of white light. She was slender and shining against the white wall, keyed to the background, part of it, but not the center. It had no center. It was a pattern, all surface.

The party had not been hers, and she knew it. She realized, as Mrs. Siddall could not, that Mrs. Siddall's society no longer existed. Polly Brant had come, out of sheer insolence, to prove that. To smile at the dowagers, and sneer at the dowdy earnest folks like the Dickersons, and snub Gina with allusions to the really smart people, who were not there. There were half a dozen smart groups, quite arbitrary in their composition; nobody could say how or why anyone was accepted; they were drawn from old families and new rich, they included a few recruits from the stage and other professions, with an occasional titled foreigner taken in capriciously. They met abroad, of course, at the recognized places and seasons. Polly was a leader of the polo and hunting set; but all the smart sets acknowledged the others, touched at the edges. And they still had a half-amused respect for the authentic leaders of the old guard, like Mrs. Siddall; but her authority did not suffice to open the inner circles to Gina.

Gina hurried the nightly beauty ritual, and let her maid go. Then she stood absently, tense with suppressed irritation, in front of her mirror, biting her lip. She hated Polly …"Come," she answered Arthur's tap mechanically. He looked sleepy and cheerful; he put his arm about her tentatively and kissed the back of her neck. Gina picked up a scent bottle and twisted the stopper in her fingers. It was impossible to unburden her secret bitterness to Arthur, because he could not understand it. He was not shut out as she was.

He did not specifically belong to any of the smart sets, not sharing their interests; but he could if he chose. He would be accepted anywhere. It just didn't matter to him. And even if he chose to go, though Gina would have been admitted as his wife, still she would have been outside. And he wouldn't know it.

He had that terrible simplicity; and he had never had anywhere to climb to.

Mrs. Siddall was so used to the part of a great hostess that it had become second nature to her; this gave her a certain self-sufficiency. She validated her own acquaintances in her own eyes. Arthur had been bred to that attitude unconsciously, but with a difference, because he happened to be incapable of snobbery, even the snobbery of the elect. In a way, everybody was alike to him. He was fond of Poliy and embarrassed by Mrs. Perry's gush; but they were both in the family. Outside the family—if he met people he assumed they were the people one met; that was the nearest one could get to it. The peculiar effect of his special position was that he had no social discrimination. Gina couldn't analyze nor define his attitude, but it was so. It went deeper than she could understand; he didn't speak to the servants kindly; he spoke to them in the same tone he would use to anyone else. He had a gentle and grateful nature, and all that he had been taught as a child of courtesy and consideration to others, the obligation of his privilege, imposed upon his immediate position as a child among older and presumably wiser people, had given him a genuine and lasting humility. It was almost incredible; and it had taken Gina several years to begin to believe Arthur was just what he was. ... And yet if he hadn't been like that he would never have married her.

She was baffled; he wouldn't help her. What she wanted was before her eyes, just out of reach. From earliest childhood she had felt shut out and bitterly resentful. Especially when she heard her grandfather talk about old times. ... Grandfather Brennan should have made a fortune, before she was born. Other men did, men he had known in the early days. The same opportunities had been open to him, in that new wild country. There were half a dozen millionaires on the Northwest coast whose names moved Grandfather Brennan to reminiscence. He had known them when they were poor; one had been a ship's carpenter come ashore with barely enough money to buy the tools of his trade and set up as a builder; one had borrowed five hundred dollars to start in business with a little grocery shop; another had begun with a fishing boat and ended with a big salmon cannery. Some had made their first stakes by less reputable means, which Grandfather Brennan did not fail to recall. And some had made and lost and made several fortunes, going broke in the Nineties and winning again in the golden years of the Yukon. Middle-aged men when the gold rush began, but seasoned to hardship and familiar with the wilderness, they had done better than younger and rasher adventurers; they knew the hazards. They brought back the gold and built their city. And their wives and daughters and granddaughters formed Society. In his last years, Grandfather Brennan went down to Seattle occasionally, and the other old-timers still remembered him. But Gina had never met their granddaughters. She used to read about them, in the society pages of the newspapers. When she went to the State University it was with a vague hope of meeting them. She didn't know till then that the girls she wished to join went East to finishing schools, or to Europe. And if she had by chance met them, they wouldn't have known or cared about Grandfather Brennan. All that was a long time ago, picturesque but boring, old men's talk. …

None of the Brennans had made any money. They had grown poorer, drifted out to the edge of things, turned to farming or taken to the sea. Mysie's father had worked in the sawmill—uncle Joe, mother's brother. Worked for newcomers like Michael Busch, who were making new fortunes. … Gina had been glad, finally, that her own name wasn't Brennan; she liked to think her father would have grown rich, if he hadn't died young. Her mother was the beauty of the Brennan girls. Even that bounty of nature had been spent without profit in widowhood and ill-health, so that she had to go back to Sequitlam and live on Grandfather Brennan and five hundred dollars a year insurance money. Never another chance. …

And now, after all. … It was like encountering a wall of glass. It was too fantastic; she had married the greatest catch, one of the richest men, in an enormously rich country, good fortune beyond her wildest dreams; and still she was shut out. She hadn't realized it immediately. On their prolonged honeymoon, she and Arthur had been entertained abroad by Mrs. Siddall's old friends. Mostly very old, late Victorian, great names, but no longer smart. On their return to New York, Gina had been included in all Mrs. Siddall's social activities. And though Mrs. Siddall had remained happily unaware, nothing had come of it. Gina had been anxious first to strengthen her alliance with the old lady. In that she succeeded; Mrs. Siddall repaid Gina's attentive deference with confidence and affection. Between them a tacit understanding was established;

they managed Arthur. For three years Gina had been beset with anxiety because she had no child. That too was sufficiently ironic, considering the alternate apprehensions and resolutions of the months before her marriage. She was healthy and young; it was her obligation to provide an heir. When at last she knew she was with child, the expectation occupied her mind sufficiently to banish lesser discontents; and her luck held, with a son. If she had loved Arthur, she might have been slightly jealous of his doting fondness for the baby. Instead she was glad of the assurance; it was a permanent title.

But she perceived at the same time that she had got nothing of what he had represented to her imagination. The younger women she envied wouldn't let her in. She didn't see that she was no worse off than if she had been a plain and awkward débutante, ignored by the smart cliques. But she felt desperately that Mrs. Siddall's contemporaries were as remote from the present as Grandfather Brennan's old-timers. Their world was dead. ...

There was no need for her to think this in words now, after the party. She had known it long enough before. ... Gina set down the trinket and picked up another. She said abruptly: "What does Bill Brant do, what is his position with Helder & Dickerson?"

Arthur answered out of his own preoccupation: "Something in the investment trust department."

"But he's away half the time, hunting or exploring. Besides, has he any financial ability?"

"Oh, well, I believe his connections bring in estate funds, discretionary accounts, that sort of thing." Customer's man, Arthur might have said, but didn't; the arrangement seemed obvious and proper to him. "And—I don't know—" Arthur checked himself. There was a historic rumor that Bill's elder sister Elena had been the mistress of Wyman Helder, twenty years ago. The old man had a dozen mistresses in succession, and was very liberal with them; he picked them wherever they caught his fancy, carried it off with a high hand, introduced them to his daughters. Some of them married well, and he always made handsome settlements. Some were from his own social environment; the Brants considered themselves distinctly superior, though they hadn't much money, they traced back to Colonial ancestry. Elena Brant had married an English honorary title; she was now Lady Richard Devenish. Arthur concluded: "The Brants and the Helders have been chummy for a long time. Bill went to college with Wyman junior, you know; Wy is practically head of the firm since the old man has been more or less retired for ten years, had a stroke or something, doesn't go to the office any more." Arthur had a fastidious tendency to disbelieve scandal. "I suppose Bill's contacts bring in enough to cover his salary; it isn't huge. Polly is always hard up."

Gina thought, how do you know? does she get anything out of you? ... She wronged Polly. ... But her main idea was that Julius Dickerson might some day enable her to even herself with Polly Brant. Julius didn't ignore Gina; he foresaw that Gina might have a good deal of influence if Mrs. Siddall died. And even Mrs. Siddall couldn't live forever. ...

"I suppose so," Gina agreed. "I just couldn't imagine. ..." She remained unresponsive in the circle of Arthur's arm. Arthur said hesitantly: "You looked marvelous to-night, Gina. But you always do. I like your cousins. Mysie is jolly, isn't she? Easy to talk to." Gina stared at him blankly. She had never found Mysie easy to talk to. And she used to try ... Arthur had no suspicion of the obscure, inverse connotation of his remark, nor had Gina. After five years of marriage, he found Gina less easy to talk to than at first. Gina did not wish to depreciate her own family, so she remained silent. But she hated Polly so much that she hated Mysie too. Yes, she had always hated Mysie.

"I expect you're tired," Arthur said, and kissed her shoulder. He wanted to rest his head there, not say good night. ... Gina started, she didn't know why. She was still facing the mirror, and it gave her a shiver—seeing herself and Arthur. He had on a dark blue dressing gown. It couldn't be the same one! Not after five years. ... She put up her hand, pulling her rose-colored negligee together at the neck. Arthur said involuntarily: "I'm sorry." And he didn't know why. There were a great many things both of them shied off from in their minds.

Gina turned to him with her company smile. "Oh I didn't mean—" She kissed him dutifully. "No, I'm not really tired."

He stayed. But afterward, he was ashamed. ... It must be his fault, his lack, if she was no more than acquiescent. Cold. He had to think that. She hadn't always been... Or had she? He felt very queer, almost sick, lying awake beside her, not sure if she were asleep, not moving for fear he might discover she wasn't. He couldn't let himself think what that reminded him of, because he loved Gina. All he knew of love.

Eleven

Thea and Mysie were driving out to Long Island to look at a cottage Thea had discovered. They intended to buy it. Mysie hadn't yet seen it, but she agreed in advance. They had to have some place for week-ends and holidays. They had been saying so for five years, and now suddenly it became imperative. Impossible to put it off another day, another hour. Mysie didn't much like Long Island, but she knew she would never find a place herself. She wouldn't know how or where to look. There was a peculiarity in the Eastern landscape. You couldn't somehow see any distance, or get any idea of what was beyond, except more of the same thing. It was all low hills and short turns. Even the flat stretches of Long Island had no perspective, no horizon.

Thea was driving. She enjoyed it, and Mysie willingly ceded her the privilege. Thea drove like unto Jehu the son of Nimshi, furiously, but skillfully too. She was accustomed to thinking through her hands, being a musician. And driving fast on a clear road released her from nervous tension. Her life had stopped when her husband died. That was ten years ago, when she was turned forty. She might, even then, have formed other ties; with her wit and energy and worldly knowledge, she could be attractive when she chose. But she had deliberately accepted the conclusion, fully aware of the cost. You cannot, in effect, stop living suddenly without desperate pain. As much as possible, she cut herself off from reminders of the past. She had a married daughter living in Boston, who bored her; and she preferred sharing a flat with Mysie to living with any of her old friends, women of her own age, simply because Mysie was twenty years younger and thus belonged to another era and came from the West and had never seen Charles Ludlow nor had any connection with Thea's married life. Their casual and cordial detachment suited them both. They needn't feel absolutely alone, but each respected the other's privacy. Thea never pried nor gave advice. The arrangement had begun fortuitously; Thea had been Jake Van Buren's music teacher twenty-five years ago, and Mysie met her at tea with Jake's mother, when Thea happened to be going abroad and wished to sublet her flat. Mysie took it, and afterward stayed on. Thea had a durable impersonal affection for Jake. She said he had always been unusual, to say the least. An uncannily polite infant, with an air of docility, though in the long run he did exactly as he pleased and gave no offense. When he was eight or nine, she had once remarked to him that he was intelligent. He replied in a grave treble: Yes, all our family are bright.

"Is this place of yours anywhere near Jake's shack?" Mysie enquired. Thea said no; Jake was at least an hour away. Jake lived on the edge of some godforgotten village on the beach, which had no railway connection convenient, so it had never grown beyond a dozen or so of summer cottages; it wasn't even any good for boats because of sandbars and shoal water; and that was why Jake clung to it. Every summer Jake invited Mysie to come out some Sunday, secure in the knowledge that she never would.

"That's lucky," said Mysie vaguely. "Oh, it's so *hot.* What's the use of being poor if you've got to live on Long Island anyhow?"

Thea turned her benevolent eagle profile for a moment toward Mysie. "Would you mind repeating that?"

"Don't pay any attention to me," Mysie said in a feeble voice. "All I mean is that I've always thought the worst thing about being rich is that you *have* to live on Long Island, and go through this every day. But they get so insensible they don't even object to Palm Beach. … If I see one more gasoline pump I'll die." She rubbed a handkerchief across her parboiled countenance. It came away streaked with grime. She had been over this dismal region often enough, the stretch beyond the Queensboro Bridge; but she didn't know the name of it because she didn't want to; it was too horrible. Mysie could drive competently; she was a careful driver, and that meant she couldn't think of anything else while driving, so it bored her. She felt with her hands instead of thinking with them, as Thea did; so Mysie liked riding or digging in a garden better than driving. But on that particular area she could not think anyhow. It stupefied her with its mean ugliness; it affected her with incipient nausea and hysteria. "There *is* something the matter with this country," she muttered, more to herself than to Thea. "It's the extremes of human nature, turned loose for the first time, to do its best and its worst. The best has been better than anything that ever was, a great splendor and pride of taking all the odds alone; but the worst is unbearable; and it's why people stun themselves with raw alcohol, to keep from facing it. We'll all burst like a chameleon on a plaid …" There were ten million fiery red gasoline pumps extending to infinity, along a white hot ribbon of concrete, leading only to more gasoline pumps and garbage dumps. With one-story glass-fronted buildings swimming in heat beside the way.

"The awful thing about New York is that you can't get out of it," she concluded, aware that she had said the same thing to Thea a hundred times. It was also part of the nightmare quality of New York that it stultified you into repetition. The aspect of magnificence, that enchantment it sometimes took on, was indescribable; one who had never seen it couldn't imagine it, even approximately. It was an inhuman achievement. In absence, it became utterly unreal; you didn't quite believe it. Perhaps that was why you couldn't stay away. The spell was irrevocable. Like those old stories of mortals trepanned into fairyland, not the small ethereal winged fantasy of childhood, but the ancient fairyland, the illusory sunless shadowless Hollow Hill; and when it seemed a week had passed and they were restored to Middle Earth seven years was gone and their youth with it, and they could never resume the kindly life they had left.

"Tell me when there is a tree," Mysie begged, and shut her eyes. After awhile Thea assured her there was a tree. They turned into a rather pleasant lane and got lost; and Thea drove on and on with serene determination, asking directions at intervals from other motorists who replied they were strangers themselves. One inviting road proved to be semi-private, intersecting two estate parks, landscaped and trimmed and empty of living creatures. The house was not in view from the road; an ample red-roofed building immediately within a stone-pillared, imported wrought iron gate was obviously the lodge and garage. Thea backed out and tried another turning.

"These big estates are rather uncanny, like a conjuring trick," said Thea.

"How?" Mysie asked obligingly.

"There are so many of them," Thea explained. "Thousands. All over Long Island and Connecticut and Westchester. Thousands and thousands, sprung from nothing. When you see the great houses and castles of Europe, you can see the social foundations, how they came to be. The land supported them. Of course they ate up all the profit from the tenants of the land, but they could go on eating through good times and bad; and they needed the houseroom in their business, for patriarchal families and stewards and men-at-arms and chaplains and visitors and all the servants to cook and brew and spin and weave. They were centers of an organic way of life, rooted to the spot. These are orchidaceous. No visible means of support. Big empty houses and foreign servants, nothing local. If you reversed the conjure, you know, said one wrong word, or got it backward, they'd vanish. This is a queer country. It's a state of mind. It usen't to be like that, even when I was young. Sometimes I think all my life since I was a child has been a dream. The Woolworth Building was the beginning of the dream. I remember going to look at it the first time, a white magic tower. And it's still the most magical of them all." Thea seldom spoke at such length.

"Whereabouts are we anyhow, and where exactly is that abandoned barn you're buying?" Mysie sat up suddenly and took notice.

"It isn't a barn," Thea replied rather crossly. "It's the other side of Glen Cove, and we must be somewhere near it." The aged motor was emitting ominous noises, which worried her.

"I thought so," Mysie exclaimed. "Oh, my goodness, I didn't pay any attention when you told me before; but I believe I know this stone wall. In a minute we'll come to another big gate and a driveway—it's the Siddall estate. If your barn is near by, we'll be right in Gina's backyard. Lookit, there's the entrance, between those blue Norway spruces. That's another thing the rich have got to have, whether they like it or not, Norway spruces. Let us flee."

Thea looked, and the diversion caused her to make some fatal error with the gear shifts. The car stopped. It declined to start again. "It would," said Mysie. Neither of them had any understanding of motor trouble. They climbed out in the August sun, which smote upon the backs of their necks like a blunt weapon. "Where did we pass a garage?" Mysie tried to remember. "I don't suppose the damn' family are here now, do you? They'd be abroad or north."

"The garage family?" Thea enquired blankly.

"The Siddalls—Gina," Mysie said. "And how do I get back to town for that rehearsal this afternoon? Blast! I wish I knew where to hit these internal works with a monkey wrench so's to do the most harm." She peered under the hood.

A shining maroon limousine slid smoothly out of the driveway. Thea and Mysie automatically removed themselves to the curb side of their derelict vehicle, to let the other pass. It slowed instead. A man's voice said: "Do you need help? Hello, Mysie, I hope you were coming to call." Arthur Siddall emerged from the limousine.

Mysie regarded his blond immaculateness with a good deal of class hatred. He wore a light grey suit, and not even the edge of his collar was wilted. "We were en route to our own country seat," she replied, and then burst into insane mirth. She explained: "I was trying to reply coldly—this weather! Why doesn't a car cross a road?"

"Let's see." Arthur did know something about cars. Mysie forgave him his appearance when he began a brisk investigation, to the immediate detriment of his cuffs. His chauffeur also took a hand. Presently they agreed on a verdict. "Yeah, that sleeve valve, she's bust," the chauffeur affirmed. He was a stocky, swarthy youth with a Sicilian accent and the expression of morose amiability peculiar to his type.

"So what?" Thea asked. Arthur said: "We'll take you wherever you were going, and send a garageman for your car. Get in—can you give the directions?" Thea endeavored to do so, and the chauffeur nodded. "Yeah, I know." They proceeded luxuriously.

Mysie murmured to Arthur: "What's your chauffeur's name?"

"His name?" Arthur reflected. "I think it's Dominic."

"Does he answer to Hi or to any loud cry such as fry me or fritter my wig? I suppose he's the seventeenth assistant chauffeur and you only take a census occasionally."

Arthur elucidated apologetically: "There are only four; the head chauffeur employs them. This man is rather new; I usually have Raymond but he drove Grandmother and Gina up to Bar Harbor." They had gone the day before; Arthur had found occasion for a day's delay on his own part. He was not quite aware that he had practically manufactured the reason. It was an inner necessity growing upon him lately, to be by himself occasionally.

"Dominic?—Doesn't mean anything in my life. Only I think I've seen him somewhere," Mysie said. "Isn't Gina here? Of course not, you just said so."

Dominic brought the car to a halt, and Arthur enquired: "What is it?" Dominic said: "Yessir, da house."

"What is it, is right," Mysie commented. The house was the last on a village street, in a shabby neighborhood. Nondescript in the beginning, the small box-like structure had become disreputable from want of care. The windows were boarded; and last year's dead leaves still lay on the paintless porch. Thea had a key to the kitchen door. They all got out of the car and walked around to the backyard, where an apple tree and several locust trees mitigated the neglected fence and ragged grass.

Arthur followed where he was led, with his disarming expression of wishing to be helpful. Mysie wondered what to do with him, but decided to wait and see. In the dismal, empty kitchen a tap yielded cold water. Arthur waited outside while Mysie washed her face recklessly. "There wouldn't be a towel," she said unreasonably to Thea. Arthur heard her. He said diffidently at the door: "Will this do?" and offered a large and very fine linen handkerchief of pristine freshness.

"There are four rooms beside the kitchen," said Thea, with honest pride.

"I'll take your word for it," Mysie declined to explore further, and escaped to the open air.

"What do you think of it?" Thea asked.

"Oh, it's just like home," said Mysie, with the bitterness of truth. It did remind her of the graceless and poverty-stricken house in which she was born. Her mother owned it, or her stepfather would probably have sold it long ago and moved on to something worse.

"It needs fixing up a little," Thea remarked, too rapt with creative vision to detect Mysie's sarcasm. "Paint, and new floors, and a bathroom, and the garden. That's a guelder rose by the fence." She pointed to a straggling bush unrecognized by Mysie because it was smothered under a stray vine. "And sweet William here." Thea had found a rusted table fork, and kneeled by what might once have been a flower border, loosening the earth carefully. Mysie smiled and sat down on the kitchen steps. Arthur sat beside her and presented cigarettes in a lordly case.

"You'd be the ten best people to take to a desert island," Mysie said gratefully. In the shade, the heat became tolerable, and the long grass was spangled with dandelions. There was rising ground beyond the house, on the clear side, giving the lift of a skyline, which is a lovely thing. Clouds rested upon it, beginning to form thunderheads; there might be rain before the day was out. The three of them experienced the pure and disinterested pleasure of being with people one likes. Mysie recognized that she didn't have to do anything with Arthur. He had that quality of acceptance which makes for ease far more effectively than any conscious effort. And Mysie reflected that Thea could and would conjure the forlorn little house into a home. With nothing but a broken table fork for a tool. That was all humanity ever had to work with. That and determination and goodwill, were enough.

Mysie said: "When the swimming pool and the pergola and the rock garden are laid out, you won't know the old place. But I can't figure where you'll put the tennis court." She observed Arthur's immediate bewilderment lighten to amusement. The suggested improvements sounded quite reasonable to his ear, against the testimony of his eyes. He had no scale of possessions.

Thea remained unruffled, sitting on her heels meditatively. "The soil is good," she crumbled a bit of it in her fingers. "I'll have to pick up an odd job man."

"You wanna man? I get you one." Dominic had returned to announce that the disabled car was taken care of. Thea consulted with him, until Mysie interrupted.

"Listen, Thea, I must be moving along. I suppose there is a station and a train somewhere?" A protracted colloquy, of that peculiar domestic kind in which the participants proceed along parallel lines, the statements of each having not the remotest bearing upon those of the other, resulted mysteriously in a practical arrangement. Thea decided to remain for the afternoon, interviewing the real estate agent and the odd job man. Arthur, since he was on his way to town, would take Mysie in.

It wasn't so bad going back; the big car made a difference. There is a great deal to be said for having money, Mysie thought; at least, for having it oneself. It doesn't seem to do other people so much good. She reflected childishly that she didn't want a million dollars, but just enough money. Ten years ago her present earnings would have seemed ample to her, but there were no reasonable values in New York, in money or anything else. And if you had enough money you wouldn't live in New York. It was baffling to find that the best she and Thea could do, both of them making good incomes, was to buy a house like this. By years of effort, she had apparently got back to where she started. And it would take over an hour of miserable tedium and discomfort to get to the place; and they wouldn't be able to manage that more than once a week.

After starting, Arthur observed that it was nearly one o'clock; they might stop somewhere for lunch.

"I can't," said Mysie. "The rehearsal is at half past two."

"Don't you ever eat?" Arthur enquired. "You hadn't had any dinner the other time."

"Hardly ever," said Mysie gloomily, "If we pass a hot dog stand— but I suppose one couldn't eat hot dogs in this car?"

"Why not?" A hot dog stand came into view as if ordered; Arthur commanded a halt and personally purchased two of those delicacies, one for himself. He supplied another handkerchief for Mysie to wipe her fingers. "Do you like hot dogs?" he enquired.

"I hate them," said Mysie, still more morosely, having con- sumed hers. "I hate Bohemianism, and bath tub gin, and sitting on the floor, and kitchenettes, and speakeasies, and riding in subways. I like bourgeois comfort, only not the suburbs. I hate Broadway too."

"Do you like acting?" Arthur ventured cautiously.

"I would if there was any."

She had never been stagestruck; the limited, vivid, self-engrossed world of the theater was too narrow. It was specifically acting which had interested her, as a mode of communication. Speech is the distinguishing mark of human beings; and every word we use is charged with the whole burden of experience. For this reason, apprehending a poetic truth too literally, men have believed in times past in words of power, secret incantations which even the blind inimical forces of nature must obey.

"I saw you last winter in *Marrying Susan*," Arthur said. "You were charming."

"It was just one of those things. All on the surface." She hadn't had a part since. But she was specially pleased by his adjective. Charming. She wished she were charming.

"What are you rehearsing now?"

"Didn't you know?" She had supposed he must, on the strength of Jake's connection with Arthur's magazine. "It's Jake Van Buren's play, *Third String*. He found an angel in Wall Street."

"I'll get a box for the first night," Arthur said. "I hope it's an enormous success."

"I hope so too," Mysie said truthfully. "Look, it's beginning to rain. I believe we're in for thunder and lightning, cats and dogs and pitchforks. It's all black ahead."

Twelve

Large warm drops of rain splashed languidly in the dust, bringing the fresh smell of washed air. Presently the rain came faster, streaming straight down, with a look of weight; the windshield was sheeted with water and the road gleamed wetly black. Mysie took off her hat to feel the moisture on her face and hair.

"I suppose I ought to shut the window," she said.

"Do you want it shut?" Arthur leaned over to attend to it.

"No, but the cushions will get wet."

"That doesn't matter," he assured her.

Well, he can buy another car, Mysie thought. "I like rain," she said.

"I'm glad," Arthur replied.

"You mean you're glad I like something?" Mysie caught him, and he looked guilty and laughed. "I like lots of things," she affirmed. "How can you really like anything if you don't know the difference? Those simpering sweet people who gush over everything and everybody indiscriminately don't care for anybody."

Arthur had a moment of disquiet, on the verge of a thought he must not admit; if he did life would become intolerable. Mysie went on, unaware: "Out where I come from it rains all winter, and the grass is always green; only sometimes there is a rime of frost, and when you walk across it, you leave green plush tracks. New York is a tropical climate. Excessive and violent. It's rather exciting. The rain is coming down in solid chunks."

"You're not violent, are you?"

"Only within reason. You needn't be alarmed. I shriek and tear my hair, that's all."

They had crossed the bridge and were driving slowly down town. The streets flowed ankle deep, and people stood in doorways, shrinking back from the spray. A girl ran through the deluge; her light dress was soaked and clung to her shoulders, fluttered about her knees, nymph-like. She was a pretty girl, and her face expressed mirth and dismay. That's fun, Mysie thought; that's the way we ought to take what happens, only we have to worry about hats and shoes; we can't afford adventure. Happiness must be unthinking. You mustn't stop to measure it by either the cost or use; the actual object one strives for is always subtly disappointing when achieved. Fame, fortune, perhaps even love—we stand awkwardly with our hands filled—now what?

"Which theater?" Arthur asked.

"Oh, don't bother; let me out where you're going and I'll get a taxi."

Arthur insisted. "All right," Mysie agreed, "you'll be taken for a stagedoor Johnny, the last one. There really aren't any more; I'm sorry they became extinct before my time. An actress has a hard time getting talked about nowadays. ... Do you want to come in and watch the rehearsal?"

Arthur did want to. He had never been backstage, nor given supper parties to chorus girls. That fashion had gone out among the gilded youth before he went to college; besides, his shyness and his upbringing and his bookish tastes would have prevented him. Yet, like all shy people who are not priggish, who are debarred from easy satisfactions by sensibility, he thought at times there must be something in that other way of living, reckless though crude. A reality that books couldn't give. ... The fact that Mysie was an actress puzzled him. He had expected her to be different; he couldn't have said just how. Glamorous, perhaps, or dangerous, or loud. Not like this—her plain linen frock was limp and crumpled from the morning's wear; she had no make-up other than a dab of powder; but above all, she was preoccupied with the necessity of being on time for her work. He thought, she's like that girl running in the rain. … He was trying to fit her to the legend of either the prima donna or the chorus girl, which she couldn't very well sustain, being neither. She had, simply, the character and manners of a woman who did work for her living. …

They didn't go in by the stage door, but the main entrance. Mysie led him down the side aisle.

She stopped halfway, with a feeling that something had gone wrong. The half-lighted stage had the dusty aspect of any theater in the daytime. A dozen or fifteen people, the cast, stood grouped in the center. It was because they were all standing there, not dispersed casually, sitting by the wings waiting for their cues, for scenes which might or might not be rehearsed that day. Mysie guessed at trouble. The leading woman, Anne Fairfield, was speaking, tragically: "But only last week, Keller offered me—"

The producer, Lew Morris, interrupted: "Well, I can't help it; good God, I'm the one that's left holding the sack. The guarantee won't even cover—"

Miss Fairfield became shrill. "Do you mean to tell me—"

"Oh, hell!" Morris flung out his hands. "Ain't I telling you? I should try to tell a woman anything—" They both talked at once, becoming incoherent.

Having no clue to the meaning, Arthur did not hear the conversation very clearly. Mysie laid her hand on his arm and muttered: "Holy cats! Please wait here a minute, I'm afraid there isn't going to be any—" She hurried on and vanished beyond the boxes. Arthur saw her reappear on the stage. He lingered uncertainly, still unable to make sense of the argument in progress beyond the footlights. He supposed it must be dialogue from the play. Mysie spoke to Lew Morris, with a motion of her head toward Arthur in the shadowy orchestra. Arthur distinguished a few words: "I brought someone … No, nobody, just… I'll go and. …"

She came back to Arthur. "I'm awfully sorry," her tone was distrait. "The rehearsal is called off, but I have to stay awhile, I don't know how long. Thanks for driving me in."

Arthur was sorry too. In the outer lobby of the theater, he stopped for a moment to observe that the rain was slackening, and debated with himself how he should fill the rest of the afternoon. He felt superfluous; it came to him occasionally, when he met people who worked because they had to. They seemed to be part of the scheme of life, while he was an onlooker.

It occurred to him that he could go to the office of his magazine, *The Candle.*

His car was still at the curb; Dominic threw away a cigarette unobtrusively and opened the tonneau door. Arthur said: "No, thanks; will you please wait for Miss Brennan—the lady who came with us—and take her wherever she wants to go? Watch out for her; I'll take a taxi."

Dominic said: "Yessir," and drew his own conclusions.

On his way to the office, Arthur reflected that the editors might be absent, since it was Friday and the end of August. They took long week-ends and holidays. There was a managing editor and two associate editors, besides the literary editor and the art editor and nine or ten contributing editors, whatever that meant. They were all very earnest and high-minded, and had the peculiar and unanalyzable faculty of getting endowed for their opinions, a sacerdotal quality. And they held those opinions whole and undigested, so that it was hard to discover the person behind the formulas. They deplored the standardization of the machine age; and at a given time they all found a new gospel in psychoanalysis, or thought Charlie Chaplin tragic, or discovered a profound philosophy in Krazy Kat.

Jake Van Buren was not an editor, though he was the dramatic critic. As he owed his job directly to Arthur, he was tolerated, but never invited to conferences. The moving picture critic, Ray Lynch, was an editor; he devoted most of his attention to Russian films, appraising them abstrusely in terms of rhythm and mass movement. The prodigious inanities of Hollywood filled him with moral indignation; he saw in them a "mechanism of escape." Nobody should escape if he could prevent it.

The Russians got into everything at *The Candle,* Arthur thought. He wondered what made him think that; it wasn't the way he was used to thinking. Young Roger Dickerson was mainly responsible. Though Roger put up only a third of the financial backing, he had most to do with engaging the editorial board and thereby introducing the sociological and economic interest in what had originally been a very precious aesthetic publication. That is, Roger had engaged Miss Sarnoff, the managing editor, and she did the rest.

Miss Sarnoff was married to a Russian. Her maiden name was Endicott; she was a New Englander of long descent. She compromised with her feministic principles by calling herself Miss with her husband's name. Arthur had never seen her husband. He existed in the distance. Though a Communist, he was mysteriously debarred from returning to Russia, for having known Trotsky or something. His main occupation seemed to be reviving *The Cherry Orchard* at Little Theaters.

The outer portal of *The Candle* was guarded by a girl sitting behind a wicket with a telephone and a pad of paper on which callers were required to state their business. Arthur had never noticed her especially, except that she was a thin, black-eyed girl with a wide mouth needlessly emphasized by a liberal use of lipstick. As he entered he heard her talking over the telephone: "Oh, Lester is a big sap; you gotta schmoos him a bit. ..." She looked up and saw Arthur. "Who do you wish to—oh!" She was flustered into a spontaneous giggle. Arthur smiled back at her as he went by. He's kinda nice, she thought. She had got her job through an employment bureau, and her private opinion of the editors was that they were a bunch of nuts.

Arthur's office could be reached only through that of Miss Sarnoff. She had a sound tactical sense. It happened she was in, and she received him almost as an equal; she was always patient with him. An athletic, handsome woman in the thirties, she had emerged from college a dozen years ago as one of the post-war revoltees, who acquired "sex experience" as a duty, whether they liked it or not. After marriage she committed adultery in the same conscientious fashion, because jealousy was anti-social and extra-marital episodes were necessary to a full life. She had a child because without maternity a woman is unfulfilled in her biological function.

She daunted Arthur. He was aware of her obvious diplomacy with young Roger Dickerson; it was, indeed, obvious to everyone but Roger. She schmoosed Roger. Arthur recognized that she didn't consider it necessary to be diplomatic with himself. She was firm and proprietary about large questions such as birth control, disarmament, and the Treaty of Versailles.

Arthur's flat-topped desk was bare except for a blotting pad, pen and ink. Miss Sarnoff fetched an advance copy of the next issue of *The Candle*. It contained the regular articles on the Russian experiment, handicraft culture in Mexico, the psychiatric treatment of criminals as victims of society, the cancellation of the war debts, Negro sculpture, James Joyce, and the art of Stanislas Prezmsyl, a Pole who modeled all his subjects in the likeness of eggs. There was also an article on the need of a literature of the proletariat.

Arthur speculated vainly why Julius Dickerson—for of course Roger got the money from his father—should subsidize propaganda for cancellation of the war debts, when Julius had been adviser to one of the debt commissions which had fixed the terms of settlement a few years earlier, terms which cancellation must abrogate as unpractical and unethical. Arthur didn't connect this fact with the subsequent fact that Helder & Dickerson had participated in various European industrial concessions which were quietly arranged at the same time as the debt settlement, though with no visible connection. Immense issues of stocks and bonds had been sold to American investors on those industrials, with commissions to Helder & Dickerson, and other big bankers. What puzzled Arthur was the argument that payment of the war debts would ruin the United States because payment must be made in either money or goods, both fatal; also, if the war debts were paid, Europe would be unable to meet the industrial loans. It seemed to him they should have thought of that sooner. And he tried to figure out why payment of the industrial loans wouldn't be equally disastrous, unless some third method, neither money nor goods, could be invented. He gave it up, assuming that he didn't understand economics. He could see that it would be a vast relief to European statesmen not to have to pay for a very expensive war; and he had the humanly kindly impulse to be generous at no matter whose expense; in effect, he fell back on the roseate theory that nobody would have to pay.

Arthur signed a check—that was what the pen and ink were for—to cover his share of the quarter's deficit on the magazine, and took his departure. The bareness of his desk depressed him subtly. In the adjoining offices girls were typing busily, or answering telephone calls about cuts and dummies and proofs, or explaining that the editor called for was out. All that, the actual work, went on regardless of Arthur. He had bought the magazine because he had a taste for letters and because he thought he ought to make some disinterested use of his money; but in the main with the unformulated hope that it would serve as an admission card to the working world. It wasn't that he was unable to understand the routine; only there was no place for him after all. He could have mailed the check; his presence or absence made no difference.

In the street again, he decided that he might as well drop in at his nearest club for a belated lunch. Then he recalled, with a bad conscience, that he had stayed over, while Gina and Mrs. Siddall went back to Bar Harbor, on the pretext of attending a meeting of the building committee of that very club.

So he really might as well go there.

Thirteen

Mysie rejoined the group on the stage. There was nothing to be done. One word had informed her of the worst. But she was bound to lend the moral support and consolation of a listener to Jake. He was lurking in the wings, too stricken to take part in the futile debate.

The backer of the play, the angel from Wall Street, had failed them. He had gone broke, or at least had lost so much on a turn of the market that he could not find money for the play. Quite as much of a gamble, Mysie reflected. It was a wonder where people got all the money they lost. The angel would have to cut his loss on whatever sum he had already advanced to cover the equity bond and expenses to date. Naturally enough he had not come to break the bad news in person; Lew Morris had been informed by telephone. Mysie was sorry for Morris, a shoestring producer with a record of one moderate success and three flops. Probably he had let himself in for bills that would mean bankruptcy, not daring to extract a safely large sum in advance from his angel. An inexperienced backer would put up four or five thousand dollars, and then keep on paying to see the thing through.

Morris had taken a chance on *Third String* because he could get Anne Fairfield for the lead. Anne's name ensured the attendance of the dramatic critics instead of their assistants; she was a recognized star. But she too had had several bad seasons, or she wouldn't have been available. In fact, she was greatly in need of a part and an immediate salary. There was the disadvantage of ranking as a star; you had to have leading parts or none, and a succession of failures, even though the fault might be in the plays, made managers shy off from an unlucky player. There were so many stars now, with so many theaters—sixty or seventy or eighty, was it? New stars every week, dimming the radiance of last week's luminaries.

Anne Fairfield went into sobbing hysterics suddenly and Vida Winship, who played dowagers, led her to a dressing room. Vida disliked Anne, but forgot it in the facile kindness of theatrical folks. Lew Morris clasped his head in his hands and enquired at large: "Can I help it?" An anxious girl who had been cast for a maid's bit whispered to Mysie: "Do you think we'll get our week's pay?" They had been rehearsing for almost three weeks. "Oh, I guess so," Mysie replied rather mendaciously; she wasn't at all sure. "Lew, can't we adjourn this lodge of sorrow? Can't everybody come to your office in the morning, when you've had time to check up?"

"You've got sense," Morris said gratefully.

Mysie went over to Jake. "Well," she said, "that's that. Let's get out of here." Jake said nothing, but obeyed.

The heat met them aggressively as they stepped onto the pavement. "This is awful," Mysie sighed. She didn't mean the collapse of the play; that had already mingled with the past. "I wish I could go to the country and never come back." Dominic presented himself respectfully. "Hasn't Arthur—Mr. Siddall—gone yet?" Mysie demanded in surprise.

"Mist' Siddall said to wait and take you wherever you wanna go," Dominic explained.

"Oh—why—thank you. I guess I'll go home—do you want to come along and have a cold drink?" she asked Jake.

"I might have known," said Jake, still amenable to orders, stepping into the car after Mysie. "Even if I did write a play, and it was accepted, it would go flooey at the last minute."

Mysie replied irrelevantly: "I don't see how that egg could lose his roll on the stock market now, with everything on the up and up. It's crazy, but what stock could he pick for the express purpose of losing?"

"It can be done," said Jake. "Internal Combustion Engine, I think. It combusted yesterday. It would."

"Good heavens," Mysie exclaimed, "I forgot to tell Dominic where to go." Dominic had started without instructions. She leaned forward and slid the glass. "Dominic, please drive to—"

"Yeah, I know where you live," said Dominic.

"You know where I live? Where?"

"You live over Gus Silver's place."

"For heaven's sake," Mysie said at random, "do I? What an elegant address. It must be the speakeasy downstairs. Or whatever it is—they call it a club. They have a chain on the door, and peepholes; and there's usually a car or two standing outside. At all hours of the day and night."

Jake said, as if he hadn't heard her, which was the case: "Maybe Morris can find another backer."

Mysie decided that a pretense of optimism would be false kindness. It was her own mental habit to expect the worst; and then when it came, it was all over. She worried a good deal in anticipation; or rather, she made every effort to exterminate each budding hope; but she seldom repined. Hardly anything ever came out right; that seemed to be the nature of things. What she found hardest to accept was the fact that so many events were negative; if one looked back, life consisted largely of things not happening. Looking ahead, one was sustained by the conviction that something *must* happen. And it did, but not ever quite what one wished or planned; so that the total effect was of a continuous double disaster. Yet, given a choice, she would have crammed every minute with events at the expense of time, though she thought that probably she was wrong. Many things need the fullness of time. The impulse toward speed, by no means peculiar to this age, is half suicidal, a desire for a short cut to experience. It drives men to war, among other follies; they feel they may for once be fully alive, if only at the moment before death. And they would be spared the great pain of thinking. Mysie sighed again and returned from this irrelevant mental excursion.

"Maybe," she said. "But I guess it's a thin chance. I'll tell you, Neale Corrigan was out in front at yesterday's rehearsal. Nobody knew it but Morris, only Corrigan told me afterward. You know he owns the Franklin Theater, and the show there will close in a couple of weeks, so he wants something to fill it. If he had seen a good bet in *Third String,* he'd have bought an interest; Morris was trying to get him to bite. Corrigan sized it up as a ten-to-one shot, and nothing in it for movie rights either; not enough plot."

Corrigan had also intimated that she could have her job back, and probably a part in a show he intended to try out next month. She omitted that item, because it wouldn't help Jake.

Jake said; "If the whole world is resolved that I shall die in the gutter, who am I to object?"

"Corrigan said the dialogue was brilliant, but that you ought to get a practical hack playwright to put in action."

"It wouldn't matter, I suppose," Jake enquired with dangerous calm, "if the action had nothing to do with the dialogue?"

"That is an idea," said Mysie. "I mean, if the characters in Uncle Tom's Cabin spoke the lines of Lady Windermere's Fan." Completely aware of the futility of advice, she was nevertheless unable to prevent herself continuing: "Still, why don't you——"

"Why don't I write a play with more action?" Jake supplied, sweetly reasonable. "I will explain why I do not do various things you might proceed to enumerate, any of which would be highly lucrative. Why, in short, I do not write a play that will run for two years, or a best selling novel, or even toss off a few short stories. It is *because I am too dumb.* This statement applies to the human race in general and in all its undertakings. You, for instance, are said to be almost as bright as the average; why don't you write a play yourself?"

"That might be the reason," Mysie agreed.

"On the other hand," Jake continued inexorably, "Miss Sarnoff asks me why I do not write like Ray Lynch. For that I am not dumb enough. She also commends the method of our literary editor to my attention; she thinks I should acquire the proletarian point of view. I don't know where *he* picked it up; maybe at Harvard; and besides, the only proletarians I know read Zane Grey; but I admit our reviewer finds common ground. Every time literature raises its ugly head, he is there to knock it for a loop. All he asks is that a book shall be so boring that you'd sooner be shot than read it, and he announces that it is a masterpiece. However, Miss Sarnoff does her best. She edits my stuff, eliminating the point of each paragraph, or whatever portions seem to contain an idea."

"Do you mean that she cuts out the jokes?"

"She does when she sees them."

"The prosecution rests," said Mysie. "Probably she thinks you don't really mean it. I guess humor worries those owlish people. If you show them one of Rube Goldberg's contraptions for swatting a fly by means of an alarm clock, a trained elephant, a springboard and a piece of cheese, they examine it carefully and arrive at the conclusion that it is not efficient."

"They want to get to the bottom of it," said Jake.

"They are very worthy people," said Mysie. "And so prolific. They run the world, and that's where we get off. Do you mind if I put an icepack on my head as soon as I get home?"

"Not in the least," said Jake. "It is *your* head. Do you suppose Arthur would care to rescue the American drama from commercialism?"

"What?" said Mysie.

"I just wondered if Arthur could be induced to back the play. If he puts up for that magazine——"

"No!" Mysie exclaimed violently. "If you even suggest it to him, I'll never speak to you again. Can't you see——" She could see luminously the reason why not, but was unable to express it in words. She was shocked and startled, and had a confused impression that what startled her was the fact that she was shocked. "It's absolutely out of the question. On account of your job and—and everything. You must *not."*

"Well," said Jake. "They are your relatives."

"I wouldn't give a damn if you got Gina to back it," said Mysie.

Jake said: "I haven't come to that yet. The intellectual gigolo. Supported by kind rich ladies."

"Oh, anyone who got a cent from Gina would earn it—and I don't mean what you mean."

"Neither do I," said Jake. "Our kept thinkers couldn't earn their cigarette money that way."

They had reached Mysie's address and went upstairs laughing.

Dominic drove away with a casual conviction that Mysie was Arthur's sweetie, and that she was two-timing him with Jake. He did not know that Mysie was Gina's cousin, and he did know that she was on the stage, concerning which he had old-fashioned conventional ideas. His own cousin Tony belonged to the push that supplied Gus Silver's place with liquor. On his free evenings Dominic had occasionally gone around with Tony on the truck, so he had seen Mysie several times, once or twice with Jake. When old Dean Hervey went abroad for a sabbatical year, Dominic had got his new job with the Siddalls through the head chauffeur; he wouldn't have asked Gina, and did not suppose that she would recognize him, in which he was right. Natural tact suggested to him that the reminder of her briefly held position at the Dean's would have no interest for her. But he remembered driving her down to the Siddalls' the first time, and had known that she married Arthur Siddall, because the Dean officiated at the wedding.

In crediting Arthur with a mistress, Dominic merely assumed that a man with so much money knew what to do with it. He took for granted that Arthur was in the habit of leaving the car at Mysie's disposal. He had never driven Arthur before, and Raymond, Arthur's regular chauffeur, was uncommunicative. The last thing Dominic would have suspected was that there was nothing for Raymond to reveal.

Dominic was a realist. He left moral judgment to the priest, who was paid for it.

He drove to the public garage, to wait for further orders. Half a dozen chauffeurs were waiting, talking to the mechanics or shooting craps quietly. One, whose uniform was rather soiled and shabby, said: "Hello, Nick. How's the new job?" That was Chet Brody, a fresh guy. Dominic said: "Awri'."

Brody said: "They don't want another man, do they?"

Dominic evaded a blunt negative with a counter query: "You lose your job?"

"Had to quit," Brody explained. "I don't mind sleeping with the boss's wife, but when her sister came to live with them, there was too much overtime."

Dominic said noncommittally: "Sure, sure." That was an old gag. Brody never held a job long; he was a reckless driver and picked up too many tickets. He don't kid nobody but himself, Dominic thought. … My boss's wife, she's a better looker than this Brennan dame, but that's a funny business, a man gets tired of going home every night the same…

Three weeks later Mysie had a note from Arthur. When did her play open? He had been watching for the announcement and was afraid he might miss it. That's nice of him, Mysie thought. I believe he would have backed it. That's just why I couldn't let Jake. … Even if it wasn't a predestined flop, yes, if she had been sure it would go over, she thought obscurely, there was all the more reason. … It was because Arthur had so much money. Too much. Nothing else but…

She answered promptly: the play was postponed. She'd let him know when. It mightn't be till next season. She hesitated before addressing the envelope. He doesn't know that Gina detests me, she thought. But I don't suppose Gina opens his mail. … She sent it to his club.

Fourteen

Jake Van Buren's Aunt Hallie died the week of the stock-market crash. Both events seemed unreal. Jake had always been singularly detached from the visible world. He had been born in that old house on East Eighteenth Street; he had lived there all his life—and he was now nearing forty, though he did not look it—but in spirit he had always been a lodger. He was used to the house; he was equally used to his Aunt Hallie and his Aunt Susan.

The house was an authentic brownstone front, narrow and ugly, four stories with a half-basement. It had belonged to Grandfather Van Buren. There was a muddy oil-painting of the old gentleman in the parlor, with beetling brows and a cast-iron mouth and Horace Greeley whiskers. Grandfather had left the house in trust in a rather complicated manner. It was, Jake irreverently said, a Van Buren Sanctuary. Any or all of Grandfather's immediate offspring, or their widows, were bequeathed the right of residence so long as they should survive. The estate could not be finally settled until the last son or daughter expired. Jake had forgotten the original number of Grandfather's viable progeny. There had been an elder son, Uncle Martin, who took precedence of Jake's father in the line of inheritance. Uncle Martin died soon after Grandfather, but as he had had a son, who also died years ago, the house would ultimately go through that line to Katryn Wiggins. Or so Jake understood; the will was slightly ambiguous on such remote contingencies, having been drawn by lawyers. Grandfather Van Buren had tried to outwit time, and failed as men usually do. The house could have been sold profitably on several occasions, if it hadn't been so thoughtfully tied up. Those occasions had passed; it was now wedged in between two apartment houses, and probably unsalable. Grandfather and Uncle Martin and Father and the will had become history, something that ended before the present began, and had no connection with it. The house was in statu quo. Jake lived in it as we do live among historic scenes, never quite identifying them with our own affairs.

Aunt Susan was a spinster and Aunt Hallie a widow. Aunt Hallie's matrimonial term had been brief, and she returned to the house immediately after her bereavement, which was before Jake was born. It was impossible to imagine her as a young bride, or to conjure up even a hypothetical bridegroom. She was the type of widow to whom marriage is only a necessary formality precedent to her natural condition of widowhood. She and Aunt Susan invariably wore black in winter and grey in summer. Both of them, it seemed to Jake, had been the same age ever since he could remember. This could not be true, but reason availed naught against his impression. He didn't know just how old they were.

Though he saw his aunts every day, he spent very little time in their company. They existed on the lower floors. To Jake the house was an arrangement of layers. He always thought of it vertically, with himself going up or downstairs. He had contrived to secure for himself the fourth storey, under the roof. It was hot up there in summer, and cold in winter, and altogether inconvenient, having been intended for the servants. There was a front room and a back room, with a dark bathroom and closet in between. The bath-tub was of tin, and the water was never quite hot. The bedroom contained a hideous wooden bedstead with a high solid headboard "grained" in brown varnish, and a marble-topped bureau, and this and that. The front room had a Brussels carpet firmly tacked down, a small carved sofa apparently upholstered in concrete, two chairs with the backs curved in precisely the wrong places, a marble-topped table with scroll-sawed underpinnings, three framed mottoes on the walls, a filing cabinet, and a pretty little rosewood stand with a green silk pocket underneath, a sewing table. This last had belonged to Jake's mother, and he carried it upstairs from the room which had been hers, on the third floor. Nothing else had seemed to belong to her specifically; the house was furnished and the aunts in occupation when her husband brought her home, and she must have perceived at a glance the futility of attempting to change it. Her room was now called the guest room, though there were never any guests. The door was always shut.

The third floor back room had been given over to the one servant. From time to time one cook left and another came, but she was usually Irish, middle-aged, fat, and of uncertain temper. Jake kept on good terms with her by giving no trouble; he did not complain if his rooms were not dusted, and he tipped her frequently.

The second floor was sacred to the aunts. Two bedrooms, also equipped with gloomy walnut and marble, and faintly musty although aired and kept in rigid order. The aunts took their meals in the sunless half-basement dining room, and the rest of the day they sat in the parlor, by the front window. They were both rather stooped, with high noses, liver spots, and an indefinable expression of self-satisfaction. One might wonder whence they derived it from lives so negative, dull and narrow, but perhaps that was precisely the reason. They read the society pages in the newspapers and picked out names they knew, not exactly friends but names of families with whom the Van Burens had once associated, finding fewer each year. They did not read much else, nor do fancy work; they just sat.

The parlor contained a square piano, a cabinet of curios, various plush armchairs and hassocks, matched by plush curtains at the windows, and two bookcases with curtained glass fronts. The bookcases supported marble busts of Longfellow and Dante. Numerous steel engravings shared the walls with family photographs. There were two objects the like of which Jake had never beheld elsewhere: a patent rocker and a mantel drape or lambrequin of macramé cord lace.

The aunts had a formal, gelid yet doubtless real affection for Jake, as the man of the house. It embarrassed him slightly; but he was careful never to utter any disturbing sentiments in their hearing. Sometimes this was difficult. Their remarks were so shatteringly inept. Frequently Jake did not arise until noon, and the aunts assumed he devoted the midnight hours to intellectual pursuits. This was measurably true of many evenings; he did his writing in great discomfort with a bracket light glaring in his eyes and a litter of books and papers on the floor beside his chair; he made innumerable notes, and filed them, and couldn't find them again, and at intervals he spent whole nights going through the files. When he came downstairs in the morning, one or both of the aunts said: "Brain work is the most fatiguing." Therefore when, as occasionally happened, Jake had been out the night before and had come home solemnly pickled about four o'clock, creeping upstairs with bated breath, this statement threatened his equanimity. He didn't drink much nor often; but the cook was not deceived. She used to bring up his coffee, with a gleam of sour sympathy in her eye. ... Of course there were nights when he did not come home at all.

The aunts could not have been wholly unaware, but they belonged to an age when gentlemen had unwritten prerogatives, and ladies were not supposed to understand anything that could brush the bloom from their innocence. Even married women were not supposed to understand. Maybe they did not. A good many aspects of the matter were quite incomprehensible.

The break in the stock market was like a house of cards falling. It had been built up incredibly high and then a breath brought it down. It was a soundless catastrophe; it happened in the mind. Jake read the newspaper headlines with fatalistic indifference. Because he had, in his detachment, always known it was a house of cards. ... That was why he had quit his job ten years ago. He had looked *through* the figures he used to deal in; he really knew how to read a balance sheet. He had perceived a curious fact that wasn't mentioned in his accountancy course: the difference betwen a modern balance sheet and an old-fashioned inventory. The inventory listed material things and obligations dischargeable in the same kind. It was realizable in physical terms. The balance sheet seemed to do the same, but it didn't. It was a reading taken at a given time from a dynamometer. Everything depended on the continuance of the flow. If that should stop, the debit and credit items would have to be transposed to arrive at the truth. The assets instantly became liabilities. A closed factory of the modern kind is not only a net loss but a devouring expense. The accountancy thus was an enormous joke, like the careful proceeding of those rustics who built a fence around a cuckoo. A hedge of figures circumscribing imponderables. The exquisite part of the joke was that the figures were often skillfully juggled, in a quite legal manner, with depreciation and reserves and goodwill. What an amusingly futile performance, when a few months or years might turn the trick even more handsomely, though unfortunately it was impossible to be sure which way. ... It interested Jake for awhile to see this, but he got tired of the motions, and quit. To earn enough for his own imponderables—his share of the upkeep of the house which was now a liability instead of the asset it had been in Grandfather Van Buren's time—Jake did emergency work for his old firm, when they were rushed with annual statements and income tax returns. The third day of the panic they called him in, and he went downtown.

He was so driven for the next week that he worked automatically, and the successive downward plunges of stock-market prices instantly became part of the routine. He was checking up brokerage credits. ... It was fantastic, for at a given time the banks were all insolvent, but the momentum kept them going. It was all imaginary; so they continued on the assumption that the card castle was still standing at whatever height was requisite. Till they could build it up again. They did believe they could. ... Bid for U. S. Steel at 225. Wasn't that how it was done in the first place? If it would work once, why not again? Cheers for the hero who made the bid; anyhow it was a good offer! ... Jake muttered sardonically: "That bird isn't taking any chances; he can get all he wants at the price." The auditor who was checking with him looked at Jake blankly.

At the end of the week Jake wasn't very tired, though it had been a long week of long days. He worked easily under pressure; and he had put in fifteen hours the day Aunt Hallie died. ...

He had breakfasted with the aunts that morning. Aunt Hallie passed the newspaper to Aunt Susan, and expressed admiration of the Bankers Consortium for saving the situation. Jake didn't say anything. Aunt Susan read aloud that conditions were basically sound and that the Rockefellers were buying good common stocks. "Your grandfather," Aunt Hallie remarked to Jake, "said that bonds were the only proper investment for ladies. For security."

Aunt Hallie nibbled a piece of toast carefully; she had false teeth. Her thin hair was an off-color white, the same shade as her wrinkled skin. She wore half a dozen old-fashioned rings on her bony hands; for years she had been unable to remove the rings because of her swollen knuckles. Aunt Susan was stouter than Aunt Hallie, with a double chin and swollen ankles.

"May I be excused?" Jake said, as he had been taught.

In the subway, many people appeared rather sleepy, but everyone read newspapers, wedged in as they were. Nothing unusual. After ten o'clock, presumably the floor of the Exchange was bedlam, but Jake had no occasion to go there. He was working in the strained quiet of private offices. At noon, going down in the elevator, a man leaned against the side of the cage; when it stopped at the bottom he walked out groggily, sat down on the steps of the vast smooth indifferent building, and cried, with his head in his hands. He was quite conventional in appearance, well-tailored, with a neat clipped mustache. People walked by, glancing sideways at him in an embarrassed manner.

Jake sent out for sandwiches at dinnertime, and remained till one o'clock in the morning. He took a cab home. Wall Street was empty and silent, but half the office windows were alight, a checkered pattern of small golden squares, up and up. It was a fine night.

As he got out of the cab at Eighteenth Street he thought that the house also had something strange about it; he did not realize why until he was unlocking the door. A thin line of light glimmered under the parlor blinds and from the second floor windows. As he closed the door softly, Aunt Susan appeared at the head of the stairs, in a brown flannel dressing gown. "Oh," she said, "we tried to telephone you, but nobody knew the number."

Jake said: "Is anything wrong?"

"Your Aunt Hallie—" Aunt Susan made muffled sounds into a handkerchief. "She passed away this morning."

It was an accident, with a gruesome touch of the absurd. Aunt Hallie had gone to the corner grocery, to do the day's marketing. A small boy on a "scooter" ran into her; she stumbled over the curb and fell, striking her head against a lamp post. She got to her feet, got home, and while explaining what had happened, she bent over to brush the dust from her skirt. That was all. She fell again. The doctor arrived too late.

The rest of the night was rather grim. Jake sat up with Aunt Susan. And he had to see Aunt Hallie. She had the grey serenity of the dead. She was secure now.

It was fairly awful till after the funeral. Jake had to go to that. More aunts appeared for the occasion, and a few cousins, all with that left-over air characteristic of a family in decline. Those of the Van Buren connection whose fortunes had risen instead of sinking were absent. The final formality was the reading of Aunt Hallie's will. Jake was completely surprised to learn that he was the sole heir.

Aunt Susan was severely annoyed by a misprint in Aunt Hallie's ten-line obituary notice. "Widow of the late Daniel Blakeny"—it was spelled Blackney. Aunt Susan clipped the item to keep. "Your uncle Daniel," she said, "was a brilliant young lawyer. It was thought he would go far in his profession." A faded photograph of the long-deceased Daniel, in a black frame, hung in the parlor. He had a lean hatchet face and sideburns. Aunt Susan said: "It was I who met him first, at Narragansett. He asked permission to call on me. He died of the Spanish influenza, in 1889; he had a weak chest, and did not take sufficient care of himself."

For some obscure reason Jake did not really hear what she said until the next day; then the words came back to him irrelevantly. And he thought: Aunt Hallie stole Aunt Susan's beau! And Aunt Susan never forgave her, all these years; she probably believes he wouldn't have died if he had married her instead of Aunt Hallie. She'd have taken care of him.

Yet he understood that Aunt Susan mourned for Aunt Hallie. Like the majority of people, who remain within the restricted circle to which chance allots them, lacking initiative or desire to go beyond it, Aunt Susan had whatever emotions are prescribed for a given situation. She mourned for a sister, just as she had mourned, as long as the newspapers indicated, for President Harding, or as she admired the Bankers Consortium, or believed that prohibition was a noble experiment, or that Mr. Coolidge was a silent man even while she was reading his speeches.

Jake thought, it's incredible that Uncle Daniel and Aunt Hallie were once alive. They were young and perhaps Aunt Hallie was pretty. Aunt Susan too. And innumerable millions of people, famous or unknown; some were very much alive and the rest at least had blood and breath they might have put to use. You won't live forever either. More than half your life is gone...

A few of the female relatives hovered about for the next two or three days, and Jake went back to work the day after the funeral. He had to escape from the house. In the evening he telephoned to Aunt Susan that he was detained downtown, and went to the theater. On Sunday he telephoned to Mysie to ask her to dine with him. He hadn't seen Mysie for weeks.

Mysie said: "You'd better have dinner here, since we'll be going on to that party." Jake had forgotten there was a party. Mysie had no means of knowing about Aunt Hallie. So he said thanks, he would. He smuggled his dinner clothes out and dressed at a hotel. Maybe a party would do him good.

Fifteen

The party was large and expensive. Neither Mysie nor Jake knew their host very well; they had got on his invitation list in some casual manner and came when asked. Jake wasn't quite sure how he made his money, but thought it was either a hotel or a taxicab company. People made huge incomes in New York in so many ways. It didn't matter. Apparently he had plenty. He gave his parties with indifferent good nature, not expecting any chop-for-chop return, presumably deriving a sense of prestige from them. Though half his guests were no more than casual acquaintances, there were no hard feelings. Nobody cared. Sometimes they were fun. The apartment was immense and somber, decorated in pseudo-Spanish style, with iron lanterns for lighting, and galleries and balconies. It didn't make sense, high up over Park Avenue, but what of it?

Jake said misanthropically: "This is going to be dumb. Too many celebrities. They always blight a party." There was a jazz orchestra to dance by, but not enough room. Jake was soon lost in the shuffle of guests circulating in and out of the pantry bar. Mysie had intended to go home early, but stayed out of inertia. Some people were getting squiffy, and she usually left before the maudlin stage. She was to remember the occasion afterward as the last of the drunken parties that marked the boom years; at least, it was the last she happened to attend.

Before supper, the floor was cleared for entertainers. Someone did imitations first; Mysie couldn't see, being penned in a corner. She edged her way out, and then wished mildly that she hadn't. The next turn was a girl dancer, attired in a fringe of beads and with bells on her ankles. She was young and her pretty face had nothing coarse or hard in expression; the dance left very little to the imagination. A man breathed heavily into Mysie's hair; and a stout middle-aged woman said bravely: "How artistic." Mysie reflected irreverently: I suppose this is an orgy. As near as honest folks can manage. But we ought to be lolling on Roman couches. … The chairs were all taken; Mysie perched on the arm of a sofa, and by degrees was shoved over onto the knee of a strange man. The dancer was succeeded by a limp youth who gave an interminable pianologue.

Mysie murmured to her involuntary supporter: "Excuseitplease." He replied: "But for my part I am delighted." He contrived to make her comfortable, on both his knees, holding her thoughtfully about the waist. Numerous couples were more closely entwined, kissing at intervals perfunctorily. In the penumbra of the spotlight, Mysie could see across the room that Jake was almost extinguished by a woman with taffy-colored hair, in a red chiffon frock that did not quite cover her knees. Holding a cigarette in one hand and a cocktail glass in the other, she clasped Jake about the neck. Nevertheless, she looked like a suburban matron on her evening off. Probably she was. Jake blinked the smoke out of his eyes and listened to her with that intense simian melancholy which, to Mysie, indicated that he was rather bored. The lady was not his type.

Mysie surveyed her own polite stranger. He was quite presentable and amiable. He spoke with a foreign correctness and a faint accent. French, she thought. She asked him. He said he was; she did not hear his name clearly, and was never to find out. She gleaned—their conversation was gravely formal—that he had something to do with metallurgy, and had come over to study American methods in structural steelwork and factory and foundry organization. She asked him if he would take back a skyscraper.

He said: "They do not belong anywhere but in New York. In Europe they are a mistake. Perhaps even elsewhere in America?"

Mysie agreed. "The skyscrapers don't pay, you know," she said. "They do not pay?"

"No. Not in money, interest on the investment. Two or three per cent, I believe, on the older ones; so if they go on building them, with the costs increasing, they haven't a chance." An architect had told her so.

"Then why do they build them?"

"To the greater glory of God. Or because we're all crazy."

"I believe you," he said, and asked her about herself. She said that she worked for her living.

"Publicity, if you know what that is." Though she happened to be playing at the time; Corrigan had kept his word and given her a part; but she was always disinclined to say she was an actress, because it was a bore to have people try to remember whether they had seen her on the stage, when they hadn't. "In France," she said, "I guess there aren't so many of these odd-jobs. You have a profession, and can see your life ahead."

"It appears so," he agreed, "but I am not sure. Perhaps that is an illusion. For example, my grandfather was a scientist, and he died at Sedan. My other grandfather was a physician, and he died of yellow fever at Panama, with de Lesseps. But my father was a soldier, in the engineering corps, and he served over thirty years and retired to a farm in Touraine, dying there peacefully in 1912, on the land of his ancestors. How should one know?"

"You must have been in the war?"

"I was fortunate, a liaison officer in the transport service. I had a dear friend, who was a poet—killed at Verdun. There is no sense in that."

Mysie reached backward over his shoulder to set down her glass on the table. She had a dim recollection of Grandfather Brennan telling how he had seen machinery left by de Lesseps crumbling to rust in the jungles of Panama.

"Would you like another drink?" the Frenchman suggested.

She shook her head. "That was nothing but seltzer. I take it in self-defense, so nobody will pester me with cocktails. This bootleg stuff must taste poisonous to you."

He smiled. "I hid mine behind that lamp; have not touched it. But truly, in New York one does not need a stimulant."

"I daresay New York strikes you as a madhouse?"

"Not mad—but Atlantean. It confounds judgment. The spirit as much as the scale. All races and nations strive in turn to rebuild Olympus, reach the clouds. We French abandoned Versailles, our

Olympian gesture, and asked only to be let alone to become good bourgeois. This is your venture. I cannot think what you will do after."

Mysie laughed at the fantastic turn of the encounter. The enforced proximity enabled her to observe the undertone of his olive complexion, the flecks of brown in his grey eyes, a nick he must have given himself while shaving. He was fortyish, reasonably good-looking, a sound physical specimen; also he kept his hands to himself. ... They were insulating themselves by this conversation. ... She would have disengaged herself, only he must be sufficiently bewildered by the customs of the country, so that it might seem she had taken offense when he was so scrupulously giving none. Or perhaps he was at a loss how to extricate himself from the situation without rudeness. She said hastily: "The Olympian attitude is beyond the individual, isn't it? Take off the wig and the high heels, and nobody is any taller. And we cannot reach the top of our skyscrapers without elevators. One has to scramble for a living just the same, or snuffle with a cold in one's head. The undignified details persist. Look at these people; I suspect they are entirely respectable. They are trying to be something more, but it's no use. The drinking and—and the rest—it just doesn't mean anything. They remain ordinary. Pathetically innocent."

"You don't drink?" he said.

"Not as an Olympian effort."

"But you are not ordinary."

"Oh, yes," said Mysie. She was not sure if there was a further implication in his remark.

The entertainers ceased and the orchestra resumed. Would she care to dance? Mysie accepted, as an admirable solution of the situation. "That is a good tune," he said. *You Saint Louis woman with your diamond rings ...* Mysie acquiesced. "It is good. And quite apropos. The Beale Street Blues." *The graveyard is a nasty old place; They lay you in the ground and throw dirt in your face.* The floor was overcrowded; another couple cannoned into them, and everybody apologized. The other girl was a statuesque beauty, with her left arm covered with bracelets from wrist to elbow. Her voice blurred, and she broke off in the middle of a sentence to affirm: "It's too hot."

Mysie said: "It is hot." Her partner suggested: "There is a balcony." That seemed a good idea. It was an outside terrace, a narrow ledge protected by a coping. He shut the door after them.

The night air was soft and mild, with a thin mist in which the multitudinous street lights were diffused; the sky was a strange color, grey-lavender above the yellow glow.

He put his arms about her gently. "May I see you again?"

"I don't know," Mysie said. She had half a mind to tell him she appreciated his courtesy. Whatever his intentions, he had given them value by consciousness and privacy. … She thought, we are looking at the sack of a city. London Bridge is falling down, my fair lady. … She gave him back his kiss. The world seemed to rock a little, a ground swell of the force that made it. All passionate endeavor flowed from this. … He said again: "When shall I see you?"

She didn't know what she would have answered; they heard the door opening, and she stepped out of his arms. Some more people came. The tune was going on. *Ashes to ashes and dust to dust; If my singing don't get you, my shimmy must.* She shivered and he said: "Are you cold?" She laughed and went inside. They were elbowed by the crowd again; she caught sight of Jake Van Buren. He had detached himself from his clinging vine. She signaled him by lifting her eyebrows and he obeyed promptly, asking her to dance; they had a system of communications. She turned back just long enough to say to the Frenchman: "Call me up if you like. In the telephone book …" She was certain he had not got her name correctly, and their host wouldn't be able to identify her if asked who she was—one stray guest out of so many. It was better not. Meeting again might prove to be just an assignation. Quite ordinary. They mightn't even like each other.

"I don't want to dance," said Mysie, half-way around the floor. "I'm going home. But you don't need to."

"You women," said Jake, "think a man is made of iron."

Mysie said: "Then let's duck."

In the taxi, Jake remarked: "I'd have gone an hour ago, but I didn't wish to tear you from your paramour."

"And who was the lady I seen you with?" Mysie rejoined, yawning.

"I haven't the slightest idea," Jake said veraciously. "She told me her husband was a fine steady man, and she was so tired of him she could scream; and ought she to get a divorce? I advised her to do so. It would be a break for him. When she wandered away in the supper room an egg named George Gish or something confided to me that he was an old college chum of mine and that he had lost his shirt on I. T. & T. He seemed to think that was news. What worried him most was that he meant to sell a month ago, right at the peak, but he didn't because Professor Irving Fisher said there was no possibility of a crash. He was brooding over the Professor."

"Then I guess there wasn't any crash; the newspapers are kidding us. A professor couldn't be wrong," Mysie said. "He'd better just put the professor away and forget about him. Same as my Consolidated Nickel." She also should have sold her fifty shares a month ago. There were lots of things she should have done, and some she shouldn't have. Maybe she should have been a professor. They get paid for pulling boners.

"So that is why," said Jake, "I'll use Aunt Hallie's legacy to put on my play."

"What on earth are you talking about?" Mysie gaped.

"I forgot to tell you," Jake explained, "that Aunt Hallie died last week, and left me some money."

Mysie grasped the fact by degrees, after Jake had begun at the beginning and given full particulars. She then contributed the opinion that Jake was insane.

"How much money?"

"About twenty thousand dollars."

"Cash value, right now, with everything shot the way it is?"

"There's about that much in government and municipal bonds."

"It would give you an income for life," Mysie argued.

Jake said: "Aunt Hallie lost more than half her income when the New York New Haven dividends faded away. That used to be considered her best investment; it was the widows' and orphans' special."

"Wasn't that in the panic of 1907?"

"No; it was along about 1912 or 1913. In what are called good times."

"I don't remember," said Mysie. "What happened to it?"

"The bankers got it," said Jake. "Old J. P. Morgan cleaned it out. Blew it up and busted it like a toy balloon. Aunt Hallie never could understand about that."

"But good bonds," Mysie returned to the main point.

Jake again replied obliquely: "There were some odds and ends in Aunt Hallie's tin box, street railway bonds; and then there was a big envelope at the bottom, of relics that must have been left over from Grandfather's time. Rather weird. A canal-boat company."

Mysie waved this ancient history aside.

"You're crazy," she repeated.

Jake declined to discuss his mental condition. He said: "Lew Morris has got one of those play-doctors to go over *Third String* and jack up the plot. Most of his suggestions are too horrible to dwell upon, but he knows all the surefire hokum. If I survive the operation, the part you had will be more important. Would you take a chance on it again?"

"Sure," said Mysie. "You've got to have a keeper. Listen, are we going to spend the rest of the night in this taxi?" It had been stopped for some minutes at Mysie's door. 'Yes, here's my key; good night."

She climbed the gloomy narrow stairs and let herself in quietly, to avoid disturbing Thea. The precaution was unnecessary.

Thea was awake, reading. She sat in her accustomed chair, in profile against the light. The inclination of her head, the sweep of her hair, drawn up from her forehead, its sorrel color dimmed with grey, ash over ember, and the spread of her hand holding the book, were strikingly feminine. Tall and spare and straight as she was, with no trace remaining of the soft contours of youth, ordinarily she seemed to have resigned the special business of being a woman. When she played, she was a musician, not a woman displaying an accomplishment. Always she had an unasking air. The traditional feminine manner is expectant. Women wait upon the pleasure or necessity of others—of men, children, a domestic routine. Thea never looked like that. And now obviously she was not waiting for Mysie. She looked, simply, like a woman alone.

"Aren't you back early?" she enquired. "Or am I so late?"

"Both," said Mysie.

"I couldn't sleep," Thea said. "This panic—" She did not finish the sentence.

"Have you any stock?"

"I?" Thea invested the syllable with harsh ironic finality. She added, in a more guarded tone, "No, of course not. It was stupid of me to read the papers. I'll take a sleeping powder; but it wears off, and I didn't want to wake at six in the morning. Did you enjoy the party?"

"So-so. But you can't guess what Jake is planning to do; reason totters on its throne." Mysie repeated the news of Aunt Hallie's bequest and Jake's intention.

Thea commented: "You don't care how Jake spends his money?"

"Certainly not; Jake is like the weather; there's no way to stop it. Besides, I just don't care."

"Then he may as well please himself. Everyone might as well," said Thea.

From habit, Mysie picked up a book before going to her room. "I hope there's hot water," she said in parting.

She undressed, washed, brushed her hair, with automatic motions. … She thought perhaps she ought to be more concerned over money. It was the most important thing in the world. But if you gave it first place, it left no room for anything else. For love or disinterested work. … Or even for fun, she thought, doubtful whether life is real and life is earnest. Maybe it isn't; at moments it looks like a bad joke. She meant—she meant—what did she mean? That if you could even once do a thing right, however perishable the visible result, nevertheless the perfection would exist forever. As one hears a true note in song after the actual sound has ceased.

And you must do against the odds, without favor. It's no use asking to be endowed, exempted from the common and immemorial adventure of getting a livelihood. Wisdom and beauty are not to be had for nothing. Endowments produce only university dons, grammarians, commentators, stalled oxen. How should they understand the nature of work? Work is something that *must* be done.

And love …Quantities of solemn and public-spirited investigators compiled statistics and wrote books giving technical instructions. First you carefully choose a suitable person and then you proceed according to plan. … Those bewildered revelers getting drunk and tiresome were nearer right, though they were completely wrong. For even passion has its own dignity. It rejects the forced occasion, and takes fire from scornful sobriety, at the kiss of a stranger. …

Why can't people be let alone, Mysie thought gloomily. Between the blasted reformers and the earnest immoralists a pretty good country has been darned near ruined. Neither will recognize that there really are different kinds of people. There used to be room for everybody to be what they were. Cities, small towns, suburbs, farms, backwoods. Rigid respectability with the alternative of doing as you pleased at your own risk. Take it or leave it.

The reformers got us, tried to legislate us into righteousness, a concrete-walled sanitary plan. At the same time a flood of money seeped in and loosened the foundations they were building on. And everything floated in an indiscriminate welter, with the advanced thinkers paddling about on their separate chips like water-beetles, telling us we must all be alike but quite different from what we used to be.

But we were like that because that is what people are like. To produce only one kind of people you must have a way of life so hard and exigent that it kills off automatically every variation from type. There were never vast numbers of Indians. Those who weren't born good Indians died very young. Sparta perished of uniformity. The Peruvians were dead long before the Spaniards came.

And if, whether by accident or force, you lift a man out of a mental horizon that agrees with his capacity for vision, he remains the same person but becomes more so …Henry Ford belonged in a small town. The old small town was illiterate, gossipy, petty and busy, with a comfortable slack for minor eccentricities because nobody had much of an edge over his neighbors. Henry Ford would have been thoroughly in place running the local hardware store. He might have been the village atheist, or a Fundamentalist deacon. Or the only Socialist in the community, and no harm done. He could have got on happily with a limited stock of borrowed ideas that he did not comprehend and was not required to connect with reality. He was rather appalling when fortuitously hooked to a conveyor belt, a stream of power. Being what he was, he had no use for money except to buy little red school houses and old grindstones for a museum; and no use for leisure except to pry into the private conduct of his workmen, or advise the young to dance the polka on the village green of Detroit. No capacity for magnificence or ease.

Most of those people at the party—it suits them to have a neat house in the suburbs, with shrubbery and two cars and three children, one of them called Junior. Why shouldn't they? Very decent people, monogamous, with twin beds of maple, and a guest room, and all opinions ready made. It doesn't bore them. … But they've been nagged into believing they've got to drink too much and change partners, with the agreement that it doesn't matter as long as they Tell Each Other Frankly. … If it doesn't matter, then why go to the trouble? You might as well sleep at home. Respectability, the domestic virtues, are genuine accomplishments. If you want anything more, then it must matter a great deal. More than an easy conscience or convenient physical satisfaction. It must have a special value.

It *does* matter, Mysie thought obstinately.

You can't have it both ways. … On the terrace—he understood. I won't see him again; he isn't the one, but he knows that even a kiss is important. He was nice.

But if only that burning core in the very center of your being would cease sometimes, not be there forever while you have to keep on cutting bread and butter or brushing your teeth or checking the laundry list. … Mysie thought, that is the reason for sleep. We have to die every night to enable us to live through the day.

Sixteen

Afterward Geraldine was ashamed that it had taken her a month to discover how much Leonard had lost in the stock market. Of course he had lost every cent, not only his winnings but his original small savings. Some of hers too. And of course she had guessed accurately enough to refrain from questions. She was kind, passed it over tactfully. That was why she was ashamed.

She was so busy, and she had to keep her mind on her work. It astonished her when she reflected how strictly she stuck to routine. Nothing could have been more alien to her secret self. She had effected a compromise by the simple device of living in an apartment. In the nature of things, an apartment is a temporary expedient.

She could at least have bought a cottage in the country. She had not even considered doing so. If she owned a house, she would be trapped, would never get away.

Her reluctance must be a memory of the house in Hoboken. Not that she had been unhappy there. Though it was shabby and ugly, it was home, and had the comfortable atmosphere of long use; and she had a room to herself, a room not much bigger than a closet, warmed by the kitchen stovepipe; even in winter she could go up there and be herself and look out of the window at the river and write stories. In summer there was a hammock on the porch and a tree in the garden; she and her two sisters played at camping out under the lilac bushes. Her sisters had a larger room together, but Geraldine preferred her own refuge.

The house owned mother. Leaving it even for an afternoon was an onerous undertaking. The children couldn't be left unguarded in it. Father came home for dinner at noon sharp as well as supper at seven in the evening. If mother were to absent herself, father had to be told in advance to get his midday meal at the hotel, and he made a small grievance of it. Very rarely mother went over to New York by ferry to shop. She always returned out of breath, whisked off her hat and changed her dress immediately, and put on an apron as if she were afraid of being caught without it … Geraldine and her sisters had far more freedom. What Geraldine liked most was to go by the docks and look at the ships. When she grew up, she resolved, she would go aboard a liner and sail around the world. Perhaps she would never come back. … Mother had come from the Pacific Coast, when she married. And she had never gone back. That seemed unreal and sad, especially because mother hadn't come by boat, but by train.

Geraldine hadn't gone around the world. But as long as she didn't have a house, she still felt that she could if she chose. A flat was not the same. Even furniture did not grow into a flat as it did into a house. A flat could be stripped in a few hours, leaving nothing but so much impersonal space. A house became desolate and the furniture itself died, became mere sticks and rags, if the owners moved out. Geraldine had lived in four apartments successively since her marriage. She hardly recalled the earlier ones. This latest apartment was unusually pleasant, with its spacious high-ceiled rooms and tall windows. But its chief charm was that it was not a house. One could walk out and shut the door and think no more of it. The routine was bearable because each story she wrote was a job and could be got through with, finished. The children would grow up and she could live with Leonard anywhere. Sometimes she felt guilty; perhaps she ought to have a house for the children to remember as home. Still, they didn't seem to miss it. In summer she rented a flimsy bungalow on some Jersey beach, and they ran on the sands and swam like mermaids and were healthy and good and merry. In winter it was necessary to live in New York because of Leonard's work.

Geraldine always rose at seven. She had been obliged to when the babies were small; now it was habit, and it gave her almost an hour for her bath and coffee, a breathing space. Then she woke Judy and Dina and dressed them and served everybody at breakfast and kissed Leonard absent-mindedly and bundled the children into hats and coats and took them to school. When she returned it was nine o'clock and the apartment was beautifully empty. Geraldine wrote in the living-room. She ought to have a study, but it wouldn't have made much difference; she had to submit to a certain number of interruptions. She wrote with her eyes and hands and lent her ears to external affairs. If asked a question, she answered without turning her head. If called to the telephone, or to the kitchen to give instructions to the cook, she left a part of her mind at her desk. The household ran smoothly because Geraldine was quite competent to do the actual work herself, so she could command it intelligently. But she knew she was extravagant; she couldn't have said just how the money went. Her two sisters were married and not well off; she enjoyed giving them small luxuries, paying their expenses to the beach, or in town for a winter holiday, theaters and restaurant dinners. One sister lived in East Orange and one at Hartford. … It was marvellous not to have to think about money. Geraldine had made seven thousand dollars in the past twelve months, with short stories and a serial.

She sat at her desk faithfully till mid-afternoon. There were hours when her pen ran, and unaccountable intervals when she twined her hands in her hair and frowned at the wall, wishing she had gone around the world. … Soon after three o'clock the part-time nurse-maid brought the children home from school. The rest of the day belonged to them and to Leonard, with a slight margin for friends and parties. There was no time that belonged wholly to herself.

And yet all the time her life fitted into its domestic setting only at the edges, like a cog. She never felt like a wife and mother. … She had an uncanny suspicion that maybe she didn't exist at all. Not here and now. When she thought of *herself,* she saw a little girl looking out of a window. … The branch of a maple tree, just the leafy tip, extended across the lower panes, cutting the blue of the river down below in the distance. … She could think of herself at nineteen also, very unhappy and yet glad to be alive. And very real.

When she used to cry. ... Over a silly love-affair, a quarrel and an estrangement; she didn't think now that she had cared so much for the man she had been engaged to, but she had gone about with him one summer, and been light-hearted and young; and then it ended suddenly, and he went away, and she couldn't go away because her mother was not very well and they were poor and anxious. ... Leonard had never made her cry.

Why did she feel so far-off and helpless while Leonard was hard hit? The first day of the panic he was dazed; he couldn't believe it. The next day, he was in such obvious distress, Geraldine urged him to stay at home, send word to his office that he was ill, which was true enough. He had a cold anyhow. For herself, when she was depressed, solitude was the best remedy, to wear it out. ... Leonard said, with pathetic irritation, that he had to be downtown, "in touch with his brokers." He added that he "didn't know whether to hold on or not." He couldn't admit even to himself, so soon, that everything was gone. Geraldine said that it must be difficult to decide. Leonard rejoined that he would have to put up more margin—and he didn't see how. ...

Geraldine knew that margin meant money. She had over a thousand dollars in her bank account. She wrote a check instantly. Leonard said: "There's bound to be a rally soon—the big men like Mitchell say that prices are below the true values." Geraldine was glad to hear it. She had the more faith in the big men because she had never heard of them before.

A few days later Geraldine was giving an impromptu cocktail party when Leonard came home half an hour early. A few of her friends had come unexpectedly; they were gay and noisy, telling how much they had lost in the stock market. Leonard glanced into the room, hesitating as if he would rather not join them; but Geraldine called to him. He took a drink; only Geraldine noticed his silence. Then she was busy for awhile, mixing more drinks. When she turned to him again she saw. Leonard looked so—so thin and empty. It was terrifying.

She thought her guests would never go. When at last they trailed out, they left an utter vacuum. ... The nurse brought in Judy and Dina from a walk in the park. Geraldine exclaimed: "Doesn't this room look horrid? Children, when you grow up, don't ever put cocktail glasses on the piano. It's low." She began emptying ashtrays. She was not perturbed by the children seeing her smoke or drink a cocktail. They had a great deal of common sense. They were real. … The maid announced dinner; Geraldine knew the cook must be cross, as they were late.

"I don't think I want any dinner," Leonard said. "I have a headache."

There was nothing Geraldine could do but offer aspirin and coffee …

No doubt she should have persuaded him to tell her he was broke. She couldn't. He was stripped and disarmed. For the next month, they avoided the dangerous ground. It made a distance between them.

Against her will, Geraldine read the newspapers every day … She thought, things happen to us now at a distance. Of course they always did, but now we see them happening far away, and feel them quite awhile later. Like the Red Queen, shrieking because presently she would cut her finger. Perhaps it was better to live in a world where one didn't know in advance. We have to go through everything twice. Even the weather—we read that there is a low pressure area in Kansas and we shall have rain in New York as a result …

The stock market plunged and paused and plunged again; and every day some prominent banker or politician assured her that to-morrow, or next week, or next month, all would be as it had been.

Their assurances were shocking. They are fools, Geraldine thought, with sick dismay. Telling us it isn't so, when it is before our eyes. These are the men we depend upon. … Sometimes their pictures were printed. Foolish fat faces. … What has happened to men? Every loss can be made good except that. They are not grown up; they are pretending. They won't admit anything.

But she had her own work to do. After all, she had lived through the war, the dollar-a-year men and Victory loans and Liberty cabbage. Probably the sum total of fools was constant; only under stress it became visible, finding a common denominator. They were funny, too, in a desperate way, like the comedy which invariably creeps in at a funeral. Possibly her apprehensions were exaggerated by the measure of Leonard's personal bad luck. … She remembered her father and mother telling about the hard times of the Nineties, which had passed. … Fear was the worst thing; all that imbecile optimism was the meanest kind of fear.

Six weeks later Mysie sent tickets for the first night of Jake's play. Geraldine thought, things do go on just the same. She was amused to find herself mildly thrilled by the occasion; she had never been to a first night. She might have easily enough; tickets could be bought. Living in New York, one never did anything that the name of the city connoted.

Dressing for the evening, Geraldine found that her evening frock, two years old, had grown perilously tight, strained at the seams. I'm matronly, she thought; can such things be? Thirteen years of matrimony had had an opposite effect on Leonard; he was rather thinner. As she straightened the bow of his tie, she had a fleeting recollection of going to the theater with him before they became engaged, herself in a high-waisted blue frock with a ruffle at the neck and her hair done in a top-knot like Billie Burke. And she had been pleased by his recklessness in getting the best seats and taking a taxi.

The children came in to be kissed good night and to admire her loyally. Judy promised to be a real beauty, with her straight fine limbs and "moth eyebrows." Dina's round roguish face and curled lashes would serve her as well as beauty. Whenever they were in the room, Geraldine thought, being matronly became natural and almost painless.

It was a very smart first night; all the regular first-nighters were there, and recognized one another in the lobby, and felt prominent. Geraldine didn't know anyone, and stayed in her seat between acts, assembling her impressions of the play. There was a twist to it, an almost imperceptible burlesque of conventional situations—Jake had taken a subtle revenge on his collaborator. Its chance of success was fine-drawn; reckoning in terms of her own métier, Geraldine decided it was like a novel which is a cut above the popular level, but which may reach the best-seller list if the public is mysteriously seized with the conviction that it is the current book one must be able to talk about, must keep on the library table.

As leading lady Anne Fairfield was professionally competent; one could take her for granted. Geraldine gave most of her attention to Mysie. When she realized suddenly that for minutes she had forgotten

Mysie in the part, Geraldine knew she had seen good work. There and there, when Mysie was merely listening, when she said nothing but Yes, she caught it, what it's all about. The flash…That time I went to the theater with Leonard, Geraldine thought, and we drove back through the park, and I had a gardenia pinned to my coat, I wasn't in love with Leonard but with life, and it seemed as if I had it all in my hands …

At the memory, Geraldine felt treacherous. It was nobody's fault if those moments were only moments, and must be reckoned against years and years of the commonplace. Besides, we couldn't endure such delight always; we should die of its intensity. But it's queer how it can be brought back like a ghost by such simple devices as a dab of greasepaint, the cadence of a phrase, a gesture … Geraldine could see why a man might fall in love with an actress across the footlights, unable to separate her from the illusion she created. Mysie had somehow resolved herself into another creature, slender and delicate, with great soft black eyes. The effect was achieved by a material irony, by laying it on with a trowel, rouge and mascara and a theatrically simple gown of pale yellow crêpe cut an inch in advance of the fashion, nothing but crossed straps to the waist in the back, the skirt showing her ankles but emphasized by an artless train.

Gina and Arthur were in one of the boxes. Geraldine didn't notice them till the second intermission, and stopped on the verge of pointing them out to Leonard. She didn't want to meet Gina to-night. Gina wore a narrow band of diamonds in her hair, and was applauding at the correct moments, with her set smile. Geraldine thought, Arthur does see the quality of the play, and what Mysie is doing. He has taste. Why under heaven he married Gina—only if one regards her as an *objet d'art,* yes, one might collect her for her points, her hands and feet and the curve of her neck and the texture of her complexion. There's the curse of being rich, God help you, you can have what you want. … Meow, Geraldine accused herself.

They couldn't avoid Gina. Mysie had invited them to come to her dressing room after the play if they wished; Gina and Arthur were there. And Jake, and two or three others unknown to Geraldine. Everyone talked at once, asserting enthusiasm and conviction of a hit.

"I'm sure it will be a great success," Gina said. Geraldine thought, why does she always make a visible effort to utter even the most banal remark. Like a child "speaking a piece," learned by rote. Afraid of everybody—but what should she have to fear? Gina addressed Jake: "How you think of all those clever things I can't imagine."

To his own immediate horror, Jake heard himself answer: "Brain work."

Gina said: "It must be. Mysie, could you come to dinner next Thursday—and you, Mr. Van Buren?"

"I have to be here every night at seven-thirty," Mysie explained. Arthur caught her eye and smiled, silently reminding her of his question: Don't you ever eat?

"Oh, yes, of course—but you're free Sundays, aren't you? Next Sunday, or the next?" Gina said. "And Geraldine too," a palpable afterthought. Geraldine said hastily that on Sundays she went to the country, which was a lie and rather flagrant considering the season and the absence of any other inducement.

Mysie reflected that perhaps she had better accept, for Jake's benefit. She said: "All right, next Sunday." It would be completely boring. No, she didn't mind much, she liked Arthur.

Mysie asked Geraldine: "Do you think it went over?" She meant the play.

Geraldine answered: "Certain. Don't you?" They both glanced sideways at Gina; Geraldine's look said: *She* thinks so; it's worth a dinner. Mysie's unspoken retort was: Sure she thinks so, but how would she know?

"Maybe ten or fifteen weeks' run—about long enough to pay out," Mysie guessed cautiously. "By the pricking of my thumbs."

"All winter," Geraldine affirmed. "What a lot of flowers."

Mysie was put in mind of her manners. "Thank you," she said to Arthur. He had sent enough roses to fill a bathtub. One couldn't say anything more in that crowded cubicle, with its bleak painted walls, unshaded lights glaring above a merciless mirror on the crudity of rouge-pots, rabbit's foot, canister of face cream and crumpled face cloths. "Sticky stuff," she made an impatient gesture before her face. "Like a mask. I can't speak through it except my lines."

"It really is a mask, isn't it?" Arthur agreed. "But I'd know you by your eyes. You were charming. ... Can we drive you home?"

"I'd be glad to, only I can't leave right away, the first night."

Gina was drawing on her gloves. "Then we shall see you Sunday, at eight?" She departed, taking Arthur. Geraldine lingered, to say once more: "Honestly, Mysie, you were splendid."

"Oh, gosh," said Mysie. "This is all there is to it, and then you start over again. Eleven telegrams and a bushel of roses." What could one keep? A babble of compliments from people hurrying away, leaving a litter to be cleared up by the dresser. "I never could figure what percentage there is in telegrams; I don't own the Western Union. But roses are something. You'll have to carry them for me, Jake. And if you'll please get out I'll change; go and tell Anne Fairfield she's your dream girl. ... Not you, Geraldine; it's mean of you to dodge that dinner."

"I couldn't," said Geraldine.

She had refused the dinner instinctively, on Leonard's account. For herself, she might have found it diverting, even useful. The worst of being a writer was that one needed all experience, all knowledge. And one did not even know how the janitor lives, where the maid goes in her off time, what a policeman thinks. ... Or what was behind Gina's brittle unfocused smile, Arthur's unfailing gentle courtesy. ...

In the taxi going home, Leonard said: "If a play does make a hit, I suppose the royalties run up to forty or fifty thousand dollars?"

"I suppose so," Geraldine agreed, with the liberality of Americans when imagining profits. "Well, that would have to be a big hit, a very long run," she remembered the popular belief that all writers make forty or fifty thousand dollars. "Most plays fail, more than half; oh, I guess nine-tenths. And lose a lot." *I hear that your brother-in-law Abe Schultz in Chicago made twenty-five thousand dollars last week. That's right, except that his name is Schwartz and he lives in St. Louis and he didn't make it, he lost it.*

It occurred to Geraldine that she had never been able to believe in large sums of money. Her last year's earnings, seven thousand dollars, would have seemed a fortune, in a lump. When it came at intervals, and was spent, one had no sense of the whole sum.

Leonard said no more until they reached the apartment. Geraldine wriggled out of her tight gown into a kimono. With her bobbed hair ruffled and her pretty red mouth stretched in a yawn, she became girlish again. She went to peep in at the children, to make sure they had not thrown off the blankets. Naturally they had, and lay in fantastic attitudes in their white pajamas. Judy, the scamp, had been reading in bed, a forbidden indulgence, and had fallen asleep with the book on the pillow and the light still burning. Dina slept with her doubled fist under her chin. The napes of their necks, their bare feet, were enchanting. Geraldine drew up the covers and turned off the light. One dared not look too long. That untouched and unsuspicious quality in children made one's heart come up in one's throat.

Geraldine returned to her bedroom. Leonard stood by the dresser in his shirtsleeves, with his head bent. His dark hair was brushed very smooth. He had told her years ago that in high-school he and the other boys wore stocking caps at night to ensure that indispensable uniformity.

He said: "I'm sorry, Geraldine, I'm rather short this month. If you could make out … I got caught when the market broke."

He too looked very young. Not boyish, but like an untried young man, slight and diffident. Precisely the same as when they were engaged, only then he had been eager and hopeful.

"Why, certainly, it doesn't make a bit of difference," she said quickly. "I sold a story this week."

"Your money," Leonard said, "is tied up too." What money, Geraldine almost asked, but recalled that he had "invested" a couple of thousand dollars for her some time ago. Besides the last thousand. "It's safe enough," Leonard continued, staring at his keys and small change on the dresser. "But this is a bad time to sell." He had to insist to himself that Geraldine's money was safe, it would "come back." His speculative account had been wiped out; he had used the thousand dollars in hope of recouping and seen that go too. What he intended now was to assign to her the stock allotted to him by his company as an employé. He had not put that up with his brokers; it would not have been acceptable, as he had paid only twenty per cent of the issue price, and it was quoted thirty per cent off now. The company held the stock until it should be fully paid by deductions from his salary. It would take four years … And his brokerage account had closed with a small debit. The avalanche had crashed through stop-loss orders. … When he had been thirty thousand dollars ahead, last summer, he could easily have paid for his company stock. It had seemed foolish to draw out money from marginal deals that might double any day. He would have sold and taken his profits when they touched a hundred thousand. He *would* have, he told himself.

"Yes, of course," Geraldine said. "I'd just as soon leave the money there. Don't bother." She hung up Leonard's dress coat. "It's too bad the—the stock market went wrong, but it doesn't matter, does it, as long as—" She floundered in the fatuousness of mere words against facts, and laid her hand on his shoulder. "We were just as happy at first, when we were so poor."

"Yes," he said. He felt the worse for the reminder. Because while they were poor he had supported his family. When he went to the chemical company, at seventy-five dollars a week, the first week's pay was riches. Now the future was blank. … As a boy he had worried about whether he could ever make a living. His father was chief clerk in a large law firm, one of those steady low-salaried men who do the detail work with no expectation of a partnership. They were a small family, four children, and they lived in a careful way in Brooklyn. The world appeared to be arranged on that plan, everything fitted together and all the places filled. Leonard studied hard in school, because he wanted to go to college, having read that one made useful friendships. In fact, he had been rather lonely in college. He specialized in chemistry not because of any unusual aptitude, but the head of the department wanted a reliable assistant, not a rival. An instructorship was secure, once you got it. Leonard had let Geraldine believe he was keen on research; it gave his poorly paid position dignity. When he went to the chemical company he knew he was doing the best he could with his moderate ability; he would never rise above routine work. Like his father, he was steady.

His stock-market winnings were the realization of an impossible dream. Temporarily he had been transformed into one of those nonchalant young men he had envied in college—with cars and expensive clothes and cash in his pocket. He was proud of his talented wife, his pretty daughters. He wanted nothing more. How could the structure of his happiness have vanished overnight?

Geraldine said: "Don't let's worry about it; your luck will turn again; you're tired." He could not refuse the comfort of her kindness.

Geraldine lay awake for a long time. She thought about her child-hood. Her mother did not worry about money; there were a great many things they could not afford and therefore did not expect. They were, it seemed, in about the same circumstances as everybody else. Within that limitation, they had no misgivings. Father would take care of them. Perhaps their confidence was delusive; when father died, it went with him. But as long as he was alive, they had it. Mother was middle-aged at thirty. By no stretch of fancy could Geraldine picture her father as a young man. He was heavy and taciturn, with a drooping greyish mustache and a bald spot on the crown of his head. His clothes were unpressed and a substantial gold watchchain reposed in a crease across his waistcoat. When he came home of an evening, he planted himself in his special armchair and smoked and read the paper. ... It was as if father and mother had given up youth as a pledge in exchange for peace in their time. They married and settled down.

Geraldine saw she had never depended on Leonard. In marrying, having children, she had counted upon herself. That was why his win-nings and losses were of no conscequence. She had never believed in them anyhow. The knowledge was darkened by remorse, as if she had wronged him. She had an equable affection for him; she was inseparably attached to him by the years they had spent together, by the children, even by their lack of other common interests. And he had supported her while the children were babies, literally borne in her arms. Nothing could change that. So he must not ever know. ...

In the morning, at breakfast, though Leonard was quiet, she fan-cied he was more cheerful. They read the reviews of Jake's play, which were highly favorable. Geraldine was glad. If somebody could still be lucky, then anybody might. Leonard might again ... She refrained from following the thought to its conclusion; he could succeed only by luck ... After he was gone to work, Geraldine made telephone enquiries and went downtown herself, to insure her life for the benefit of the children. She must take care of them.

Seventeen

Mrs. Siddall was not altogether surprised when Polly Brant came to her for financial assistance. She guessed the object when Polly telephoned. She also knew that Polly was still abed, at ten in the morning. Mrs. Siddall had risen at eight, her regular hour, and breakfasted in the morning room, armored for the day in unyielding corsets and a garnet velvet gown of majestic amplitude which made no concession to either fashion or informality. Her hair was firmly coiffed; and she sat upright in a straight armchair, before a damask-spread table loaded with heavily embossed Georgian silver. Mrs. Siddall's tradition did not permit a lady to be seen in deshabille except by her personal maid; and breakfast in bed, unless in case of illness, suggested other, more reprehensible laxities. She tolerated the custom for guests; but as mistress of the household she felt bound to set an example to the servants. Mrs. Siddall was an admirable example of good conscience and a good appetite. She had disposed of two hours' work with her correspondence before Polly arrived.

Polly's explanation of her situation struck the older woman as fantastic, like viewing a familiar object through a refracting medium.

"You mortgaged your house to speculate in the stock market?"

"No," said Polly, reciprocally astonished, "we bought it on mortgage."

"But that was nine or ten years ago," Mrs. Siddall reminded her, "when your father-in-law's estate was settled; I thought Bill's share paid for the house. You said it was a great bargain."

"So it was," said Polly. "Real estate went up like mad around Southampton afterward; we could have sold last year for twice what we paid. Of course you can't sell anything now. Bill only got fifty thousand from the estate. We paid half down on the house and left the rest on mortgage, only twenty-five thousand. Now it has to be renewed, and the mortgage company insists we should reduce it at least five thousand. Everyone said it was better to have a mortgage."

"Better to have a mortgage?" Mrs. Siddall echoed.

"It keeps down the taxes."

"But you have to pay interest, far more than the taxes."

"I don't know exactly; that's what they said," Polly repeated. "Everyone said so. I don't know much about it; Bill's secretary always looked after that sort of thing, at the office. Bill has drawn his salary three months in advance now, and the way things are, he doesn't like to ask them to do anything more. I tried to get a loan on my trust fund, but the trust company says I can't; but the income seems to be cut in half, I don't see how they could do that, if it mustn't be touched, only they said some of it is in foreign bonds and there was a default. The rest is guaranteed mortgage bonds; they say those are safe," Polly was happily unaware of any discrepancy in her summary of prospects. Her trust fund had been two thousand a year, a perfectly miserable sum in her estimation. If she went abroad even for a couple of months, it barely covered traveling expenses, and left nothing for clothes. "Even if we shut up our town apartment, the maintenance goes on, with those coöperatives. Bill says he'd sell his polo ponies, but I don't want him to; what would he do? and besides, who would buy them? We can't afford to keep them either. I don't know what has happened to *everything.*"

Mrs. Siddall did know, so far as Polly was concerned. She could add and subtract. She was not to realize yet awhile that "everything" was a strictly accurate term. She persisted: "The twenty-five thousand you lost in the stock market would have paid off the mortgage. That was very reckless."

"Well, we made a lot more than that," said Polly, with what she considered extreme reasonableness. "Everyone did; Julius

Dickerson bought Kennecott Copper himself. We had to have something to live on. Bill's salary is only fifteen thousand, and he says that may be cut any day. Because the accounts he handles are mostly invested in City National Bank stock and things; he says those bear raids oughtn't to be allowed."

"Yes, perhaps, but Julius Dickerson could afford the risk," Mrs. Siddall said, not unkindly. She looked at her niece with absent-minded appraisal.

Polly was forty-three, but even in the cold light of noon she could have passed for thirty, to the superficial gaze. Riding, swimming and dancing had preserved her figure, all but the resilience and grace of youth. Her gypsy coloring was coaxed to maintain its natural tone by sunbaths and oil rubs. If she had taken off her hat, one would have seen that her dead-black hair had changed to a silvery lead color; she was too clever to resort to dye, knowing it would coarsen her face, so she dressed to the frosted high light of her coiffure, especially for evening. Her legs, delicately emphasized by rose-beige stockings of cobweb thinness, justified the shortness of her skirt. She had tossed off a brown ermine coat as she sat down. Her frock, of black crêpe with a tiny green flower, made with a little jacket, couldn't have used more than five yards of material, and cost not less than two hundred dollars. With every stitch of her undergarments added, the lot would have weighed under two pounds. A close black felt hat was pulled down over her ears; it was untrimmed except for a triangle of jade, to match the clasp of her handbag and her imitation jade costume jewelry, expensive but valueless.

Mrs. Siddall remembered distinctly that at forty—that was in 1897—she dressed in a manner suitable to her age and position. Gowns from Worth, of the heaviest silk, stiffly boned, with skirts nine yards around the hem, and gigot sleeves puffed out with buck-ram. Two or three petticoats, rustling with taffeta ruffles; and velvet hats loaded with ostrich tips. She had rejected the tailored fashions which were introduced about that time. And jewels were jewels, sets of diamonds, rubies, emeralds; they showed the money invested in them, and at the Opera one recognized the famous adornments of the acknowledged leaders of Society.

Mrs. Siddall was seventy-two, and all her life she had been rich, securely and enormously rich. The panic and the depression did not shake her mind immediately. She had seen several depressions. Though she might have talked nonsense if required to defend her position, she had a genuine practical intelligence, consistent with her experience. Her natural and instinctive morality was so fully accordant with her time, place and circumstances that she had never needed to formulate it. In a complex society there are many moralities. They do not necessarily conflict, being complementary. There would be no virtue in ascetic or voluntary poverty if there were no wealth or luxury to reject. Any morality is posited upon choice and freewill. Confusion arises only in the mind of the individual who professes a morality at variance with his way of life, refusing to meet the terms. He asks instead that it shall be imposed by force, through a vast uniformity, abdicating as a moral being. This is the way of death. Mrs. Siddall's life was logical and all of a piece, proceeding from the axioms of property, the virtues of which are thrift, tenacity, and faith in the visible world.

The great and durable fortunes, accumulated by men such as her father, Heber Crane, had been made in bad times as well as good. Mrs. Siddall held her father's memory in respect and affection, the only decent sentiments as long as she benefited by his money. It would have been easy to turn his careful and laborious career to satire. During the Civil War he hired a substitute for four hundred dollars, made large gains out of army contracts, and afterward subscribed half the cost of the local Soldiers' Monument. His brother James, who was "wild," volunteered and died in Libby Prison. Heber considered himself more useful at home. Satire could readily compute that he was worth four hundred dollars to his country and four hundred thousand to himself. Yet if the glory is to be stripped from war, James fares no better as cannon fodder. One must commend either prudence or valor, else the satirist too is out of employment, for want of any measure; he must go to the ant and praise only anonymous negation.

There was no hypocrisy in Heber Crane's condemnation of the first Wyman Helder, founder of the firm, who bought up obsolete and defective army rifles, cast equipment, and resold them to the War Department at a profit. Crane considered Helder's trick immoral because it undermined the basis of business. For the same reason he denounced Jim Fisk and Jay Gould; they destroyed business, left only wreckage. Speculation he considered allowable for a man at the beginning of a career if the odds justified the hazard of being compelled to start over again. Having once acquired a competence, it was wrong to imperil it; his dealings were confined to what he could afford to lose. No gain without risk; cut a loss quickly and take a profit before it vanished. He regarded material possessions as the ground anchor of wealth, and got out of money into merchandise in time to profit by the inflation after the Civil War. Therefore he supported the sound money candidates; one might cross by a rotten bridge once or twice or even a dozen times, but in the end it would break, and those upon it would go down, and traffic cease.

Gradually, as the great corporations came into being, he let go his foundries and oil-wells on good terms to the nascent trusts; he saw that the big fish were going to eat the little fish anyhow. His caution served him as a social conscience; the Pullman and Homestead strikes alarmed him. Something wrong, too much pressure, dangerous. They were going too fast. He did not want power but possessions; the two are inimical to each other. He was building what was perhaps the last of the great private fortunes, gathered mainly by personal ventures and personal risks, and concentrated in such form as a man might hold under his hand, pass on to his descendants. One could not do that with corporate control, which is the instrument of power.

Charlotte was his only child, and it gratified his fond vanity, the egotism of the proud parent, to think of her as the richest girl in America, as perhaps she was for a time. He lived to see the upturn after the mid-Nineties, and reckoned his wealth conservatively at twenty millions when he died. In the next twenty years it tripled with rising prices and the unearned increment, and Heber Crane rested in peace.

Mrs. Siddall was shocked by Polly's talk of "only fifty thousand," only twenty-five thousand, only fifteen thousand. Her grandfather, her mother's father, too thoroughly Pennsylvania Dutch to become a millionaire, had left an estate of fifty thousand dollars, which in 1873, the date of his death, ranked him as one of the first citizens of Lancaster. On her sixth birthday he had given her a silver mug; she still owned it. Strange, she remembered that birthday party, a timeless moment of it, vividly; she had red-tasseled shoes, which Grandfather did not altogether approve; and a round-necked cashmere frock trimmed with narrow bands of velvet ribbon, and a birthday cake with candles; and it must have been in 1863, in the dark years of the Civil War, but there was no Civil War in her memory. That occurred in the mysterious lives of older people; it was an abstraction.

Twenty-five thousand dollars is a large sum of money. ...

"However, I daresay we can arrange—" Mrs. Siddall conceded. Polly was down in her will for fifty thousand; the mortgage could be taken over and deducted from that, without mentioning the contingency to Polly. "I'll speak to Mr. Lutzen," Mrs. Siddall's lawyer for estate transactions; "you can tell Bill to make an appointment with him," Mrs. Siddall considered it her duty to assist her family, and equally her duty to do so in a manner which should discourage extravagance.

"It's awfully good of you, Aunt Charlotte," Polly said, much relieved though not beyond her expectations. "Anyhow, we're lucky that our place is small; the big estates are eating their heads off. You know the Marston Stukeleys aren't opening their Florida place this year, and they've laid up their yacht and dismissed most of their servants, and Mrs. Stukeley is having a nervous breakdown, with five trained nurses. They had a million dollars a year income, and Bill says it has shrunk ninety-five per cent—isn't that awful?"

"Five trained nurses," Mrs. Siddall repeated, unconscious of any humor, "what does she do with the odd one? The Stukeley income was from railroad stock, wasn't it? My father always said railroads were too speculative; they suffer first in a depression, besides watered stock and radical legislation. Like the Erie; that was a shocking scandal. And what good did the money do? squandered by that horrid little French count, and a family law-suit after everything."

Polly hadn't the slightest notion what Mrs. Siddall was talking about; and even if she had been fully informed, she would have been unable to understand Mrs. Siddall's inherited conviction that "tainted money" brought a curse. *Pecunia non olet* was Polly's creed. Money, to her, did not come from any specific source, or physical origin. It materialized out of the ether, by a benevolent dispensation. It was privilege without responsibility. And she spent it mostly for intangibles, for things perishable and fragile, for the evanescent quality of smartness, for speed, for exclusiveness. Mrs. Siddall in turn would have been puzzled by Polly's idea of exclusiveness, crowding with dubious strangers in some expensive speakeasy, to drink bad gin in a stale atmosphere shattered by jazz.

"Well, they say Conant Hacker was completely wiped out, and he was worth a hundred and fifty million last year. That's the second time; he made two hundred millions once before and lost it."

"Hacker?" The name meant nothing to Mrs. Siddall.

"Motors. Of course he made most of his money in stock-market pools."

"My father said that a gambler always dies poor," Mrs. Siddall commented. She did not believe in two hundred million dollars made in the stock market. That was not real money. Gambling was immoral; how could it pay? Not in the long run. … But Mrs. Siddall did not perceive, as her father did in his time, that power is a shifting stream, forever finding new channels. He had seen that the railroads signified the obsolescence of inland waterways; she did not realize that Hacker's incredible millions from motors presaged the obsolescence of railroads; nor did she suspect that gambling on a scale so vast might overbalance the property basis of wealth, leaving the prudent minority to be held for ransom for the spendthrifts.

"Bill says the worst is over now," Polly said resiliently. "He says it's wonderful how the bankers got together and supported the market. If we had any money now we could get in on the rise again; it's just our luck to be broke. And Bill will have to give up that Greenland expedition he was planning to join next summer."

"That is too bad," Mrs. Siddall agreed, overlooking the suggestion. "Though why anyone should want to go to Greenland—Wasn't it snowing this morning?" She looked toward the window. Even if her eyesight had been keen, it would have told her nothing. She was cut off from the weather. Her boudoir was ventilated by invisible hygienic flues. Between the heavy window draperies of amber satin the net glass-curtains softened the bleakness of the street with a delicate illusion that left no hard surfaces or sharp edges. A lively wood-fire burned beneath a mantel of yellow faïence tiles. On an Italian table of yellow marble pale bronze-pink roses unfurled in a cloud of white gypsophila from a cloisonné vase. In furniture as in clothes Mrs. Siddall was faithful to her own era, when money was expected to show. She found the *decor* of Polly's apartment incomprehensible: black velvet divans built against silver-painted walls, a silver-grey rug on a red-lacquered floor, a black marble mantel, and two pictures of angular nudes with dislocated hips. Polly had had it done over only a year ago, at preposterous expense. It wouldn't last, Mrs. Siddall thought firmly.

"Only a flurry," said Polly. "Spring snow."

"The winters used to be much more severe," Mrs. Siddall recalled. "After a snowstorm we drove out in cutters; you could hear the bells all along Fifth Avenue."

Yet she had a conviction that she had lived in a world of permanence, which had mistakenly changed, very much for the worse, only temporarily. It would have to go back. ... Healthily incapable of introspection, she did not perceive that to herself she was simultaneously and miraculously the six-year-old child with red-tasseled shoes; and the dashing young woman in a sealskin coat, holding a sealskin muff to her face to shelter a bunch of violets from a spray of snow in the Park; and her immediate self, a repository of ripe wisdom and authority. The permanence she felt consisted in whatever secret and persistent filament of flesh or spirit preserved those continuous memories.

"That must have been fun," said Polly. "You'd have to go to Greenland now. Thank you, Aunt Charlotte, I'm sorry but I can't stay to lunch; I promised to go to a bridge luncheon for the Unemployed." She kissed her aunt, with moderate gratitude and affection, and departed.

The month's accounts were waiting; Mrs. Siddall checked them thoroughly. "We shall have to economize, Mrs. Enderby," she said. "Yes, madam," the housekeeper agreed. "I don't think I shall open the Bar Harbor cottage this summer," Mrs. Siddall said. She told her secretary to make a note about the greenhouses on the Long Island estate. Perhaps one could be shut down, dispensing with a couple of under-gardeners. There were so many calls for charity. To do her justice, Mrs. Siddall did not consider reducing her regular contributions; there was her favorite hospital, and St. Stephen's parish fund, and a settlement house, and an orphanage, to all of which she subscribed generously; they had long since become fixed charges. They were appealing urgently for larger benefactions; she decided to increase the various amounts, say ten per cent, this year. Unemployment relief—yes, that was a duty, in the present emergency. She paid a number of small private pensions—old servants, and remote poor relations to whom she was not inaccessible for extra sums when there were children to send to college, or in case of illness. None of them was nearer than second cousinship; several she had never seen; the law of averages had kept the total fairly constant for many years by death and birth and superannuation. Disaster seemed to be hereditary. Mr. Lutzen had told her that young Mr. Fraser, in the estate office, had tuberculosis. Fraser was the grandson of one of Heber Crane's early associates who inexplicably ruined himself backing inventions which were afterward successful. Mrs. Siddall had employed the grandson out of sentiment. He had been doing well enough, was married and had a child; now he was stricken, with no resources. Mrs. Siddall gave instructions that he should be sent to Colorado on full pay, with his family, until he recovered. She was a genuinely kind woman, one of the limited percentage of the rich who give as a matter of course. If she had been a farmer's wife she would never have refused food to a tramp, and though she would have required him to chop wood in return, she wouldn't have been astonished if he had evaded the chore. Her sympathy was practical and unimaginative; she did not suffer vicariously over social injustice. Her comfortable benevolence was of the type which rouses the scorn of idealists and the fury of social revolutionaries. She would have driven either or both to apoplexy by listening to their arguments and then replying that if all the money in the world were divided, in six months there would once more be rich and poor. Neither she nor her opponents would have realized that both sides were assuming their own axioms. Few people do perceive that all logic proceeds from axioms.

After Polly had gone, Julius Dickerson arrived for lunch. Business was not discussed at the table, but later, in the library, Julius discussed the financing of the Siddall Building. His characteristic mode of conversation was soothing and encouraging; only a thoughtful listener would have observed that it was impossible to recollect subsequently exactly what he had said or not said. One was left with the general impression that all was for the best.

About half the bonds for the construction of the Siddall Building remained unsold. Some of those which had been sold were not fully paid. The building corporation was legally empowered to pledge the unsold bonds for seventy per cent of face value. Mrs. Siddall owned none of the bonds, and held no shares of the building corporation, to which she had leased the land. Money must be found if the work were to go forward. The depression made it practically a public duty to proceed, and since building costs were down, Mrs. Siddall could acquire a majority ownership in the building at a reduced price, by assuming the unsold bonds, and taking over at a discount some of the bonds which were not fully paid. She would thus protect herself on the lease also; an unfinished building couldn't pay ground rent, and bankruptcy of the building corporation would be prejudicial to the immediate enterprise and the Siddall name. Julius Dickerson forgot to stress the point that ultimate returns depended upon rentals when the building was completed. In fact, he never thought of that. Of course there would be tenants.

Mrs. Siddall remembered that her father had acquired his choicest bargains in New York real estate at the low mark of the Nineties.

She signed the necessary papers. Naturally, she did not keep millions in cash on hand, but that would be taken care of through her bank, by loans; the presumption was that ultimately the building would liquidate its costs. She could see no risk whatever; she was lending the money to herself. Nothing could be safer. It was impossible to contemplate the stopping of the work, letting the name of the Siddall Building stand for failure.

Julius mentioned that he must hurry away to a conference on a municipal loan issue. He was saving the city. With the other leading bankers, he had in the course of years sold—and taken his percentage—on so many city bonds, credit was exhausted. He would now demand economy. The taxpayers must be roused to protest against Tammany graft. He expected to be in Washington next week to urge a moratorium on international debts, also a necessity, he said. ... To sustain credit. This reasoning seemed luminously clear to him.

His soft, greyish face, with its flat clerical upper lip, was irradiated with altruism. His private life was blameless, and he had a pious veneration for the aged Wyman Helder, who had saved the country during the panic of 1907, at a handsome profit; and was the leading vestryman of St. Stephen's until locomotor ataxia forced him to retire. Wyman Helder senior had given Julius his career.

Every afternoon, before tea, Mrs. Siddall was accustomed to visit the nursery next door. To-day Arthur forestalled her, bringing his son to call. Young Benjamin, named after his great-grandfather, was two years old, and just promoted to approximately masculine garments. Arthur carried Benjy on his shoulder, and the child squirmed and laughed, holding on with both hands.

"Do be careful," Mrs. Siddall warned him.

"I'd better be," Arthur agreed. "He's got me by the ear. Come down, Colonel." Set on his feet, the little boy ran to Mrs. Siddall.

"What have you been doing to-day, Benjy?"

"I bwoke my duck."

"Your duck?"

Arthur said: "One of those celluloid objects floating in his bath."

"We'll get you another duck," Mrs. Siddall promised.

Benjy struggled with the dawn of thought. It wouldn't be the same duck. He couldn't express the idea, and shook his head. He had Gina's dark hair and Arthur's blue eyes; his dark lashes were tipped with gold. His round face and dimpled knees retained the plumpness of babyhood; and he was as good as gold. Mrs. Siddall's fat white hands, with their burden of rings, held him competently. The superficial haughtiness of expression which had been fashion in her youth and habit in her middle years had almost vanished with age; her hair was now snow white; and tiny purple veins showed through the powder on her cheeks and nose; her double chin suggested amiable indulgence.

Benjy gazed solemnly at the roses. "Flowers," he said. Then he yawned, with the comical candor of infancy, and leaned against Mrs. Siddall's whaleboned bosom. He had been playing very hard with Arthur, and it was time for his nap.

"I'll take him back," Arthur said.

"He's such a lamb," Mrs. Siddall rejoined.

On the stairs in the other house Arthur met Gina coming down. For a second he did not recognize her. She was dressed for the street, going out to tea, tall and slender and elegant in a close-fitting jacket suit with a sable collar and a small hat that hid her hair completely. She was as smart and stylized as a fashion drawing. The fashions had changed suddenly, and women with them, flowing into longer skirts, curving lines, swaying movements. ...

Arthur had not seen Gina since yesterday. That happened occasionally of late. Increasingly often.

She stopped, with a startled air, one hand on the baluster. "Oh," she said, "what——"

Arthur said: "He's asleep." They stood a moment, with an immense distance between them, not six feet in actual space. And yet there was the child in his arms. Gina had had a bad time when Benjy was born.

"You know the Wigginses and the Averys are coming to dinner," Gina said, "and the opera afterward."

Arthur said yes. He went on up to the nursery, and gave Benjy to the anxious stout nurse. Then he went down to his library, a new library built in the new house, and there were some recently purchased books to look over, before finding place for them on the shelves. Dinner and the opera meant a long evening; Katryn Wiggins would talk through it, but that was of no consequence; he didn't want to hear music, and spend a wakeful night. Sometimes he couldn't face the hours past midnight; and Gina never refused him. He almost wished she would. When he slept afterward, the distance between them increased. ... Then what were all the books about? So much passion and beauty shut between dustproof covers, locked away and silenced by possession. In a great rich house full of beautiful dead things. ... *A bracelet of bright hair about the bone.* ...

Eighteen

Mysie went home, a flying visit, and stopped over a day to see Michael Busch. They wrote to each other at intervals, so he expected her and met her at the train.

"Does anyone know you're here?" he asked.

"No. I'd rather not."

"That's good. Would you like to come to my apartment and powder your nose before dinner?"

"It might be an improvement," she said. "You live in town now?" He had, or used to have, a country place out toward Bremerton.

"It's more convenient," he said. He meant since the death of his wife, three years ago. "I go over Sundays; my girls are living there. The youngsters are better off in the country." Two of his daughters were married, and his sons-in-law had gone broke, or as near as made no matter, in the general collapse of business. There were two grandchildren. Michael was very fond of them, but he disliked being a grandfather. As a visitor—though he paid for the upkeep of the place—he felt less definitely fixed in that status.

He had brought his car, and drove it himself. By the time they were out of the station, the clear June twilight had begun, and the lights were coming on. As they zigzagged up the steep streets from the waterfront, Mysie felt inexplicably homesick. She had come back to her own country, and she was homesick as she had not been while away. The soft Pacific air carried familiar reminders of salt water and tide flats, the smell of the docks, of fish, timber, and the Orient odors of corded bales of tea-matting. The hills rose from the harbor in terraces; as they climbed, Mysie tried to place herself.

"The town has changed," she said. It was fourteen years since she had gone away, six since her last visit, a brief one. Eight years since she had spent six months here; yes, it was changing then, but she hadn't expected a clean sweep. "I don't remember this apartment house—I don't seem to remember anything."

"I guess it is new." Michael parked the car, and carried in her suitcase. The doorman took it and gave it to the elevator boy. Mysie suppressed a smile; she thought, Mike is doing that on purpose. It was characteristic of him. He was cautious up to the point of decision; then he didn't care, he was obstinate and dependable. Nobody could crowd him; he would or he wouldn't, and they could go to hell. He stood by whatever he did. Only if she had declined his suggestion, he would have let it go at that without comment; it was for her to say what *she* would do. He unlocked the apartment door.

"This is the spare bedroom," he put down her suitcase, "I'll be ready whenever you are."

Mysie took a shower, brushed the train-dust from her hair, and changed to a dinner dress, because it would please Michael to see her "dressed up." A pink dress, for the same reason; he liked bright colors. The bedroom suggested a hotel room, with varnished mahogany and a sheet of glass on the dresser. The living-room had the same anonymous aspect: leather club chairs and an oak table with magazines laid in a row. No books; he didn't read books; and the magazines were seldom disturbed. He read newspapers.

Michael was waiting, with champagne cocktails. He clinked glasses. "Here's luck. You're famous now, aren't you? I knew you'd get ahead. But you don't look a day older." He kissed her cheek, with the slightly awkward restraint of shyness, as if uncertain how she would take it. That was strange, considering …

"I daresay I don't look a day older than I am," she smiled. "But one lucky break is a long way from fame."

The apartment was high up; a tall window looked over Puget Sound, with the riding lights of ships flung like lost stars in a gulf of ether. They distracted her … The first time Michael had ever kissed her, it had been like that, abrupt and tentative. At dusk, in the mill office, looking out over the water. She had stared at him for a moment, and then burst out laughing. Because she had thought of him as so assured and solid and competent, knowing what he wanted and how to get it. She had not supposed he wanted her. She had thought she amused him, that he talked to her easily because he had no need to be on guard against anyone so insignificant as herself, indeed against anyone. It did not occur to her till long afterward how much he had risked, and how well he must have been aware of it. He must have told himself that he was a damn' fool; that he would appear to be worse than a fool. A man of his age, forty. She was only nineteen. He had everything to lose and nothing to gain. For he expected nothing. He really had only generous intentions.

She looked at him now. He looked older, but not essentially changed; she had been right, he was substantial, dependable. Rather tall, he stood very straight, with his head up because he was far-sighted. He had put on some weight under the belt, and his dusty-colored hair was thin, receding at the top. Though he was a farmer's son, and had done heavy work in his youth, his hands were smooth and shapely; he dressed well. Clean shaven, with long upper lip, straight nose, pale blue eyes, a poker face, his features expressed no emotion except an occasional flash of youthful and amusing exasperation, though he never lost his temper. He had a watchful patience that baffled Mysie, as her oblique and sudden gaiety, her nimble mind, baffled him. He managed things as far as they were amenable, and put up with the rest.

He had displayed that unfailing patience with her from the beginning. She remembered now almost incredulously how young she was, and how happy for a time, light-headed with happiness over having a job, money of her own, the world before her. That year was a breathing spell between childhood and maturity. … Having once given himself away, Michael made no reservations; he kissed her sometimes, and she allowed him for courtesy, though she didn't care much for kissing, and often turned her face away, slid out of his arm, and laughed. She used to pry into his pocket, literally; ask him staggering questions out of her ignorance …

She remembered, that summer, she used to wear a blue serge suit and a white blouse, and her hair in a double braid wound on the back of her head; it was not till later that she decided to have it bobbed. And she remembered that funny flash of exasperation on Michael's face as he let her go, answered her, permitted her to rummage his pockets. As if she had been a squirrel sitting on his knee, which she did sometimes. He would write and tell her when he was coming, or if he was delayed; she knew a lot about his business. He had an astonishing, complete confidence in her.

And though she didn't tell him, he knew about her beaux; she was an incorrigible flirt, the sign of a cool temperament. He did not mention her beaux; except once. Saturday nights, during that summer, the young people usually went over to the next town, a bigger town, to dance at a new pavilion, a harmless excursion by twos. For a couple of months Mysie's escort was the assistant manager at the mill; what was his name? Dick Chisholm, a quiet steady young man. Michael asked her, was she engaged to Chisholm? If she was, he would promote, him, give him a better job at the head office; Dick was all right. ... Mysie said no—she did not explain, though it was the truth, that she wouldn't marry anyone in Sequitlam. Michael said no more on the subject.

Late in the summer she had two weeks' holiday; Michael asked her where she was going. She had not decided; she had been counting up how far she could go. Living at home, she gave half her pay to her mother. She couldn't even let herself think of Japan or China; they were too far, too expensive. Perhaps to Alaska. Because she knew that next year she must really go away, go East; she must and she didn't want to; she wouldn't like the East, nevertheless she knew she wouldn't be able to come back, not to stay. ... Michael said it was a fine trip to Alaska. He had been there in the gold rush, made his first money there, not mining but building boats on Lake LeBarge. After a couple of years he came back to Seattle because that was where the money was going from Alaska. His elder brother had staked him his passage; his brother ran a gambling house, he told Mysie. She remembered how incongruous it seemed that Michael should have such a brother; but she saw now that he had a gambling streak in him too, though it came out in other ways.

He said he would see about a steamship ticket for her; and then he handed her a hundred-dollar bill. Have a good time, he said.

She said: But I can't——

He said: Sure, you've earned it; you work hard; I'd have to pay a man bookkeeper more. I meant to raise your pay, but I didn't know how to fix it without the manager thinking something. She still hesitated; she didn't want anything from him except—she understood her own motives later—the wisdom of his maturity. For she then had the childish illusion that years bring compensating certitudes. … Go on, Michael said, keep it; it's nothing. He stood there with his hands in his pockets. Look here, he said at a tangent, I've been thinking— would you like to go to college? The same as your cousin. I'll pay your way. … Of course he knew about Gina; in such a small town as Sequitlam, though he didn't live there and came up only once a week or less often, he couldn't help knowing local news.

Mysie said: Why? She was rather stunned by the offer. Four years of college would be expensive, a considerable sum for even a rich man to give away. He said: You've got brains. She said: I don't know; of course Gina would; she goes to church. … A ridiculous answer; but Mysie meant that Gina wanted to belong, to be inside, secure and certified; and Mysie didn't. … Michael said: Well, think it over; you can make up your mind when you get back.

She did have a good time, made the most of it, aware that she might never again feel so carefree. For she must be away from Sequitlam before the year was out, before her twentieth birthday. She had a superstitious notion that one could do anything if one began before twenty; but afterward it might be too late. *Time is, Time was…*

On her return, Michael met her at the boat and took her to dinner. There wouldn't be a boat to Sequitlam till morning. She hadn't expected him to meet her; he told her his family had gone abroad. He was stopping in town, in a hotel apartment. After dinner he gave her the key, and then he came up and they talked. She said she would not go to college. She had known at first, but it seemed discourteous to refuse without consideration. She asked: Why did you offer to do that for me? He said: Because I think a lot of you. She said: *Cultus potlatch*? (A free gift?) He said: Sure, *cultus potlatch*. He had his arm around her and he kissed her hair; she could feel the quickening of his heartbeat, even and strong. The place, the hour, made him scrupulous; she was his guest.

She said: But don't you—

He said: Hell, yes, you know it. What of it? We can't have everything we want.

She said: Why not?

He held her very hard, and tipped up her chin with his hand. He said: Do you mean that? You won't be sorry, honey?

She said: No.

Do you have to go home in the morning?

No, she said again. Can I have something to drink?

Yet it made no difference, being his mistress. She wouldn't have objected to the word; it had a traditional grace. Though she was not sorry, what she had done was a mistake. Not in the ordinary sense; that had no weight with either of them. They wouldn't turn on each other with the mean excuse of conscience. But what was her motive, when there was no compulsion and no advantage? She did not understand herself till later; it was because Michael had handed over to her all his advantage, offering her his money and leaving himself disarmed. She couldn't let him believe he meant nothing to her. Also she wanted to forget Johnny Disston by learning what it was could shake one so. And she did not realize that she had required Michael to throw over his scruples, as he did without hesitation.

She was unable to define the nature of their attachment. In some respect they were alike; they saw the world from the same point of view. They were tough-minded, ruthless, matter-of-fact and romantic. He would have said he was in love with her, and believed it. He had a great regard for women; and none of the ordinary masculine resentment against his need of them. Not even against the women he had paid. He was logically willing to pay for his pleasure and their risk. But Mysie doubted if he had ever been in love with any woman. No more than she had ever been in love with any man. Not altogether—with nothing left over. He was capable of love. But neither of them had found it. They were out of luck.

After so many years of absence, with such separate lives, they were still friends. Mysie was glad to see him; she felt irrationally safe again. Michael was the one person she could count upon. The impersonal, tasteless room somehow strengthened that confidence; they had always met in the wilderness, shared nothing material; so it seemed they must remain to each other even if everything else were swept away.

Mysie drank her cocktail. Being temperate, Michael insisted on having something fit to drink.

"Well, you're a star, aren't you?" he said. "I read all about it. I'd like to see you play, but I can't afford to go East."

"I've had two or three leading parts," Mysie said, "but that's a long way from being a star." Mike wouldn't understand how little it might mean. Jake's play ran four months, and gave her sufficient prestige to get a featured part in a trivial melodrama which made an accidental hit. Then Neale Corrigan placed her cautiously in a couple of his plays which did not call for stars but good ensemble work; still, he gave her the most desirable rôles, and she got enthusiastic notices. … What you need is genuine comedy, Corrigan said, gruffly pessimistic. You could play it on your head; and what would that get you out in front? The stage is shot. What the public wants is movies; glycerine tears the size of an egg and a synchronized megaphone, nothing real. Mysie was astonished by the intensity of his contempt. Who would have thought the old man had so much blood in him? But he had lived. She too disliked the movies irreconcilably: that empty, passionless, monstrous, two-dimensional world appalled her.

If Jake ever finished his next play, and if Corrigan took it, and if he didn't have some star under contract needing a production, he might give Mysie the lead. Success in the theater depended on an endless series of contingencies.

She said to Michael: "Has the depression hit you here as hard as it has New York?"

Michael shrugged. "I can just about meet my taxes and grocery bills. You can't give lumber away, unless you pay the freight. Maybe business will come back; 1 don't know. I guess the war sent us all crazy, with the idea that you can borrow yourself out of debt. My father fought all through the Civil War, with Grant's command; he was wounded twice, and he was in the guard of honor at Lincoln's funeral——"

"Was he?" Mysie tried to seize a fleeting clue to a larger pattern; the Civil War was only one lifetime distant.

"Yes; he was a German, you know; grandfather came over when my father was about knee-high; the joke is that he came so his boys wouldn't have to do military service. Well, what I was going to tell you was, in Ninety-eight I got a notion to join up, go down and fight in Cuba."

"*You* did?" said Mysie. "What for?"

"Damned if I know now. I guess it was mostly to see New York on the way, and come back a hero, of course. Hot time in the old town. My mother was born in New York; her folks were Irish, and she was a cashier in Stewart's department store. Not many women had jobs then. She was smart, like you; she could do anything. When she and father were married, Horace Greeley was advising young men to go West. Father got as far as Minnesota and homesteaded and made up his mind never to move again. I ran away from home when I was eleven; not that there was anything wrong with home, Father wasn't hard on us; but I'd saved up two dollars and forty cents and decided to travel. I hid in a box car, with two other boys. At the next siding a hobo got in the same car, and he took my money. So we went back home. The other boys got a licking, but my father just chuckled and gave me a dollar. I couldn't quit on him again; I stuck at home till I was grown up. Father wasn't much of a talker, hardly ever mentioned the Civil War, and didn't ask for a pension, though he could have had one. When the Spanish-American war started, I told him I was going to enlist. He said: Ach, so? Wait, I will show you something. He dug into his wallet and brought out a dirty piece of paper, creased and frayed; he had it in an old envelope. Paper money. He said that after Petersburg—that was pretty near the end—he was sent out with a scouting detail, and they captured a Confederate soldier who had straggled off foraging. The reb was ragged and hungry; and my father gave him some grub, bacon and coffee. The reb said he'd pay for it. Father said no; he was kind of slow on a joke. The reb said: Keep your hair on, Dutchy; this is the most expensive cup of coffee I ever expect to drink, and you're welcome to the change. And he handed Father that bill. A thousand dollar bill, Confederate money. Father said: Nah, I got a chunk of shrapnel and maybe a bullet on account already. ... When he had told me the yarn, Father said: That's what you get from a war, bübchen. You keep this to remember by. … I did keep it; I've got it yet. I went to the Yukon instead."

When Michael quoted his father he lapsed into a faint German accent, as if it were a buried part of his personality brought to the surface. There was no trace of it in his ordinary speech. "Ja, I used to speak German with my father," he said, "and it always made Mother kind of mad, put her Irish up. You know, two of my nephews, my brother's boys, went over in the war, and one of them was killed."

"What became of your brother that was a gambler?" Mysie asked, at a tangent.

Michael gave her a quick look. "How did you hear about him?"

"From you," said Mysie.

"He went down to Tia Juana ten years ago, and died there. I guess he was in the right business for these times, I was just thinking, while the Civil War was going on, they didn't know how it would end."

"No, of course not," said Mysie. "Oh—I see what you mean, I never thought of that."

"That's what I mean," said Michael. "We knew how it came out, and it seemed as if it couldn't have been any other way. But they didn't know till they fought it through. It seemed to us as if everything was settled."

Mysie said: "I suppose we did feel that. So the future was nothing to be afraid of. We had only to go ahead and take care of ourselves. But wasn't it like this in the hard times of the Nineties?"

"The times were just as hard," said Michael. "But people weren't so scared. They'd never had it easy. I don't know why everyone shouldn't have things easy; only it does something to them. I got my first job when I was seventeen, at twelve dollars a month. My sons-in-law—oh, well, they play a first-rate game of golf. And they figured this was like the panic of 1907—that nice little hand-made panic that was called off the same as it was called on. … Shall we split what's left—I guess you're ready for your dinner?"

He held her coat and kissed her cheek again, and she made a friendly gesture, brushing her face against his shoulder like a cat. He thought again, she hasn't changed at all. … Mysie thought, Mike is a good man. She meant that he had the masculine virtues, a constant mind, a fidelity not exclusive but enduring.

They dined at a hotel. It was new. Mysie asked about others she remembered. They were torn down or run down, Michael said. And the Klondike Club?—she had dined with him there in the old days. He said it had been moved to another building over ten years ago, and he didn't use it much now; most of the original members, the real sourdoughs, were dead or broke. Nearly all the Alaska fortunes had vanished.

The dinner was excellent. But the hotel might have been in any other city; it was simply a big, new, expensive hotel—running at a loss. Not many guests. A man passing their table spoke to Michael, not quite looking at Mysie. "Good evening, Mr. Busch; ah, by the way, I phoned your office to-day, missed you. Perhaps to-morrow?"

"I'm afraid not," Michael said; "sit down and have coffee with us—waiter, bring another coffee. Miss Brennan, Mr. Hambley. Take a chair, Hambley; glad to have you."

Mysie maintained her gravity carefully. Mike was showing off his girl again; he was proud of her. "I expect to be driving Miss Brennan up to Sequitlam to-morrow," Michael said. "What did you want to see me about?"

Mr. Hambley explained: "Mr. Mackentire is back from Washington; it was thought the Committee should meet as soon as possible. ..."

A relief committee, Mysie gleaned. She didn't listen closely; it was difficult to listen to Mr. Hambley. There are people who make listening practically impossible, she thought idly. They present a collocation of words squeezed of vital content. It couldn't be wholly accident; there must be a psychological reason, the opposite of her own when she was studying or playing, when she was intent upon charging her lines with significance and emotion. That was hard enough if the lines were thin. Therefore it was certainly an accomplishment to desiccate one's entire vocabulary, deprive a rich language of the values accumulated by centuries of purposeful use. ... Michael dragged her into the conversation several times; Mr. Hambley asked her about "conditions" in New York. "Terrible," she said. Hambley was middle-aged, bloodless, with thin, flaccid lips and nothing behind his eyes. He reminded her of somebody—Julius Dickerson! An abridged edition. At Gina's party, Mysie had tried to listen to Julius.

Men didn't use to talk like that. Not even the stuffed shirts, the pompous orators; their large phrases had some original reference which gave them consistency. What baffled Mysie was that no two of Hambley's sentences held together. After ten minutes he made a formal excuse and departed. As soon as he was out of earshot Mysie exclaimed:

"I don't understand anything any more. He said he had confidence in the leadership of our big bankers because they haven't speculated. Is he an imbecile?"

"Well, he's one of our prominent citizens," Michael replied noncommittally.

Mysie said: "But then he said he had made a turn in the market himself last week. And he's on a committee getting money for local relief from Washington. I can't say why, but the men now, since the panic, remind me of the women while the war was on. Especially the fat middle-aged women puffing around in uniforms, very broad in the beam. And giving their male relatives to the country. They seem to have given the wrong ones. They were awful—the women, I mean. Made you sort of seasick. I wonder if history tells us the really important events—the things people finally can't stand. Perhaps nobody cared a snap who Nero murdered, but they wouldn't put up with a torch singer. I felt something give way like the last suspender button when J. P. Morgan unloaded five million dollars' worth of bankrupt Missouri Pacific railroad bonds through the Reconstruction Fund and then made an appeal over the radio for unemployment relief, with the microphone brought to his private library because he couldn't be expected to go to a broadcasting station; and he hadn't paid any income tax since 1929. Historians tell us lately that it doesn't matter how dumb anyone or everyone is, the result would work out the same; but it seems to me it might make a difference. … Listen, I'll register for a room and leave my trunk check." She would have to go back with Michael to his apartment to pick up her hand baggage.

She walked through the lobby while Michael paid the check; she would find him outside with the car. Turning away from the registry desk, she wasn't sure if a man standing near tipped his hat to her or to another woman, but she gave him a slight nod and an indeterminate smile, passing quickly. Yes, his face was dimly familiar; possibly he was an acquaintance; was it in Sequitlam? No matter; she did not wish to meet people if she could help it; she hadn't time, only she must call up Clara Carson at least, in the morning, before starting to drive out with Michael; and see her on the way back. Clara had been her chum in school. Married now, and not very well off; she'd be hurt if Mysie overlooked her.

Nineteen

In Michael's apartment again, Mysie took off her wrap and sat down; it was early and they had so much to talk about. "Oh, do you want to drive up to Sequitlam to-morrow?" she asked. "It's all right if you were only giving Mr. Whoozis an alibi; I can take the boat."

"I have to be there this week anyhow," Michael said. "And there's a good road. … Unless you'd rather not. Will your mother think——"

"She'll think it's very nice of you," said Mysie. "Mother thinks whatever I do is all right. You know, Mother is really good. And she's had it pretty hard, with no money and six kids, besides two babies that died; she's always felt she let us in for it, marrying my stepfather. Moral men are so damned moral, always making laws and preaching sermons about bathing suits or lipsticks and peering through keyholes with their eyes bulging; I hate to think what they're thinking. But really good women have no time for such performances. They have eight children and make them wash behind their ears and get up in time for school in the morning and stop squabbling and not bolt their food; and they hope the boys won't turn out loafers and that the girls won't marry loafers and have eight children. They want the kids to amount to something, so it will have have been worth while."

"Aren't you ever going to marry?" Michael asked.

"I don't know," said Mysie; "it doesn't look like it. Maybe my father dying, and Mother marrying again, stopped me—I can just remember my father. I don't mean that Mother shouldn't have, even if she did make a mistake; you can make mistakes about everything, and you have to try just the same, but you see most girls grow up counting on getting married and living happy ever after. Oh, I guess it's me; I'm not domestic. The truth is, Mike, women aren't domestic; men are. A man has to own things, a house and stuff piled up around him, to be sure of himself. He wants something to tie him down, because he—he's centrifugal. A girl marries for the opposite reason, and she finds she's taken on a job, she's got to stick to it; the same as a man has to earn a living for his family, he can't run out on it. But look at all the elderly widows, traveling around the world. It's too late, but at least they want to see what else there is, outside their experience. You wouldn't believe what my mother would like to do—the one thing—she's always wanted to go to South America and see an eclipse of the sun. It happens there regularly, doesn't it? and astronomers go down to observe it. Mother got that in her head as an impossible dream. Because it's the furthest thing imaginable from her own life."

"I guess I don't understand women," Michael said. If he had been sufficiently subtle and articulate, he would have perceived that a man is bound to be disconcerted by feminine intellectual processes, since he regards a woman either emotionally or not at all. He cannot separate her from his own impulses toward her; he is disconcerted to find ideas wrapped in rose-colored taffeta, tied with bows, shod with insubstantial scraps of satin.

Mysie rested her chin on her hand and turned her round brown velvet eyes on him; the curve of her eyebrows imparted an expression of sympathetic enquiry. Michael said abruptly: "You know my wife was—the last few years—part of the time she wasn't quite herself."

"No, I didn't know," said Mysie. She knew nothing about his wife.

"She'd been out of sorts for awhile; she wouldn't speak to me for a day or two; or else … All of a sudden she went to a lawyer and had him file suit for divorce. No warning; I got the notice one day in my office, the surprise of my life. I went home and asked her if she really wanted a divorce. She said she'd never give me a divorce; talked as if I'd been trying to put it over on her. The doctor said it was a nervous breakdown; and sometimes she was all right, and sometimes she said pretty hard things to me. Then she came down with appendicitis; the doctor said perhaps that had been causing the trouble, toxemia I think he called it. She wasn't expected to recover from the operation."

"Yes," said Mysie. She knew that. She remembered with exactitude, Michael was aware that she knew it. He had told her at the time, but only the bare fact, in the fewest possible words. Eight years ago, during the summer she had spent here on her own affairs—she didn't know yet if he had ever learned the reason for her six months' sojourn, but the question he had asked her this evening indicated that he had not. During that summer they had seen each other, but not often and not as lovers. Michael accepted the situation without reproaches. He knew when she had planned to leave for the East. The last evening, he telephoned; she was staying with Clara Carson, and didn't want him to call at Clara's, but he had an apartment at a hotel and she went up. He had left the door unlocked, for her to walk in.

For a moment she had thought the room was empty, though the light was on. Michael was sitting in a big chair, with a newspaper dropped on the floor, where it had slipped from his hand. He was asleep. He woke with a start, and apologized.

You're going back to New York to-morrow? he said. As if she might have changed her mind. She said: I've got to get back to work. He asked: How are you fixed? She said: all right. She'd had a temporary job, enough to pay her way. He said: Well, let me know how you're getting on. I suppose you won't be here next summer? She said: I don't suppose so. It's too far.

He dropped a cigarette while lighting it. He said: I was up all last night. At the hospital. My wife is sick. Not expected to live. ... He looked at Mysie, straight.

She was stunned into stillness. His absolute honesty was slightly terrifying. She had never known another human being with courage to face his own actions. He was hard, but hard enough to sustain full responsibility.

There was nothing to say. She was deserting him; but she couldn't marry him; it would be a repetition of her original mistake. Perhaps he understood her silence.

Michael said: Is it raining? ... She had come afoot, and her hair was meshed with infinitesimal crystal beads of moisture. They could hear the sirens in the harbor at intervals. She said: Not rain, a little mist ... Michael picked up the newspaper, and they remarked on the headlines, nothing of importance. ... She said: You must be tired. She thought she had better go. He said: I have to wait here in case of a telephone call. Will you be sure to take a cab—it's not very safe, in the fog. She said: Yes, I will; good night.

Mysie took the train early in the morning, without hearing from him. Now, after eight years, Michael was telling her the rest.

"She did recover from the operation, but not the nervous trouble. We had to keep a nurse, never the same one for long; she'd take a dislike to one after another. She was restless; used to roam around the house. She managed the housekeeping just the same; of course the servants had to be paid extra. ... She accused me of all sorts of things. The doctor suggested a sanatorium, but I couldn't do that. It was her home."

Mysie thought, there is that about Mike; he'll stand the gaff ... He had stood it to the end. After five years, his wife died of pneumonia, which had nothing to do with her mental condition.

Michael said: "But if women do—maybe she hated the house?" Certainly she had said often enough that she hated him. He supposed he had it coming to him. None of her accusations was specifically true; she named women he had never thought of, scarcely known. And the possibility of divorce had never entered his mind. But he had been unfaithful. He hardly knew why. Before his marriage, he had gone on the loose occasionally, various affairs more casual than mercenary—which meant that he paid somewhat more. With women who knew what they were about. He had a queer kind of reasonableness and no remorse whatever. He married at twenty-six, soon after he had got his start in business. A man was better off married. She was a fine girl, handsome, capable, energetic. He considered himself lucky; she pulled with him, never ran him in debt, had a sound business head. And the children were a credit to her; three girls, of course the third ought to have been a boy. She said that was enough; he had a notion that she resented his hope of a son, as if it implied a slight upon herself and the girls. She said: Yes, if *you* had to go through with it—After that, he couldn't mention it again. And he was unable to pretend that she gave him cause for straying. She had a temper, but he didn't mind it much; that was a woman's privilege. He watched his step for four or five years. Then—well, there was no special reason. He hadn't, in fact, quite intended anything of the kind; but he had to be away from home occasionally. Not very often. Not with anyone she might meet. No, he had no excuse; only it was like a vacation, or taking a drink, not to get drunk but for the kick. An extra. Women were interesting. The way they could put it over on a man. But he knew his wife hadn't paid him in his own coin. He had cheated. And she knew it somehow.

Of the other women, Mysie had counted most. And he had never had her, never would have her. The physical fact was immaterial. Now, after so long, when he kissed her cheek, he saw her face as he used to see it, half averted, her head bent; if he kissed her mouth, it would be fresh and cool. She slid out of his arm … The first time, when she said: Why not? his instant thought was that she must have had a lover already—why not? He knew better afterward, beyond question. The shock of it recurred to him each time, a sensation beyond sensuality. … He used to think, in straightforward vernacular, what if he got her in trouble? And he tried not to wish it. That would be a hell of a thing to do; though he would take care of her. He asked her sometimes, did she know…was she all right?…Looking away from him with stubborn shyness, she would answer almost inaudibly, Yes. But he didn't believe she knew anything; obviously not. Only it just did not happen.

And then she left him, and now she had come back, exactly the same. It gave him pleasure to see her in this apartment, which belonged to him; he wasn't going to bother her. Maybe the twenty years between their ages had been impossible to span; and he had grown no younger. He wanted her still, but a desire of the mind more than the flesh—that she should be near him, and kind, and happy.

Mysie realized that he alone regarded her as a girl, defenseless in her youth and ignorance, needing to be sheltered. Since she was past thirty, she felt the charm of that relationship, whether it is traditional or instinctive; for she too liked to think of him as a man, strong and able to be protective. There is, after all, an unarguable reason; for women are helpless when nature traps them.

"Oh, no," she said, "women don't hate their homes. But we'd all like more than one life." He ought to understand; he had not been satisfied with one. *Lord, we know what we are, but not what we may be.* Passion itself is intellectual, not to be quenched with a sop of transient sensation. It asks for everything … Mysie reckoned

herself a fool in the main, and therefore did not see how she could
have acted with wisdom; how would that have helped her? There
were periods and places in time past when such as she might not
rest in holy ground. Fair enough; indeed, she would rather not be
so huddled up. *How do they pass their time, I wonder, Nights and
days in the narrow room, Six steps out of the chapel yonder…*

"I'd better be going along to the hotel," she said.

"You needn't unless you choose," said Michael; "there's the spare
room." He wished to remember her here, a matter of sentiment. She
was touched, unable to deny his offer.

As she said good night, she was aware that a faint expectation
lingered in his mind, and was instantly suppressed. "You'd better
give me a call in the morning," she said. "I usually oversleep." In
the cloudy borderland of oblivion, she was glad to be under his roof.
Then she slept sound; it was past nine of a sunny new day when
she woke. The particular quiet of emptiness told her that Michael
must have gone out. A note slipped under her door confirmed it.
Gone to the office for an hour; he'd be back before eleven with the
car. If she called the neighboring restaurant, they would send up
breakfast. While she drank her coffee, she decided to telephone
Clara Carson. Clara's name was not in the directory; as she hunted
through it, she heard Michael's key in the lock.

"You got something to eat?" he said. "I didn't want to disturb
you; I looked in on you and you were dead to the world."

Yes, she was ready. But would he mind driving by Clara Carson's
former address, to enquire?

"Sure," he said. "Dexter Avenue?"

"On Denny Park," she explained. They were stepping into the
elevator; and she thought she must have misunderstood Michael's
answer. He said:

"Maybe the house is gone; they've torn down Denny Park."

"Cut down the trees?"

"The whole thing. Anyhow, we can take a look-see."

How could a park be torn down? As Michael was starting the
car, she postponed the question. What he had said made no specific
impression. She was remembering Denny Park. She had loved it for
its peace; nothing had ever happened to her in connection with it.

That was where she used to leave tracks like green plush in white plush, on the rare winter mornings when the grass was rimed with frost. It was at the top of a hill; the hill rose sharply, a sudden angle of at least twenty degrees; a street went upward for a long block, with houses alongside set on slanted foundations, old homely frame houses with people living in them; and one reached the top unexpectedly and there was the park, a little park about a block in extent spread out level. The trees had attained the nobility of respected years, and the grass was not forbidden to wayfaring feet. It was all verdure; and it looked over the city, so that it was like hiding in the top of a tree, looking through the leaves. She used to run up the hill, for fun and to shake off melancholy; then she always loitered across the grass, and in summer rested awhile in the shade. It was so serene in the midst of the city, so lifted up, one cherished it as a secret happiness in the heart. It was high above the tops of the tall business buildings; one could see the harbor traffic, and barely hear the remote thunder of the cable cars on the stepped streets rising from the waterfront; distance and the soft air subdued the note of strident power to an almost musical murmur, like a grumbling bumblebee under a leaf.

"I don't remember this part of town," Mysie remarked to Michael. The homesickness came over her acutely. "Where are we?"

"We'll be there in a minute," Michael said. "I guess it's been graded down since you were here. You know, they washed down the grades with hydraulics … Here's Dexter Avenue; what was the number? I'm afraid the house is gone."

"No, it was facing the park," Mysie repeated.

"This is Denny Park," Michael said.

"What do you mean?" Mysie was unable to connect his words with the visible facts. She was gazing at an open square of naked and infertile sand, with not a stick nor a stone nor a blade of herbage on its arid surface. A new concrete pavement bounded it rectangularly, one city block in an extensive grid of dismal blocks, of which the others were meagerly built over with new bleak small buildings and gas stations; nowhere a tree nor an inch of sod. It was uniformly flat; it resembled the squalid portion of Long Island which she loathed to the point of nausea, beyond the Queensboro Bridge.

"Here," Michael reiterated, pointing to the blasted spot. He had stopped the car.

Mysie said, in a daze: "Denny Park was on top of a hill."

"They washed it down," Michael said once more. Mysie thought she must be going mad.

"But it was quite a high hill, very steep. It was lovely. How could—what for—?" She put her hands to her head. "I used to walk across it every morning. There were big trees. And the grass was green all winter."

And it was gone. It no longer existed. Wiped out, trampled flat, by a herd of Gadarene swine. Where it had been was this desolation.

"Why did they?" she said.

"Well, they were planning an industrial development further out, factories; and they wanted a level road, a main artery, straight through. Of course, the grades all over town have been washed down as much as possible, and the tide-flats filled in; so the business center has gradually moved over toward the filled ground, because it's level. I guess the town has changed a lot. ...Would you like to look anywhere else for your friend?"

"No, for God's sake, let's get out of here," Mysie said. Michael drove on. She asked: "Are there any factories?"

"Nothing much," said Michael. "The depression hit the project."

"The grading must have cost enormous sums," she reflected. "And loaded the city with taxes."

"Sure," said Michael.

"I'm glad," said Mysie vindictively. "Whoever was responsible, I hope they're dead broke. That's what the planners are going to do for us everywhere. I hope they rot in hell. A flat hell, that goes on forever and ever." They didn't care about anything but money. And the money had gone back on them. Men had built the city for pride; and those who came later had destroyed it for profit. But there was no profit, only futility and fear. ... Every cycle has its representative figures; do they make it or are they made by it? Ours are masks and puppets of fear, jerky little dictators, with trick mustaches, staring white blank eyes, stage frowns and vacuous smites, the blaring mechanical voice of the radio switched on and off. They move stiffly, collapsing from one expedient to another; they have no private lives; they are impotent—men without women. They occupy a meaningless mindless interval in history.

"Nothing goes on forever," said Michael.

The car crossed a high viaduct by the inlet. Two airplanes, on divergent courses, giant dragonflies, hummed across the blueness of the sky. "Are those navy planes?" Mysie asked. "Passenger planes; there's a regular service, every half hour," Michael said. "Every half hour?" That destruction of beauty had been altogether unnecessary; there was not even a temporary financial gain to be had from the spoliation. This had been the last built of the old cities, and it might be the first of the new. They could just as well have let it alone. ...

The future is unmanageable because it is formed by desire and not by will alone. Men wanted to fly. Not for any use, or even for knowledge: just to fly. Knowledge was painfully won to enable them to satisfy their longing, and use was found afterward. Sometimes nations and races grow weary, cease to want to do anything new, and then they don't. They stop, fall back slowly, for centuries. They are tired. The planes, the motors, operate by mechanical laws, but they are driven by a force in the men who invented and built them. They won't go of themselves. And you can't gear everybody to the machines for efficiency; nothing would get done. Michael drove his car easily. If he were told he mustn't on any account stop, he would drive into a smash through boredom. We're smashed now, she thought dreamily. And they talk about strapping us to the wheel as a remedy. It won't go.

"What beats me," she said, "is that your prominent citizen last night seemed to think he's staving off revolution—by borrowing money for relief, and speculating for profit. He's scared. To start a revolution in this country now—even if anyone knew which way to revolve—you'd have to drag most of the able-bodied men out from under the bed by the feet. You're not scared, are you?"

"Not much," said Michael. "The next time I cross the street, a truck might hit me. What of it? If the whole set-up goes bust, I'll be on the Skidroad with the rest of the lumberjacks out of a job. I'll roll my blankets and go up in the woods and build a shack where there's some fishing. And the government can take over my sons-in-law." They expected places to be made for them. He had nothing against them. White collar boys, very pleasant; they'd gone to college on allowances and graduated to jobs ready-made by family influence. The way they talked, he was out of date. No use arguing with them. They had read a book.

"Well, if there aren't going to be any more men," said Mysie, "I don't care what happens either."

"Fine," said Michael, "you can come along with me." She smiled at him. He continued: "Anyhow, I've had mine. All you get in this world is the side-bets. With wars and governments—what I mean is, you've got to live *around* them somehow."

Gulls floated and skimmed over the inlet. ... Every single gull had to be able to fly. *Every soul got to get saved by itself.* You can touch hands with another, borrow a little comfort and instruction, stand by or step into the breach at the worst; that is all. You've got to make-do. You are given an impermanent physical body to do with, and it goes to pieces by inevitable degrees. When she was tired, sometimes she had a singular vision of life itself, its brevity, its certain end. So many years, more or less, inexorably allotted; and nothing would stay. Yet it was not a vision of despair but of consolation. What was it could mark the changes? Something permanent, else one would be unaware of impermanence, for all things are distinguishable by their opposites.

The car left the city; in half an hour they were in the country, on the peninsular highway. Sleepy shabby small towns, then farms with orchards and pasture fields; and then long stretches of wilderness, cut-over timberland, stumps and deadwood and second growth. Some of it had been burned last year, but already summer had clothed the waste with bracken and blackberry vines. There were shacks in small clearings by the roadside, built of raw boards, with stovepipes projecting from lean-to kitchens, and flowers blooming at random in the unfenced front yards, flourishing in that soft air and clean soil. The shacks were not sordid but absurdly cheerful habitations. They had the validity of primitive necessity: shelter and fire and bread.

Mysie thought, Mike would be all right in the backwoods. He'd keep the woodbox and waterpail filled, and manage to bring in food as long as earth or stream would yield; and he would be even-tempered as competent men are. Mike is a good provider. Whatever else he might do, he wouldn't run out on any responsibility. He was permanent.

At home, that evening, Mysie helped her mother wash the supper dishes. Whenever she came home she went through an indescribable Alice-in-Wonderland reversal of experience; time turned backward in a loop. For half an hour the little old house was shrunken and alien; and then by some instantaneous adjustment it became familiar and natural as no other place could ever be. And she herself became a daughter again, existing as it were solely in that relationship. She felt as if she had actually grown smaller, resumed the unimportance of childhood. This emotion was unaffected by the fact that she was inches taller than her mother, standing beside her at the sink. Her mother was a small woman, and had been very pretty as a girl, with delicate features, a trim slender figure, and thick dark hair a yard long. Now she was slightly stooped, an old woman; only her hair, turned to a soft grey, was still abundant enough to twist into a double knot; and her brookwater-brown eyes were bright and gentle. She moved about the housework quickly and quietly, preferring occupation to idleness, and when she rested she sat still in a low rocker, with her hands folded in her lap. She was noticeably frailer and older since Mysie had seen her last. She was sixty-three. Perhaps five years more. … She didn't even want to be young again. Her work was done, and she was ready to fold her hands.

Her husband, Fred Kennedy, Mysie's stepfather, was the same age as his wife and looked ten years younger. A stout, rather handsome man, he tried to be genial to Mysie and she answered with indifferent brevity. She could just about stand him for the two weeks she would be staying. He'd keep out of the house most of the time to avoid her. He had gone uptown immediately after supper. Mysie's eldest brother, Joe Brennan, and his wife, had been over for the afternoon. Joe was forty-two, tall and large-boned and red-haired; his long jaw and straight nose reminded Mysie of the sculptured effigies of Norman knights she had seen in pictures of ancient churches, a singular throwback, not in the Brennan blood. It was Grandpa Brennan's first wife who had brought the red hair into the line, for Joe and Geraldine. Joe had a farm not far from town; he was quiet and hardworking, and said he guessed they'd get along somehow. Mysie's eldest sister, Kate, was married and lived in California; the next girl, Nellie, was also married and lived in Idaho. Johnny and Charlie, the two youngest boys, Mysie's half-brothers, were Kennedys; Johnny was working half-time in a garage in Aberdeen, and Charlie had a summertime job on a coasting steamer that touched at Sequitlam, so he was home Sundays. Mysie scarcely knew them, as they were small boys when she left home fifteen years ago. And the three older than herself were equally removed from her by the fact that they had grown up and married while she was still a child. Kate and Nellie were only two years apart; they had been playmates; Mysie was the odd one, a reserved and solitary child. She did not know what the others thought of her; no doubt they seldom thought of her at all, for there is a natural statute of limitations which acts through distance as well as time, exempting her from judgment. They all came home at intervals to see their mother; as long as she lived they would remain a family.

Mysie emptied the dishpan, hung it on its accustomed nail, and put her arm about her mother's shoulders. Mrs. Kennedy answered with a hug and a smile. What grief there is in loving, Mysie thought. Especially children, who grow up and go away. … "Let's sit outside awhile, mamma. For goodness sake, what's become of the old pear-tree?"

Mrs. Kennedy said: "The fruit didn't set last spring; so Fred chopped it down; he was going to plant potatoes there."

Mysie had a simple healthy impulse toward homicide. Not murder, merely the removal of Fred Kennedy as a detrimental object. He hadn't even planted the potatoes … He used to have a habit of walking across the newly scrubbed kitchen floor with muddy boots, grinning as if it were a joke. It would have been a keen pleasure to hit him with an ax.

Unfortunately, such direct measures are too idealistic; the intricate knot of human relationships cannot be resolved at a stroke. Mysie said, nothing goes on forever; no, and yet perhaps nothing ever ends, either. Time supersedes old problems with new ones growing out of the old… At supper, Kennedy had been vocal about the hard times, declaring the government ought to Do Something. With J.P. Morgan at the head of the breadline and Fred Kennedy at the foot, both asking for handouts, it was tough on Joe and Mike, who had to get along somehow and carry the others, good times or bad.

Twenty

Geraldine felt as if her mind had divided neatly into two compartments, one for thinking and one for receiving external impressions; and the connection between them had lapsed. Perhaps what she was hearing was luncheon conversation, peculiar to such occasions. Geraldine never went to formal lunches; they took all day, the hours she devoted to work. She had accepted Gina's invitation as a temporary relief from herself, from the apartment, from the inertia which slackened her hand, stopped her working—when it was imperative that she should work. Mysie would be there; that was an inducement. But Mysie was at the other end of the table. It was a hen party, a dozen women, expensively dressed, massaged, marceled, into bright, earnest vacuity. They talked, in public voices, about parity and Hitler and subsistence farming. Geraldine found herself marooned between Mrs. Perry and a massive female in blue velvet and a lace tucker and Queen Mary hat, a museum piece, from Washington, who said we must stand behind the president. We must have confidence. Geraldine wondered, confidence in what? And how do you get it if you haven't any—order it in packages? The lunch progressed through soup, creamed eggs, sweetbreads and broiled squab. Geraldine had had no appetite for days, and the sight of so much food was repulsive to her. She waited for coffee… Gina, at the head of the table, in pansy-blue crêpe, addressed each guest in turn, with laborious tact. The white-paneled dining room was sterile and shut off, dedicated to this strange ritual.

Mrs. Perry, as a delicate compliment to Geraldine, spoke of books. She named several which she said she had not read; she had heard they were clever.

Geraldine said: "Very." This was her sole contribution to the feast of reason and flow of soul; she had tried in vain to produce some remark which would fit in.

Mrs. Perry said: "But don't you think modern novels are terribly morbid? So much sex. After all, there is enough unpleasantness in the world without reading about it."

Geraldine said: "I suppose so." The pistachio ice cream might be delicious, but if she ate it she would never be able to eat again. There was a weight at the pit of her stomach and her head felt tight. Coffee at last. She was smoking too much, but she couldn't quit. … When Gina rose, Geraldine upset her empty coffee cup in her haste to follow; then she dropped her handbag, bumped her head on the edge of the table retrieving it, and emerged dizzy. She wasn't ill, she told herself; there was nothing the matter with her except nerves. She crossed over to Mysie, and they both experienced the relief of the rescued.

Going out, they encountered Arthur in the hall. "Hello," he said, "if I'd known you were here, I'd have been here myself."

"And if I'd known you wouldn't be, neither would I," Mysie replied. "But you'd have been torn limb from limb among so many women. G'by."… On the steps outside, she added to Geraldine: "I can't figure why he isn't spoiled; but he's a darling. Let's walk down Fifth Avenue; can't you come home with me? What was that lunch for?"

"It wasn't for anything. They read Walter Lippmann," Geraldine explained. "They have to fill in time. I'd like to walk." She felt light-footed as well as light-headed. Everything appeared sharp and clear and unstable as things do in a dream, as if the whole scene might shift and vanish without warning, giving place to something unpredictable and irrelevant and unaccountable, without rational sequence. It did not so change, but it might any moment; there might be no pavement when she put down her foot; or the wall of the building beside her might not be there if she stretched out her hand to touch it.

They gazed in shop windows and commented at random. The sun-shine was warm and runlets of water gurgled along the curb as last night's snowfall melted, in the February thaw. When they crossed into shadow Geraldine shivered and Mysie exclaimed: "Let's buy a taxi." They got in. … Mysie tried to put out of her mind a beggar who had asked her for a dime and Teddy McKee who had come to borrow ten dollars and the statement of a prominent banker that he had been forced to make foreign loans which would never be paid, but that the fingers of a new dawn were stretching their tips above the horizon. … She had given the beggar five dollars, buying herself off.

"Aren't you thinner?" Mysie asked. Geraldine's black tailored suit and little black hat set off her pale red hair; she had no other color about her except her reddened lips.

"Yes, quite a lot," Geraldine assented. If you don't sleep or eat, you get thinner.

While Mysie paid the taxi, Geraldine dodged around a huge truck that blocked the pavement, directly in front of Mysie's door. After the dazzle of the sun, the hall was dark. She bumped her shins against some heavy object on the floor—a keg. "Oh," she said, and stumbled to her knees. Several men emerged from the gloom at the back of the hall. One, the tallest, picked her up easily.

"I'm sorry," he said. He seemed very strong. "Get that stuff out of the way, Tony." Someone else rolled the keg back, under the stairs.

"It's all right," Geraldine said. "I'm not hurt." The sense of being sustained, the muscular certainty of the man holding her, gave her an instantaneous comfort. She put up her hands and smoothed her hair.

Mysie opened the street door wide as she let herself in, and day-light with her. "What's the matter?"

"Nothing," said Geraldine. "Thank you," she disengaged herself from her supporter. "I tripped myself," she explained to Mysie. Another man, in the background, tipped his cap; Mysie acknowl-edged the salute with an inclination of her head. Geraldine and Mysie went on upstairs. Geraldine wasn't sure she could make it; her knees were unreliable; but she did.

When they were out of earshot, Mysie said in a discreetly lowered voice: "You fell over a beer-keg, didn't you? About once a week they unload a truck. The one who nodded to me, did you notice him? I couldn't think where I'd seen him, but I believe he was that

Wop chauffeur of Arthur's. I guess this is his day off and he drops in for a drink with his friends; it's none of my business."

"I'd be afraid to live here," Geraldine said.

"What of? All they want is to be let alone to pursue their nefarious occupation, same as me. Anything for a quiet life. I'll tell you what strikes my funnybone, though; I found out after living here ten years. This building belongs to Arthur. Or anyhow, to his grandmother, the Siddall estate. An agent collects the rent; that's why we didn't know. There's an estate corporation, not their name. Thea made them reduce the rent since the depression, cut Arthur out of twenty dollars a month; I hope he doesn't have to deprive himself of yachts or such necessities. I'm sure he hasn't the least idea I'm his tenant. Maybe he'd repaint the bathroom if I insisted. He supports a reform ticket with money from a speakeasy. ... Hello, Jake, who let you in?"

Jake was there ahead of them, waiting patiently, in the living-room. "Your trusty slave, Mirabelle, said she guessed you'd be home if you wasn't detained elsewhere. Sound deductive reasoning. So I've been improving my mind." He displayed Geraldine's latest novel, published the previous autumn.

Geraldine regarded it with indifferent distaste. "It didn't sell," she said. "How can anyone write ... Yesterday I managed to pull myself together and had just begun on a story, and a woman telephoned me to inform me she thought she was going mad."

"Why can't she go mad quietly like the rest of us and say nothing about it?" said Mysie.

"The things that happen every day now won't go in a novel," Geraldine said. "They're not plausible. And then the things that people say. One woman asked me what really happened in that book, you know, over the weekend. What did she imagine would happen, in the circumstances? Last week I went to East Orange to visit Effie. Effie's husband has a distant relative named Mrs. Hedrick. She was an old maid; she trained as a nurse forty years ago, but she had to give it up and stay at home to look after her aged parents, till they expired. Then she took care of another invalid, who also died, leaving a disconsolate widower, Mr. Hedrick, aged sixty-nine. By that time she was fifty-five. After a suitable interval Mr. Hedrick married the nurse. In about three years he died, and left her plenty of money.

She is sixty now; she cherishes his memory as the one love of her life, and I guess he was, as far as that goes. She is active in good works—but that isn't what I was leading up to; you see my brain won't stay on the track because there is no track and probably no brain. The point is, she asked me severely if I believe that people do go around breaking the commandments as if they were taking a cup of tea. I said I didn't think it was exactly like taking a cup of tea. … And Mrs. Perry, at lunch—she said sex is morbid. What did she mean?"

"The trouble with you," said Jake, "is that you assume everyone has a low mind, like you and me. Many people, in fact, do not do that sort of thing at all. They take it out in talk. In these days, if you choose two persons of opposite sex, and lock them up together, and at the end of a week open the sealed compartment, it will be found that they have spent the entire time doing a jigsaw puzzle."

"Would they?" said Geraldine. "I forgot the point after all. She, Mrs. Hedrick, said: My dear, believe me, it Doesn't Pay."

"Even if you could get it to do," Mysie quoted.

Thea had come in. "But it's true," she said suddenly. "What Jake said. They don't go through with it and they don't pay for it. Not even three dollars. It's very bad for them. For men."

"What an immoral statement," said Mysie. "Thea, I'm surprised at you."

"You'd be surprised," said Thea grimly, "at what I think."

"All action is highly immoral," said Jake. "Morality is order. Action produces incalculable consequences and thereby disturbs order. Hence it is immoral."

"Does that mean anything?" Mysie demanded.

"Nothing whatever," Jake replied cheerily.

Jake had come to tell Mysie that his second play, *Jack and Jill,* had at last been revamped sufficiently, and Corrigan promised a production next month. Mysie remained cautiously skeptical. Geraldine was wondering how she should summon energy to go home. When Jake said: "I must be going, I have a heavy date. Exit, pursued by a bear," Geraldine accepted his offer to take her uptown. She talked all the way in the taxi, though not quite certain that the words made sentences or the sentences made sense. She was resolutely not thinking of a great many things.

Jake was going to tea with Gina. He had not mentioned his destination because he had a rule never to do so. There was nothing clandestine about the engagement. He had fallen into the habit of calling on Gina occasionally at tea-time because she had invited him to dinner and to her At Homes repeatedly, and as he hated formal affairs, a compromise was effected. He had to be polite to her. Besides, she interested him mildly. What did she get out of her youth and beauty and wealth and great house and position? He did not harbor any coxcombical delusions; he knew she merely added him to her list of acquaintances because his play had succeeded moderately, given him a certain rating. She wanted everything desperately, but she had no use for anything. No use for men, as either friends or lovers; no use for the material elegancies money afforded, since she was devoid of coquetry; no use for him, indeed, since she had neither wit nor gayety. She liked to hear gossip about well-known names. Jake found that rather pathetic. It placed her with the great majority of the deprived. Readers of movie magazines, or the paying guests who attend public dinners, or the gazers who march in line at official functions. There was a wistful quality in her *arriviste* attitude. She did not have any fun. An hour or two of her company did not bore him; he had sufficient æsthetic detachment to appreciate the sight of a pretty woman in a luxurious setting. That was why Mysie said he wasn't human; his various tastes were so separate. His friendships were intellectual. When he fell in love, as he did at intervals, it was with some stormy melodramatic fickle creature who made scenes and tore his quiet existence to tatters for a month or two or three, with violent delights that came to a violent end.

But he had also an aloof general sympathy which enabled him to detect that Geraldine was in distress. He got out of the taxi with her, accompanied her to her own apartment door, and there left her unobtrusively. He knew she didn't want him to come in; she was in flight.

In the living-room, Judy was reading, with her silky dark hair falling over her serene brow. Dina was dressing a doll. Geraldine stood a moment looking at them. Their perfect, unconscious trust finished her.

Geraldine took off her hat and sat down on the sofa. Then she couldn't get up again. She could not stand on her feet.

The fact was blankly appalling. For a moment she could not speak either. With an immense effort, she controlled her mind, answered the children's greetings. "Darlings, one of you please hand me the telephone."

What was the matter with her? She waited five minutes. The weakness did not pass. She must not frighten the children. "I've turned my ankle," she said. That might have been true, though it wasn't. "No, Judy lamb, don't touch it; I'll call the doctor. It's not serious." She called the doctor and told him the same lie, because the children could hear. It didn't hurt, she assured them truthfully. She was in no pain. That might be all the worse, she reflected.

Dr. Jamieson arrived promptly. He was sixty, a deep chested sanguine man with thick white hair. Third of an honorable line, he had the kind and assuring presence of the born physician. Geraldine had confidence in him; he had seen her through with both the babies. "Let's have a look at the ankle."

Geraldine made a slight sign, indicating the children. "Could you help me to my room first, doctor? It would be more convenient."

"Nothing easier." He lifted her deftly and carried her in his arms, laid her on her bed and shut the door. Again she felt a personal gratitude for a man's strength. "Now, what's this?" he enquired.

"I don't know," she gave him a brief explanation. "Am I paralyzed?"

He laughed heartily. "No chance." A rapid examination sufficed. "You've been worrying, haven't you? Yes, of course. Rest is what you need; I'd suggest a sanatorium, away from the family. Nice family, but you need absolute quiet, peace of mind."

"If I could afford a sanatorium, what would I be worrying about?" Geraldine exclaimed furiously.

Not thinking of it meant thinking of nothing else but how not to think of it. Every moment, waking and sleeping. … She had not sold a story for five months. Leonard's salary had been cut, and then he was put on part time. Twenty dollars a week was all he got now. One might live on twenty dollars a week, but not in an apartment that cost two hundred dollars a month rent, a month overdue, and with two months miscellaneous unpaid bills stacked up. The apartment lease had a year to run and the landlord refused to cancel it. Magazines were not buying stories. Besides, she couldn't write. And Leonard might be let out of employment altogether for the summer, with only a hope of being taken on again later … The debts crushed her. They had accumulated from day to day, from month to month, because she could not imagine nothing would sell. Not after years of prompt acceptances.

"I've dreamed this sometimes," she said. "Some awful danger and I couldn't run away; my feet wouldn't move. Exactly like this. What is it?"

"Nerves. Nothing organically wrong."

"How long will it last?"

"That depends. You should rest for three months."

"Three months." It was her turn to laugh. She sat up against the pillows; it was only her legs that refused to obey her. She could move them, but they refused to carry weight. "Don't be silly, doctor. You've got to give me something this minute to cure it. I can't lie here. I won't."

"I see." He was too intelligent to destroy her courage. She might break the deadlock by main strength of will against the subconscious surrender. "You can have a sedative to-night, and if you sleep, you can have a tonic tomorrow. It won't cure you; it will only whip you up temporarily. Can't you possibly manage at least a change of scene?"

"I will," she said fiercely. "Put me on my feet, and I'll take a boat for somewhere. Anywhere. I'll borrow the money. This is—— ridiculous." She could get the money from Mysie.

Having reprieved herself for a short term, the tension relaxed. She realized with astonishment the conditions of her existence. She had gone on like a primitive savage woman with her children at her heels, picking up a precarious livelihood from day to day, sleeping at night under whatever shelter was at hand, owning nothing and with no provision for the morrow. For children one ought, after all, to own a rooftree, keep a store of food. She had refused the responsibility. She had been wrong.

"But where did the time go?" she demanded of Mysie. "Only a minute ago I was young. And now I'm thirty-eight. There didn't seem to be anything in between."

"You don't look thirty-eight," said Mysie. The outline of Geraldine's face was fined down and her collarbones showed faintly; she did look younger.

"But I *am* thirty-eight," said Geraldine.

A week later she lay in a steamer chair, rolled in a rug, watching the fluid semicircle of sea and sky, chill blue against blue, swelling and sinking slowly, rhythmically past the rail.

Going aboard had been the last of the nightmare. Still not quite sure that she could stand, she walked aboard, with Leonard holding her by one elbow and Jake Van Buren the other. Mysie had brought Jake. One wouldn't expect it of him, until it became obvious that he could be counted upon in any such capacity.

Her sister Effie was staying with the children. They had promised to be happy in Geraldine's absence. She could count on them too; they had character and intelligence. She mustn't think about them while she was away, so they could be happy; it was a tacit bargain. She mustn't think about Leonard either; it would not be fair. Humiliation breaks a man. It isn't the same for a woman, because women know anyhow that life can strip them, bring them to their knees, as the price of life…

A long white-crested wave rushed down the slope of the curving sea. Hold your breath, keep your head down; you have to go under the breakers…

Twenty-One

The reflected sunlight flickered between Geraldine's lashes; and passengers pacing the deck went by as shadows. She wasn't quite dozing; she was aware of a substantial shadow passing, hesitating and returning. A man sat down in the adjoining steamer chair. Geraldine paid no attention; she felt extinct and invisible. This was the second day out. The first day, she had remained in her stateroom, sodden with sadness.

After he had gone by once, he looked back, caught by the gleam of her hair. He had seen it before. He made the round of the deck and at the second opportunity scrutinized her more closely. Yes, it was—the dame he had literally picked up in the hall at Gus Silver's. He had asked Nick Spinelli: Who's the red-headed cutie? Nick said: I dunno; the other one, she's an actress. He retorted impatiently: I know that; lives upstairs; name of Brennan. The Brennan didn't interest him; he had a hunch she must be one of those highbrows; he never saw her around at the swell night clubs or anywhere, and the older woman who shared her apartment was a teacher. Of course Gus and Tony knew who lived in the same apartment house with them. All they knew about the red-head was that she called once in a while. He always fell for red-heads… He sat down in the next chair.

The tag on her chair said Wickes. That didn't tell him anything. Looked like musical comedy. Dimple in her chin. She held onto him when he picked her up. If it hadn't been for the mob around, and checking off the truck, he might have got her telephone number right then. And here she was on the boat for Havana, only a week later.

He had taken the boat, instead of flying down to Miami and then across, because he thought it might give him the edge to drop in unexpectedly. In Florida, he would have run into some of the boys, and the tip would have gone ahead. That last lot of Bacardi had been cut twice; they were double-crossing somewhere along the line. Since the election, in fact ever since the conventions, when repeal became a certainty, they thought they could get away with anything and clean up, figuring the racket wouldn't last more than a year or two. Probably not that long. Well, he'd be there in person for the pay-off. Might tie up direct for legitimate business; he had influence enough to get licenses; there would be decent saloons again. Always too much overhead on the speaks. The old saloon was honest, he thought sentimentally. … Like most men who live on the edge of the law, he was very sentimental about honesty. He believed in "straight" gamblers and big-hearted bad men. He also spoke well of good women, and would go miles out of his way to avoid one. You had to marry them.

He lit a cigar. It was too early to go down to the bar. He was a temperate man, retaining the habits of his early years, when he had been a pork-and-beaner. Welter weight. He never got any further than the preliminary bouts at twenty-five dollars; he could take punishment but hadn't the speed.

Scratch lot of skirts on board, mostly round-trip tourists. Red-head was the only one that looked like a live one. And she was asleep.

A gust of wind scattered the ash from his cigar; stray flakes blew across Geraldine's face. She started and rubbed her eyes. "I'm sorry," said a deep voice. Words and tone struck her ear as familiar. The man sitting next to her tossed his cigar overboard.

"Oh, you needn't," she protested, too late. "It didn't do any harm."

"Well, it can't do any harm now, unless a flying fish samples it," he said.

Geraldine smiled vaguely. His voice was singularly agreeable, and he was handsome in a bold masculine way. Black-haired and blue-eyed, with a ruddy complexion and a bluish shadow on his jaw in spite of a close shave. He must be somewhere about forty-five. Perhaps he was a little too well-dressed, and he wore a cabochon ruby ring on one large manicured hand. "Steward," he called. The deck steward paused attentively. "What will you have, Miss Wickes?"

"Nothing," said Geraldine, taken aback by his immediacy. "No, really, thank you, but it's too cold to keep my arms out of the rug." Too cold for comfort on deck, even in the sun; but she stayed as a duty, to get the sea air. "Did you say there were flying fish?"

"Not yet. Sometimes you see them the last day. You haven't been to Cuba before?"

"No, never. How did you know my name?"

"Well, you're labeled. Excuse me," he took a card from his pocket and offered it to her. F. I. Matthews. "Here you are, Miss G. Wickes. What does the G stand for?"

"Guess. And F. I.—for instance?" I sound like a halfwitted flapper, she thought. It doesn't matter; I'm so cold, and he has a nice voice. Deep and warm. Comfortable.

"Suppose we trade," he said. "The boys call me Matt. I don't usually tell my first name. But it's Florence. Florence Ignatius. Now laugh."

She did laugh. Florence! With those shoulders. "That's right," he said. "My mother used to call me Flurrie. I had to lick every boy on the block."

"I'm sure you could," she said. "My name is Geraldine." She thought, he'll be calling me Gerry in ten minutes.

"It's pretty," he remarked. Then he was silent for awhile, and she was gratefully aware that he had a capacity for repose, the ease of perfect physical coördination. That was what his voice expressed, the rhythm of a balanced organism. He looked at her quietly and openly, without offense, a simple tribute to her femininity. She felt less forlorn. She thought, to be alone and unnoticed is to be a ghost. The boat, to her, was rather ghostly; being old-fashioned in its appointments, white paint and gilding and red carpets. Ships were like that when she used to go down to the docks at Hoboken and imagine herself stepping aboard and sailing around the world. The world she would have seen then had vanished, unless in forgotten faraway corners. If one could find such a lost port and go ashore without farewells and stay long enough to recover the lost years. There might be glimpses of them in Havana. Behind green jalousies or through the grilled gates of high-walled courtyards. If there were a fountain… And no skyscrapers…

The ship's bells struck; she failed to count correctly, but it must be tea-time. Dutifully aired and frozen, she thought she might go down and revive with a hot bath before dinner. Struggling out of her cocoon, she stood up unsteadily, saving herself with an outstretched hand as the deck slanted slowly.

"Better take my arm," Matthews was beside her. She was glad to accept.

"I turned my ankle last week," she said, defensively mendacious. It was so stupid to be ill, grotesque not to be able to stand up.

"I'm sorry," he said for the third time. "You did hurt yourself on that damn' keg?"

"How did you know?" The question was superfluous as she stared at him. "Was it you caught me?"

"Sure. I spotted you right away, this afternoon."

"How extraordinary," she said feebly.

"So I owe you a drink," he said.

She let him guide her down to the smoking room, where she ordered coffee, and he insisted on adding a pony of brandy. The brandy, the smoke, the after effects of sea air and nervous exhaustion, induced a not unpleasant stupor; she could not rouse herself to go below until the first gong sounded for dinner. Matthews talked very little, but his silence was soothing; she sat with her chin propped on her hand and smiled drowsily at intervals, to indicate politeness. When she was obliged to go, he asked: "How about having dinner with me?" He walked down the stairs and along the corridor with her, toward her stateroom.

"I don't know—don't wait for me," she temporized. An elderly female tourist shared her stateroom; as Geraldine opened the door Matthews stepped back with noiseless celerity, to avoid being seen. He was not seen. Geraldine went in and sat down on the sofa, waiting for the other woman, Mrs. Carroway, to finish dressing. Afterward, by herself, she got her clothes off, with a dim intention of putting on a dinner dress. She would nap for fifteen minutes first. … When she awoke, she knew by the texture of the darkness that it was past midnight. Mrs. Carroway had come in, gone to bed and to sleep. Geraldine burrowed into the blanket and slept till morning. She had not slept a night through for months.

In the morning she still felt nebulous but not ill. She managed to reach the dining saloon for lunch. Afterward, she went on deck. Matthews was there. Two young men were with him. She saw them instantly as a pair; it would be hard to tell which was which. It wasn't that their features were similar; one did not exactly observe their faces, only their sleek hair, the exaggerated Broadway cut of their clothes, their narrow heads and thin chests. As Matthews rose to meet Geraldine, the two young men moved away, keeping together.

It seemed as if a habit had already been established as Matthews sat down beside her. The afternoon passed lazily, ending as before with coffee and brandy in the smoking room. At seven Geraldine managed to stay awake, dress, and go to dinner. The young men were once more with Matthews, and again they removed themselves. "Weren't you busy?" she asked. "How?" Matthews said. "Oh you mean Eddie and Spud—no, they've got nothing to do." He did not offer any further elucidation of Eddie and Spud. It was remarkable how little he could say and still seem friendly, even sociable. His black tie and pearl studs were obviously expensive; it was somehow not vulgar of him to be slightly overdressed. She thought, men used to wear ear-rings and gold chains and scarlet plumes and velvet cloaks.

She had put on a black crêpe dinner dress. For five years she had worn nothing but black for evening, through indifference and because it made her look slimmer. Now she had lost so much weight, her frock was falling off her shoulders; a silver girdle took in the waist. She did look ten years younger, slender and brilliantly flushed, with her blonde cendré hair curled by the damp. The tiny coppery freckles across the bridge of her nose had come out frivolously in the sun; her neck and arms were of that translucent whiteness which goes with red hair. An inconvenient complexion, immune to tan and subject to sunburn, but dazzling at propitious moments. Her sleepy smile was misleading. Matthews watched it consideringly. He asked her where she expected to stay in Havana. She looked in her handbag unsuspiciously and gave the name of a hotel which had been recommended to her as cheap enough and quiet.

After dinner they watched the dancing until Geraldine was once more overpowered by drowsiness. Matthews walked with her to the companionway.

"I suppose that lady in your stateroom turns in early?" he remarked.

Geraldine said: "I suppose so."

"I've got a bunkie too," Matthews said. "Would you care to take a turn around the deck?"

Geraldine thought it might blow the cobwebs out of her head. She wasn't expecting what happened. She had given him no provocation.

In a dark angle of the afterdeck, Matthews folded her in his arms and kissed her thoroughly. He was not rough but competent and unhurried. His vitality, as real as a magnetic current, dazed her, and she was shocked by her own acquiescence. Her bare arm slid over the soft broadcloth of his sleeve, and when she ducked her head the smooth satin lapel caressed her cheek. He lifted her off her feet and kissed her hair where it curled about her ear.

"Let me go," she gasped. "You mustn't—there are people——"

He set her down. She ran, but got back her wits before entering the lighted corridor. How ridiculous! As she paused to regain composure, Matthews was at her elbow. She couldn't say anything. He took her arm and escorted her to her stateroom. "Go away," she whispered. He nodded and obeyed.

The next morning she was ashamed of having slept again profoundly, almost happily. But why was she here, except to rest? ... There was nothing for it but to avoid the man and forget the incident. She packed and went to lunch late. Matthews was not at table. When she ventured on deck he found her. She bowed curtly, without speaking or stopping.

"You're not mad?" he said.

"Don't be silly," she retorted. He reduced her to the elementary repartee of the elementary female. She was afraid she would be saying next that she wasn't that kind of girl! In spite of herself, the reflection made her giggle. "I was very much annoyed," she said.

"I think you made a mistake." How idiotic—she mustn't argue with him about it.

"Don't stay mad. I kind of lost my head," he said. She could not imagine that he understood she was rebuking him for his careless choice of place and occasion; though he did. "I apologize."

"Very well." Drop it … The situation was resolved by the sudden discovery that they were in sight of land. Then there was luggage to see to, and the crowd on deck. She grew fatigued again in the prolonged bustle of passengers pressing to the rail, the tug and quarantine boat edging alongside, the tender standing by. That must be Morro Castle … The harbor was very blue, and Havana was a city, that was all … On the tender she was very shaky, and Matthews locked her arm in his; she was unable to resent it, since she would have sunk down in a heap on her suitcases without him. Nobody paid any attention; the dancing motion gave most of the passengers sufficient uneasiness on their own account. Geraldine surrendered temporarily. At the end of the confusion, Matthews was handing her into a cab with her belongings, outside the dock. Eddie and Spud had materialized silently. Matthews said: "Listen, Spud, I'll be along in about half an hour; you see if they got my reservations, and have my baggage sent up." Spud said: "O. K." Matthews stepped into the taxi beside Geraldine and gave the address of her hotel.

Powerless against an apparently natural sequence of events and enmeshed by circumstantial evidence, Geraldine perceived her cabin companion, Mrs. Carroway, watching her departure. She had not conversed with Mrs. Carroway, beyond the unavoidable forced civilities of their proximity; but she knew precisely what Mrs. Carroway must surmise. She protested: "Mr. Matthews, I'd rather you didn't—"

"Now don't worry; I'll just drop you at your hotel," he said calmly. She clutched at the fact that he had told Spud he would "be along in about half an hour." And he had reservations, doubtless at some more expensive hotel. "I couldn't leave you to get lost in a strange town," he said. … In any event, she couldn't scream and jump out of the cab. At least, he had given the right address to the driver. In her bewilderment, she got no specific impression

of Havana, except that there were street cars and business blocks
such as one might see anywhere. When they drew up, she sprang
out of the cab with no recurrence of her inability to walk. A porter
took her suitcase. Though Matthews went with her into the hotel,
he stood aside while she registered. He tipped the porter liberally;
and when she said: "Thank you so much; good-by," Matthews said:
"That's all right. Take care of yourself."

In her allotted room, she got rid of the porter instantly, bolted the
door, and collected her mind.

The room was admirable for that purpose. For a bedroom, it
was immense, at least twenty feet square, with a lofty ceiling,
limewashed walls and a stone floor, clean enough and restfully
bare except for a strip of brown rug. An iron bedstead with a
white coverlet, a heavy dresser surmounted by a flawed ancient
mirror, three wooden chairs, a writing table and a bedside stand
comprised the furnishings. There was a large bathroom with
old-fashioned marble fittings. Two tall windows with green
Venetian shutters opened from the big room onto a narrow
railed balcony. The austerity of the interior was contradictorily
tropical. It suited her mood much better than elaborate luxury.
After a bath she wrapped herself in a kimono and peeped out
between the shutters. The afternoon was warm as spring, not a
Northern spring, which is cool underneath the warmth; this air
of the Antilles was warm underneath coolness, acknowledging
the dominion of the sun.

The street was commonplace, yet essentially foreign, with stone
façades and balconies and little shops. People sauntered along the
pavement. Nobody hurried. The women were mostly dressed in
black. As she pressed the shutters, they opened wider than she
intended. A man stared and called up to her from the street. Yet
nobody addressed the women going by; apparently custom permitted only a salute to a woman on a balcony. Conforming by instinct,
Geraldine drew back hastily.

Thinking of Matthews, she told herself severely that she had
been flattering herself with the pleasing terrors of sheer hysteria.
As if she were an artless maiden pursued by a villain. The state of

her nerves was her only excuse; the silliest aspect of her alarm was that she had never been alarmed when she really was an artless maiden. Matthews had kissed her. As a girl she had been kissed and mauled about by impulsive men, with or without provocation. She had flirted, being a normal girl, committed mild indiscretions, and escaped hastily with her hair pulled down and her dignity not quite redeemed by indignant reproaches. She had never given such trifles a serious importance. Men were like that. They ought to be. Life would be dull if they weren't, she was candid enough to admit. There was a line beyond which a girl must not go. An immemorial and cherished feminine tradition held—perhaps hoped—that men were dangerous if... Up to that shadowy limit, girls had a firm presumption of being in the right. They need only retreat, and then ignore the incident... At thirty-eight, it was preposterous to be indignant. The worst of being thirty-eight was that there was absolutely no danger. She had been so startled she had reverted to an attitude that was, in the cold light of reason, comic. He had been courteous enough to sustain her vanity with an apology. And he had validated it by taking care of her on the tender, driving her to her hotel. On the whole, he had behaved creditably. She had been glad enough of his company, when she was perishing of cold, solitude and inanition. The insignificant adventure on deck—why pretend otherwise?—had stimulated her drooping self-esteem. Women are like that.

To-morrow, she thought, she would be a tourist, find a sightseeing bus and view the prescribed objects of interest. For what remained of the afternoon, she rested in her spacious seclusion, dipping in Lethe. This was the purpose of her journey, this first strangeness; while it lasted, she needed no diversion.

Dusk fell suddenly. She would dine in the hotel. She put on an afternoon dress and hat, not to be conspicuous alone. When she was ready, she hesitated; she dreaded even the effort of crossing the threshold, as if grief were waiting for her somewhere.

A knock sounded on the door. It must be the room maid; who else? But she knew she was not genuinely surprised when she opened the door and saw Matthews.

"How about dinner?" he said. "I'd have asked you before, but I didn't know if I could get away; I had some business. You're not dated up?"

"No–that is, I wasn't–" She was not going to dine with him.

"I'll wait for you downstairs," he said.

She thought afterward, there can never be any Judgment Day. Even God could not sift out the truth. Nobody knows. One does things; and there is no going behind the returns, recapturing intentions, defining volition.

Twenty-Two

She thought that the next morning, waking in the lucid dark of dawn, the owl's light, which delayed in the large room as smoke may be held in a bowl. Color had not yet returned to the tangible objects; there were no shadows; the world was only a thought.

Matthews was asleep, with his cheek against her hair. She could barely hear his breathing. She knew where she was; she had known while she slept. She remembered everything; she could account for nothing; what had happened was a fact. She was here. Other facts existed elsewhere.

It must be clear daylight outside. Transverse lines of pale light crossed the ceiling above the windows, thrown upward through the slanted bars of the Venetian blinds. The greyness dissolved imperceptibly second by second. The air had grown deliciously cool, and his arm across her shoulders kept her comforted and warm.

When had she … Perhaps from the beginning, when she found his voice pleasing. Or when she had gone downstairs, where he was waiting.

They had dined at a café on the beach. Fantastically, with Eddie and Spud. Across the room several tourists from the boat occupied a table. She was aware that they recognized her … Sometimes in an absent-minded mood, on the street, she passed her destination or turned the wrong corner, and suddenly observed her surroundings. This isn't where I was going … It was like that, sitting there with Matthews. And Eddie and Spud! They were very nearly incredible. They actually did talk out of the corners of their mouths, fortunately limiting their conversation to "Yeah" and "I'll say so" and "O. K." They handled their knives and forks carefully, and were equally circumspect toward her. On account of Matthews. They weren't making any breaks. …

Whatever had thrown her into this stranger's arms, it was not a superficial impulse. She hadn't been drinking. One Daiquiri cocktail before dinner, and another later. She had not even finished the second; she didn't need it. The sensation of a tight band around her head had vanished. Mysteriously, she recaptured the innocence of the mind and senses which belongs to youth. *The foreign ships and the foreign faces* … At eighteen or twenty, she remembered, it was enough merely to go somewhere, anywhere—to tea at the old Manhattan Hotel, to a banal play, a ten cent movie, to the beach— the simplest experience was colored with the enchantment of first impressions. Everything had been created fresh and new for one's delight. … It was so last night. She could taste simultaneously the separate ingredients of the drink, sharp and sweet and cool and warm, the limes and sugar and rum. She felt no obligation to talk, and was glad of Matthews' taciturnity. Overhearing the conversation at a near-by table, she smiled to herself, discovering that the most commonplace phrases became original and significant in a strange language. Matthews was sufficiently observant to catch her listening. He asked, impressed and perhaps suspicious: What are they saying? She answered: Nothing much; they're only asking one another what will you have. Matthews said: You speak Spanish? She explained: Not really; I took a few lessons, because it's so beautiful. He agreed: That's so; no matter what a girl says to you in Spanish, it sounds like— He broke off abruptly.

So it does, she thought. Spanish is the speech of men and women. Of action and of love … And Matthews' voice was arresting, regardless of what he said, because it was distinctly a man's voice.

After dinner, Matthews said they might as well see the town. She stipulated that she must not be out too late. He assured her: We won't. He left Eddie and Spud to shift for themselves; Geraldine was with him in the taxi. What *am* I doing here, she thought …

She was being kissed. She jerked away from him; the taxi stopped before she could make her protest articulate. … There was nothing to see at the second café, a small place open to the street, a few men drinking beer placidly, two of them playing some game in the far corner, gambling without excitement for the smallest stakes. It was a way of spending the evening. She surmised: Havana stays up all night… She would have been content, sitting there indefinitely. But when Matthews proposed they should go on somewhere else, she said: I'm tired; I'd rather go back to my hotel. … She heard Matthews telling the taxi driver to drive around … She didn't know where they were, passing big houses with gardens, secret and shadowy and profoundly foreign. Once the sweetness of cassia flowers flowed by … She was ruffled and out of breath: this was why one did not regret youth too bitterly. It is crude and inept and disappointed. Don't be so *stupid,* she exclaimed, saying in despair exactly what she meant. Millions of women have said it. Some meaning must have reached him. He desisted, though he kept his arm about her, and there was not space to escape. He said: Look here, don't you like me? She wouldn't answer. Too tired? She was obstinately silent. He persisted: How is a man to know what a woman wants? She muttered: A woman! Women aren't all alike. He said: That makes it harder to guess. She said sullenly: Oh, you spoil it—such a lovely night, and—I want to be let alone. Please tell the man to drive back to the hotel. He said: But what's a lovely night for? She was angry at herself for the futility of her attempt at communication. She said: It might be just for itself.

He pondered for a long time, perhaps five minutes. His presence became like the sound of his voice, and she grew sleepy and content again. Then he tapped on the glass and told the chauffeur to drive to the hotel. He said: That's fair enough, isn't it? She said: Yes, thank you. Presently he said: You might give me one kiss, just for itself.

She turned against his shoulder and he kissed her, touching her chin with his fingers and then her hair.

When the taxi stopped at the hotel she said good night. He said: I've got a room here myself. Oh, she said, and in the lobby she repeated: Good night. She crossed quickly to the elevator while he went to the desk for his key. She had hers; and went up alone. She was unlocking her door when she heard the elevator return, stop, and start down again; and he stood beside her, very quiet in the quiet hall, where all the doors were shut.

It was because her head was perfectly clear, and the earth was steady beneath her feet again, and he was real. If she put out her hand, he would be there.

As he was now, sleeping with his arm around her. ... She thought, this must be the nature of temptation, the consent of the mind and will, against all argument.

She must have made some slight movement; she felt him opening his eyes, his lashes brushing against her hair. "It's you," he said. She thought, I daresay it might have been anybody! It was light enough now for him to see her smile. He said: "Well, I didn't think I was going to get you."

She said: "It was no trouble, was it?"

"Plenty," he said. "I don't know yet... You never told me; you went to sleep. Now do you like me?"

"Yes, that's why," she said, exactly truthful. The attraction was almost impersonal. ... In summer, as a child, she used to walk barefoot on the grass ...

He said: "I'll tell you something; a man doesn't find out how much he likes a girl till the second time. But last week in the hall, I got the feel of you in my arm, like this—l'm sorry. ..." He took her hand and laid her palm to his cheek. "Sandpaper. What pretty hands. Dimples across the knuckles. I'd better go and shave, before——"

With her eyes closed, she thought how lightly he moved about the room, for a big man. He said: "I'll take a shower and order breakfast, and as soon as you're ready you come to my room. It's the next, number forty-nine." "But won't they—" "They mind their own business. No floor clerks, and as long as you tip 'em and don't raise a row. ..." He ought to know, she thought, without cynicism. She could hardly afford to be cynical at his expense.

Because, she thought twenty minutes later, as she drank her coffee opposite him, she knew what she had to do. ...

His room was almost a duplicate of her own. The shutters were open an inch, showing a narrow strip of sunlit wall across the street. She poured his coffee domestically, thinking how guileless a man looks in the morning. Washed and brushed and in green pyjamas. Nothing could be more demure than her own pale grey crêpe kimono, lined with white. Three lumps of sugar … I am a respectable woman, she thought. A virtuous woman till yesterday. So I shall lie to him and run away …

How should we not betray each other when we are so betrayed?

He tries to be consistent. He is an outlaw; he admits no moral implications and therefore no claims, nothing to argue. But then he has no right to make any; he shouldn't ask: Do you like *me*? What if I do? The worse for him. There are others who come first; nobody can meet all the claims in full. *You must to the greenwood go, alone, a banished man…* The treachery at the root of life is that if we are capable of passion or curiosity or tenderness we must be so till we die …

He said: "How long are you staying in Havana?"

"I don't know," she said, strictly veracious. It's three days till the boat sails; is there an earlier boat? I'll have to find out to-day, change my ticket if there is. Pack while he is out of the hotel; he said he had business…

"How about taking a couple of weeks off? We might cruise around the islands; there must be boats."

There must be boats. Or if there isn't one before three days, wait till then, and walk aboard at the last minute. Don't leave a note. He doesn't know anything but your name. "I don't know—perhaps I could. I'd have to arrange. …" Let him believe so.

"You're on the stage, aren't you?"

"The stage?"

"I thought you might be, like your friend."

"Oh, yes, she is."

"None of my business, you mean."

"Oh, no, it's not that. I work for my living too, but what's the use of a holiday if you don't forget about work? It's not very interesting." Writing isn't interesting in any of its circumstances. A solitary task, composed of dissatisfactions and uncertainties… He doesn't ask me if I'm married, she thought. He knows I am; there's the ring. I don't want to know anything about him either. Never. Away from here, he does not exist. When someone dies, you go on just the same. Almost the same. Anyhow, you go on.

"You don't say nothin' and you don't do nothin', do you?" Matthews showed his strong white teeth in a smile. "Well, you don't need to; you just give 'em a look." Why, I seem mysterious to him, she thought; I am mysterious, because I don't dare tell him anything about myself; but the reason I dare not is because my life is so ordinary, so committed to the norm of conduct, all that we take for granted. An adventuress, if there is such a creature, would not be mysterious to him. So he endows me with the fascination of mystery, with unique and irresistible seductions. Is that the secret of the women whose charms become legendary: that by chance the legend begins in their lifetime, and men surrender to that, not to the real woman, whom they would not recognize if they saw her apart from it? ... But I have no means of comparison either; he may be uttering the conventional compliments of this situation, new to me. This is his commonplace: hardly an adventure. ... *There is no excellent beauty without some strangeness.*

"Where would you like to go to-day?" he asked. "I've got an appointment at ten o'clock over at my hotel; but I'll try to break away this afternoon."

"At your hotel?" she repeated. His embarrassment was comic and engaging; he was caught out.

"Sure," he said. "This isn't—well, I took this room on the off chance."

"I see," she gave way to laughter. "There's always the off chance." Patience, and stack the cards.

"You're kidding me," he said. "I guess you think I—" He couldn't get around the plain truth, lacking the sophistry to plead a special case. But he felt the injustice of the truth. He said: "I'm kind of scared of you. I mean, I don't want to get in wrong." The qualifications he had theretofore considered sufficient—he was a good spender, he could give a girl a good time—were hardly what he wished to offer.

He stood up, came around the table, and she too rose. She held him off with her hands against his chest, and he was stopped by the frail barrier. "There you are," he said. That was equally the truth. There was a physical sympathy between them of which passion was only an expression. If not love, it was a fact in nature; it flowed from the deep sources. We are sensual beings first. She was under no illusion. They had nothing else in common. Oh, nothing except that, she thought ironically—the tide of his blood against her palms. With the whole of civilization as an obstacle. That, perhaps, was the price of being civilized. And since they would get no more, they might as well make the most of it. We must also grow old and die.

"Will you be in if I telephone between twelve and one?" he asked.

She said: "Yes, I expect so. Have you got a cigarette?" There would be time enough to find the shipping office between ten and noon. For an hour now they might talk; there wouldn't be much time for that. The words wouldn't be important in themselves, only as clues for future recollection; for delight is hard to remember, so she didn't want him to make love to her for awhile, though she did want him to. She meant deliberately to separate this brief encounter from past and future, from what he was and what she was in their other lives. Even though they were common or false, this immediate relationship had its own quality. One ought to be able to save an hour, a day, from so hard a bargain.

Cigarettes—his search revealed only three, slightly damaged. "I'll get some"; he rang, and Geraldine discreetly stepped into the bathroom when the waiter came and took the order, at the same time removing the remains of breakfast.

That was why they supposed it was the waiter returning five minutes later. Geraldine hid again hastily. She failed to close the door tight. Through the crack she heard Matthews say: "What the hell—"

She did not catch the reply, but it was not the waiter. Someone unexpected, unwelcome. Matthews listened and rejoined: "I'll give you five minutes. But you can't come here again. I told Louie I'd see him at ten o'clock."

The intruder became audible: "Yeah, that's why I came here, so we could have a little talk before—"

Matthews said: "Talk fast, then. And not so damn' loud."

The colloquy became an indistinguishable murmur, at the far end of the spacious room. Geraldine didn't dare close the bathroom door; the movement might be noticed. Matthews was not saying much; the peculiar rich note of his voice occurred at intervals, curtly and with anger behind it. Geraldine remained immobile, holding her finger to her lips. A drip of water from the tap into the grey marble washbasin worried her. Matthews said suddenly, with the emphasis of contempt: "That's what *you* say." Then both spoke at once; but it was Matthews she heard: "Why, you damned—" The final epithet she had never heard before, and it was shocked out of her subsequent recollection by the thud of a heavy object and three shots. Someone shouted.

Startled beyond fear, she ran out, and stopped in the middle of the room, with her mouth open as if she had screamed but she knew she had not. The waiter was there, a thin young Cuban, backed against the open door; several packages of cigarettes lay scattered on the floor, obviously knocked from his hand. An overturned wooden chair lay against the wall.

Another boy rushed in carrying a tray, interrupted on the way to some other guest. The two waiters shouted senseless questions at each other in Spanish, neither heeding the other, both staring at Matthews. There was no one else in the room.

Matthews stood bent forward, his shoulders hunched, his hands pressed to his abdomen. He said: "For Christ's sake, call a doctor."

"You're hurt," Geraldine exclaimed.

He frowned. "Don't touch me, honey. Cut along. You don't want to be mixed up in this."

Instead she caught one of the waiters by the arm, shook him to enforce attention. "Go and get somebody. The manager." She thrust him into the hall and he went. She commanded the other waiter: "Help me get him to the bed." Her domestic training had taught her to take charge in emergencies.

"I'd better not move," Matthews said. "A chair." She righted the overturned chair, and he sat down slowly, keeping his hands in position. She saw a spot of dark blood, no bigger than a dollar, on the stone floor. A doctor, her mind repeated; but there is no telephone book. ... The plaster is broken there; one bullet hit the wall. ...

The manager arrived; he was short and stout, with a round paunch and Teutonic hair brushed up short and stiff. "What is?" he demanded, irritated and alarmed, puffing audibly from haste. He stooped and picked up the packages of cigarettes, a mechanical action.

The scene was absolutely unreal. Geraldine said: "Is there an American hospital? An ambulance." She motioned to the telephone. "Be quick."

The manager grasped the situation sufficiently to obey, and she listened while he made the call; he asked for the number in Spanish and then spoke in English; that would be for the doctor.

Then he said: "But how? There was shooting?" He looked at Geraldine.

Matthews said, with difficulty: "This lady doesn't know a thing about it. She wasn't here. I thought it was the boy with cigarettes; he knocked and opened the door. I never saw the fellow before; I guess it was a hold up. There wasn't time; the waiter did come just then, took him by surprise, I saw the gun in his hand and I side-stepped and tried to down him with the chair, but he plugged me and scrammed—got away. The waiter yelled, and I guess the riot fetched the lady and the other waiter; they came running, but the fellow that shot me was gone. They wouldn't know about it." The effort of speaking was visible; his forehead was wet with sweat. But that was his story.

"You did not know the man?"

"No," Matthews said. "Will you all get out—do you want the whole damned hotel in?" His ruddy color had faded to a grey pallor.

The manager saw the point. Geraldine backed toward the door, her gaze fixed on Matthews. His eyes told her to go.

In her own room, Geraldine stood stupefied. It was impossible. The material event could find no lodgment in her mind, had not yet occurred there, for lack of preparation. There was no sequence. … He might be dying.

She heard a knock presently, but ignored it. She watched the door opening. It was the manager. He isn't a Cuban, she thought. Probably Swiss. I don't suppose a Cuban could run a hotel. Or would want to.

"Excuse me, madam; this is your room?"

"Yes." She thought, words are absurd.

"With your permission, may I enquire—did you see the shooting? Or the man escaping?"

"No. I heard the shots, and something falling; I ran out. Only the waiter was there, and the other waiter came immediately afterward."

He looked at the unmade bed. She was beyond feeling for the moment. She thought, he knows well enough. Matt's bed wasn't slept in. At least the breakfast tray had been taken away before. …

"It will be necessary to notify the police," he said.

She said: "It puts you to a good deal of trouble."

"Trouble?" he echoed, his guttural accent stressed by exasperation. His whole person indicated grotesquely that a hotel is compact of trouble. He had grown fat, his garments were baggy and wrinkled, his hair stood on end, with trouble. He glared at her vindictively; he would have been glad to turn her into the street if he had dared. Did he want the police? He asked no questions of his guests; he did not interfere with their business or their pleasure; the least they could do in return was not to involve him in their troubles. Not to get caught, get shot, bring in the police...Geraldine appreciated his point of view disinterestedly. The knowledge steadied her. She understood Matthews' prompt lie, his denial that he knew who shot him. It was no punctilio of honor among thieves. Even if he were in the article of death, he could not take his injuries into court, risk the inquisition of the law into his affairs. Why, none of us can, she thought; nobody is innocent enough. And the wild satiric conclusion followed—perhaps the police would be equally reluctant.

She may have been right. For in fact she simply walked out of the situation, and nobody stopped her... The manager muttered darkly: "Yes, well, but what can I do?" and left the room. What can anyone do, she thought. It's done... She locked the door, packed methodically, dressed. It was almost nine o'clock. The shipping office would be open. She went downstairs. It was like fulfilling the terms of a game of forfeits; if she did not look around, nobody would look at her; if she did not think or feel, nothing would happen. A tall dim mirror on the wall of the hotel lounge was half obscured by a dusty potted palm; she had an irrelevant impression that it was an artificial palm—here, in Havana! She saw her own reflection cross the surface of the mirror and disappear as she went beyond its range. A woman in a neat blue tailored suit and a little blue hat pulled down on one side, walking across the room and vanishing.

The clerk in the shipping office was an American, professionally civil. He couldn't possibly have heard, she told herself. Obviously he had not. There was a boat next day; he would have to enquire if her ticket could be transferred. He consulted someone beyond a glass partition. His matter-of-fact air enabled her to wait, leaning upon the counter, studying a map under glass. The steamer route was a black line through the blue. … The clerk returned, filled out a new ticket, handed it to her. Sailing to-morrow at noon …

Now there was only that gulf of time to bridge safely. Twenty-four hours. She thought of removing to a different hotel, without leaving an address; no, it would be more unpleasant if the police had to search for her, follow her up to question her.

She had never before had such an exact consciousness of the pace of time itself, time merely passing, not to be either hastened or delayed. She would have gone sightseeing, but feared to risk fatigue. Leaving the shipping office, she lost herself after a few turnings of the street. A confectioner's shop offered an excuse to rest. It was empty, and she loitered over a cup of chocolate for an hour. Common sense, brutal in its restored authority, informed her that since she must return to the hotel sooner or later, there was no advantage in a temporary absence. She took a taxi back.

Her room was a refuge, with its large airiness, and a bolt on the door, and the shutters filtering the noises of leisurely traffic going along the street below, and she out of sight… No one came. During the afternoon she slept, and forgot about dinner. …

The changes of the hours of the night proceeded by such fine shades that only silence and solitude made them perceptible: by the varying density of the atmosphere, the spaciousness after midnight, the coolness that runs ahead of dawn. Geraldine sat propped against the pillows, reading by a small dim light: Hakluyt's Voyages… *Columbus himself had neither seen America nor any other of the Islands about it, neither understood he of them by the report of any other that had seen them, but only comforted himself with this hope, that the land had a beginning where the Sea had an ending …* What endurance men had then; how feeble to assert now out of self-pity that yesterday possessed certitudes we have lost, an established heaven and earth and everyone safe within marked boundaries.

It was dawn … it was daylight … it was nine, then ten o'clock. Now she could go to the boat. She went down, paid her bill; a boy carried her luggage out. She followed him; the image moved across the mirror and was gone …

She was clean away. On the dock, her resolution faltered. She did not know if Matt would live or die, if he were dead already.

She might have contrived to learn. Even yet, she could try, enquire in the dock office about hospitals, telephone at a venture. No. She went aboard.

Lying face downward in her berth, she was aware, by a tremor in her nerves, when the gangplank was raised. The propellers began to beat steadily ... She thought, what women want in men is courage. That they shouldn't be afraid of life. But even the best of them fail us in the dark cycles of history. They used to go into cloisters, ask God to save them. Maybe they had to, to gain time to think their way through. And the reckless ones turned to fighting; getting killed was a way out. They've tried fighting now, and they are too much afraid to think; they are retreating to a horrible imitation of child-hood, submission and dependence and anonymity; grown-up boy scouts in black and brown shirts, marching to catchwords with no goal. Turn over the women and children to the state... When men cloistered themselves, they did know they weren't men any more; they became celibate; that was the condition ...

Matt has a kind of courage, she thought, even if it's the lowest common denominator. He is bad; those creatures, Eddie and Spud, are sinister, they give you the creeps; and they are a part of his life. He has shuffled off responsibility too, by turning outlaw. But at his own risk. So he seems like a man, by comparison.

Twenty-
Three

The second footman informed Gina that Mrs. Siddall was having tea in the garden. Gina laid down her gloves and handbag in the hall and went through the library to the terrace, without delaying to go to her room or take off her hat. Under the same roof with Mrs. Siddall, Gina unconsciously observed an approximation of court etiquette. She was more at ease with Mrs. Siddall than with Arthur, more naturally fitted to the duties of her position as dauphiness than to the intimate personal relationship.

Mrs. Siddall's Long Island house antedated the consciously rambling style and the Colonial revival. It was built when the hallmark of value was that everything should be imported; Caen stone, English oak, Italian marble. Especially marble. The hall floor was tessellated black and white marble; there were enormous carved white marble mantels; the white marble balustrade of the terrace sustained alabaster urns filled with pink geraniums. The house itself was ponderously rectangular, and of high visibility from all sides. Its sole connection with the landscape was established by force of gravity. Trees and shrubbery stood apart, affording no hope of seclusion. Marble benches invited a maximum of publicity. Every thing seemed to be in full view from everywhere: the sunken garden, the lily-pool, the rose-garden, now over-bloomed, at the end of July. Three thousand rose bushes were set in circles and

rows and trellis arbors; possibly the head gardener knew the names of
all the varieties, but no one else; they blossomed and faded in mass.
Roses to be cut for the house were grown specially under glass, and
the gardener delivered them every morning to the housekeeper. The
establishment was not only palatial; it *was* a palace, enforcing a ritual
of living unchangeable by the idiosyncrasies of the inhabitants.

The nearest shade was at some distance from the house, under
a pair of cedars. Gina walked slowly across the lawn, checking up
the guests as she approached. Mrs. Siddall sat in a peacock-backed
rattan chair; the others endured the picturesque discomfort of more
modern garden furniture. Mrs. Perry, Sam Reynolds, Mrs. Reynolds,
Katryn Wiggins, Marion Townley, Polly Brant, and two men brought
by Polly and Katryn.

Beyond the cedars, a high wall of smooth masonry separated the
stables and kitchen gardens and greenhouses from the formal grounds.
A grass-walk led through a circular opening in the wall, the grey curve
clear against the green. Benjy and Arthur came through it, followed
by Benjy's nurse and an unnoticeable youngish man, who might
have been a guest but wasn't. Benjy's abbreviated blue linen suit, his
socks and sandals, showed most of his straight brown legs. As he saw
Gina, he ran ahead to meet her. "Oh, mother-r," he called, "I rode my
pony by myself." He slid his hand into hers happily. "Did you? that's
splendid. Have you hurt your foot, Benjy?" He swung his weight on
her arm, keeping his right heel from the ground. "Yes," he agreed. "I
rode all around." Gina picked him up in her arms and carried him the
rest of the way, her tall slender figure swaying gracefully. When she
set him down he shook hands gravely with the guests, with sidelong
ingratiating glances; he had already Arthur's charming deference
of manner. A baby is royally ignorant of dependence; its necessities
are imperative commands. At five, the child has begun to look up,
to admire, to wish to please. Mrs. Siddall beamed at him, and he
climbed onto her lap. "How did you hurt your foot, dear?" The nurse
came forward anxiously, and knelt to take off his sandals. "Which
foot, ma'am? I don't know how he could have hurt it; does it hurt,
Benjy?" "No, thank you," Benjy replied. "There isn't any mark," the
nurse said. "He must have been just hopping on one foot, for fun."

The butler and a footman, arriving processionally, set out trays and
glasses. "You may have one of those little cakes, Benjy," Mrs. Siddall

said. Benjy took it and thanked her, but after one bite he held it in his hand uneaten. The nurse murmured: "I think he's sleepy, ma'am; he missed his nap, he was so excited about the new pony." "Very well, you'd better take him," Mrs. Siddall relinquished him to the routine. Benjy bobbed his head inclusively: "Good-by." He stood with his right foot eased. The unnoticeable youngish man said: "Let me carry him." He was Benjy's guard, taken for granted by the child. Even Mrs. Siddall, Arthur and Gina had grown forgetfully accustomed to the reminder of constant peril. "Good-by daddy," Benjy called to Arthur.

Everyone looked after him, smiling. "Fine little chap," Polly's escort volunteered. "Regular sportsman." Silence ensued, and the momentary sentimental accord dissolved. … Arthur, acutely conscious of Gina as he always was now in her presence, thought elliptically: No, I can't…Nothing…

Polly's eyes, dark and discontented under her stormy brows, rested on the man she had brought. Guy Fletcher. Tall, thin and carefully weatherbeaten, his mouth slightly open, his hand clasping a glass. No occupation. He belonged to her set; he hunted; he had an income of ten thousand a year—if anyone had an income now. Subject to the same reservation, he would presumably inherit fifty thousand a year from his mother in the course of nature. He had suggested to Polly that she should get a divorce and marry him, if he could gain his mother's consent. Ten thousand a year was hardly enough. He had been following Polly around for five years… My God, she thought, what's the use? He's just like Bill, but there's more to Bill, if it's only bone and muscle. Solid ivory. I used to be crazy about Bill. I'm fond of him yet. He drinks a little too much, and snores. Getting too heavy for his fences. Some day he'll come a cropper, or he'll just drop in his tracks, probably after dinner. And my life will be over. There isn't time to make another. Might as well stay the course. If I did chuck Bill, and married Guy, and Bill died afterward, me not there, I'd feel worse—it would finish me just the same. Greenland! It's lucky he can't raise the cash; if he strolled off for six months, Julius Dickerson would have him out of his job. So I've got to go back to the yacht to-night, keep in with Wy Helder; but the sight of the old man gives me the creeps; he's gaga. … Marion Townley's had three husbands, and look at her—hungry as a hawk …

Gina was looking at Marion Townley. Marion asked Arthur for a light, and took his wrist in her fingers to steady the briquet. A platinum blonde, with perfect make-up, and smooth curls gathered at the back of her neck. Arthur disliked her. Nobody could have guessed it from his extra shade of attentiveness. The two fair heads bent together were striking.

Gina thought: Impossible. Arthur doesn't. … But he might. They all do. Arthur is different. But it's months, I can't remember how long, since he asked me; they say a man has to have somebody. He cares most about Benjy. But if some woman got hold of him… Mrs. Siddall would be on Arthur's side if it came to a choice. … I haven't a cent of my own. How could a trust fund stop paying? It was a trust fund. I'll have to make it up to mother out of my allowance. Mrs. Siddall said we must economize; how can we? unless we shut our house—I don't want to go back and live with her now, she'd notice about us. …

Mrs. Perry broke the pause by resuming a conversation with Sam Reynolds. She said: "But why was the bank kept open if the examiners knew it was insolvent? Nobody told the depositors."

"Nobody could tell you," Sam pointed out. "They'd have been sent to jail—it's against the law."

"What is against the law?" Mrs. Perry's natural muddleheadedness had at last encountered a subject entirely fitted for it.

"Telling the truth about a bank. Injuring its spotless reputation. And of course its reputation is spotless as long as nobody tells the truth."

"But I would have taken my money out if I had known," said Mrs. Perry plaintively.

"Then you're in luck; you might have been sent to jail for that too," Sam consoled her. "That is, if it was real money and you tried to keep it. Cheer up; you can't win."

"I wish you wouldn't make a joke of everything," Mrs. Perry was goaded to rebuke. "I never know what you mean."

"Me?" said Sam, his bald head and moony countenance as free from guile as a new-laid egg. "If you want to laugh yourself to death, get some of the big boys talking—get Julius Dickerson to explain things to you. Ask him why is a standstill agreement and what to do with a discretionary account and how to unload building mortgage bonds and how much a guarantee is worth and who's going to manage a managed currency—who'll take care of the caretaker's daughter? And if you have any money left, maybe he'll sell you some nice copper stock at a bargain; I don't believe he got from under that in time. There weren't quite enough widows and orphans to go round. Unless Julius handed his copper to old man Helder; he's paralyzed."

"Mr. Dickerson is on the bondholders' protective committee," said Mrs. Perry.

"Ow!" said Sam. "Excuse me; I've got a stitch in my side!" He rolled about in his chair.

Mrs. Siddall stared at him broodingly. She knew he was talking at her; and he knew she knew it; but he shouldn't make a fool of poor Annabel, especially before strangers. Of course Annabel was a born fool, no more sense than God gave a goose; nevertheless she was one of the family; and besides, the loss of money was not humorous. Mrs. Siddall meant to have a private chat with Sam; she had asked him out for that purpose; but she had expected to see Julius Dickerson first. She had had an appointment which Julius was obliged to cancel; he was summoned to Washington. The testimony of the leading bankers before the Senate Committee disturbed Mrs. Siddall profoundly. It reminded her grotesquely of the way Polly had spoken of "only fifty thousand, only twenty-five thousand"; though they mentioned millions, even billions. They had sold to investors *only* so many hundreds of millions of worthless paper, European bonds, South American bonds. And there was the Kreuger affair, the Insull scandal... These things produced a physical tremor when she thought of them. They brought back her sensation when she was ill, with that maddening bandage over her eyes, and everyone speaking soothingly to her... The heat was oppressive this afternoon. It was years since she had spent July on Long Island, but she had stayed on from day to day going over the estate accounts. Almost half her capital was tied up in the Siddall Budding—that was what Sam was jibing at. And the bonds had defaulted on interest. Indeed, since she had borrowed the money to take over the bonds, putting up her soundest collateral as security at the bank, it was she who was paying interest, an insanely incomprehensible reversal of the first principles of her existence.

The building was eating up her income on her remaining capital. Sam's brutal cynicism offended her sense of propriety, but Julius Dickerson's bland generalities, which used to be so reassuring, had begun to increase the doubt and irritation at the back of her mind. After all, it was Dickerson who had advised her throughout the transaction, floated the bond issue and arranged for her to take over the unsold bonds in order to complete the building—which didn't pay. She had depended on Dickerson's wisdom, followed his counsel. The returns were inadequate in the form of phrases on the debt structure, reflation, parity, maldistribution, the New this and the New that. Conservative men used to anticipate hard times, prepared for them, weathered them; hard times were the test of their ability, and wealth their just reward. Men like her father and Wyman Helder senior. Though her father disapproved of the first Wyman Helder's record—those Civil War rifles!—that was a very long time ago, and at least he made money, he didn't lose it. She was annoyed by Sam's callous phrase; Helder was not paralyzed, he was retired. About once a year. Mrs. Siddall dined at the Helders', and paid a brief, ceremonial call on the old man, in his wing of the Helder house. He had a collection of coins and medals, the finest in the world in private hands; and a cabinet of precious stones. Jewelers had standing orders to show him unique or historic gems. His hobby was more or less a secret; even to Mrs Siddall he had never shown the jewels, though they had been friends, after a fashion, for forty years. He was only two or three years older than herself; it was his father who had been her father's contemporary. Mrs. Siddall realized suddenly that he was practically the only other survivor of her own generation and group. Now she thought of it, she hadn't seen him for three years, not since immediately after the stock-market crash. And he hadn't talked like Julius Dickerson then. He said: It looks bad…After a protracted silence, he added: They've been on a big drunk, and this is the morning after… His lapse into the vernacular from his usual laconically noncommittal habit, fixed the conversation in her mind.

Polly touched up her face and rose to go. "Must you?" Mrs Siddall had a genuine affection for Polly, in spite of her settled disapprobation of Polly's extravagance and her attendant swains.

Polly made a sulky mouth. "There's no discharge in the war. I accepted the invitation for a week; I thought it was to be a cruise. But the old boy can't travel this year, so they brought him onto the yacht in his wheel chair and we steam up the Sound in the morning and back in the afternoon and anchor for the night. The yacht has to be kept very quiet, so we play bridge in whispers and would like to cut one another's throats. Awfully jolly."

Again Mrs. Siddall was baffled by a tone, an attitude, so subversive, that reproof could find no point of approach. She preserved her dignity by silence, but her mental disquiet affected her bodily. She was conscious for the first time of age as a process of loss, authority slipping away. She looked to Gina for support and was slightly comforted; there at least was a vindication of her own judgment.

Gina smiled back at Mrs. Siddall mechanically... She thought, Arthur scarcely knows Marion Townley. Marion tries the same tricks on every man she meets; and Arthur isn't interested, didn't even catch her intention; he's talking to Guy Fletcher now. But why has he changed?...

Gina could not recall precisely when the estrangement had begun. Arthur's mannner toward her had not changed—except in the one particular. She had thought nothing of it—for how long?... The answer, which did not occur to her, was contained in the fact that she had thought nothing of it.

Arthur was instantly aware of Gina's oblique concentration on him. For the remainder of the evening, throughout dinner, while Mrs. Perry made conversation with an inconsequence that frustrated all rational rejoinder, Arthur speculated what Gina wanted of him; he felt the tension in the dark, as they sat on the terrace after dinner.

Mrs. Siddall thought, really, Annabel is too tiresome. All these silly women chattering, running about and making speeches and getting their pictures in the papers, with prominent teeth... Mrs. Siddall's reflections were incoherent, and the connection remote; Mrs. Perry had never made a speech in her life, nor had her photograph published even as an indistinguishable smudge in the background of a group of patronesses of this or that. But Mrs. Siddall felt suddenly that there were far too many women in the world, and no men at all. Only committees and mobs. She rose and excused herself brusquely. Arthur gave her his arm to mount the marble stairs, and Gina came to say good night.

Arthur would have gone down again, for no particular reason except that there was no reason for anything else. Gina said: "Were you—if you're not busy—"

"Why, no," Arthur's invincible courtesy constrained him. He followed her into their sitting room, one of five immense rooms forming their suite. There were also nurseries reserved for Benjy on the same floor. Arthur sat on the wide window ledge and watched Gina move about nervously, her backless white satin gown rippling around her pretty ankles.

"Just a moment—it was so hot in town to-day—" Gina said.

"Very hot," Arthur agreed. There was thunder in the air; the night was thick dark, and a sultry sweetness rose from the garden. He waited... She couldn't touch him any more. Strangely, desire troubled him least when he was near Gina, because all his emotional experience was identified with her, and it was over. Even the nights when he couldn't sleep, or when he woke at lonely hours, the knowledge that she was there beyond an unlocked door, that if he asked her she would not refuse, subdued his senses. *The expense of spirit in a waste of shame...* He had schooled himself to be fair to her, to admit the failure must be his. Now it was as if she merely reminded him, by the poise of her head, the downcast eyelids, of someone he had loved. Someone who had never existed. A picture, a fancy. There was nobody else, and he doubted if there ever would be. Not caring was easier, once you had attained it. One couldn't, he thought, go through that twice. He was still young enough to believe in the efficacy of such resolutions.

Gina returned in a lace negligee, having sent away her maid. Arthur was lighting a cigarette; he said: "May I?" since this was her room, and he no more than a guest.

"Of course; give me one." But she laid it down immediately. "We haven't seen much of each other lately," she said.

The few feet of distance between them became absolute. She couldn't mean... Would she say it? He had enough unregenerate human nature in him to feel that it was her turn, yet he felt also that to let her speak was a tacit treachery, since it was too late. No, he didn't want her to. Leave it alone. "I suppose I have been in town more than usual," he said quickly. "A lot of editorial conferences—rather futile, I'm afraid."

"Perhaps it's my fault," Gina said. His manner, polite, attentive and disinterested, struck her with dismay. That was how he had conducted himself toward Marion Townley. "I've been worried about other things—but that doesn't matter."

"Of course it matters, if you're worried. What is wrong?" He was sincerely insistent, making amends for his ungenerous first thought. They must go on as they were …

She knew later she had committed a folly in telling him what he asked, but she too was under compulsion to fill the dead space between them with words. … She had had a letter from her mother. Soon after his marriage, Arthur had made a settlement on Mrs. Fuller, with reversion to Gina. Five thousand a year. At the time, it was half his own private income, money inherited from his grandfather. It made no material difference to him; Mrs. Siddall had always allowed him much more; but it solved a painful problem for Gina. She could not leave her mother in poverty, and she didn't want her living with them as an unofficial pensioner, another poor relation like Mrs. Perry. Mrs Fuller had retired to Santa Barbara, where the climate agreed with her health and she was the most important figure in a group of elderly left-over women of sufficient means, who played cards, went to lectures and the movies, and exchanged reminiscences of deceased husbands, absent children and vanished friends. Gina's amazing marriage had left her mother permanently dazed. Once a year she visited Gina and Arthur, a proud but uncomfortable pilgrimage. Once a week she wrote, and Gina answered. The money came through the bank every month.

Three months ago the remittances had dwindled to a quarter of the accustomed sum. Mrs. Fuller supposed it was a mistake. Her bank made enquiry for her; she was informed that "owing to unprecedented conditions" the income had diminished. She sent the letter to Gina, with a timid bewildered note. What did it mean? Assailed by a frightful suspicion that the gift might somehow have been revoked, Gina spent the day in town pursuing information.

Deferential but ambiguous gentlemen assured her that the trust was unaltered, but some of the securities were "frozen."

"Never mind," Arthur said. "I'll send a check to your mother to-morrow, and I'll ask Mr. Lutzen to look into the trust fund. He'll straighten it out." Arthur couldn't imagine any other issue. Certainly Mrs. Siddall had told him that they must cut down expenses, as the estate income was diminished by the depression. He had refrained from buying various rare editions for his library, items he had coveted, which were going cheap. So far as he could see, he had no other expenses. Household bills, club dues, that sort of thing, were paid through an estate account. Of course there was the magazine; Mrs. Siddall had hinted at that; it was hard to decide what to do about it. … Some time ago Mrs. Siddall had transferred to Arthur a minority interest in the estate corporation; but as it carried no control, he accepted it as a formality. He really never thought about money, unlike most young men in his position. He was neither stingy nor spendthrift; his point of view was very like that of a well-behaved child with a good home and sufficient pocket money. He took it for granted. If money was what Gina wanted, she could have it, he thought, with the high-minded contempt of endowed virtue for the ethics of necessity.

"Don't worry," he repeated. Gina saw that he was going, and she couldn't hold him. He would stay as long as she furnished a pretext; he would not be rude. But her advantage had slipped from her. Theretofore he had been the one who asked and she who granted favors.

She did not even know how to—to make love to him, to win him back. She had never needed to…

There was a light tap on the door. Gina blushed, an involuntary betrayal. "Who is it?" she called sharply.

It was Benjy's nurse. "Excuse me, perhaps I shouldn't disturb you; I expect it's only that he was so active this afternoon. Benjy has been restless, and he has a slight temperature."

"You should have told me at once," Gina exclaimed. She hurried to the nursery, while the nurse protested that there had been no delay. Benjy had waked and asked for a drink of water, saying that he was hot.

The dim glow of a shaded night-light showed Benjy lying flat on his stomach, in blue pyjamas, with one knee drawn up, and a calico doll on the pillow beside him, his favorite toy. "He's asleep again," the nurse whispered, with relief. "I daresay it's only the heat."

Benjy waked, instantaneously and completely, as a child does. "Hello, daddy, is it morning? Can I go and see my pony?"

"No, dear, it isn't morning yet." Gina stroked his head. His forehead was cool, and the tender hollow of his neck slightly moist with perspiration. "You shut your eyes," Arthur said, "and it will be morning in a wink." "I didn't fall off, did I?" Benjy asked. He had dreamed he had fallen off, and was not quite old enough to distinguish between dream and reality. "No chance," Arthur said. "You rode like a trooper." "Lucy can have a ride tomorrow," Benjy said. Lucy was the rag doll.

"Certainly," Arthur stooped for a kiss; and Benjy flung his arms about Arthur's neck and hugged him tight.

The nurse returned to say she had telephoned to the doctor, as a precaution, though Gina agreed the child did not seem feverish… Dr. Haines was out. The nurse had left word for him to call in the morning.

"I think I'll go down and get the air," Arthur said. "It's the hottest night. …"

He paced the terrace for an indefinite time. He had read books explaining how marriage and divorce should be made easy and painless. When love ceased, there should be an amicable parting. Presumably, under some unspecified anæsthetic, one dissected out from the intricate living tissue of nerves and cells whatever held the imprint of the years spent together. What could be simpler?

A flicker of summer lightning picked out the night watchman making his round. Arthur leaned on the terrace balustrade. Down there was the lily pool, smothered in darkness. Carp swam in it, sluggish creatures with gasping mouths and dull goggling eyes. They ate and swam about in the circle of their marble tank. Patches of moss or fungus grew on them as they aged. They lived to be very old. They were imported. Generations of them had been fed by hand; when a shadow fell on the water they thrust their snouts to the surface, anticipating food. Arthur disliked them. The sight of them made him queasy. They were invisible now, but they were there, in the dark.

It was past midnight when he went upstairs again. He might look into the nursery—or perhaps he'd better not; it might rouse Benjy. As he glanced down the hall, Gina was standing at the nursery door. She had her hand on the knob; then she drew back and went away. They had had the same thought.

She cares about Benjy, Arthur thought. It is more decent to feel kindly toward a woman you once loved. The heat deadened all feeling. He sat by his window until a gust of rain brought coolness from seaward; and sleep took him stealthily. His valet woke him at eight o'clock to say that Dr. Haines had come to see Benjy.

Dr. Haines had a good bedside manner, serious and encouraging in just the right measure to indicate to wealthy women that their ailments were important but curable. His lucrative practice had been acquired by social connections as much as professional skill; he had married a rich widow and lived on an impressive scale, with a house near Sutton Place and a summer residence on Long Island. As a young man he had worn a Van Dyck beard; at fifty he was clean shaven, with a golfing tan, keeping up with the current model for fashionable physicians.

The nurse had kept Benjy in bed; he sat up, drowsy and bright-eyed, submitting to the examination with sweet docility. A slight temperature—yes. He had better stay in bed for the day. Children ran a temperature very easily, the doctor reflected; but prognosis was difficult, because they could not describe incipient symptoms. Dr. Haines began to write a prescription for a mild febrifuge, and hesitated. Had Benjy complained of any pain? The nurse said no, he was not a complaining child. He must have bruised his foot yesterday, but he said it didn't hurt. Ah, said Dr. Haines thoughtfully, and got Gina and Arthur out of the room. He remained about ten minutes, having implied that he wished to give the nurse instructions.

Dr. Haines's gravity was genuine when he left. He did not want to believe the dreadful possibility, but he dared not put it aside. The symptoms were irregular, especially the lameness before any other manifestation. But it was a disease so little understood, and cases varied greatly.

Dr. Haines said he would return before noon. He did so, and suggested that Benjy should be removed to a hospital. He was so tactful that Gina and Arthur did not immediately apprehend his meaning.

Poliomyelitis. Dr. Haines was obliged to repeat the word. He would be glad to call a consultant. He would be very glad to find himself mistaken.

"How could Benjy have got it?" Arthur asked numbly.

"Nobody knows. The mode of infection, or contagion, has not yet been discovered." A grimly indiscriminating disease, striking the most tenderly nurtured children as readily as the neglected offspring of the slums.

The discussion was renewed when the consultant arrived; then Mrs. Siddall had to be told. The same phrases were repeated over and over. Quarantine. The resources of science...All the time Arthur knew what must be. The worst was when he saw the nurse carrying Benjy down to the ambulance. They wouldn't let him say good-by; it was better not to excite him.

Dr. Haines offered an encouraging remark. Arthur winced and said: "But even if he lives, he'll be—lame."

"By no means necessarily. In many cases there is complete recovery."

You've got to believe that, Arthur thought. As long as possible.

For the remainder of the day Mrs. Siddall and Arthur and Gina stayed together. They told one another what the doctors had said; Mrs. Siddall played solitaire; and at intervals they telephoned to the hospital. There were no new developments; Benjy was no worse. The evening passed in the same manner, till Mrs. Siddall nodded over her cards. She was flushed and spoke slowly: "We had better not wait for the Senator." Hearing herself, she started from her doze; for a moment she had fancied herself giving a dinner, in Washington, and that her husband was delayed by a debate in the Senate. On Free Silver. Why, that was forty years ago. ... Arthur persuaded her to go and rest.

"Are you—going down again?" Gina asked Arthur. She dreaded being alone. "You must try to sleep," he said. "I can't," her eyes were dry, and she twisted her hands together. After awhile he coaxed her to try; he held her hand, and before morning they both slept.

They went to the hospital mornings and afternoons, but regulations were strict; they weren't allowed in the room with Benjy. The nurse was human and occasionally managed to let them have a glimpse through the door, when Benjy was asleep. They could see the round of his dark head on the pillow. The rest of the time they sat waiting in a separate room. Arthur thought that was an ingenious kind of hell, waiting, with only a wall between. Dr. Haines expressed increasing hope of a wholly favorable outcome; the child had not developed acute symptoms, no delirium or unconsciousness. Some weeks must elapse before the disease ran its course, but he was doing remarkably well. The nurse said Benjy had asked when he could go home. He was a good patient.

Gina broke down and cried on Arthur's shoulder. He was kind, without bitterness or desire. Presently she said: "You don't love me any more."

"Of course I love you," he said. She clung to him and he kissed her; his resolution vanished.

But he did not love her any more. He knew it most certainly after the brief oblivion of pleasure. He thought, perhaps that is of no consequence in marriage. The experience of the race has never found it to be sufficient; it will not endure. It was children made marriage permanent. The rest is habit and the occasional urgency of the blood.

On the sixth day Benjy died.

Twenty-
Four

By a misunderstanding, it was Mrs. Siddall who received the message over the telephone, instead of Arthur. She said: "What? I can't hear you … I don't believe it!" She had heard clearly enough; but how could Benjy be dead? Though she could not continue to deny it, she would not speak of it afterward; and her silence was respected as an evidence of grief. It was, in fact, a wall built up obstinately to shore her tottering world.

In his decline, Napoleon continued to give orders for the disposition of regiments which had ceased to exist, because he regarded himself as the image of victory. Deprived of that derivative mode of being, he was nothing. He could not contemplate his own nothingness; that was a logical impossibility. The alternative was to see himself as a little sick fat man, a cuckold, a broken adventurer. His ego preferred the illusion, and strove to maintain it by the most puerile devices. This is the weakness of temporal ambition, the seed of ruin ripening in the fruit of success. The man whose achievement is measured by externals must ever entertain a doubt that he commands events; else what is he? Too rudely forced to a reckoning, he may die of chagrin.

Mrs. Siddall, being unimaginative, had no specific image of herself; but she had functioned through her wealth. So great a fortune required an heir. If any part of the scheme failed, all might fail; the event she was denying actually occurred before Benjy's death. She had been able to postpone acknowledgment so far; but she was impatient of Julius Dickerson's evasions because she had already exhausted that recourse herself.

She delayed the interview for another month, and came to it at the end of her patience. Listening to him was like fumbling along a blank wall in a fog. "But, my dear Mrs. Siddall, what would have happened if——"

The wrath so long smoldering under her fears rose, bringing the blood to her head. "What did happen?" she retorted. "Can you suggest anything more that might have happened and didn't?" Julius said: "Of course we have all had losses—" "Have you?" She couldn't see that it was any recommendation of a financial adviser that he had had losses. An incidental suspicion sprang from the question. Julius said deprecatingly: "We could not foresee—" "Why couldn't you foresee?" Mrs. Siddall demanded. "If you can't foresee, what are you paid for?" She marched out, an angry old woman, more formidable in that native character than in her customary complacency of privilege. Even if it wasn't any use to speak her mind, it was a satisfaction; and it gave her the impetus to face the worst. She ordered her chauffeur to drive to her estate office.

Mr. Lutzen, her manager, braced himself as he caught the tone and import of her request. The information she desired should be obtained; it would take only a few days. "Weren't those bonds registered?" she demanded. "Yes, Mrs. Siddall, but to examine the records—" "An hour should be time enough," she said. "Meantime, please call Mr. Reynolds for me."

An hour was time enough; Mr. Lutzen knew it had better be. And Sam Reynolds obeyed her summons with slightly malicious alacrity.

Mrs. Siddall had never before let Sam look over her investments to such an extent. With an effort, he refrained at first from unsolicited comment, but it was rather staggering. He admired the variety of ways in which Charlotte had been stuck. At that rate, the Siddall fortune was terribly depleted; and if you figured in the building, which wasn't even paying its upkeep— whew! Finally she handed him several memorandum slips. Julius Dickerson had taken some of the Siddall Building bonds, on their first issue, as a private investment for himself. These bonds originally registered as his purchase had been resold to her. They had gone through an intermediate ownership, but if there was no sale for the remainder of the bond issue, how had Julius found a purchaser for his lot? Obviously he had used a dummy to work them back on Mrs. Siddall, while urging her to complete the building. He had taken pains not to show the transaction directly. "Isn't that the record?" Mrs. Siddall asked.

"Absolutely," said Sam. "Is it legal?" she asked. "Perfectly legal," Sam assured her. "You authorized such purchases under your own signature. I don't think you'll catch that sanctimonious son-of-a-bitch outside the law." "But Mr. Dickerson was morally in a position of trust." "Oh, morally—I guess you must be talking about two other fellows. Fact is, the same dodge was worked on quite a few corporations, with promotion stock. After the market blew up, the insiders turned back their stock for cash, cleaned out the last nickel."

"Then there is nothing I can do?"

"I see by the papers that the King of Siam is over here on a visit. You might call him up and make a deal. He specializes in white elephants."

Mrs. Siddall swept the papers together. "Yes, I called you in," she said enigmatically.

"You said a mouthful, Charlotte," Sam agreed. "What the hell—it's rather late in the day. All your life you've had fifty million dollars, and anyone like me who hadn't was a poor sap. Julius handed you thirty million dollars' worth of soft soap, and he was a big man. You didn't get any from me and I didn't get any of the thirty millions, so I don't owe you anything on account. You don't suppose anyone is going to sympathize with a busted millionaire? All there is to being rich is holding onto your money. It gives me a hearty laugh to see Julius and his friends sawing off the limb they're sitting on. Those rotten bonds they sold—what did they care as long as they got their commission? It didn't occur to them that they weren't leaving themselves any safe place to salt down their profits. Now they're in favor of unredeemable paper currency because they think it will prevent any chance of another showdown; and it inflates their book values so they can make their ledgers balance—on paper. Damned if they don't seem determined to cut their own throats by every means that dumbness can devise. They kept passing the buck till there was no one to take it. I'd like to point out that the prime condition of owning anything is that you can lose it. You either own it or you don't. You needn't expect anyone else to wipe your nose for you. Look at Mr. Astor offering to hand over to Uncle Sam his slum properties that are running in the red—he's willing to accept long-term bonds in payment. Ain't that nice of him? Of course he expects to hang onto his good stuff. Who does he think is going to pay the bonds? And what with? Every government bond is a mortgage on whatever you've got left. These birds think they are going to save their incomes—by mortgaging their capital. It's all to be paid out of thin air. They'll find the air getting thinner and thinner. If you want to know what's happened to you, it's simply that they got you on a short circuit. It will come around to Julius in good time. And you and Julius running a Communist magazine; now that's a fancy touch. Honestly, you don't need to do that. Just let nature take her course. God help the rich, the poor can beg."

Mrs. Siddall listened with an expression of detached comprehension. It puzzled Sam, when he stopped for breath. He had seen that expression before—but where, when?

"Oh, Arthur's magazine?" she said, after a long pause. "How can you tell it is a Communist magazine? I didn't know anyone could read it. I tried to, once. They have fifteen hundred subscribers. Does it matter what they call it?" She glanced at her black dress.

"By gum, Charlotte, you've hit it; what does it matter, when we're being run by politicians who've always lived on inherited incomes and intellectual ambulance chasers on endowed salaries out to do us good? They've got ten million voters on the payroll already. ... You want me to go over this stuff for you?"

"Yes, I'll see you to-morrow, perhaps," she said. "Of course, I can't trust you, Sam—that's an advantage." The gleam of humor was an echo of her father's manner of speech.

Sam thought, Charlotte was the best of the lot. She took it on the chin. Not like most of the hen-brained rich women his wife cultivated so assiduously. He had barged into a bridge party at home last Saturday, and one old cluck was saying we ought to have a Mussolini. He told her that if she needed a dose of castor oil, she could get it at the corner drugstore. His wife said he was a low brute.

Mrs. Siddall wondered remotely at her own tranquillity. The heavy sense of age had lifted; there was a faint singing in her head, not troublesome. ... As the car progressed up Fifth Avenue, she found herself thinking back—the Martins' house used to stand there, on the site of that department store; and the Pearsons' there, where the closed bank stands; even the Public Library was a "new" building to her; it used to be the reservoir. The Union League Club—ladies were not supposed to lift their eyes to the windows as they passed. On Sundays after church one drove up the street in a victoria, bowing right and left to acquaintances. ... There was one remaining landmark. Mrs. Siddall took up the speaking tube. "Raymond, stop here at the Helders'."

It was a huge but undistinguished house in Italian Renaissance style, with barred lower windows and a bronze door. The footman recognized her, bowed her in. "I think Mrs. Helder is out, madam; I will enquire." "I wish to see Mr. Helder senior; thank you, I know the way." The footman appeared uncertain, as she walked past him; he did not know how to prevent her. The east wing. ...A valet-nurse interposed ineffectually. "Good morning, Morrison; how is Mr. Helder?" "Not so well, ma'am." ... She advanced; the immovable body gave way to the irresistible force.

Wyman Helder senior sat in a wheel-chair, with a rug spread across his knees. He had been a stout man, deep-chested and bull-necked, with bushy black eyebrows; but he was stricken in years, shrunken, his broad shoulders bowed, his jowls pendant and the ridge of his nose bleak. The bones showed in the backs of his hands. He shut the sliding drawer of a cabinet beside his chair.

The room was sound-proof as well as burglar-proof. No rumor of the world's traffic and disorder could penetrate. A dozen famous paintings spaced the walls, among them a Holbein, a Rembrandt, a Velasquez, acquired at fabulous prices. There were also a small set of tapestries, Diana at the chase, reputed to be from Chenonceaux; and vitrines containing rare examples of enamel and goldsmith's work: jeweled reliquaries, covered cups of state, a Golden Rose presented to a queen by a pope, a salt cellar credited to Cellini, wrought in an elaborate and rather ugly design representing Venus on a shell, borne by Tritons. It was a private museum, a treasure chest.

"How are you, Wyman?" Mrs. Siddall had a moment's misgiving; the old man glared at her with defensive annoyance, quickly mollified into a formal welcome. But she thought his wits must be wandering; he said to the valet: "Give Dayrolles a chair." He was tolerably well-read; more so than Mrs. Siddall. "Sit down, Charlotte," he added. "Is Evelyn giving a reception?" He referred to his daughter-in-law. "No," Mrs. Siddall explained, "I was passing and it occurred to me—" "Umph," he grunted, and a gleam of distrust came into his sunken eyes. "They keep things from me. The newspapers. Pretend they forget. I don't forget." Mrs. Siddall was uncomfortably conscious of the valet-nurse hovering in the background, obviously wishing her away. And the fleeting changes in Helder's features, almost imperceptible, were like the shiftings of a mask, sly and cunning. "I had a talk with Mr. Dickerson this afternoon," Mrs. Siddall approached tentatively the object of her call.

"Oh, Julius." Helder grunted again. He was fingering a handful of coins on his lap-robe, specimens from his collection, Mrs. Siddall assumed. Silver coins. "They all talked too much," he said. "Got to believing themselves. The New Era. In my time. ..." His hands twitched, and several coins rolled to the floor. He made a convulsive, ineffectual effort to catch them, and uttered a whimpering noise. He seemed to disintegrate. The valet sprang forward, and Mrs. Siddall instinctively helped to pick up the bits of silver. She noticed, with astonishment, that what she had retrieved was an ordinary quarter dollar. The valet had two dimes. "Give them to him, madam," the valet muttered urgently. "He has an idea ..." The valet laid the coins on the old man's lap, and he clutched them feebly. "There isn't any more money," Helder said in a hoarse whisper. "There isn't any more money."

Mrs. Siddall fled. In the anteroom, she came to herself; the valet had followed her and was saying: "Excuse me, madam" … She said: "Thank you, Morrison; by the way, you need not mention my call to anyone else; I think I had better not wait for Mrs. Helder." "Thank you, madam." The valet was more than thankful to avoid any such mention.

The incessant and varied stream of life along the Avenue struck Mrs. Siddall with fresh force as she emerged from the guarded house. People going about their own affairs, busy, anxious, gay, indifferent. She was carried along with them. Energy flowed into her.

At her own door she stepped out of the car firmly. She felt as if she had been away a long time, a great distance. The butler opened the door. She enquired: "Arkright, will you see if Mr. Siddall is at home?" The butler took up the house telephone connecting the two houses. "No, madam; he is expected to return shortly." "Very well, say I should be glad if he would come over when he does return." She hesitated, and then went through the party corridor into the other house, and upstairs. A housemaid, seeing her enter the empty nursery, was touched by a sincere impulse of sympathy. Benjy had been such a darling little boy, laughing and affectionate. The house did seem mournful without him; and Mr. Siddall looked as if he'd never get over it.

The nursery was sunny and still and desolately tidy. Toy cupboards shut, the bed made, rugs spread straight. Only the rag doll, Lucy, sat uprightly limp in a small chair. Benjy's nurse, bringing back his things from the country, had placed it there, a pitiful act of piety. Mrs. Siddall picked it up. Careless of observation, she carried it back to her own house. Her maid, Trudi, was shaken out of a lifetime's training. *"Herr je!"* she exclaimed. Mrs. Siddall dismissed her: "I shan't need you for awhile, Trudi."

Left alone, Mrs. Siddall sat for awhile holding the calico doll. She shook her head; there were tears in her eyes.

She took up her patience cards, and laid them out. The first game failed. She shuffled, cut, started again. There, it was going very well.

That singing in her head …But her mind was remarkably clear, and her eyes; she saw the cards through brightness. A knock—that was Arthur. "Come in. One moment, my dear, I believe I have it." Looking down again, she saw her hand moving more slowly, stopping. She said: "Why, what—I can't——"

She never spoke again. The doctor, arriving too late, said that at her age the first stroke was sometimes fatal. She must have had a shock. He said consolingly that she had not suffered. Lying in her coffin, she looked dignified and kind; the last trace of haughtiness was wiped away.

Twenty-Five

After the probate of Mrs. Siddall's will, Arthur spent his days at the estate office with lawyers and managers. At the end of a month he could not determine whether he had inherited a vast fortune or a handsome deficit. He asked the question bluntly and the executors didn't know either. The lowest valuation of the Siddall Building and the two big houses would call for an inheritance tax that would eat up practically all the quick assets; and a sale would involve an equally disastrous sacrifice, assuming that purchasers could be found, which was highly improbable. It would, the executors remarked sagaciously, take some time to arrive at a settlement. They omitted to say where they would be when they arrived.

Thus enlightened, Arthur made an unpremeditated excuse and took leave for the day. He was desperately inclined to drop the whole business, walk away and leave it without a backward glance. The desire to escape was so literal that he dismissed his car and walked uptown. He was tired of possessions. His feeling was sincere, just as one may weary of the confinement of walls and roof after being indoors too much; the more so since he had never experienced the inclemency of the untempered wind to the shorn lamb. … A cup of coffee, mister. … Arthur gave the suppliant the loose change in his pocket hastily, looking guilty and ashamed. Am I my brother's keeper? Like most humane and sensitive souls, he wished vaguely for some impersonal super-power to take over the load of responsibility. It is especially the dream of those who cannot manage even their own affairs, a secret and unconscious excuse. Man is the naked animal, the stepchild of nature. The limit of his freedom is his ability to carry a pack on his back. He envies his fellow animals their fleet-foot grace, their ignorance of yesterday and to-morrow. His gods are winged and timeless.

Arthur's one personal venture had failed. If the money was lost, that let him out. Gina had married him for the money. ... *All, all of a piece throughout; Thy chase had a beast in view; Thy wars brought nothing about; Thy lovers were all untrue.* ...

Gina was in the library with her social secretary, an efficient middle-aged woman, acknowledging messages of condolence. Hundreds had accumulated, a drift of dead leaves, a funeral offering. When they were disposed of, Mrs. Siddall's shade would vanish with them. Gina took up a letter, glanced at the signature, and varied the formula of reply to the importance of the name. She looked up as Arthur entered; she didn't expect him so early but she had just been thinking of plans for the future.

"We can finish these to-morrow," she said; the secretary took the hint and effaced herself. Gina said to Arthur: "I've been wondering, wouldn't it be best to close both the houses as soon as possible and perhaps go abroad? For the winter, at least."

"The houses will have to be sold," Arthur said. "I'm afraid there won't be much left when the estate is settled. Practically nothing—we really haven't any income now. Gina, it's no use going on, is it?"

"Going on with what?" But she understood.

"You could get a divorce in Paris, or somewhere. I'll meet whatever arrangements you decide on; I expect there'll be enough to—to provide for you. Even if the estate is wiped out, I could sell my library."

"A divorce?" She heard her own voice, flat and thin. "Why?"

Of all things in the world, he could never tell her why. How could he explain the humiliation of a man who has been seduced by a virgin?

"I thought you might prefer a clean break," he said. "Since it's always been—distasteful to you; and there is no reason now why we should—keep up appearances. ... Anyhow, I can't go on."

"You're not going to leave me? Now—so soon after ..."

He winced. "No, of course not; we needn't bother each other; and if you want to go abroad you can take your own time and avoid all the—the talk."

What took Gina's breath away was the completeness of the disaster and Arthur's matter-of-fact tone. As if there were nothing else to be said. He hadn't thought out what he was going to say or even meant to say it just then. Simply he had come to the end. After he had left the room she realized that she had apparently acquiesced. She thought she must be mad. Such a conversation could not have occurred. Mrs. Siddall was dead and Benjy was dead. The Siddall fortune had vanished, and Arthur was asking her to divorce him. All that couldn't have happened so suddenly, leaving nothing. ...

The butler appeared, the door being open; he paused discreetly, and said: "Mr. Van Buren is calling, madam."

"Who?" said Gina.

"Mr. Van Buren, madam. I said I would enquire if you were at home. He is in the drawingroom."

"Oh—yes," Gina said. She moved like a sleepwalker. She had no motive except the necessity for action of some kind.

Jake had not written any letter of condolence; he thought they were ghastly. Since Benjy's death, two months ago, Jake had refrained from calling, out of delicacy; she wouldn't want to see outsiders. He came now to express a genuine sympathy.

Strict mourning enhanced Gina's beauty, gave it a classic elegance; she resembled a lady on a cameo, under a willow tree. Her hand was cold; as she listened to him she put out her other hand instinctively. "Why," she said, "you really are sorry for me!"

"Of course I am."

"Nobody else is." Tears welled out of her eyes; she made a pathetic effort to stop, puckering her face like a child. "I don't cry," she said wildly. "I haven't—this is——"

Jake really was sorry for her. He was perhaps the only man since the world began who was touched, not terrified, by a weeping woman. And he knew what to do about it.

"Cry all you want to," he said.

Six hours later he was wondering what he had let himself in for. On such occasions, one said things intended only for the emergency. He didn't suppose Gina would take them seriously; but he considered it obligatory to afford her full opportunities for a graceful repudiation. He'd have to telephone her in the morning, call again in the afternoon if she gave permission, and so on diminuendo, until they resumed by imperceptible degrees their former footing. The episode would be closed with affirmations on his part of unalterable devotion, of his readiness to hasten from the Antipodes if she should summon him at any time during the remainder of his natural life. The least a woman could do, in acknowledgment of such an offer, was to let it go at that. Oh, the very least, Jake reflected ruefully; usually they insisted on doing ever so much more. But surely not Gina, in her position. Ten to one she'd be "out" when he telephoned, transmitting polite regrets through the butler. She would be glad to let time obliterate an hour of pardonable hysteria. Jake really couldn't quite remember all they had said. ... The usual things. ...

He had it on his mind while he waited to take Mysie to supper. It was her last week with a show that was going on the road. She had only a secondary rôle; but she was lucky to have got anything that summer. After many postponements, Jake's play was to go into rehearsal in two weeks. Corrigan had promised her the lead. Meantime she would have a few days' rest. She was tired and cross. "Well, that's that. Where do we eat?" "Anywhere that suits you." Jake had brought some pages of his play, bits he had rewritten and wanted to talk over with her.

"The nearest quiet place," she said. "I'll scream if there's an orchestra." "Julio's?" It was an ex-speakeasy, only a block away. "I don't care. Weren't they awful—speakeasies?" Mysie commented. "Dingy basements and gratings. The sight of a corner bar makes me ill. I'm so tired."

"Now don't *you* start," Jake said incautiously.

"Start what?" Mysie scrutinized him. "Uhuh, I see what you mean." They had alarming moments of insight with each other. Some woman had been putting Jake over the jumps. "All right," she said. "This is a delightful joint, and we're going to have a gay party. ... Oh, my gosh, we are too," she lowered her voice. "Look who's here!"

Arthur Siddall and Roger Dickerson occupied a corner table. As there were only half a dozen other people in the room, an encounter was unavoidable. Arthur rose and welcomed them eagerly, with an urgent invitation to join forces. Mysie accepted, since it was advis-able for Jake to keep on terms with his editors. They needn't stay long; and Jake could stop in at the apartment for an hour, to talk about the play, when he saw her home. She ordered a club sandwich and slumped with her elbows on the table. She was too tired to eat.

The combination was wrong; they didn't click. She certainly wasn't in any sparkling mood; Jake obviously had something on his mind besides the damn' play; Arthur was distrait. Roger Dickerson was a pain in the ear anyhow. Mysie couldn't guess that Jake's principles, such as they were, squirmed at the bad taste of accepting hospitality from the unsuspecting husband. Even though it wasn't serious, they shouldn't meet. Not until Jake had been definitely rejected.

Mysie ignored Roger Dickerson, also on principle. She was unable to decide whether a millionaire's son going Communist on father's money was a more obscene spectacle than college youths on allowances, who had never done a lick of work in their lives, volunteering as strikebreakers. It was a nice point. I know what's so queer about the rich in this country, Mysie thought suddenly; they're aliens. They have no function. The men who actually make money have a function, of course; but not the wives and sons, the heirs. All they can inherit is the money itself, just a lump of something. The job doesn't go with it, except once in a hundred times, where the son is a born moneymaker too. Because there's no technique, it can't be taught. So the heirs are encysted objects. If they'd keep quiet nobody would mind; they used to, they petrified unseen at Newport and places. But when they go around pestering busy people it's almost more than one can bear.

Roger resumed, with forensic earnestness, an argument he had been conducting with Arthur, concerning the policy of the magazine. It was very boring, and Jake suffered visibly.

"One must belong to the future," Roger asserted. Mysie thought: *Such instructive ardor filled him, Clarence would have further gone, Had not someone kindly killed him, With a handy paving stone.*

She had been gnawing her sandwich in an unladylike manner; she discarded a clammy slab of tomato, and said: "Why must one? Maybe you ought to be liquidated, but that's a local issue, like the tariff."

Yes, you're doing Jake a lot of good with his editors, she told herself. She couldn't help it. She had restrained herself when Roger remarked previously, with a distinct trace of the paternal unction, that Russia was the only country in which he would bring up his children. She thought it was a splendid idea. And he could take father along too.

Arthur upset the salt, and was extremely embarrassed. "If you pour ink over that, it will remove the stain," said Jake, with abysmal gravity. "Ink?" Arthur excogitated the suggestion for a moment, before he laughed. He reached again, more successfully, for the glass which had been his original objective.

Good heavens, Mysie thought, how dumb I am; the poor darling is soused.

Probably it didn't take much to make him tipsy; Mysie had noticed other times how little he drank. She couldn't know what had kept him abstinent; it was the memory of those drunken girls.

Someone ought to stand by, Mysie thought. Roger Dickerson was distinctly spiflicated too; but she didn't care if a caterpillar tractor ran over him.

"I positively must go," she came to a sudden decision, and rose with sufficient emphasis to bring them all up standing. Arthur was at the suggestible stage; it was easy to lead him to the door. She said: "Arthur, will you take me home? Jake is going in the opposite direction." "Certainly," Arthur agreed. Jake looked astonished, but she gave him a warning nudge, and whispered: "Call me up."

She meant to see Arthur home, but he retained sufficient control of himself to ask for her address and repeat it to the taxi driver. Well, then she would take charge of him until it was safe to send him on.

In the taxi, he gazed at her with hazy intensity. He was bareheaded, holding his hat in his hand. She thought he was a dear, drunk or sober.

He said: "Mysie?"

"Yes?"

"You're not like Gina, are you? You said so."

He couldn't have known what I meant, she thought. "No two people are much alike," she said.

"And when you find out, it's too late," he said.

Mysie answered at random: "I suppose so; experience isn't much use, because the same thing doesn't happen twice—not exactly the same. And if it did, maybe we'd have to act just the same, being ourselves."

"But I've never done anything," Arthur said.

"You don't need an assistant, do you?" Mysie enquired. "I'd like to do nothing, for ever and ever." Arthur said: "You're always busy—I never see you." She did not guess he was remembering her excuses for not coming to dinner two or three times Gina had asked her.

The taxi stopped; as she paused on the pavement, fumbling for her key, she glanced up, wondering if Thea was at home. The windows were dark, but the moon, almost full, rode overhead, thin and pale, spoiled by the garish lights of the city. "There's the moon," she said.

Arthur shrugged and shuddered. "I hate the moon."

My God, she thought, does everyone feel that? I thought it was only me. It pulls your heart out, and you're all alone.

She was afraid Arthur might stumble on the stairs, but he was steady enough. The blinds were up in the living-room, so she could see her way dimly to the lamp. Arthur said again: "Mysie, where are you?" As the light came on, he rubbed his hand across his eyes. The warm enclosed air of the room made him dizzy. "I'm sorry to be like this," he muttered.

"Sit down," Mysie said, "you'll be all right in a minute." She didn't dare understand what he had been saying.

He said: "I haven't anything to offer you."

It wasn't fair to let him talk. Mysie said: "Never mind; it's all right." She fussed about purposely, taking off her hat, moving a small table, straightening a cushion. "Wait till I—" She went into the kitchen and found herself staring at a row of saucepans. What had she come for? The coffee-pot—she filled it and plugged in the cord. Then she returned to the living room. Arthur was asleep, with his head on his arm, against the arm of the sofa.

She thought: You haven't a chance, my girl. You could get him the same way Gina got him, and what good would that do you?

The light was in his eyes; she swung the lamp about, and he sighed and relaxed. He was as unprotected as a child. ... That was his extraordinary quality; he was precisely what his training was supposed to make of him. Like Don Quixote, who was not only the last true knight, but the first; there had never been another. ... In theory, if you give people security and leisure and means, free them from the pressure of toil and the narrowing anxiety of breadwinning, they ought to be gentle, generous, considerate, sensitive and cultured. In fact, they are usually greedy, snobbish, undisciplined, and equipped with a vocabulary of about eight hundred words. Spoiled children. Arthur was a good child. He had even the heart-breaking charm of a good child. What else could he be? For after all, those are the conditions of childhood. The qualities of maturity are fortitude, enterprise and forethought; they are formed by adversity.

She heard the coffee bubbling; after awhile she turned it off, set two cups on a tray, and waited again. An hour ought to be long enough. ... It is not quite fair either to watch anyone asleep. Even in the shadow, his features were modeled in light; a summer's tan was only a glaze over his fairness, as if the sun had glanced off. He was frowning slightly; his head was bent forward and his face pressed into the cushion. When you are unhappy, Mysie thought, you sleep like that, face downward.

The hour was almost past when the telephone rang. She answered quickly. Jake's voice said: "You got company?" "Yes." "Need any help?" "No, but where will you be?" "At my dilatory domicile." "I'll call you back."

Arthur woke and sat upright. "I'm awfully sorry," he said. "I'm afraid I've been——"

Mysie said: "I went to make some coffee and you took a nap. Great presence of mind. Do you want sugar in yours?"

He drank it black. "How long was I asleep?"

"Oh, maybe ten minutes," she lied. "I often go to sleep while Thea is playing."

"Was I talking nonsense?"

"No; do you talk in your sleep? Thea says I do. One morning I had asked her to call me; she came into my room and said: It's eight o'clock. I replied severely: You should have told me sooner. She had absolutely no comeback to that."

"It must be very late."

"Not for theater folks." But she did not try to detain him. At the door, he paused, looking about the room curiously.

"You know, you've never asked me to your house," he said.

"Goodness, do you have to be asked?" Yes, she thought, I suppose you do. Well, I'll never ask you.

She listened to him going downstairs; then she went to her bedroom window and leaned out. There was a taxi at the corner; she saw Arthur get in. She was very tired. But she had to telephone to Jake.

"Hello; how's the boy friend?" Jake greeted her over the wire.

"Oh, he snapped out of it with a cup of coffee. He's gone home. Come over in the morning as early as you choose, and we'll talk over the play."

"You left me with that Dickerson homunculus," said Jake bitterly.

"What did you do with him?"

"He wanted to make a speech, but I headed him off. I explained everything to him, and had got as far as the Middle Ages when he sort of sagged across the table. So I put him in a taxi and told the driver to deposit him at his club."

"What club?"

"That's what the taxi driver wanted to know. I left them to argue it out. They didn't seem to be getting anywhere, but I didn't want to get mixed up in the class struggle. Anyhow, he stuck me for the drinks."

Mysie went on talking to Jake purposely. The world was entirely comic while one talked to Jake. When she rang off she read for some time; it was three o'clock before she went to bed. She turned restlessly half a dozen times, but at last she lay quiet, face downward, with her head on her arm.

Twenty-Six

Mysie was not thinking of anything when Dick Chisholm telephoned; especially not about Arthur; that was no use. Her empty mind refused to attach any significance to Chisholm's name; she had to pretend she couldn't hear, asking him to repeat it. Dick Chisholm—of course, she hadn't seen him since she left Sequitlam; why did people expect to be remembered forever for no reason? Someone she had danced with fifteen years ago. She hadn't the energy to snub him off, but she moaned at his suggestion of going out, to a theater or night club. "Oh, *no*—I *can't;* but if you want to drop in. … It's the top floor."

Thea was at the little house on Long Island. Mysie intended to drive out. She had been in town all day, shopping; and seeing Neale Corrigan. He always managed to extort overtime. He was darkly pessimistic about the play, rather a good sign. … When she got to the flat after snatching an unsatisfactory dinner at a restaurant, she sank on the sofa and lapsed into a vacuum. And then this. … She remained inert until Chisholm arrived.

Mike had had an idea she might marry Dick; she couldn't imagine why. In fact, Dick had never proposed. Nor even made love to her. A big, silent, shy young man. She hadn't paid much attention to him. He must be about forty now.

The doorbell—she let him in. While they exchanged the inevitable desultory reminiscences, she pondered, studying him. He was not much changed, allowing for the imprint of middle age, and something else, some detail she couldn't pick out. He was the same person. Then what is the past? If they could be suddenly transported to Sequitlam, the town was still there, the mill and wharf and houses and streets, and the eternal sea, all the material forms, including herself and Chisholm; yet they would not make up the total she remembered. Other girls were now living in the time which for Mysie was irrecoverable. We have each a personal clock and calendar, so that it is simultaneously morning for one and noon for another. Pursuing this melancholy conclusion, she lost the thread of the conversation, and bethought herself tardily of the rites of hospitality. "Will you have a drink?" He declined, and she exclaimed: "Oh, you don't drink!" He had no bad habits.

"You'd forgotten even my name, hadn't you?" he said.

"Not exactly. But I went back last year—you know how it is. Everything is gone; you aren't there yourself."

He missed her meaning. "I left the winter after you did." To her astonishment, for she had regarded him as a settled type of man, he had been half over the world. Mostly in Central and South America, selling and installing machinery, mill equipment, motors, in outlandish places. That was the change she couldn't define, the brown of the tropics, emphasized by a streak of white in the crease of his eyelids, and again across his forehead, where it was protected by the band of his hat.

"How did you know I was in New York?" she asked idly.

"I've always kept track of you," he said. "Five years ago I was here, and I tried to find you, but you were out of town. And I saw you last summer, out West."

"Where?"

"In the hotel. You were walking across the lobby and you didn't recognize me. Next morning you had checked out."

"Was that you?" He had touched his hat to her, and she had nodded. "But how could you keep track of me?"

"Clara Carson writes to me sometimes. When I was back, she read me one of your letters. Of course I've seen your picture too. Once I was in Caracas, and I found a New York Sunday paper in the Consul's office, with your photograph in it."

How can you manage your life, Mysie thought, when you can't possibly guess who is thinking of you in Caracas or sailing from China maybe to crash in on you in New Orleans? At a loss for a comment, she reached for a match. Leaning back, she encountered his arm and avoided it. He said: "I beg your pardon." Mysie laughed. "It was a reflex action," she said. "I was afraid of injuring your fragile arm."

"That's how you used to be," he said. "You never knew I was alive. Maybe I wasn't."

"How not?" He had at last secured her attention.

He said: "You used to look at me with those big brown eyes and never really see me. I knew I wasn't in the running."

"Why weren't you, as much as anyone?"

He hesitated before saying: "I thought you were Michael Busch's girl."

"Then why did you keep track of me?"

"Oh, I was going to make a million dollars."

"Did you?" she asked, mildly malicious. If he thought that. …

"No. Nor likely to, the way business has gone."

She regretted the jeer. "But aren't you married?" she asked.

"No. Clara told me about your divorce."

Mysie started. "Clara?—she broke her promise."

"So did I," he said. "I shouldn't have mentioned it."

"Did you think that would make a difference?"

"No. But I thought I'd see you once more. You have got lovely eyes."

"And are you satisfied?"

"No. I didn't expect to be. I guess nothing would have made any difference. Anyhow, I'm sailing for Rio next week, so you needn't mind."

She didn't know whether it was silly or tragic. Why must there always be one who kisses and one who turns the cheek? And why must he wander in now, when she did not want to think at all. Not of anyone. Hadn't she enough——

Apparently not. At that moment the telephone rang again. She was glad of the interruption, until she had listened a minute. It was Jake, but she thought at first he must be joking, and she couldn't see the point.

"What?" she demanded inelegantly. "Yes, I *heard* you; but what's the catch?" He said it again. Mysie exclaimed: "With *Gina?* Are you crazy or am I?"

Jake replied, taking pains with his enunciation: "The propositions are not mutually exclusive. Now listen—I've only got a minute—I'm in a pay booth, at a gas station—and she's waiting in the car." He repeated for the third time the statement which had stunned Mysie, and added: "Can I count on you?"

"You're delirious," said Mysie. "I'll be there."

"Good girl." The pay phone clicked off. Mysie clutched her hair with both hands. Jake had informed her that he was eloping, reluctantly, with Gina. They were driving down to his beach bungalow. Even if he was merely out of his head, Mysie was obliged to investigate. She looked about for her hat and coat and saw Dick Chisholm. "You'd better come along," she said. It would be a wearisome drive, and perhaps not altogether safe for a lone female.

Chisholm did not ask where to. After she had snatched up a suitcase and run downstairs and started the car, she explained that she was going out home, and had to call on a friend en route.

Gina had run off with Jake.

That was flatly incredible; but Jake had said it three times.

With luck, it was a run of an hour and a half, or two hours in heavy traffic. Fortunately, this was the slack hour, between nine and ten o'clock, and a mild October night. After crossing the bridge, she apologized to Chisholm. "I'm afraid I can't be very sociable." The one and only time she had been to Jake's place, Thea drove.

After an hour, she had to diverge from the main road, and pray for guidance, watching the signs. The flying darkness on either side of the headlight made her sleepy. She identified the last village thankfully; beyond that she must follow the beach for several miles, till she came to a dozen cottages in a row. Jake's bungalow was not directly on the beach, but a few hundred yards apart, inshore. It stood on a low hill, and there was a windswept tree by the porch, so she was reasonably certain when she saw it.

I don't believe any of this, Mysie thought. Probably I'm dreaming. ... It did not seem advisable to drive immediately to Jake's door. She said to Chisholm: "Do you mind waiting in the car? I won't be long." She hoped not.

A path led to the porch; the window was dimly alight, and a car stood parked in front. Mysie peered under the blind. Jake and Gina were there.

Jake had had a bad half hour since arriving. The key stuck in the lock; then he had to find and light an oil lamp. The interior of the cottage was damply chill. He begged Gina to rest while he kindled a fire on the hearth. She was silent, an elegant incongruous figure, sitting on the edge of the convertible couch.

On several previous occasions his fatal facility had led him on to an undesired success, from which he could extricate himself only by ingenious lies or ignominious flight. The most awkward affair was with that girl—what was her name?—who was just out of college and theoretically an advocate of "free unions." In a fit of innocent idiocy he proposed marriage to her, to see how she would "react." She reacted with the instant precision of a steel trap. He broke off with her finally by telling her that insanity ran in his family; that his mother was insane. Later he confessed the subterfuge to his mother. No one else could so well appreciate it. She said: "There must be. Who will get you out of your scrapes when I'm gone? I don't blame Mysie for declining the job."

He had played up to Gina one step too far. When she said: "Take me away with you—now," what else could he do? Here they were. He certainly couldn't leave her stranded in his own house. To-morrow it would be even more impossible. If Mysie didn't come. …

Gina took in her surroundings with bleak dismay. She had little appreciation of beauty or harmony, but she had grown used to luxury. It was years since she had been inside a house so small, cold and shabby. The cheap rug was worn and needed a cleaning; there was a stain on the wallpaper where the rain had beaten in the window. The limp dotted Swiss curtains were the worst. The same kind of curtains they used to have at Grandfather Brennan's house, when she was a child. Twice a year they were taken down and washed. Those curtains were the trailing banners of defeat.

She had been so terror-stricken by Arthur's defection, by the collapse of the Siddall fortune, that she had clung to Jake blindly.

In the last four years she had seen and heard of such incalculable reverses, people who had been enormously rich actually penniless, men lately in control of vast wealth broken, disgraced, under indictment; women who had been reared in affluence looking for any kind of employment. It was like an earthquake. ... And she had no one to turn to. Certainly no other man, since she had been absolutely circumspect in her conduct. ... Jake was a successful playwright, a rising genius.

And he had a light touch. Arthur's youthful, untaught ardor repelled her, perhaps her body protested and would not forgive the compulsion she had put upon it in the beginning.

But Jake's house too wakened unwelcome memories of her girlhood. Jake saw tears trembling on her lashes. He succumbed again and sat down beside her, coaxing her with endearments.

He thought, with a detached corner of his mind, this is getting worse and worse. He wasn't immune to the natural impulses of a man holding a beautiful woman in his arms. Her hair was fragrant, with a dry, delicate odor. A little more and he would be sunk. He'd better talk, spin out the time somehow. ...

"Darling, don't cry; if you hate it here, shall we—" he couldn't think of an alternative; certainly not a hotel. ...

Gina said, in a small voice: "You don't really live here?"

This was his opportunity. "I couldn't write anywhere else." He had to have isolation, simple things. "You must realize, darling, that I am poor, I have to earn my living. This is all I can afford."

She said timidly: "But your plays———"

Second plays, he explained, practically always failed. His first play had brought him next to nothing. As he had backed it himself, the production ate up his presumed profits. And he had family obligations—the upkeep of the house Aunt Susan still occupied, and various other indigent relatives. ... Besides, he did not wish to become a popular playwright, nor to make money. "Money runs through my fingers," he said. "No matter how much I made, I'd be broke; if I haven't got it, I can't spend it. I'm better off without it." He almost convinced himself.

Gina said: "But I shall have—something." Her upbringing, on the inadequate annuity from her father's insurance, had taught her to loathe the mean economies of genteel poverty. ... Arthur had said he would do the best he could for her. If there was anything left. … He hadn't said how much, but the law. … No, it wouldn't, if she put herself outside the law. She had only Arthur's provisional promise to count on. He mightn't keep it; lawyers would give him more prudent counsel.

"I can hardly," said Jake, with stern nobility, "live on your husband's money, after stealing his wife. How am I ever to repay your sacrifice? Darling, I've been a selfish brute; thank God it's not too late." He kissed her hands, a gesture of resignation.

For a similar attitude, Mysie had once slapped him. She then burst into laughter and exclaimed: You priceless imbecile—thus laying the foundations of a durable friendship. No hope of Gina taking it that way.

It *was* too late. She could go neither forward nor back. Self-pity flooded her; she began to cry again.

Jake had tried his whole repertory. He began over again. "Darling sweet, listen, we'll find a way; don't spoil your beautiful eyes. Do you know you've got the prettiest ears in the world too?"

The screen door clicked. Mysie's voice interrupted: "The family ears." Jake and Gina sprang to their feet; Jake was taken by surprise as completely as if he had not invoked the visitation. He had been so nearly gone. Gina backed against the wall by the mantel, rigid with anger.

"It used to be my ears," said Mysie. "We seem to have a good deal in common. Don't mind me, Gina; I'll be going right away."

"How did you get here?" Jake achieved this inanity.

"I was motoring home, and I had a message for you from Corrigan; that's what you get for not having a telephone. I looked in and was going to back away till I saw who it was. Of course you'd like to kill me, Gina; I would, in your place. But I've known Jake longer than you have. I introduced you. I feel bound to tell you; you can't depend on Jake. He doesn't mean any harm, but he's a born bachelor. You can take my word for it."

Gina said: "Do you mean that he is your lover?"

"Worse than that," Mysie said. "He was my husband once. Not for very long, of course; and not much of a husband, but the best he knew how."

"Your husband?" Gina clutched the mantel.

"Well, a justice of the peace said so. It's eleven years ago. Maybe you remember the first time you met Jake, at my apartment? He was there to talk over a divorce. We'd been married about six months before. We met in Providence. I was playing in stock, and he was trying to write a play as usual. We used to sit on the beach for hours and talk about our ambitions. When the stock company closed, Jake saw me to the train, and then he decided to see me to New York; and so on. We went straight to City Hall and got the license and were married the same day, and we took a boat to Norfolk for our honeymoon; I can't think why. Jake was seasick. Before we got back, we discovered we really didn't want to be married. We had one grand row and several good laughs. Jake hadn't told anyone but his mother. It was so silly; we just liked to talk to each other, and I guess he had a brainstorm when he saw me going away on the train from Providence. His mother asked us to think it over, but after six months she saw it was no go. So I went back West and got a divorce. I stayed with Clara Carson, and nobody in Sequitlam knew about the divorce. It wasn't in the papers, an undefended suit." Artemisia Van Buren vs. Jakobus Van Buren, both utterly unknown to fame.

That was a long speech, Mysie reflected, almost two "sides."

Gina swayed and slipped toward the floor. "Look out—catch her, Jake," Mysie exclaimed. Gina did not hear her. Everything else she had heard, but remotely, as if it were of no importance. Mysie and Jake had been divorced. ... In the middle of a sentence Mysie's voice stopped, the last words sounded loud and strange, echoing like the note of a gong; the meaning was lost in the sound. ... This has happened before, Gina thought. ...

She was mortally cold; Jake was lifting her to the couch; and Mysie appeared out of nothingness, holding a glass of water.

Gina protested: "Don't. ..." Her head was heavy, and her forehead dewed with cold sweat. If they dashed water in her face she would be sick. She couldn't bear it, before Mysie and Jake. ... She knew when this had happened before, knew what it meant, with absolute physical certainty. ... If she had ...why, she could never have been sure whose ... "Go away. Let me alone," she said violently.

Mysie seconded her. "Get out, Jake; I'll call you." He effaced himself with grateful alacrity. Leaving was one of the best things he did, Mysie thought. "Take it easy," she said to Gina. "You look nice anyhow, fainting." Gina certainly was not the swooning type of female, Mysie cogitated; then why did she now? Why do women faint? There was one possible sound reason. If true, it wasn't funny to Gina. One of those appalling jokes on women. ... Mysie suppressed her unseemly curiosity, casting about for a way of letting Gina know this evening would remain a secret forever.

"Gina, will you promise not to mention that Jake and I were married and divorced? Especially since I'm in Jake's play—it would be a tabloid news story. We'd be utterly ridiculous."

Gina understood. "Of course I won't."

I'll bet she won't, Mysie thought. "How do you feel now? What you need is to go straight home and rest. I'd take you myself, but if I don't show up after telephoning Thea two hours ago that I'd be along soon, she'll be worried. Can you manage it?" "Of course I can," Gina said angrily. Jake was lurking in the kitchen; Mysie summoned him: "Gina's ready; she's going home; please drive carefully. Where's your hat, idjit?"

Jake whispered imploringly: "Couldn't you?"

Mysie whispered back: "I could not. It will be a lesson to you." She went with Gina to the car and said good night in a casual tone, as if nothing had happened. Well, it hadn't. She could tell. ...

Gina sat back in the corner of the car rigidly withdrawn. ... She thought: Arthur can't leave me now. He can't. ...

When they were out of sight, Mysie walked down the path to her own car, where Dick Chisholm waited patiently.

"Will you drive?" she said. "I'll get on the road first." She backed the car; there was a short cut at the last turning. After ten minutes she found it, and drew over to one side, stopping so they could change. It was a byway; no other cars were in sight.

"You can't imagine what I was doing," she said.

"No."

"I was stopping an elopement."

"Did you succeed?"

She nodded. They could see each other plainly. The yellow glow of the headlights picked out a clump of grass and fern by the roadside, drawn in sepia and gold. The moon too was pale gold, large and warm.

"But it really seems too bad," she said. "On such a night. Someone ought to."

"I've always been in love with you," he said.

"No, you haven't," she said. She had represented the unattainable to him. Most men have an element of snobbery in their attitude toward women; there was that in his long remembrance of her. He would make a fortune, and then he would be as good a man as Michael Busch. But Mike hadn't been like that; he backed his own choice. Dick Chisholm wasn't a bad sort, but the fault, the shortcoming, was in himself. He wouldn't take the odds. It takes generosity to love, to be happy. ... She didn't want Dick to be in love with her. But he would do for a barrier. She wouldn't mind having someone to talk to, at two o'clock in the morning, so she couldn't think of anyone else. And why shouldn't Dick have his desire? He could then go away and maybe find some woman for himself. "It doesn't matter," she said, "let's go."

"Straight ahead?" he asked, spinning the wheel. The sound of the motor almost muffled her reply.

"Whichever way you like. I've got two days."

Twenty-Seven

"I wish," said Thea, "that you two would agree on a selection before you begin. It's rather distracting to have you singing and playing two different songs at once."

Jake was on the piano bench and Mysie leaning over his shoulder turning the music. Thea was adding up her accounts methodically and grimly. The livingroom of the cottage had to serve as study and music-room also. Even for week-ends in the country Thea could not dispense with a piano, though for lack of space it had to be an upright. Thea said that the installation of a cozy corner would make the room a complete period exhibit, American middle class of 1900. There was a Morris chair, occupied at the moment by Geraldine reading the Saturday Evening Post. Geraldine and Leonard were week-end guests, which meant that Mysie had to sleep on the convertible davenport sofa. Jake was there only for the day. If necessary, they could have made him up a cot in the diningroom. The accommodation of a large house is fixed, but a small house will shelter almost any number of people.

"What bothers you," said Mysie, "is not merely that Jake is determined to soothe his savage breast with the strains of the Bird in a Gilded Cage while I prefer the works of Thomas Haynes Bailey; but if Jake had a voice it would be a tenor and if I had one it would be a contralto; and no song is written for exactly that arrangement.

Did you ever notice, Thea, that all songs are in the wrong key for whoever is asked to sing them?"

"I've noticed something of the sort," said Thea. "It is a great comfort to me that I have lost practically all my savings on the very best advice." The abrupt change of subject did not disconcert her auditors. It was their customary mode of conversation, each resolutely following his or her own line, with amiable acknowledgments of the separate interests of the others. The transitions were made as by the quantum theory, with no intermediate process.

Mysie said: "It's no use worrying; they've got us whipsawed. I tried to figure out lately what I should have done to hold onto my miserable savings. There wasn't any way. New York real estate, or mortgages, or stocks, or bonds; I'd have had to leap from one to another like Eliza crossing the ice. And if I'd got across, there would be the tax-eaters waiting with open jaws; besides, nobody knows how much a bank account will be worth to-morrow in German marks. Maybe it doesn't matter; God didn't mean people like us to have incomes. You know Mr. Gates McGarrah said we weren't to be trusted with real money. Never give a sucker an even break. We were born to earn our livings from day to day. We can't be anything but what we are."

Nobody was observing Geraldine. There was no reason to do so. She merely sat very still, conscious of her own heartbeats, hearing the echo of a voice she'd never hear again. ... For two months after her return from Havana, she had not known whether Matt was living or dead. Then one morning she answered the telephone ... Mrs. Wickes? The warm deep note vibrated through the insensate wire. ... Yes, she said ... It's you? Matt said. You know who this is? ... Yes, she said again ... You alone? he asked ... No, she said, the children are here ... He said: I get you. I suppose I couldn't see you? ... She said: I can't ... He said: I've thought of you a good deal ... She repeated: I just can't. How are you? ...He said: Oh, I'm O. K. I guess my number wasn't up yet. ... They were both silent for a moment, still aware of each other by some mysterious mode of communication of which the telephone was only a materialized form. That which divided them was equally imponderable and immeasurable, not steel or stone or space. She felt that her respectability was as dangerous to him as his outlawry was to her. Respectable people were bad medicine to him. All the presumptions were on their side. … He said: I guess you can't. Well, good-by, girlie—good luck. … She said: Good-by. …

She had to face it cold. It is much nicer if you are able to supply a pretty phrase for what you've done. Elective affinities, Goethe called it. But you really can't call a rumrunner an elective affinity. Goethe didn't make any phrases either about settling down with his kitchen maid. The less said the better. We can't be anything but what we are. With a husband and children and a living to earn, there certainly isn't much time to be anything but what you are. She had sold two stories recently, and moved to a three room apartment—the landlord had to let her break her old lease since she simply couldn't pay him—and Leonard still had his twenty dollar a week job, though one couldn't be sure how long it would last. In sum, they were back where they began. That didn't matter in itself; only she did not dare look ahead; what kind of a world would the children grow up into? She had to be cheerful, for Leonard; she would, literally, rather die than hurt Leonard. She didn't care how much Matt might suffer; anyhow, he wouldn't. He could pick up plenty of women; he couldn't be anything but what he was either. And she didn't care about the other women; the thought caused her no pang; only she was puzzled by the—the unrelatedness of life. That nothing should come of an emotion so powerful and complete; that they should have it for each other, being what they were. … Already it seemed to her that it had happened a long time ago.

"Maybe we can't be anything but what we are," said Thea, "but circumstances may cramp our style. In my opinion, there are a lot of men at present miscast as financiers and politicians. They ought to be pimps."

"Such language!" said Mysie.

"I'm old-fashioned," said Thea. "Yesterday I got two letters by the same mail. One was a statement of what happened to a bond I bought; it was highly recommended by all sorts of prominent names. I may get ten per cent out of the wreck; but the lawyers get ten thousand dollars for foreclosure proceedings and the trustees get a management fee just the same. For what, I ask you? The other letter was from my sister-in-law, burbling about how she had turned in her gold teeth to save the country. Of course if she didn't a lot of able-bodied men would fine her as a hoarder. I could stand it if they didn't talk such drivel, but it wears on me."

"Young men must live," said Mysie.

"I do not perceive the necessity," said Thea. Neither did Charles, she thought. … He shouldn't have done it, but she could not blame him now. Fifteen years ago, her husband, Charles Ludlow, shot himself, after losing his last cent in the stock market. He left a note asking her to forgive him. His health was broken, and his insurance would provide for her. No, he shouldn't have left her; she could have supported both of them; but that was what he feared. He had always been reckless, but till then he had been lucky. They used to quarrel wildly and make it up laughing. She had no heart to patch up the broken bits of the life she had had with him. Nothing could give her back her youth, when she had been brilliant and happy—and Charles thought her beautiful. She wouldn't touch the insurance money; how could he imagine such a thing? Her daughter Drusie accepted it gladly. When she heard Drusie say it was fortunate father was insured, Thea knew she was really alone. Let Drusie have it then; it enabled her to marry a prudent young man who might otherwise have jilted her. But Thea never wanted to see either her daughter or her son-in-law again. No doubt that was unjust; Thea did maintain indifferent conventional relations with them; Drusie never knew what her mother felt. What was the use of talking? … Charles had gambled and lost and taken the consequences. Thea forgave him.

My love he built a bonny ship and set it on the sea, And the name of the ship was the Golden Vanitie; And he sailed it to the Lowlands low. … Jake and Mysie had compromised on a book of old ballads unearthed from an immense miscellaneous stack of music which belonged to Thea. Years ago she had made a general collection, partly a joke, ranging from the best to the worst. Charles had shocking bad taste in music; he went to sleep at concerts, Thea thought, and dragged me to musical comedies, and made me play the most terrible popular trash to him—and I did! I was flattered, because my talent meant nothing to him; he loved me as a woman—whatever that means. Perhaps he'd even have loved me now, as I am—but I wouldn't be like this if he had lived. I'd have loved him still. I do. Dear Charles. He's dead, but he must be somewhere. It was wrong of him, so I have to pay for both, by waiting. It doesn't hurt any more, it's only watching the clock.

"Aren't you going to the Siddalls this afternoon?" she asked Mysie.

"We are not. We did our duty last Sunday. Now there's what I mean; your odd-job man says Arthur has lost all his money, but they are living in that awful marble mausoleum the same as before, and they're going abroad in a few days. And Gina is going to have a baby."

"Did the odd-job man tell you that too?" Geraldine asked, roused to professional curiosity.

"No, the grocery boy did. He knows that Wop chauffeur, and the chauffeur probably heard it from Gina's maid. You can't have any private life if you have servants," Mysie said. "We're learning all about how the other half lives. How the Stukeleys are letting their thirty servants stay and work for their board; and the Averys have moved into their gate lodge and make the gardener's wife do their laundry for nothing; and the Van Eycks filled up their wine cellar with canned spinach and stuff a year ago in case of revolution; and young Jelliffe Pearson goes around in person to collect his rents in New York; he's one of the stingy kind. At first I thought we were hearing mythology in the making, but it's all true. And after last Sunday I can believe anything. Dean Hervey told me that none of his parishioners come to him with spiritual problems any more; they bring him their financial problems. Asking for the miracle of the loaves and fishes. But when I said so he was shocked. And I had a long conversation with Bill Brant; he told me how disappointed he was over having to give up an expedition to Greenland. Apparently his idea of the good life is to sleep in a furlined sack on a pile of rocks and ice; he showed me a snapshot of himself in that blissful situation. But it's beyond his means at present; fate has condemned him to spring mattresses and steam-heated houses. It's pretty sad. They say those things and nobody finds anything funny about it. I don't know what Jake and I were doing in that galley, but I'll be darned if I'll put in another day off with our best people."

Of course she did know what they were doing there; but that was strictly private. They were doing their duty. It was an act of oblivion. Arthur had asked them, and Gina could give no reason for objecting. Mysie would have evaded the invitation, when it occurred to her that Gina might be easier in her mind if she met Jake once more. Jake was absolutely inadaptable to ordinary human relations; but he had a genius for the impossible. How else had he shared the same roof with his aunts for forty years, and contrived to build an indestructible friendship out of the wreck of a marriage and a divorce? ... Mysie had watched Gina's terror at the meeting change, within the space of fifteen minutes, to simple bewilderment and then to condescension. Nobody but Jake could have turned the trick. By assuming the rôle of a humble, discreet and rejected adorer, he convinced Gina that she was a kind but inflexible goddess. Mysie thought, Gina has to have her lines and cues. It was perfectly silly of her to run off with a man. None of the conventions will cover such a situation in actuality; you have to improvise; and that's where she's lost. I can imagine what Jake's shack looked like to her; it looked exactly as it is. Perhaps that's what's extraordinary about Gina. She sees everything literally. As if the world were an immense department store. ...

Being what we are, we must each have a separate world. They tell us we are going through enormous changes, that everything will be different. But it will last our time; it must, for you create and hold your own world around you, so it can end only when you die. And none of us can know what the other's world is or looks like. ...

"How did you ever happen to hear the songs of Thomas Haynes Bailey?" Thea asked suddenly, for no reason.

"Oh, there was an old songbook that had belonged to my grandmother. And a parlor melodeon. She died before I was born; but Grandfather Brennan kept the things. The Young Ladies Album of Musical Selections."

"Was that the dance hall girl?" Jake asked.

"The dance hall girl? No, the dance hall girl was grandfather's first wife. Gina's grandmother. Georgie Gay. I don't suppose that was her real name; she was the family scandal. Gina was shocked pink when she found out who she'd been named for. My grandmother was a New England schoolteacher. I must have inherited my Puritan conscience from her." "Yes, you did," said Jake, cryptically. He wasn't in a position to argue the matter.

Thea went on with her accounts, Geraldine turned the page of her magazine. Jake continued to strum gently on the piano. Mysie leaned out of the open window with her elbows on the sill. It was November, but a lovely sunny day, steeped in an exquisite melancholy. Probably the last fine day of the year. ... *The weary winds began to blow and the sea began to rout, And my love and his bonny ship, Turned withershins about. ...* Mysie thought, I daresay I'll never meet Arthur again. ... His father and mother were drowned at sea. ...

She was looking at the rise of land which gave the little house its individual charm. It was lovely in its bareness, with one small evergreen against the brown slope. And as she was absorbed in the scene and thinking of Arthur, she didn't see him drive up to the gate until he stopped and was stepping out of his roadster.

"I thought I'd stop by and make sure you were coming over this afternoon," he said.

"I am glad to assure you," said Mysie, "that we are not. You are witnessing the revolt of the middle classes. Come in."

"I can't stay," said Arthur; whereupon he came in and stayed half an hour. There you are, Mysie thought, smiling at him; and he smiled back. He doesn't know what amuses me, and I've no idea what is in his head. But I was just saying good-by forever to him, when he appeared at the gate; and he couldn't stay, but he walked in while he was saying it. We have to make the gestures, but they practically never coincide with the occasion; we say good-by ten thousand times, every time except the last, because we don't know it's the last, not till afterward.

She walked with him to the gate when he left. Returning to the livingroom, she broke into the middle of a story Jake was narrating to Geraldine. Some misadventure with a motor launch, floating in darkness and mist without direction; the motor had broken down. Icy water and darkness. "Where was this?" Mysie interrupted. She hadn't heard of his encountering any such perils of the deep. And what started him telling it now, chiming with her thoughts? Perhaps the song was what summoned the same images to both of them.

"In South Bay, last winter," Jake replied.

"How were you saved?" Mysie asked.

"By wading ashore," said Jake.

He gazed at Mysie with intense solemnity. "We bumped onto a sandbar," he amplified. "We must have been within a few yards of the beach all the time."

Mysie said: "You damn' fool!" And shouted with mirth. She rocked to and fro, held her sides, and slid from her chair to the floor. Jake continued to regard her with deep sadness for about thirty seconds; then the spirit moved him also; they were disarmed, dissolved, destroyed with laughter.

But Mysie thought, we'll never touch our shore again. That landfall is lost forever, down under.

THE END

For Product Safety Concerns and Information please contact our EU
representative GPSR@taylorandfrancis.com
Taylor & Francis Verlag GmbH, Kaufingerstraße 24, 80331 München, Germany

www.ingramcontent.com/pod-product-compliance
Lightning Source LLC
Chambersburg PA
CBHW071547110726
47908CB00007B/2025